THE
WICKED
AWAKENING
OF ANNE
MERCHANT

THE
WICKED
AWAKENING
OF ANNE
MERCHANT

By Joanna Wiebe

BenBella Books, Inc.
Dallas, Texas

BenBella
10300 N. Central Expressway, Suite #530 | Dallas, TX 75231
www.benbellabooks.com | Send feedback to feedback@benbellabooks.com

Printed in the United States of America
10 9 8 7 6 5 4 3 2 1

Library of Congress Cataloging-in-Publication Data
Wiebe, Joanna.
  The wicked awakening of Anne Merchant / by Joanna Wiebe.
    pages cm
  Sequel to: The unseemly education of Anne Merchant.
  Summary: "Thrust back into the cryptic world of Cania Christy, Anne Merchant finds herself tangled in a mystic plot she can't escape"—Provided by publisher.
    ISBN 978-1-940363-29-5 (paperback)—ISBN 978-1-940363-58-5 (electronic) [1. Supernatural—Fiction. 2. Good and evil—Fiction. 3. Boarding schools—Fiction. 4. Schools—Fiction. 5. Wealth—Fiction. 6. Islands—Fiction.] I. Title.
  PZ7.W63513Wic 2015
  [Fic]—dc23
                    2014027912

Editing by Heather Butterfield
Copyediting by Brittany Dowdle
Proofreading by Greg Teague and Jenny Bridges
Cover design by Sarah Dombrowsky
Cover illustration by Chad Michael Ward and Ralph Voltz
Text design and composition by Silver Feather Design
Printed by Lake Book Manufacturing

Distributed by Perseus Distribution | www.perseusdistribution.com
To place orders through Perseus Distribution:
Tel: (800) 343-4499 | Fax: (800) 351-5073 | E-mail: orderentry@perseusbooks.com

Significant discounts for bulk sales are available. Please contact Glenn Yeffeth at glenn@benbellabooks.com or (214) 750-3628.

CONTENTS

SEMESTER ONE

SEMESTER TWO

SEMESTER
ONE

INTO THE FIRE

FIRST IT'S BLACK AND THEN IT'S BRIGHT. I'M RUNNING.

Someone has me by the hand. He's shouting for me to hurry as he drags me over tangled roots and under sharp branches.

I realize I'm back in this world before I know I'm racing up from the shores of Wormwood Island, between its craggy trees, and toward its dark, beating heart: the Cania Christy Preparatory Academy, a stately campus of mossy stone buildings veiled in ocean mist and secrecy.

Oh, God. I'm back.

My heart's pounding at double time.

I'm staggering. Lumbering. In bare feet.

"Come on!" Teddy hollers at me. I recognize his voice at the same time my eyes adjust to the bluish light. Sunlight through the trees. Sunlight trapped in swirls of low-hanging fog. I trip, and he yanks me back to standing, to running. "Wake up, Anne, before it's too late. Before we're there."

Teddy. Teddy brought me back here. He was next to me in California only moments ago—or what seems like moments ago. And he was taking my blood, doping me, telling me—what was he telling me? My mind feels stuck back in that damn hospital bed, back with my body, back where I'm supposed to be. Remember. Think.

Ben helped me. Ben risked it all to help me escape Wormwood Island.

Ben Zin.

I'm back here, where Ben is. A silver lining I'll think about later. *After.* After I wrap my brain around the here and now.

"Can't you move any faster?"

"Teddy?"

"Good. You're alert. Now hurry. He'll be here any minute."

"*Teddy,*" I repeat and stop suddenly.

He jerks my arm like it's the leash of a disobedient dog. I pull back. He yanks again, harder. I free myself from his hold, stumble away, and stop cold against a tree. My feet sink into the chilly, wet earth of the forest floor. Standing here, feeling the ground beneath my feet, makes this all real.

My efforts with Ben were for nothing.

Flashes of last night—*God, was it just last night?*—strike me like furious fists. The glowing interior of Valedictorian Hall. That short-banged girl named Hiltop P. Shemese transforming into Villicus, and Villicus revealing he's none other than Mephistopheles, the not-so-fictional devil who makes exchanges with humans. And then came Pilot Stone, my very own Judas, to help the devil do his dirty work. I see the vials—his, mine, beautiful Ben Zin's—glinting in the firelight; I see myself grab them and flee, in flames, into the rain, up to the cliff. And then…and then Ben joins me, holds me, frees me. Kisses me. We jump. I vanish. Wake. And then Teddy…

"I need a sec," I tell Teddy.

"I didn't say we could stop!"

"I'm not *asking.*"

He's panting when he halts to glare at me with those pale eyes of his. This demon-boy.

Behind him, the woods double and conflate. I brace myself against a tree, clear my head. I know what's happening. I know I've just been vivified, created anew. I know Teddy's got vials of my blood in his satchel.

I know all those things.

But I can't intellectualize away the fact that I feel like my body, mind, and soul are bricks that have yet to be cemented together.

"Don't give me that look," I growl his way. "You've ruined everything."

"Everything? You had nothing. What's to ruin?"

"I was awake. After years in a coma, I was awake."

"You're not needed in California. I need you here. So does your mom."

Teddy told me I had a purpose on Wormwood Island. Over the racing beep of my heart rate monitor and the slow drip of my IV, he said I should trust him, that my mom trusted him. My deceased mom. How could he know my mom?

"Why?" I ask him. "Why did you bring me back here?" And then I ask the question I should have been asking all along: "What don't I know?"

"We could fill the world with what you don't know."

"Then start with the big stuff, Teddy. The life-and-death stuff."

"We don't have a moment to spare, Miss Merchant." He goes for my arm again, but I jerk away. "You're going to make this difficult?"

I hold his glare. "No more secrets. I'll call my dad, tell him I'm being fed poison, and he'll get me out of this coma faster than you can blink."

"Don't you realize Mephisto will bring you back? There's no escape. He wants you here."

"Why?"

"Naive little girl. Do you think he needs a reason for everything?"

"Yes."

"Well, if you're going to waste time," he says. Kneeling, he swings his satchel down and rummages through it.

I glimpse two of my vials.

"Just two?" I ask. "You took three vials of my blood."

"I sank one into the earth by the dock. I needed to vivify you. I thought you understood: this island is enchanted."

"You mean *cursed*."

"*Enchanted*, Miss Merchant. Those with the power to vivify the dead have enchanted Wormwood Island such that the moment a bone or a strand of hair or a vial of blood touches any part of the island, that person returns to life in an immaculate version of their past body."

"Yeah, I know. The escape plan you foiled was kinda based on that whole idea."

"I am not gifted with the talent to vivify merely by touching a vial, so I had to connect your vial with the earth. Now." He tugs a heap of navy, gray, and yellow clothes out of his satchel and shoves them at me. Tall boots follow. It's my Cania Christy uniform. "Put this on."

"No."

He looks up at me. His teeth are clenched. The kindness I thought I saw in him in my hospital room—the kindness that made me trust him for the faintest moment—has vanished like the dream it probably was. Only a monster would bring me back to this place, knowing what he knows about it. The vivified high-schoolers. The deaths narrowly escaped thanks to a devil's trickery and outrageous sums paid by desperate parents. The cutthroat competition for a second life off this island, which is the reward given each year to one—*and only one*—valedictorian, the reward known as the Big V. I'm just a girl in a coma. I shouldn't even be here.

I look at the uniform, held up to me like a peace offering when it's anything but. I look at Teddy. My long, lanky, gray-skinned Guardian who seemed, until I woke to find him standing over my hospital bed, like just another Cania Christy garden-variety demon. Now I'm not sure.

"Put it on," he repeats.

If my Cania education has taught me anything, it's that you should never do something without getting something in return. That's what Pilot taught me when he betrayed me. That's the foundation on which Cania is built: tit for tat.

So I say, "One piece of clothing for one answer."

"An exchange?"

I nod.

"Underclothes don't count," he says.

"Yes, they do."

As he grumbles about the clock ticking, he pushes the ball of clothes into my hands and turns so I can drop my hospital gown; evidently, you vivify in the clothes you were last wearing.

After checking to be sure there's no one around, I stand on the gown, rub most of the muck off my feet, and yank on my underwear, bra, and tights. I'm about to ask my first of three earned questions when Teddy whirls to face me again.

"Hey!" I hunch and cover myself with my balled-up uniform and boots. "This isn't a peep show, dude."

Ignoring me, he raises his hand and swirls it down as if he's drawing a tornado in the air. I see a faint glimmer like a low-hanging cloud. It begins over our heads and curls around our bodies. When his fingertips pass my shoulders, the sounds of the island—croaking frogs, distant barking sea lions, the omnipresent wash of waves— vanish as if they've been sealed out, leaving us in a vacuum of silence.

Now we can be honest, he says. Actually, he doesn't say it. His lips don't even move.

"What the—" My voice is gone.

He shakes his head. *Don't speak to me, Miss Merchant. Think to me.*

Think *to you?*

We're in a silencer. It's a common spell for preventing others—

Oh, the joys of being surrounded by devils.

—from overhearing a conversation. It gives voice to your private thoughts, but only for those within it. So, for God's sake, don't start fantasizing about Ebenezer Zin, that foolish boy who parades his eternal youth and beauty like—

Fine! I cut his tirade short. *Where was I?*

You've got three items on. So you've earned three questions.

First: Who are you?

My demon name is Ted Rier. I've been living in the underworld for the last 150 years.

Doesn't seem long for a demon.

Is that your second question?

Definitely not. Okay, you said something about my mom trusting you. But if you're a demon, how could you know my mom? I saw her in my hospital room. She looked more like an angel than, like, a dark soul.

You saw her?

Briefly.

He pauses. *After she passed away, I met her soul.*

My stomach knots. *In Hell?*

No, no, no.

Well, don't scare me like that!

That's three questions. Put on your shirt to earn a fourth.

I do. *Where did you meet her?*

Outside the realm of what you can understand. The spirit realm is very different from what you know here. The best way I can answer that question, Miss Merchant, is to tell you this: I've been masquerading as a demon.

I zip up my skirt and ask question five. *So you're telling me you don't actually play for the devils?*

I do not. I'm what you might call a secret agent.

I can't help but smile.

Teddy scowls. *I amuse you?*

The only secret agents I know are, y'know, made in Hollywood. Like James Bond.

I don't look the part?

My thoughts betray me: *Not even in Bizarro World.*

My sincere apologies, but the face and body you scorn are the visages that suit the tastes of Mephistopheles, whom I serve. I was once quite striking, I assure you. But physical beauty—

I didn't mean to hurt your feelings ...

—is hardly as interesting to Mephisto as the ways he can torture and manipulate a growing number of you simple-minded humans.

Got it. Sorry.

Which brings me to the point, if you can collect yourself for a minute, Miss Merchant.

I'm not even laughing! I barely smiled.

He glares at me. *To answer your fifth question, I met your mother in secret when I was convening with the rest of the benign spirits aligned in our mission.*

Which is ... ?

Put on your cardigan.

Oh, for the love of ... I hastily button the sweater. *What's your mission?*

Our mission, Miss Merchant, is to stop the expansion of the underworld into this world.

So just a small mission, then.

Your mom specifically asked for you. She believes you can do this.

I saw that coming. Taking a deep breath, I nod. *If it's for my mom.*

Very good. Mephisto's reach is growing, in spite of his recent humiliations at your hand and the subsequent loss of at least one of the Seven Sinning Sisters. Now is the perfect time to strike. Or it will be, when we've built up enough supporters and we get the right plan in place.

Wait, who are the Seven Sinning Sisters?

He looks at the boots I hold, the last part of my uniform.

I tug them on. *There. Boots count as two.*

Boots count as one.

There are two of them.

They count as one.

After what you've done to me, Teddy, I'd say you owe me as many answers as I want. They count as two.

To my surprise, he relents. *Two. Fine. The Seven Sinning Sisters are Mephisto's most powerful followers. They are seven beautiful dark goddesses, each one a keeper of one of the seven deadly sins. They're behind everyday destruction, making them exceptionally valuable followers Downstairs and here on Earth.* He tilts his head. *And now you've got just one question left. Hurry up with it. We're wasting precious time.*

But you hear my every thought! No matter what question I think, that'll be it.

Suddenly, noises rush at me. I wiggle my jaw to pop my ears, and the low caws and sea lion moans that possess the island whoosh around us.

"Is that better?" Teddy asks.

I glimpse someone in the shadows. Both Teddy and I look in time to see Mr. Watso, dressed in fishing gear and looking 100 feet tall, sneer at us, growl a little, and trudge away. I haven't seen him since the night his granddaughter Molly was cremated; he had to destroy her body because, if it remained on Wormwood Island, she would vivify—and Mr. Watso's always seen the evil in letting a devil's spell vivify the dead. The cremation happened the night after she was murdered—not for a crime, but for befriending me. Suffice it to say, I've made a lifetime enemy of Mr. Watso.

"Miss Merchant, we must hurry to campus."

"Wait!" I've got to make this question worth it. But Teddy's gritting his teeth like the world might end if I don't spit out my next thought.

"Your question?"

"When I first came here, I—I didn't wake up on the edge of the island. I was just suddenly at Gigi's house, which is in the middle of the island. The first thing I really remember is waking up and getting dressed for school on my first day. But my head was clear. I knew everything I had to do, and I had this sense of where I'd come from and why I was here. I knew the name Cania Christy, and I knew Gigi. But, when I think about it, I don't know how I could have known anything." I look at him. "So how did that work?"

"*That's* what you want to spend your last question on?"

"You rushed me!"

"You want to know *more* about vivification. You don't want to know what's become of Mephisto? Or who's about to take control of Cania Christy?"

"There's someone else in control?"

"You don't want to know why your friend Molly allowed herself to be killed?" he continues in disbelief. "You don't want to know if, after you destroyed the Stone boy's vial, he's gone Upstairs or Downstairs?"

"Now that you mention it…"

"You don't want to know if Mr. Zin and his father are being punished for what the two of you did? You don't want to know what punishment *you'll* endure now that you're back?"

God, I've really messed this up. There's so much to know here, and it's like I'm always a step behind. Teddy's already glancing up-island, looking desperately through the trees toward something I know nothing about. So many secrets for such a small island.

"Just answer the question, Teddy," I say in exasperation.

"I wasn't there," he reminds me, "but, as I understand it, you were vivified sometime in the early morning of your first day of school. Dr. Zin brought your vial to Gigi's house, where Mephisto was waiting to vivify you and Star Wetpier was waiting to…" he hesitates, "rewrite your past. Your recent past."

"Star Wetpier. The history teacher?"

"She's a demon. Everyone who works here is either a punk—that's what we call new lost souls—or a demon of some rank. Demons have powers, you see. Star's gift is to rewrite the past. When you were in the initial fog of vivifying that day, she fed you details that kept you from questioning why you were here."

"That's a lot of work to get a coma victim into a snobby school for dead kids."

"If you come with me, I'll explain more."

Teddy grabs me by the arm, and we're running again. He tells me, in short gasps as we race to the road, what's been happening in our absence. He knows because he's bound to Mephisto, his master, who has brought him up to speed, like, telepathically or something.

"The underworld has been in an uproar since you and that Zin boy jumped off the cliff." He charges on. "Mephisto has fallen from the status of devil to archdemon, which is still far above a demon but is, nonetheless, below where he once was. He's been removed from Cania Christy."

"*What?*"

"Gone. Until he can prove himself again, which will require him to rebuild his legions, he cannot lead this school."

"We've got a new headmaster?"

"Don't be too excited," he warns. "Better the devil you know than the devil you don't."

"I'll take my chances."

"Prepare for madness on campus. Everyone's arguing, switching sides," Teddy explains. "Alliances are forming and breaking. It's chaos. And, yes, it's all your fault." He barely pauses for emphasis. "The powerless punks, scheming succubae, darkest demons— everyone that served Mephisto is questioning him. Your escape was like nothing seen before. Many of Mephisto's followers lost faith in him—"

"Faith in a devil!"

Teddy shoots me a glare. "Everyone needs to believe in something."

We bolt out of the woods and onto the road. The massive iron gates to Cania Christy loom ahead. I hear the commotion Teddy's been warning me about: warring staff members trading sides and creating volatile new alliances.

"You should be safe now, though," he says. "The demons won't battle you. And the parents have all left."

I happened to escape on one of the few nights of the year that parents are allowed to visit their kids—and my cries for help as I raced out of Valedictorian Hall, chased by Villicus and Pilot Stone, did not go unnoticed. Not that any of the parents raised a finger to help me. No, they closed their blinds and turned out the lights.

"What does that mean, I should be safe?"

Teddy's breath is fast. "The parents see you as a threat. You killed one of their own. Pilot Stone."

"He had it coming!"

"If that settles your conscience."

He *did* have it coming. Pilot's scheming ways could have jeopardized my life. It was him or me. None of the Cania parents would understand that. I've been an outsider among wealthy people all my life—first back in Atherton, and most definitely here. It'll be a cold day in Hell before they take my side above one of their own.

"The new headmaster is about to arrive. I can feel him." Teddy pauses to focus on whatever he's feeling. I'm never going to get used to living among mystic oddballs like Teddy. "Oh, it's *him*," he says, seeing something I can't imagine. "*He's* the replacement. I should have guessed."

"Who?"

"A liar. A terrible being. A devil we will destroy. Someone you should stay away from."

"*Who?*"

Ignoring me, Teddy pushes through the gates of Cania Christy. We stumble into the closest thing to pandemonium this side of Hell. It's late afternoon. In the half day that separated my departure from my return, the order of Cania Christy has collapsed into chaos as the school has found itself without a leader. An absent headmaster wouldn't be a problem if the staff and faculty weren't composed entirely—save Garnet Descarteres, my art teacher and Ben's ex-girlfriend—of Mephisto's legions. In his absence, they've gone off the rails. I watch as secretaries, Trey Sedmoney, and a teacher named Levi Beemaker board up Goethe Hall's stained-glass windows. Below them, housedads, chem teacher Dr. Naysi, and my sculpting teacher ol' Weinchler curse and throw anything they can get their hands on at the building. Near Valedictorian Hall, the janitor is fielding attacks from a cafeteria lady, who has broken a makeshift switch off a tree and is brandishing it.

"It's so loud!"

At the opposite end of the quad, near the shore, student noses are pressed against the glass in the dorms, where most people must have been when the madness erupted. I search the crowd for the one face I most want to see. But he's not there.

"It's a wonder the parents escaped this madness. Come, to the quad," Teddy says, pointing into the eye of the storm.

I follow him with my head down. Not just because I want to avoid the fighting faculty. But also because I get the sense that, among the student body, there's a warrant out for my arrest. The coma girl who shouldn't have been allowed here in the first place has caused more trouble than she's worth.

I call after Teddy, "Why are they fighting like this?"

"Like I said, they're choosing sides and forming alliances. Those who serve Mephisto are trying to defend themselves against those who've turned. This kind of upheaval isn't rare Downstairs."

"You mean in Hell?"

He nods as we back against a tree in the middle of the quad. And wait. Teddy keeps looking toward the Atlantic.

"This will all be different any second," he says, and I hope he's right.

But I'm not just hoping for peace. Or a new, better leader.

I'm hoping that, if and when this chaos subsides, I'll see the boy I've been trying not to be too obvious about looking for. Ben Zin. His dad's mansion is all the way on the other side of the woods, toward the village. Is he there now? Does he know I'm back? Is he, as Teddy suggested, being punished for helping me escape last night? Will I, too, be punished?

For the last few weeks, I was neighbors with Ben. I lived in the attic bedroom of a house that belonged to Gigi Malone, who sadly took her own life last night. She asked me to throw her body in the ocean, but I didn't. I couldn't. I had to go to Valedictorian Hall, where my vial of blood was stored, and free myself. If I'd stayed, if I'd done what she'd asked, or if I'd gone to Ben's like he'd asked, would this mess have happened?

"Who's the new headmaster?" I ask Teddy. "You saw him?"

A woman's shout interrupts me: "There he is!"

The hollering and smashing stops. We look toward the small dock just north of the dorms, just south of the cliff. There, a caravan of canal boats like you might see in Venice is being nudged against the dock by thick, burly rowers in red-and-white striped shirts. The men and women that fill the boats are dressed like members of the most spectacular circus; they begin, one by one, on shaky feet, to come ashore.

Students file onto the quad, veering away from the unstable staff as they do. I spot my archnemesis, Harper Otto, quickly; it'd be impossible to miss that red-haired Southern beauty queen, especially with her entourage of too-perfect followers. She sees me and mouths, "*Murderer.*" Behind her, someone I like even less—Hiltop P. Shemese, whom I didn't expect to see again—shuffles out of the

woods, smoothing her short bangs and bobbed hair as she flicks a
glare at me, a glare that morphs into a thin grin. She offers a little
clap for Teddy. Only when she's turned back to the caravan do I
smack Teddy.

"I thought you said Mephisto was gone," I say. "Hiltop's obviously still here."

"*Villicus* is no longer in control of Cania. Even if he hadn't
been demoted, the parents wouldn't have stood for it after seeing
him chase a student down like he did you. But Mephisto will never
leave this place, and so his avatar Hiltop remains." He shoots me a
pointed stare. "Until we destroy him—and his replacement—he will
be here in whatever form he can skulk around in."

"And how do you propose *we* destroy him? What's the plan? I'm
not exactly a demon slayer. Unless I can paint him to death, I'm not
gonna be much help."

"I don't know the plan yet."

"Sorry, what?"

"Patience, Miss Merchant," he hisses. "You're rushing like a
common demon. We'll work on it shortly. There's time."

"Here's an idea: let me go home, and come get me when you've
got a plan."

He points hard at the people around us. "Don't talk so loudly,
and don't look so familiar with me. I brought you back here against
your will, remember?"

"How could I forget?"

"Well, then, you're supposed to hate me. Play the part."

That shouldn't be a stretch.

"And remember," he says so quietly I have to read his thin lips,
"no one can know about my secret identity or our plan, when we
create it. Tell them I put you in an unbreakable coma. Tell them
whatever you must. Fight for the Big V to make them believe it. But
do not let on that I'm involved in anything, Miss Merchant, or I will
be killed. No one must know. *Trust no one.*"

"So I've gone from discovering secrets to keeping them?"

"Let's hope so."

Teddy stands on his tiptoes. Everyone is leaning and jumping to
see over the heads of the crowd, to see the man of the hour. Playing
the part of a loyal follower of Mephisto, Teddy grumbles that he

thinks he can see "that egotistical little freak." So our new headmaster has a big ego? I'm not sure that distinguishes him much from Villicus, who was anything but humble.

I watch Hiltop from afar and realize that I'd be a fool to believe that she—the only remaining avatar of Mephisto—is going to take this upheaval lying down; she's probably already knee-deep in a plot none of us can imagine.

"Dia Voletto. He's here," Teddy whispers to me as he points at a man. "See his boldly tattooed arms—I believe you call those *sleeves*? That's his mark; his followers wear tattoos the way Mephisto's followers wear jewels. Those tattoos represent their powers." He charges on. "Look at him. You're not looking! Come, get closer and you'll see little tick marks all over his body. That's how he keeps track of his legions of followers. Anne, come. See your new headmaster. Tell me what you think of him."

But I'm not paying attention to Teddy. Or to Dia Voletto. Or even to Hiltop.

Because Ben has just walked into my line of sight.

two

SAME AS THE OLD BOSS

IN THIS MOMENT, I CAN'T HELP BUT WONDER IF MY RETURN to Wormwood Island isn't the best thing that's ever happened to me. Demons aside. Devil Destruction Challenge aside. Medically induced coma that could kill me aside.

Ben and his dad, Dr. Zin, the recruiter for Cania Christy and a former plastic surgeon, are walking in what could be slow motion directly across from me, only steps from me—and they don't know I'm here. I want to call out, but more than that I want to pause time and simply *look at* the guy I thought I'd never see again. Ben, with his precisely brushed ashen hair. Ben, with his uncannily green eyes, eyes the color of a breaking wave in a Turner shipwreck painting or the sky in a Cézanne seascape. He is tall, his back is straight, and his chin is held high, like his mother must have told him to hold it back when she was alive, and his sister Jeannie was alive, and his life was headed on a different course. Back before a drunk-driving accident brought him to my family's funeral home and changed everything.

Around me, everyone is saying, "Look, look."

I watch Ben and Dr. Zin pass me by. It's only when Dr. Zin falls against a sophomore girl that I realize this is not the picture of a father and son out for a walk. It looks like Ben's hoisting Dr. Zin up, like his dad might fall over at any moment.

"What do you think of him?" Teddy nudges me.

16

"I think he's drunk."

"Voletto?"

No, not Dia Voletto. Dr. Zin is clearly intoxicated. I close my eyes, certain he fell off the wagon after learning about the reckless, destructive escape plan his son was involved in. Now I can see the far-reaching effects of what we'd tried to do: Dr. Zin nearly lost the only child he has left, the son he chose over his daughter. And, without question, Ben will be punished for helping me. What might that punishment be? The worry about it could easily push a recovering alcoholic like Dr. Zin beyond his will to be sober.

I call Ben's name. But the crowd is too noisy.

Taking me by the arm, Teddy ushers me in the opposite direction, through the throngs, up to the front of the crowd where Hiltop is quietly observing the arrival of the new headmaster. The underworld leader known as Dia Voletto is, to my surprise, on his hands and knees just on the edge of the shore. He seems fascinated by something he's spotted in the water.

Hiltop looks angry enough to kill. Which kinda makes me like Dia, her replacement.

"Master," Teddy says to Hiltop, with the slightest bow.

I shudder at the sound of it. *Master*. If my mom wasn't on Teddy's side, I'd be grabbing his satchel, throwing it into the Atlantic, and praying for a miracle in California.

"You've brought her back," Hiltop says to him without deigning to look his way. Or mine.

"I promised I would, Master."

Teddy's convincing enough that I almost believe he was lying to me about this whole celestial takedown mission. Of course, he's had a few years of practice as a fake demon. If he wasn't believable, he'd probably have been destroyed—*I think you can destroy a demon, but hell if I know*—or, at minimum, Mephisto wouldn't have brought him to work at his precious school for dead kids.

"Dia Voletto will need the vials," she tells Teddy with a glance at his satchel. She turns her glare on me. "I told you you'd be back. You thought you got away."

"I did. Your little peon had to abduct me to bring me here. But I guess breaking the basic rules of humanity is the norm on Wormwood Island."

"A bent rule is not a broken rule," she says. "You were signed over to me, and not just until something better came along. You were signed over to me until the day of your graduation. Only I may sever that contract; you may not. There are no refunds at Cania Christy."

"Well, given that you're not even in charge here anymore, whatever contract my dad signed is null and void."

She clenches her fists. "All the contracts have been revised, to be sure, and Dr. Zin will begin traversing the world to have Cania's 200 parents sign their precious children over to Headmaster Voletto," she says. "Of course, he'll have help."

"Help? From whom?"

"I've found myself a second recruiter, you see."

While Hiltop watches Dia Voletto, who is still transfixed seemingly by his own reflection, I watch Hiltop. This small, nearly invisible girl with a face so simple, she could be a doodle; she's hardly fleshed out human. I'd never given much thought to her before—I'd barely even seen her on campus before last night—but now I see her: dots for eyes; long, thin nose; scribble of lips. Designed to be overlooked. The avatars of Mephistopheles are more perfunctory than artistic. If Mephistopheles is the devil with the strongest hold on mankind, he is interested in something beyond the aesthetic beauty of this world.

"A second recruiter?" I repeat.

"Surely you knew you'd be punished for what you did, Miss Merchant," Hiltop says.

The main reason I tried to escape Cania Christy was to keep my dad from being as enslaved to Mephisto as Ben's dad is. Could this be my punishment?

"Your father agreed this morning. It took very little to persuade him."

I practically growl at Teddy, hoping he realizes just what he's done. I may be the one being punished, but my dad's bearing the brunt of it. To atone for my rebellious behavior, my dad—Mr. Stanley Merchant, funeral director in the most expensive zip code in the United States—is Cania's newest recruiter.

"Why would you punish *him*?" I ask Hiltop. "I'm the one to punish. Punish me instead."

"Hush. I would think you'd be more interested in the arrival of Dia Voletto."

"I'm not. Not in the slightest."

"I thought your *prosperitas thema* was to look closer. And yet you're missing everything."

A burst of activity near the water draws my eye. Dia Voletto is getting to his feet, and a dozen of his servants have bolted toward the student body to make room for their leader. Two part the crowd, shoving me and Hiltop back, while two follow closely behind and roll out a deep purple carpet. Six more men cart wood and a gauzy fabric up to the middle of the quad, where they hurriedly pound together pillars and string tulle over them, creating a gazebo. A platform and podium are placed within.

Dia's entourage, all dressed fantastically, start up to the podium. Dia is in their midst. He glances around, searching the crowd. I'm stunned by how attractive he is, how very different he looks from his predecessor. This twentysomething who could be mistaken for the front man in an Oregon indie band is Villicus's replacement?

"Is he searching for you, Hiltop?" I elbow my little enemy.

"Guess again."

No sooner has she uttered those words than Dia's gaze lands on Teddy, who's standing next to me. Dia stops in his tracks. His eyelids are heavily lashed. His eyes slide my way and back to Teddy. Most of the students have continued on to the quad, but some stop to watch Dia approach us.

"You," he says to Teddy. "How do you know this girl?"

A cold sweat breaks out under my uniform. The last thing I want is attention.

"I'm her Guardian," Teddy tells Dia.

"Her Guardian? You oversee her. You influence her. If I understand right, you brought her back here after she liberated herself."

"What is your point, Dia?" Hiltop interjects.

Dia and Hiltop meet eyes. You don't have to read souls to feel the tension between these two. I wish I could slink away unnoticed, but that's unlikely.

"Ted Rier," Dia says, "you have a new mission. You will scout the planet for a new home for Mephisto." He grabs Teddy's satchel and snaps his fingers.

And Teddy's gone.

Stunned, I turn and catch my classmate Augusto staring, gape-mouthed, at the now-empty space between me and Hiltop. His gaze meets mine. And then he looks away, busying himself. Has he known all along that we're dealing with the darkest of all arts here? Does everyone secretly know? Am I the only person who thinks it's nuts to live like this? Are the rest complacent? Or are they simply smarter than I? They know it's best not to look closer, as my *prosperitas thema*, or success thesis, would have me do, but to look the other way. Not to fight the madness of this island's leaders as Ben and I tried to do, but to play along.

How did we ever think we'd outplay the likes of Mephistopheles?

How does Teddy think we have a chance of destroying him or Dia Voletto? And now that Teddy's gone, what am I going to do? Take on these devils by myself?

Without the slightest look in my direction or another word to Hiltop, Dia continues up the path. I follow the crowd. I keep my eyes open for Ben.

"Miss Merchant," Hiltop says, catching my sleeve.

I shove her away. "Stop. Touching. Me."

"I thought you might wish to meet your new Guardian."

New Guardian. *Dammit!* Because Teddy's gone now. Thanks for nothing, Dia.

"How could you possibly know who my Guardian is?" I ask her. "You're not in charge anymore."

"He's the only Cania staff member available to take on a pupil right now."

I turn and cross my arms. "Who?"

That's when I see him. Over her shoulder. He's standing by the water. I recognize him instantly: his short, cropped hair and his stocky build. The scowl he wears is vaguely familiar—for weeks, he faked friendly smiles for me.

"Pilot Stone," I whisper. In place of his Cania Christy uniform are janitor's coveralls. "I shouldn't be surprised."

One day I won't flinch at the endless life cycle possible in a world run by demons. I'll accept that a boy can die in a house fire he set, live again here, die by my own hand, and yet live again here.

"You're like a cockroach." I watch Pilot stride toward me and Hiltop.

"You can't keep a good man down," he says. "After you so cruelly ended my life, I found myself in Mephisto's domain."

"Hell. Where you belong."

Hiltop interrupts. "But I couldn't leave my protégé to burn like some common lost soul. Especially not with my followers fleeing in the one moment I could actually use their allegiance."

"I will always be there for Master Mephistopheles," Pilot says. A beam of sunlight catches the brooch near Pilot's nametag. He is one of Mephisto's now.

"Because you're loyal? Or because you want to avoid, oh, say, the fires of Hell?"

"Get your student under control," Hiltop warns Pilot.

"His student?" I repeat.

"Miss Merchant," Hiltop says, "Mr. Stone is your new Guardian."

"Hold on, *what?*"

Pilot's my Guardian? Whether a student wins the Big V or not rides almost entirely on how much their Guardian is willing to fight for them during the debate on graduation day. If my Guardian hates me, I don't stand a chance.

"Pilot's my punishment?" I guess.

Luckily, I'm only in a coma. I don't need the Big V the same way everyone else at Cania Christy does. So I don't need Pilot the way other students need their Guardians. Hiltop is silently following my line of thought.

"If you think you can simply wake up and escape the competition," she says to me, "never forget that it only takes the tiniest increase in your pentobarbital drip for your coma to become a little less…terminable."

"You can't kill me, Hiltop. There are rules."

Fact: I don't *know* if those are the rules, but it seems like they ought to be! Demons can't just run around knocking off the people they want to abuse.

"Rules can be bent. Accidents happen." She forces me and Pilot to stand shoulder to shoulder and holds us tight, watching us squirm. "Now, if the two of you can try to get along, I'm going to watch Dia Voletto bumble his way through his introduction."

As she strolls away, Pilot shoves me. "You're gonna regret the day you ever met me, Merchant."

"'Gonna'? As in, future tense?"

"Let the record show I have no intention—zero, zilch, nada—of helping you," he says, his chest puffy with some delusional sense of power over me. "But I will insist that you change your PT. *Looking closer* is total crap, plus you're kinduv good at it, so that doesn't work for me. I'm thinking something like ... fitting those birthing hips into a size two. Or having a straight smile." I run my tongue over my teeth; the tooth Ben inadvertently straightened for me last week is crooked again. "That should guarantee your death."

"Piss off, Pilot."

Leaving him swearing after me, I take off to the quad, where I look high and low for Ben. I wind my way closer to the stage. I try not to react when students, noticing me, jab me with their elbows and whisper, "Murdering Merchant." I don't care; I just want to find Ben.

Far beyond Valedictorian Hall, I spy Hiltop walking with Dr. Zin. He has his suitcase and his black doctor's bag. He's leaving. I stand on my tiptoes, looking for Ben. Where did he go? He wouldn't get expelled, would he? He couldn't! Ben isn't even a student here.

"Attention, students," calls Dr. Weinchler, who is at the podium with a dizzying array of new-to-our-world demons sitting, leaning, and standing behind him. He's notorious for speaking quietly and stammering through his words; when almost no one notices him, he glares around in frustration and his wispy white hair floats side to side.

"Attention," Weinchler repeats. "Be quiet."

Pilot arrives at my side, grumbling, just as a striking woman dressed in green, with emerald-colored streaks in her wavy hair and a long jade vine tattooed on her arm, swaggers up behind Weinchler. She whispers something to him that makes him grin and replaces him at the podium.

Unlike Weinchler, this woman commands attention.

She doesn't have to do more than *be here* for the hundreds of people in the crowd to fall silent and stare, in jealous awe, at her. I've always thought of myself as relatively comfortable in my skin and cool with how I look, but looking at this woman, all I can think is, *How easy it must be to be her.* No, in truth, all I can think is, *I wish I could be her.* Hating the insecurities that thought reveals, I force myself to stand straighter, hold my head higher, and hope that Pilot's looking at me now just because he's plotting ways to hurt me, not because he's taking pleasure in the jealousy written all over my face.

The island as a whole, barking sea lions and rustling leaves included, goes silent waiting for the woman in green to speak.

"Good afternoon," she says at last.

I want to have her voice.

When I tear my eyes from her, I notice everyone else is transfixed, too. It's not because this woman is beautiful, though she is. No, it's like she's the sum of the parts I wish I had; maybe everyone else is thinking the same thing. We all envy her.

"My name is Invidia, and I am pleased to welcome you, students, to the inauguration of the second headmaster in the sixty-five-year history of the Cania Christy Preparatory Academy."

As we applaud, I wonder about her name. I know Invidia is from the underworld; it goes without saying that she's a demon of some kind. But while all of Mephisto's followers have common names, like Kate Haem and Eve Risset (two of the most evil secretaries that ever lived), this woman's name is classic Latin. *Invidia*. Perhaps all of Dia Voletto's followers have Latin names. I make a mental note to look up the meaning of *Invidia* after the ceremony.

"Without further ado," Invidia says, "allow me to introduce the gentleman you have all been anxiously waiting to meet." She pauses to allow more clapping. With an elegant flourish, she welcomes Dia Voletto to the podium. "Headmaster Voletto!"

If Mephisto and his legions are physically simple or unattractive by design, Dia and his crew might have been created just to be gawked at, stared after, and maybe even yearned for. I could never see Dia Voletto as anything but the underworld führer he is—but that doesn't mean I can't appreciate art when I behold it. Like most interesting art, Dia is composed of imperfect pieces that, together, are unlike anything the world has beheld before. He's beautiful. And I'm not the only one who's noticed that: in the corner of my eye, I spy Harper and the Model UN from Hell preening.

"Look at this!" Dia exclaims as he takes his place at the podium and gazes at us all. "Such wonder! Such splendor! Such beauty! Students, thank you for this warm welcome, and please accept my sincere apologies for thrusting such a change on you so swiftly. I assure you, under my leadership, this school will rise to be the haven of joy and opportunity you all wish it to be."

The sunlight, which has been flooding the normally cloudy island, glistens off his dark, wide irises. If you didn't know better, you'd swear there was something charming about Dia Voletto.

"That, of course, brings me to the matter I wish to discuss with you."

I watch Harper and her gang move closer to the stage, the better to bat their fake eyelashes at Dia. When they move, they reveal Ben, who's standing just behind the gap they've created, the gap that two large boys quickly fill. I try to peer between their massive shoulders even as they snap at me to turn around. I'm *this close* to waving to get Ben's attention when I stop.

Because he's not alone.

Garnet Descarteres is standing next to him.

Garnet. As in, Ben's ex-girlfriend, Garnet. As in the former valedictorian who traded her soul to be with Ben again. What's *she* doing with him? Hold on, why's she stroking his arm?

I face forward before either of them can see me looking.

My heart is thumping so loudly, I'm sure it'll give me away.

That can't be what it looks like, I think. Maybe she was dusting a bee off his sleeve. Or maybe not. I want to look again, to pick up cues, hints, or suggestions, but I don't dare. I tell myself what Ben told me: that he wasn't interested in her, that it had always been me, that from the day his funeral service was held in my family home—from the day I saw him in his open casket, and felt compelled to sketch him in those few moments before the mourners arrived, and tucked that sketch into his casket… and, finally, hoping no one would come into the reception room, kissed him on the cheek—it had been me. Ben told me I was the girl with the blonde hair he'd been waiting for. Not Garnet. *Not Garnet.*

"Hey," Pilot jabs me hard in the side. "Pay attention, psycho."

I ignore him like the pesky blackfly he is.

"Oh, wait, your mom's the psycho."

Ben wants to be with me. I'm sure he does. Yet I can't seem to fight the clouds of doom, self-loathing, and sadness rolling into my mind. Ben and Garnet? Could it be? So freakin' *soon*?

"And she tried to kill you, didn't she?"

That's enough! I hiss at Pilot, "Let's not compare parents. Your dad's Sexcapade of the Century hardly qualified him as Father of the Year."

I gave him what he wanted: a reaction. He smiles.

"I'm gonna make your life a living hell," he says.

I glance at Ben and Garnet again. Yup, still there. Still side by side.

"Take a number," I tell Pilot.

On stage, two men position a large, covered canvas on an easel. Dia stares in wonder from the men to us to his team to the world he's about to call home, with its woods colored in 100 shades of green, with its jagged stone still wet from last night's ice storm, with its vast and wild Atlantic Ocean spreading toward an azure and butter yellow horizon that is, only now, clouding over. Dia seems to be in love with it all.

"This, my friends," Dia has his fingers on the canvas' cover, "is the matter at hand."

He whips back the cover and reveals an architect's sketch.

"It's called Cania College," he says as he runs his hand over the surface of the large drawing. "And it is my masterpiece."

If he was trying to start his reign with a bang, he's done it. His audience, imaginations captivated by the possibilities that a college—something to graduate to—presents, explodes with applause. I'm a little less enthusiastic. Just last night, Mephisto told me he planned to expand. And now Dia's doing it. Could they be plotting something bigger together? They seem to loathe one another, but I'd be a fool to take anything at face value here.

"You see," Dia explains when the clapping finally slows, "with the recent emptying of that strange little village on the southern tip of the island, an opportunity to expand has presented itself.

"We have yet to secure a contractor to manage the job, but we have unwavering faith that the right person will be found. The right person can always be found, for the right price."

The subtext: some mourning dad, or mom, somewhere is about to give up his contracting business to get his dead kid into this place.

I glance in Ben's direction. He and Garnet are gone. Are they together because he thinks I'm in California? Or could there be more to it? Perhaps Ben and Garnet were playing me. But to what end? As the ceremony comes to a close, as everyone fans out, and as

Pilot continues whispering to me all the ways he'll ruin me, I realize what's happening: I'm letting all the darkness here get to me—the devils in charge, the slimy Guardians. Ben isn't like them. He's not.

But then why was he with Garnet?

"You're on your own," Pilot snaps at me. "Enjoy the long, slow walk toward your own death."

Ignoring him comes easily. I head toward the woods—so I can go to Gigi's and dispose of her remains like I promised—but I run smack into Harper. She has her hands on her hips. Her clones are arranged in a circle around her, but they're one short: Tallulah Josey isn't here.

"You've got a lot of nerve coming back, Murdering Merchant," Harper says.

"It wasn't by choice."

Plum chimes in. "Is that your excuse for that big hair of yours, too?" Chorus of *oh snap*s. She high-fives the Model UN from Hell. "As in, not by choice? Get it? Your hair?"

"Yeah, thanks for explaining that, um, sick burn."

Harper eyes me. "So how does it feel?"

I hope she's not talking about Ben and Garnet. I haven't even had time to sit with that yet; I'm sure as hell not ready to talk about it, especially not to *her*.

"Having my life stolen from me?" I ask. "Or standing here and gossiping with my favorite gang of dead girls?"

"How does it feel to know you're going to lose the Big V to me now that Headmaster Voletto is here?" Harper juts her butt out and begins gyrating on the spot. "I'm gonna be twerking up on that fine man, and you can kiss your chance to win good-bye."

"What's twerking?"

"How long have you been in a coma?" she asks in a fluttering, glittery huff. "Look, just keep your stuff neat 'n' tidy on your side of the room, got it? I don't know how small your trailer was back in C-A, but we keep it spick-and-span 'round these parts."

Wait. She's not saying what I think she's saying, is she?

"I'm rooming with you?"

"There's gotta be a reason your boxes of poor bitch junk are all over my place. Nothin' to keep secret from you anymore, moron. You've graduated to the big leagues, I guess." She crosses her arms.

"And don't get too excited. You can't kill me like you did your last roommate."

"What?"

"Murdering Merchant on her murdering rampage. You shot Gigi before you offed Pilot. You're a total psycho."

She and her team whirl—in unmistakably perfect timing—and strut away. I'm about to shout that I had nothing to do with Gigi's suicide, but why bother? The truth doesn't matter on Wormwood Island. Avoiding a thousand death stares—do people really think I killed Gigi?—I head toward the dorms. Reluctantly.

I stop dead when I spot Ben and Garnet standing outside the boys' dorm.

They don't notice me. So I tuck behind a tree. And peek out to watch them.

Six or seven boxes are stacked against the dorm's stone walls. Garnet is holding one as she leans, balances, and kisses Ben, who's crouched to hoist up another box, on the cheek.

Feeling hot all over, I watch his reaction. This will be the test. Was he faking with me? Is he still into her? Did he lie to me about the two of them?

He smiles at her.

And I want to die.

Maybe I'm already dead, and this is Hell.

This is definitely Hell.

Garnet disappears through the front door, leaving Ben outside. My stomach is in my throat. It was only *hours* ago that Ben was kissing *me*. Was that all BS? Who kisses someone and then goes back to his ex-girlfriend?

A dead branch snaps under my foot. Ben turns at the sound. I try to flatten against the back side of the tree, but I'm not fast enough.

"Hello?" he calls.

Did he see me?

"You. Behind the tree. Hiding."

I know I'll look like a total spaz if I keep hiding. So, holding my breath, I step out.

three

THE SACRIFICIAL LAMB

"HI, BEN," I SAY WITH THE LAMEST WAVE IN THE HISTORY of waves.

Ben drops the box he's holding. He mouths my name, but I just keep standing like a moron. I feel naked. I have to glance down to be sure I'm still wearing this idiotic school uniform because I've never felt so exposed in my life.

"Are you a ghost?" he asks in a breath, like he's not sure if I'll float away at the sound. I can't speak, not with the memory of Garnet kissing his cheek and, earlier, stroking his arm. "Anne?"

Oh, God. My name said by his voice. This is why people have names. This is why people have voices.

He glances over his shoulder, checking the open doorway, and looks back at me like he's worried I'll be gone. But instead of appearing relieved to see me, his face falls.

"Tell me you're not here," he says. He must see my chest moving, my breath struggling to flow. "God, you're really here. You're back."

I nod once, almost imperceptibly. But he's watching me closely enough that he sees it. He closes his eyes. It's my chance to get a little closer to him, but I do so only tentatively, on tiptoes, like he might bite if I cross an unseen line. Wormwood Island and its uncrossable lines.

His head is down. He looks the same, but different. I knew him only briefly and left him only hours ago—but he doesn't seem to be the unaging sixteen-year-old I left behind.

"Did you die?" he asks without looking up again.

"Teddy was waiting for me in California," I tell him and struggle to keep my voice even, certain it will betray my feelings.

I've always known I'd be a fool to believe Ben Zin could ever want to be with me; I should have expected him to reunite with Garnet and forget me as the fleeting memory the universe might have planned for me to be. I should have known better, been smarter. But when's the last time a person *reasoned* with a heart?

"That skinny beanpole Teddy?" he asks.

"He's got some sort of crooked nurse giving me just enough meds to stay in a coma. There's no escape. Mephisto wants me here, so…"

"He was in California when you woke up?"

"He got there fast. The perks of being a demon, right? Transcending physicality and all that." I awkwardly search for words to fill the dead air. Ben keeps his head down.

"Of course, he had to fly back here like a normal person. Because he had to carry my vials. Can't just vaporize into spirit form when you've got three real, physical tubes of blood to tote along, I guess. Though how he got them through security is beyond me." I laugh a little.

He groans. He's not taking this as lightly as I'm trying to.

I glance at the doorway just as he lifts his head and looks there, too. The doorway's still empty.

"Garnet's inside?" I ask.

"She'll be back any second."

"So. You and Garnet."

He doesn't say anything. He looks down again.

Silence is worse than admitting it. It feels like I could freak out— just totally blow up—at Ben, but in truth only a part of me is angry. The other part, the bigger part, the part that tries to protect my aching heart, is whispering madly for me to avoid saying or doing anything that might prompt him to tell me what I don't want to hear: that he and Garnet are, in fact, together again—a fact that would make everything that happened last night, including my first real kiss, anything but real.

"I can't believe this is happening," he says.

"Neither can I."

"Anne, listen, I've gotta get my head together. I mean, what was it all for? This is…horrifying."

Bad, yes, but horrifying?

"Please, get out of here before she comes back down."

"So you're," I hesitate over the words, "back with Garnet?"

"*No!* No. Of course not."

Thank God. I want to pause time, to stop him from saying anything that might dull my relief. Why does it always seem like the good things will vanish long before I can appreciate them?

"She's nothing, Anne. A means to an end. Or that's what she was gonna be." He finally looks at me fully. The tears blurring his pupils make his eyes seem to be made of pure color. "I thought you were free. I thought I'd actually done something good."

"You did. It's just that evil trumps good here."

"Look," he says, running his hands through his hair. "Meet me at Gigi's. Give me ten minutes, okay?"

Without a second look and without even waiting for me to agree, Ben disappears into the dorm. I hear him storm up the stairs and stop midway. He says something, and Garnet says something. And she laughs.

Is she laughing at me?

Are they both? Are they laughing together? As a couple?

The slap in the face that was Pilot's betrayal still stings; it reminds me that being two-faced is a survival strategy, a universal PT. Just because I want Ben to want me doesn't mean he does. Just because he kissed me doesn't mean it meant something to him. And what does that mean, Garnet is a "means to an end"?

I turn to go. But not south, where Gigi's house is. I go north instead, to the cliff.

I don't feel the grass under my boots. I don't hear the whispering of frustrated kids taking pleasure in the humiliation of the Coma Girl they've loathed since the day I arrived here, but especially since I killed one of their own—and Gigi, too, as the rumors go. I don't notice the clouds drift over the sun as I cross the empty parking lot and start up the hill. I don't wrap my arms around myself as the wind picks up and thick, slushy raindrops start to fall, then cease. I don't even notice, when I make it to the top of the hill turned pink by the setting sun's light cast over slick gray rocks, that Dia Voletto is here already. It's not until he speaks that I realize I've got company.

"Anne Merchant."

"I didn't see you here, Headmaster." I move to leave. There's not enough room up here for his malevolence and my frustration.

"You don't want to know how I know your name?"

"It's a Cania pre-req, knowing my name. Everyone knows everything about me. More than I know about myself."

"That may be true."

I glance at his feet, expecting to see Villicus's old jeweled bag, the one he used to transport vials in only to throw them off the cliff. Has Dia got someone to expel? There's no bag at his feet. It's just him. He's traded his ringleader attire for normal human clothes: he's wearing Doc Martens, fitted jeans, and a big woolly cardigan; his hands are stuffed in the pockets. The cold evening air has colored his cheeks and made his dark eyes glossy. Looking as he does, he could be on a photo shoot for J.Crew.

"Come," he says. "Stand by me. Take a look at this spectacular seascape."

The last thing I want is to make nice with the newest devil to curse my life with his presence. When he notices my hesitation, he chuckles.

"Are you cold? Take my sweater."

"I'm fine."

"It's no problem. I've got fire and brimstone built into my bones. Keeps me toasty warm." He waves to get my attention when I don't react. "Hello? That was a joke."

"Right." I wonder if Ben's on his way to Gigi's already. Is he planning to break the bad news to me that he and Garnet have finally declared their love for one another? "I should get back to campus."

"What did you come up here for? Planning your next escape?"

"I don't know why I'm here."

"To celebrate your victory over Mephistopheles."

Our eyes meet. I'm the first to look away. "There was no victory."

"I beg to differ." He holds his hand out for me. "Come."

I don't take it, but I reluctantly shuffle to stand at his side. Thick rain has started to fall again. We stare through it and over the pinkish-gray ocean. Droplets make disappearing divots in the low waves across the water. The setting sun will soon take its warm glow to the mainland. I should leave, but I don't know where I'd go.

"Imagine all of this as your kingdom," he says. "Only a fool would risk losing something so beautiful."

"Some people don't feel worthy of beauty."

"Those people are the world's biggest fools. Beauty is a human birthright. Your souls are by far the loveliest entities I've ever beheld, but this landscape—this world—is a close second. Fools turn from it."

"Physical beauty is impermanent," I counter absently. "Some would say fools fixate on it."

I see his mouth drooping in disappointment for perhaps the first time since he glimpsed his reflection in the water. I don't want to risk the ire of this devil leader; as nice as he may be acting, I know it's all just an act. So I backtrack. If he wants to be dazzled by beauty, who am I to stop him? Ben dazzled me, and I would have rather never been woken from that trance.

"That's what artists are for," I offer. "We preserve beauty as we see it, Headmaster."

"Call me D."

That's not gonna happen.

"So," I say, wishing he would leave and wondering if I should, "when did you find out you were being sent here?"

"Sent here?" He tsks. "I came. Intentionally."

"To build the college?"

"If you think any devil gives a damn about educating the masses."

"So why, then? Why are you here—aside from replacing our shamed ex-headmaster?"

"Why are *you* here?"

I scoff. "A devil wants my dad's network, and he got a demon to bring me here."

"Is that really the reason?"

He stares ahead. I glance at him, wondering what he means, and in that second, I can't help but deconstruct his profile as any artist would do. Each of his features is flawed, yet in combination they're striking. Little wonder he was as taken by his reflection in the water as Narcissus.

"You're an artist, Anne?"

"In some sense of the word." I wipe raindrops from my face. "It's hard to be an artist when your every move is graded. Not much room for creative license." I catch him looking at me in the strangest way, as if he's deconstructing me like I did him. There's something about him. A familiarity. "Have I seen you before? Did you visit Cania last week or something?"

He shakes his head no. He looks like he's about to add something, but his glistening stare drifts to the entry point of the cliff-top. I follow his gaze to find Ben, out of breath and looking bewildered, standing in the shadows at the top of the slick hill. He is watching us just as I watched him and Garnet. How did he know I was up here? Or did he?

"Am I interrupting?" Ben asks us.

"Mr. Zin," Dia says. "This must be a popular spot."

Dia moves to help Ben up the last step of the steep hill. The three of us stand awkwardly—at least, it feels awkward to me—until Dia realizes Ben and I are not leaving. He wraps himself tighter in his cardigan, nods our way, and retreats easily down the slippery path to campus, vanishing in the brush.

That leaves me alone with Ben.

"Did you already go to Gigi's?" I ask him.

He's still trying to catch his breath. "There and back. Mr. Watso was there, and so was Gigi—vivified Gigi. They were dragging her remains into the water."

"You saw them?"

"They told me you hadn't come by. I had a hunch you'd be here."

Silence settles over us like the cold rain on our hair. Ben and I are separated by a mere three feet. That's not a lot of room to cross, but right now it feels like the English Channel. Whatever miracle brought down the walls around him and around me last night is unlikely to make a reappearance. Too much has happened.

It's not just Garnet.

It's that the thing we created together—my escape—failed spectacularly. How can we move past that?

"You're shivering," Ben says at last.

I hadn't noticed. I feel like we've been standing in the cold for a lifetime—a proper one, not a Cania one—when Ben takes off his school blazer and wraps it around my shoulders.

I thank him.

He says it's no problem.

Our voices are quieter than they should be. They are, like the inches of physical space between us, bricks rebuilding the walls. If I were Garnet, I could get close to him, I could kiss him like she easily did and laugh with him like she easily did. Instead, I rock on my heels and try not to shiver too noticeably. He's going to think we ought to go in to escape the rain, and then what? And then it's all over, like it never happened? We can't leave. I need to say something. Do something.

"I'm sorry about the way I was on campus just now," he says at last. "Please don't be angry."

"I'm…confused, Ben."

"What you saw with Garnet, it wasn't real. She doesn't know that yet, but trust me."

I slip his jacket off and hold it out to him. "You can understand how that might be a little tough for me."

"I really can't."

"Well, then there's even less hope for us than I'd thought."

We both eye his coat, this symbol of something much bigger than polyester lining, itchy wool, and the Cania crest. He surprises me by taking my bare, freezing arm and sliding it, clumsily, into the sleeve. He shuffles behind me to drape the coat, and he bends and shifts my other arm into the other sleeve, trying to be delicate, until I think my shoulder might pop out of its socket.

"Could you make this any harder?" he says under his breath. "This is why I work with clay."

Trying not to smile, I shift my shoulder and shape my hand so he can pull his coat up and over me. He adjusts it a little. Rolls a cuff. Unrolls it. And stands back to admire his handiwork. Girl in a school blazer. Major success.

He tugs the collar up. And, in doing so, pulls me onto my tippy-toes. Close to his face, close to his lips. Not close enough to be *close*, but close enough to make me believe that we could close the gap in little time.

Am I wrong to think his jaw is more defined than it was just yesterday? Or that small lines now run in thin rivers at the corners of his brilliant but sad eyes? Or that his shoulders are broader and he's at least an inch taller? Ben looks the part of the twenty-one-year-old guy he is, the guy who was trapped in a teenager's body and doomed to live forever as an unaging, beautiful sixteen-year-old boy, the eternally youthful boy Teddy scorned.

"You think there's no hope for us?" he asks me, still holding me by the collar. "Is this part of your dark, brooding mortician's-daughter façade?"

"Is stringing along multiple girls part of your hot-guy-in-school façade?"

"Is that what you think of me?"

"That you're a philanderer?"

"That I'm a hot guy?"

I smirk. Was there ever any doubt? I've been a gelatinous mess since he first uttered my name.

My gaze moves back and forth between his eyes and mouth. I see myself reflected in his darkening irises, his dilated pupils. I look away. Because I don't want to lose myself in him—God knows that would be easy.

"I'd say there's hope for us, Miss Merchant."

"Hope is the worst of all evils," I whisper. "It prolongs our torments."

"You're quoting Nietzsche?"

"Loosely."

"Here, all we have is hope," he says.

"Well, isn't that ironic?"

"The irony of hope in Hell on Earth?"

I shrug. "'Abandon all hope, ye who enter here'—isn't that written on the gates of Hell?"

"In the *Inferno*." He smiles, and his bright eyes meet mine. "Do you have any idea how much it turns me on when you quote Dante and Nietzsche within seconds of each other?"

I'm about to laugh when he, at last, presses his lips to mine. I'm on my tiptoes, so I stumble a little until he wraps his arms around me, steadying me. How this happened, how we've crossed the chasm that seemed greater than the distance between Hell and Heaven, is a testament to either our humanity or our divinity here. We're either completely weak and foolish or part of something bigger. This kiss is part of something bigger.

"My Anne," he whispers into my hair, near my ear, as he pulls gently away, leaving me in shivers. "We tried to outsmart the devil, and we screwed it up royally, didn't we?"

"Like Charles and Camilla," I say. He laughs a little. "*Royally*. Get it?"

He leans back. "That's pretty bad."

"You could've done better?"

"Working with 'screwed it up royally'?" He thinks about it. His hands are on my lower back. I pray we'll never, ever move. Let the rain freeze us in place. "Maybe something like, 'Like a lightbulb in Buckingham Palace.'"

I wrinkle my whole face.

"Not good?" he asks.

"Worse than mine."

His grin grows. But as our shallow breaths come and go, as rain collects on us, and as his eyes darken, it fades. At least his arms stay around me. And mine around him.

"I heard your dad's working with my dad now," he says. "So we were right about what Mephisto wanted with you."

"I've never wanted to be wrong so much."

"Always the A student," he says. "I assume your dad's new job was your punishment?"

"That plus two cherries on top."

"Two? Lucky you."

"Harper is my roommate."

"Ouch."

"And Pilot is my new Guardian."

"Double ouch! Damn, I thought *I* had it rough."

"What's your sentence?" I ask him. "You're being forced to produce twenty more soulless copies of the Dance of Death sculpture?"

His smile is weak. "You're wearing it."

I glance down at his blazer. He's always worn a school blazer; it's part of the reason I'd assumed he was a senior. But I understand his meaning in little time.

"They made you a student," I guess.

He doesn't respond; that's response enough. I stumble out of his hold and steady myself against a tree stump, which we soon sit on, side by side. In silence. I drop my chin onto my hands and stare ahead, piecing together the implications of Ben's punishment. The reason he looks like he's twenty-one now is because the curse that kept him young has been lifted; he's now cursed with a fraction of the life he could have had.

"Tell me you're a junior," I say hopefully.

He shakes his head. "Cania's newest senior."

So much for hope! Ben's only got a little over eight months until graduation at the end of May, when they'll award the Big V to one senior—and kill all the others. Eight months in which to prove himself. Not impossible, but most seniors started the competition in their junior year and, thus, have a whole extra year on him.

"I can't believe this is the fallout of what we did. You're going to need the most insanely motivated Guardian to help you win this late in the game, Ben."

"Let's be real. Winning is unlikely," he says. "You don't know who my Guardian is."

"Oh, God, who?"

He raises his gaze to mine. "You saw her kiss me on the cheek a half hour ago."

"They gave you Garnet?" I jump to my feet and start pacing as he looks on. "*She's* your Guardian?"

"Did you think I was helping her move her own boxes into the guys' dorm?"

"Is that why she kissed you?"

"That's why I let her." His voice is a whisper as I stomp back and forth. "I thought you were gone. Sucking up to her is—was—my only chance of being with you again. She was, as heartless as it sounds, a means to an end."

"*She'll* be fighting for you?"

"Ha."

"Ben."

"And you'll never guess my PT."

"I don't want to know." I stop pacing and roll my head up to the sky. "You will succeed in life by giving crazy ex-girlfriends second chances. You will succeed in life by making out with girls formerly known as Lizzy who sold their souls to be with you."

"It's to make sacrifices," he says. "That's my PT."

I sigh. And give it some thought. "Well, that doesn't sound *that* bad."

But he's a step ahead of me, explaining before I can speak. "She wants me to be with her. The first sacrifice, if she had her way, would be you."

I close my eyes. The rain is letting up, but it feels heavier and colder than ever. I was *this* close to being with Ben. *This close.* And now she'll have him again. I'll have to walk the halls and see them holding hands, eating lunch together, and kissing. I'd tear my eyes out rather than watch that.

"So that's the last nail in the coffin. In *our* coffin," I say, resigned to our doom.

"No, Anne, listen." Ben joins me and cups his palms around my face so I can't help but look into his beautiful eyes and watch his lips—lips that were *juuust* about mine. "It's you I want."

I shrug out of his hold. I can't pretend that being with Ben makes sense. Not if his life will be even shorter because of it.

"You have to give Garnet what she wants if you're going to win."

"Who said I wanted to win?"

"You've been hanging around Pilot Stone too long."

"Har har."

"She's a wily one, Ben—I'll give her that. She figured out how to separate us. No wonder she won the Big V last year."

"She may be clever, but she misjudged my feelings for you."

His feelings for me are perhaps the only topic I'd ever like to discuss, if given the choice, but that's not in the cards right now. Hearing about his feelings will only make it harder to sever our ties so he can play, and win, her game.

"Anne, I want to opt out of the Big V competition."

"That's not an option."

"I'm already dead."

"Everyone is."

"You're not."

"Yeah, and I'd like to live again. With you."

He blushes. "What if we could just treat these next months like the gift they are?"

"Sorry, but where you see a gift, I see gift wrap on a ticking time bomb."

I'm pacing again.

His gaze follows me patiently. His calm resolve only frustrates me more. He can't actually be serious about this. Give up the chance to live again—and be with me *for real* off this island—just because he doesn't think Garnet will fight for him? No. He has to be with her. She thinks he's into her again; he needs to roll with that, and I'll just have to wait until he wins...then wake up and join him in California.

"Anne, come on," he says, interrupting my scheming. "Stop thinking about tomorrow."

"I'm thinking about tonight. I'm thinking about you tracking down Garnet and throwing yourself at her within the hour. Kiss her. Tell her you love her. Do whatever it takes to win your life back, Ben."

"That's crazy."

"*Not* doing it would be crazy."

"Come on. Be young and reckless with me." He stops me mid-stride. "Just live in the here and now, where we're together and we can be as connected as I've been dreaming about."

Before I can list off the many, many head injuries he must be suffering from, he presses his lips softly to mine, then more powerfully. I stagger on the spot. He draws his hands down to my shoulders and, with a need that surprises me, pulls me about as close to him as a person can get without actually melting into him, which it sort of feels like I'm doing. I wonder if the lines around us are blurring, like they do when he holds my hand. To test the limits, I curl my fingers into his soft hair.

Definitely melting into him.

I'm kissing Ben Zin. I'm kissing Ben Zin. In the moonlight on an island, I'm kissing Ben Zin.

And he's kissing me. His lips trail away from mine and run up my cheekbones, to my eyelids, and down my jaw, softly, wonderfully, to my throat.

Definitely melting into him.

I open my eyes to see his are closed. I close my eyes and imagine his open.

I think he says my name. And I'm pretty sure I say his. Warm shivers replace the cold ones. His lips find mine again. His breath is fast, and I'm not sure if I'm hyperventilating or holding my breath— air intake is, frankly, not high on my priority list right now.

It's not until I begin to unbutton his shirt—just one button— that our eyes open. Ben looks at me, his face flushed, and grabs my hands, stopping me.

"Anne," he breathes. Then he shakes his head.

"You're right. It's too cold out here. Let's go find my dorm—we can kick Harper out. No one will see you."

"That's not what I meant." With the most unusual expression, he steps back and releases my hands. He pats his hair back in place. "I don't want to do this with you."

four

ENVY

THIS IS THE PART WHERE I DIE.

"Anne, I moved really fast once before," Ben says, his tone pleading but firm. "And, God help me, I'd love to repeat that mistake right now, but it *would be* a mistake. I'd never forgive myself."

I am standing with my hands still in the air, positioned where his top button was. I am a statue memorializing the purest moment of rejection any girl has ever known. A plaque rests at my feet: *The Easy Girl*. Somehow, this is what I've become, what he's made me. Somehow, the boy is telling the girl she's moving too fast. I'm that girl. Even though I'm not.

I drop my hands.

Embarrassment heats my skin, making me feel so hot all over, I'd take his blazer off if he wouldn't think I was trying to seduce him. If I could die, I would be dead right now. Death by sexual shaming.

"Anne, please don't take that the wrong way."

It's a line he's made famous for me. *Don't take my cold shoulder the wrong way. Don't take the implication that you're a total slut the wrong way.* He repeats my name, but he keeps his distance. I shake my head like it's no big deal. I need to disappear. I need to rewind to the moment he first appeared at the top of the cliff and do this all over again, but this time I'll make *him* feel like a sexual deviant.

"You're angry."

I shake my head again. "It's cold. I should go find my room. Unpack. And stuff. I'm really sorry you got Garnet for a Guardian, Ben."

"*A-Anne.*"

"Please don't," I whisper, stepping past him and shaking him off when he reaches for me. "I wasn't suggesting what you think I was. I just liked… It doesn't matter."

"Don't leave," he says, following me. "I don't know why you're taking this so poorly."

You wouldn't know, I think. *You're always the one doing the rejecting; I'm always the one receiving it.*

"Good night, Ben."

"Anne, please!" he shouts after me.

My head is in a daze as I rush down the hill, cross the quad, and run toward the girls' dorm. All I can think about is Ben with Garnet. Sure, he talks like she was a proxy for me, but I'm damn sure that he got a lot closer to my would-be understudy than he's willing to get to me.

I reach the girls' dorm before he can catch up with me. I shove the door to the squat stone building open and dart inside, closing it behind me to distance myself from him. The whole way here, I could hear his breath as he ran a timid five or so paces behind me. He could've overtaken me at any point, but evidently he's smarter than that.

The lights are dim inside the dorm. The stained-glass windows won't let me see if he's still outside.

"Doesn't matter," I whisper. I stare at the wall next to me. And then lean into it.

Here, with my forehead pressed against a copy of the Cania Christy Code of Student Conduct—featuring BS rules like *no fraternizing with the villagers*, who are basically gone now anyway—I close my eyes and see Ben with Garnet. Doing everything he says he doesn't want to *rush into* with me. I relive the time I cowered at the edge of the Zin property and watched as, standing with Ben in his kitchen, Garnet lifted his hand to her mouth; there was nothing innocent about that. I'd be more than a little naive to believe they never slept together. Ugh. They totally did. They *def-in-ite-ly* did. Ben slept with Garnet. And the mechanics of it! I can't help torturing myself with each painstaking step in a process I'm unqualified to imagine. The taking off of clothes. The selection of a suitable location. The spoken or unspoken agreement that *this* is going to happen. I squeeze my eyelids until I see bright orange dots instead of two intertwined bodies. Where I'd be a tense, awkward mess, they probably weren't even shy about it. Garnet's so damn confident, and Ben's so impossibly gorgeous. They slept together. Naked. Skin to skin. Probably more than once. Oh, God. Probably a lot. In a bed. In his bed. Where else? Anywhere else? Everywhere else.

"Wake up, loony bird," Harper calls down to me, her twang thicker than ever.

I glance up to see her leaning over the railing of the second floor and snickering at me. Her long bangs are pinned back perfectly, and she's wearing pajamas that look more comfortable and less overtly sexy than I would have expected.

"Not sure how y'all do it in Broke Assville, California," she says and drums her fingers impatiently on a newel post, "but here we sleep in actual beds, not leaning against walls. So haul ass up here and make yours."

I trudge up the creaky wooden stairs, worn in their centers by decades of dead girls coming and going. Most of the bedroom doors, which are nine feet tall, intricately molded, and heavy-looking, are closed, but some are ajar just enough that I can hear a girl practicing the violin down by the second-floor bathroom and another girl reciting Shakespeare just across the way. I round the top of the stairs and glance away from Harper, who's tapping her foot like I couldn't be more irritating if I tried, to see steam flooding out of the bathroom. It's Sunday night. Back to school tomorrow. Since the last time I sat in a Cania classroom, everything has changed, yet nothing is different.

"Don't look so excited. This isn't the beginning of a lifelong friendship, Murdering Merchant," Harper says. She points to the door behind her. "We're in here."

She saunters into our room ahead of me. I step warily through the open doorway as she grabs a hairbrush from a dresser, flops back on her fluffy duvet, brushes the ends of her red hair, and watches me like I'm some sort of half-trained monkey.

The room is just as I'd expect the room of a privileged daddy's girl to be, or at least her side of it is; it's the antithesis of my bedroom growing up, which I frankly loved but which was so far removed from this, it could have been a different species. Divided into two sides that are mirror images, though Harper's side has started creeping into mine, our room is all cream, purple, and sparkling glass. Two chandeliers hang from the coffered ceiling, shedding glimmers of light across the large lavender area rug in the center of the hardwood floor. Harper's side is closest to the door. Her four-poster bed, puffy with more pillows than we had in our entire house back home, is against the violet-and-cream striped wall in which her closet, packed so full the doors can't close, is set. Next to her bed are a desk and chair, both of which are in front of a dormer window. On the wall with our door, a marble fireplace sits unlit in the corner near my bed, beside two antique-looking dressers.

"I had it done exactly like my bedroom at home," she says as she runs the brush through the ends of her hair. A Hermès scarf is draped over her nightstand lamp. Gold-framed affirmations and vision boards make a neat row on her side of the room. I can see from the doorway that she's filled not only her closet with Tory Burch and Chanel's latest but half of my closet, too.

I feel her gaze zero in on me as I step into my barren new space. My attic bedroom at Gigi's was too narrow and slanty to be anything more than the *Before* shot in a home reno magazine, but at least it was wholly mine. No roommate. Now, on closer inspection, I see that my bed, which has been stripped bare, is paint-chipped; the wall it's pushed against is stabbed with nail holes and bruised by bare patches left behind by hastily pulled tape. A low stack of pale painting canvases are on my mattress, as are two boxes of my stuff and the flat pillow, thin sheets, and patchwork quilt I used at Gigi's. The desk under my dormer window is beat up. I look closer: someone's etched *Murdering Merchant* into the desktop. Gee, I wonder who could have done that?

"Don't unpack," Harper says. "If I have my way, you'll be back in California before the week's up."

"One can hope." I move the boxes to the floor. "Who used to live here?"

Harper groans. Because evidently the sound of my voice puts her over the edge. I look over my shoulder and wait for her to reply, which, with a huge eye roll, she finally does.

"Tallulah Josey."

"Your friend?"

She arches an eyebrow. "Tallulah thought she was slyer than a cat in a fish factory. When the teachers were all up in arms today, she took it upon herself to sneak into the front office and call her old boyfriend, who wasn't even that good-looking. Anyway, she got expelled this afternoon."

I stop unpacking.

"Who caught her making the call?" I ask.

She keeps brushing her hair.

"Who turned her in?"

She clears her throat.

"You know that expulsion means death, right? Harper?"

She flings her brush down at her duvet and scowls at me. But she doesn't say anything.

"I see," I say and start making my bed. "But *I'm* the murderer."

"I guess we'll both be sleeping with one eye open."

AFTER BARELY SURVIVING the onslaught of glares and whispers in the bathroom Monday morning, I leave the dorm to find Ben leaning against a tree. He's wearing his cardigan because his blazer's up in my room. He looks at me and smiles apprehensively. And I forget why I was angry with him last night.

Then I remember.

And now I have to decide if I want to stay mad at him to prove some sort of point or let it go so I can feel what it's like to hold his hand as I walk to my first-period workshop. Which is instructed by Garnet. Which makes me think he probably shouldn't show up there with me. Which means it's pointless to hold hands because it's only a thirty-second walk to the Rex Paimonde building.

"Still mad?" he asks.

I shrug. I'm undecided.

Out of nowhere, Pilot comes flying at us. It looks like he's going to crash right through us, but he stops short, grinning in his nasty way. Ben and I grab hands on instinct; I hadn't realized we had an instinctive need to connect. Decision made: I'm not mad at him.

"Bonnie and Clyde," Pilot says to us. "What's it like to look the guy you killed in the face?"

"Kinda like I imagine Superman feels when he destroys a villain," I reply.

Ben tugs my hand. "Come on, Anne. He's never been worth it."

As we're walking away, Pilot grabs my arm.

"Not so fast," he says. "Voletto wants to see you in his office."

"And he sent you to tell me?" I shrug free. "Doubtful."

"I'm your *Guardian*. So yeah. He wanted you there ten minutes ago."

"Fine. I'll be right there."

"I'm not leaving without you. Come on."

I glare at him. "Could you give me a second with Ben?"

"Oh, right, Clyde needs to kiss Bonnie good-bye." He gives Ben the finger but takes a few steps away.

"What would the headmaster want with you?" Ben asks me.

"Who cares? Listen, Ben, I hope you gave some thought to this Garnet situation."

"I did."

"Tell me good news."

He kisses me and smiles. "*Great* news: I'm sticking with you. I told her last night."

Crestfallen, I watch Ben as he tells me not to worry and struts happily away. I turn to follow Pilot to Goethe Hall, where we sit and wait outside Dia's office. I try to clear my head of the frustration of knowing Ben's giving up a future with me in exchange for the present; I stare blankly ahead as the janitor, Lou Knows, scrapes black letters spelling *HEADMASTER VILLICUS* off the cloudy window of the door. When he notices Pilot and me, he scowls at Pilot and hands him a stencil pack, black paint, and a thin brush.

"You're my assistant," Lou says, and starts away. "Not the other way 'round."

Pilot tugs off his jacket, revealing the coveralls I saw yesterday. So that's his role here. Not just my Guardian but also an assistant janitor.

The door to the office swings in. Hiltop stares at me.

"You're late," she says to me.

"*You?*"

But just then a smiling, dazzling Dia appears at Hiltop's side. He's a wearing a linen tunic that's partly tucked into leather pants, which hug his long legs. His feet are bare. His sleeves are rolled up. He seems to have more tattoos, brighter tattoos, than he had yesterday. I can clearly read *Dia + Gia = 4Ever* on one of the larger ones. I see also tiny tick marks representing his thousands of followers, like Teddy mentioned.

"Anne!" Dia declares, swinging the door further open and elbowing Hiltop aside as he does. "You're finally here. Don't mind Mephisto—what a grouch, hey? Come in, come in!"

"Enjoy it while it lasts, Dia," Hiltop says with a sneer.

"As long as Anne's around," he says, "I can depend on you being *constantly* outsmarted, Meph."

I step by Hiltop and follow Dia inside, where I find Invidia lounging on a raised divan and watching me as I enter the room, which has been completely renovated in the mere hours Dia has been headmaster.

"Please, sit," Dia says, swinging a thickly cushioned chair on its swivel and stopping it just as it faces me. "It's comfortable. Go on."

I'm sure it's comfortable. Everything in Dia's office is inviting. He's taken what was once an oppressively hot gothic-styled room filled with war medals, lit by fire, and hidden from sunlight, and transformed it into a whitewashed study you'd read a great novel in while sipping hot tea on a rainy day; he's even filled the bookshelves with what, I squint to see, are art books—thousands of them. Soft light glows in twinkling sconces and chandeliers hanging from the molded tray ceiling and falls on dozens of mirrors in all shapes and sizes, which hang on the newly painted panel walls. Pale white sculptures of Aphrodite, Helen, and Salome look both bashfully and knowingly at me, while toppling stacks of oversized ivory-colored cushions rest uncertainly against the walls behind them, layers of sheepskin blankets beneath. A dozen enormous canvases and an easel rest against the side of Dia's desk, where he's gesturing for me to join him.

Invidia stands. I swallow as I watch her move across the room to Dia's side with such elegance she could teach elegance a thing or two. Her emerald-colored silk blouse floats with each step. I am transfixed by her and helpless to it. Dia, too, appears enthralled by her as she leans against him and strokes his arm gently, though he still watches me. Only Hiltop looks at Invidia like she's some sort of foul beast.

Suddenly I remember! Teddy said Mephisto lost one of the Seven Sinning Sisters. Invidia must be that goddess. In the fallout of my escape, she must have chosen a new master over Mephisto: Dia Voletto. I wonder about the other six members of the Seven Sinning Sisters. Who are they? Where are they? And is Mephisto struggling to keep them?

As soon as I sit, Dia swivels me to face both him and Invidia fully, stopping the chair with his bare foot. I glance at his foot—or, more accurately, at the few inches of his naked calf that are now exposed. I shift my knee away from him and fix my gaze on my hands, which are gripped together over my uniform skirt.

"Are you okay, Anne?" he asks.

His hand passes under my eyes, and I feel his finger under my chin. He lifts my face until we're eye to eye. Life on Wormwood Island was easier when the devils looked like devils.

"Just a little nervous, I guess, to be called to the office."

"But you shouldn't be surprised," Dia guesses.

"No, not surprised."

Hiltop joins the two others standing in front of me. Under the weight of their three stares, I ought to be sliding into the chair and disappearing entirely, but something about the way they're looking at me makes me feel…the opposite. Light, not dominated. Invidia's jade gaze on me is especially empowering. But just for a moment. Just until I remember my mortality and their eternal darkness.

"You know what you did this past weekend was wrong," Dia begins, swinging my chair lightly with his foot. "You destroyed the life of Pilot Stone."

"And I was punished when he was assigned as my Guardian," I say, "among other punishments."

"Mr. Stone as your Guardian is a far cry better than Ted Rier."

"Do you have something against Teddy?"

Dia and Invidia chuckle knowingly but don't bother answering me. They can probably sense he's a good soul, and they don't like that.

"More importantly," Dia continues, "you almost jeopardized this school's reputation. We're a place of hope. And possibility."

"Is that what you're selling this place as?"

Invidia smirks, and even Dia looks amused. But Hiltop's thin lips curl just enough to make a frown.

"The world nearly found out about Mephisto and his," Dia unsuccessfully hides a smile as he and Invidia look Hiltop up and down, "various embodiments."

At that, both Invidia and Dia grin. Hiltop doesn't flinch and, for a second, I feel bad for her. Until I remember she's evil incarnate. And she can take care of herself; my pity, even disguised as empathy, is unnecessary.

"Well, I wasn't trying to expose anyone," I explain. "I just wanted to go home."

Dia and Invidia look at Hiltop. "That's a good point," Dia says to Hiltop.

I realize then why Hiltop's here: because no one else knows how to run Cania. It's a complex place, where secrets and lies are land mines you must carefully tiptoe around. Hiltop is pointing out the land mines. And it turns out I'm one of them.

Hiltop turns her flat gaze on me. "Give us your word you will not run amok with your stories of underworld führers and our followers."

"Give me your word my dad can leave you the moment I get away from Cania Christy and Wormwood Island," I reply.

Clearly, nobody saw that coming; even I'm a little surprised at myself. They all lean back. Invidia tilts her head like she's seeing me in a new light.

"Tit for tat," I say, staring at all three of them. I cross my arms. Invidia, too, crosses hers. "Isn't that the law of the land here? Oh, and, just to be clear—I know how tricky you guys can be—whether I live or die, he's free once I'm gone."

Dia and Invidia wait for Hiltop to make a call.

"I would have thought," Hiltop begins, "you'd have asked for the release of your dear, sweet love, Mr. Ebenezer Zin."

I hadn't realized that was an option! I hadn't even thought that she'd consider my request for my dad, never mind Ben. I was just experimenting, just trying to see if I could get under their skin.

"Very well," she says. "It is agreed."

I've just made my first deal with the devil.

It doesn't feel as awful as I might have expected.

"You'll say nothing to the students of Cania Christy," Hiltop clarifies.

"What about those who already know?" I ask. Like Ben.

Dia chimes in. "Anne, if the only thing you and the 'people who know' have to talk about is what *we're* doing, maybe you need to find someone new to talk to."

Dia instructs Invidia to round up the Guardians for a meeting; she glides out of the room, leaving me alone with Hiltop and Dia. When she leaves, I feel stronger and weaker; stronger because the raging jealousy she makes me feel follows her out, but weaker for reasons I can't understand.

I rise to go, too, but Dia shakes his head at me.

Just then, someone knocks at the door. It swings in, and Kate Haem enters with three people in tow: an adult couple and Dr. Zin. He's back from his travels already.

"Dr. Zin with the Smith family of Boston, here for the vivification of Damon Smith," Kate says and, on her way out, sticks her tongue out at me.

I look at Mr. and Mrs. Smith. And I look at Dr. Zin. And I stop breathing when I see his face.

Oh, God. Oh, God. What have they done to Dr. Zin's face?

five

THE VIVIFICATION OF DAMON SMITH

I KNOW, WHEN I LOOK AT DR. ZIN, THAT THE DEVASTATING effects of my faulty escape plan were even further reaching than I'd worried. Here stands a man who was once a plastic surgeon to celebrity clients, a man who struck me as dazzling when I first saw him, a man who could have been the poster boy for "the beautiful people"—and you would never know *this man* is the same man.

Raw redness covers his neck in thick flame-shaped patches. Tender-looking trails of fire disappear under his shirt collar, and the sticky, oozing tips of the flames stretch over his jaw, where they climb like thin claws up the sides of his once-immaculate face. His broad shoulders droop under the weight of a thousand invisible demons. The black bag he carries dangles precariously on his fingertips, which have uncoiled from a fist exhausted by clenching. His feet in their scuffed wing tips are wobbly. A frown is carved into the flesh of his face. And his eyes—they are the most damaged of all. Though not burned like his skin, they are puffy with heartache and black; they are like the half-open flaps of a dingy cellar, revealing a darkness stacked high with shadowy boxes and crates packed to bursting courtesy of fifty years of soul-crushing experiences, not the least of which happened the other night.

As I feel Hiltop's hungry gaze observing my reaction to this weakened, beat-down, and scarred version of Dr. Zin—a version that is her own making—I look away from it all. My horror will only please Hiltop more, but what she thinks about me right now is the least of my concerns. Because this is my fault. Dr. Zin's life would be perfectly normal (by Wormwood Island standards), and Ben would be safe in his father's house, if not for me. I want to tell him how sorry I am for what they've done to him, what they did to punish him for his son's actions. But my lips are sealed. I don't dare say a word, though I can't help but think, *God, is there anyone on Earth I don't have to apologize to?*

"What're these kids doing here?" Dr. Zin asks in a slur that can only mean one thing: AA is officially over for him.

Hiltop crosses the room to stand next to me and interlocks our arms like we're old friends. She explains cheerily to the parents, "We're writing a piece for the school paper."

I jerk my arm free.

"What paper?" Dr. Zin asks her. She glares at him. "Oh, sure, um, the paper."

Under my breath, I hiss at Hiltop, "You burned him? Will your punishments never end?"

"Burned Zin?" she whispers back. "On the contrary. He earned those burns in the car accident he caused years ago. I've simply... allowed his true self to shine through again."

"You're heartless."

"Hush. He asked for them as a reminder that *he* is responsible for Ben's situation. But never fear, Invidia can return him to his former state of enviable beauty at any moment."

Dr. Zin speaks directly to Dia Voletto this time. "May I present Mr. and Mrs. Robert Smith." His voice cracks as he offers his black doctor's bag to Dia. "And the vials, produced in triplicate now," he glares at me, "of the blood of their son, Damon, the next candidate for vivification at Cania Christy."

The Smiths stand straighter and try to mask their excitement as the stage is set for this moment they've been waiting for—this real-life act of wondrous magic.

As I watch Dr. Zin swing unsteadily back and forth on his heels, only skittishly looking my way, Dia opens the black leather bag, the very one Teddy mentioned yesterday. He reaches into it. The Smiths gasp as he withdraws a long, glistening vial of deep mahogany-colored blood. *Damon Smith in a bottle.* Dia steps forward and wraps his hands around it.

Almost the moment he touches it, a piercing shrill fills the office, ripping my gaze from Dr. Zin. I clap my hands to my ears—the Smiths do, too—as dense air whooshes over us, seeming to fly in from behind the plaster walls. The chandeliers swing. Paintings rattle. Light-colored fragments appear from nowhere and fly toward Dia, from all directions, and then fuse, with a great sucking force that tugs at my skirt and shakes the books on the shelves, into a glowing, growing sphere in the center of the room. Dia is smiling. Dr. Zin just keeps rocking on his feet; he's seen this a zillion times.

The Smiths, as thrilled as ever, cling to each other, welcoming this unearthly synthesis. I shield myself from the flying spots of blue and white light. Dia's grin spreads. Hiltop's eyes glisten—she almost looks emotional. No one can tear their gaze away as a human is re-created before us, re-created in a spectacle that is like all things on Wormwood Island: terrifying and hypnotizing at once.

And then, in a whirl that leaves me choking on my own breath, it's done.

Damon Smith stands in the suit they buried him in. His back is to me and Hiltop; he's next to Dia. His parents reach for him, but Dr. Zin holds them back.

"Not yet." Dr. Zin clears his throat and, flipping open a small notebook, reads to the boy, "Damon Archibald Smith, welcome to Cania Christy Preparatory Academy. You died of leukemia approximately five days ago in Boston, Massachusetts. You have been granted a second chance at life here on Wormwood Island by the venerable Headmaster Dia Voletto. To give you this chance, your parents have agreed to the following terms of admission: to finance the construction of Cania College on Wormwood Island and to guarantee its completion by the end of this school year."

For the first time, the mention of Cania College interests me. What if there's a chance that Ben can go there? If he's decided not to throw himself on Garnet's mercy—to date her and leave me—is there any chance he could graduate, move along to the college, and try his hand at winning life there?

But, no, surely that's not possible.

Dia wouldn't give us more time on Earth. Why would he? Is he the devil with the heart of gold? He sent Teddy away to look for a new home for Mephisto. Is this all just about broadening their reach? High school students weren't enough. Next up? College students. And then what? A junior high on whatever island Mephisto takes over? An elementary school? A bank, hotel, grocery store, airport, stock exchange?

As Dr. Zin finishes his robotic speech, Hiltop joins Dia at his side.

"Please take a moment to absorb this information, Damon, following which we will reunite you with your mother and father, answer your questions, and proceed with the rules of the school, the assignment of your Guardian, and the declaration of your *prosperitas thema*."

"It's your turn now," Hiltop tells Dia with a nudge. "Take control."

She's broken her cover, but the Smiths would never know it. Tears stream down their faces and run into their mouths as they look at the boy they surely thought they'd never see alive again, a boy who is free of cancer. You can see them restraining themselves, clenching their fists and gritting their teeth to keep from flinging themselves at him.

"Oh, Damon!" his mother cries.

Damon, I notice, has been rocking on the spot. And now, with the cry of his mother, he pivots toward her in a slow, swaying motion. He faces Dr. Zin and his parents. I can't help myself: I sigh with joy for the Smith family. I get it. I get why parents give up so much for this opportunity.

But he doesn't stop. He pivots toward me. Only when he faces me does my stomach turn. Damon looks so frail and lost.

Too frail.

And far too lost.

When I was vivified yesterday, I felt wonky for a while. But not for long. Did I look like Damon looks? His face is ghostly pale. His jaw is slack, his head tipped unnervingly to the side. His irises are thin yellow lines circling his oversized pupils.

Something is very, very wrong.

When the Smiths stop sobbing with joy long enough to realize that there may be little to be joyful for, the only sounds in the room become the low wheeze that leaves Damon's mouth in choppy spurts and the creaking of the floor as he turns toward new noises.

"What's going on?" Dia asks Hiltop through a clenched smile. "Why does he look like that?"

Mrs. Smith echoes his concern, but louder. "Damon?"

Damon shifts on instinct toward each new sound he hears, pivoting in the center of the room.

Mrs. Smith stumbles back. Away from her husband. Away from what should be her son but clearly isn't. The blood has drained from her face just as it's drained from Damon's. Mr. Smith is no less horrified by the possibility of what has happened here than his wife; he's just slower to react, slower to believe it could be so.

"Tell me this sometimes takes a while." Mr. Smith's deep voice fights a tremble. "Tell me it's normal for my boy to seem so...*soulless*. This will change. He'll be his old self soon. Tell me, Dr. Zin. It just takes a minute for his soul to meet his body. Isn't that right?"

"It looks to me like the *body* of your boy is with us," Dia says like some sort of rookie policeman poking around the scene of a murder, "but his soul's long gone. Probably moved on to its next life."

Dia raises an eyebrow in Hiltop's direction, and I realize that Hiltop's walking our new headmaster through the vivification process; this is Dia's first time. Hiltop steps up swiftly to calm the Smiths, though her message does little to end Mrs. Smith's whimpers. The child they thought they'd be holding is, once again, being taken from them.

A lump is in my throat. I can't swallow it down.

"My apologies, but this happens from time to time, as I'm sure Dr. Zin told you," Hiltop says, flicking a stony glare as she walks by an unfazed Dr. Zin. "Cania Christy cannot guarantee that every child can be vivified. Naturally, understanding that we could not fulfill our end of the exchange, your contract is now null and void."

"What do you mean *this happens*? What do you mean *no guarantee*? Why can't you do what you said?" Mrs. Smith looks frantically at each of us. She bounces on the spot as if torn between rushing to hold the animated body of her son, a body that appears far healthier than Damon must have been in his last days, and cowering from the dismal monster that teeters in confusion. "Where's Damon? Where's my baby boy? What is this atrocity? Zin didn't tell us anything about—*what the hell is this*?" She shoots a stinging glare at me and Hiltop. "Did you know this would happen, you little freaks? Is this some sort of edgy story for your stupid paper?"

My tongue knots. Hiltop looks expectantly at Dr. Zin, who, ine-briated, shrugs like it's not his problem.

"Would you like me to walk them out?" Dr. Zin asks Dia.

"No!" Mr. Smith insists. "No. That's not the answer. There's no *walking us out*. No. No, make Damon *be here*. It doesn't get simpler than that. You said you would. What more do you need? What more can I give you?"

I drop my eyes the moment Mr. Smith fumbles to remove his watch, as if this is one of those problems you can solve by hocking your Rolex. When I dare to look up again, I find him with his hands fidgeting helplessly at his sides; his fingers are stripped of rings; his jewelry is pooled in Dia's hands alongside the vial of blood.

His wife bolts from the room. She slams the door and attracts Damon's vacant stare.

Mr. Smith's reddened gaze falls on the boy. "Why is he like this?"

Hiltop nudges Dia, who hands the jewelry back to Mr. Smith and says, "Each of our souls is on a continuum. It stops in bodies—in different lives—along the way. Being Damon was just one stop on his journey. Usually we're able to vivify before the next stop. That wasn't the case today."

"Are you talking about reincarnation?"

"Exactly."

"So, wait," Mr. Smith sniffles, taking a silk handkerchief from his coat and blowing his nose as his gaze rolls to and from the rock-ing boy. "Are you saying that Damon—hold on, can you please do something to get rid of this abomination? It breaks my heart to see him like this. Even if it's just his body."

Dia holds the vial up and, without a thought, tosses it into the fireplace. In moments, the glass heats enough to shatter, drizzling blood into the flames. Damon Archibald Smith gradually vanishes; Mr. Smith turns his eyes away like he's been slapped, and I've gotta say that, as cool as I think I am with death thanks to growing up in a funeral home, even I have to glance away.

Again, Mr. Smith blows his nose. When he turns back to Hiltop and Dia, he looks more composed.

"I don't want the contract to be null and void," Mr. Smith says. "I died the day cancer took Damon, so I'll be happy for the distrac-tion of building your college."

"We can't bring your boy back," Dia says.

"I will give you what you wanted—that college in the village—if you will tell me this: Who has my son been reincarnated as? When we're finished building your college, I intend to move to wherever he is and watch him grow."

Dia begins to protest, but Mr. Smith holds his hand up to silence him and turns instead to Hiltop.

"You," he says to her. "You're the one running this, right?"

"Until recently, yes. Now I'm more of an advisor."

"And you, too?" He looks at me.

I stammer, "No. Not me. Not at all."

"So you're just a dead kid this actually worked on?"

Hiltop brings the conversation back on track. "I'm the one you want to talk to."

"Have you still got what it takes to track a deceased child's soul? Can you help me?"

I'm stunned at how much Mr. Smith knows. Do all parents know there's more to Cania Christy than a magic show?

"I am always open to…interesting exchanges."

"Good," Mr. Smith says. He glances at Dia, too. "Good. I'm not here to judge. I just want to know what my boy is doing. Where he's living. Who he was reincarnated as. Tell me that, and you'll get your college."

I follow Dr. Zin, Hiltop, and Mr. Smith out of Dia's office, leaving Dia staring after us with a particularly unsettling glow in his dark eyes. Only the clamor of the hallway filled with Guardians can tear my eyes from his. I snake through them until I spy Pilot.

"What are you guys doing here?" I ask him.

"We heard the Moron Parade was about to begin, and—voilà—here you are," he says. "Why should I tell you?"

Just as he finishes his question, his face crumples. And I turn to see Invidia standing behind me. She flips her thick black-and-green hair and, to my surprise, asks Pilot to answer my question properly. He looks tongue-tied at first, but, with his eyes downcast, he eventually gets it out.

"Dia's making a change to the Big V competition," he explains.

"And what do you have to say to Miss Merchant?" she asks him. Before he answers, she turns to me and touches my hair. "You have the loveliest hair."

"Um, thank you."

I catch Pilot's stare out of the corner of my eye. He looks a little less weirded out than I am, but pretty much pushed to the edge. Around us, other faculty members—those who serve Mephisto and those who serve Dia—are turning to watch Invidia twist one of my curls around her slender finger. Standing this close to her, I spy a tattoo under her clavicle; it's an unbalanced scale, the heavier side stacked with emeralds; the longer I stare at it, the more it seems to gleam. I think my heart skips a beat—just a slight palpitation, but noticeable.

"Pilot," Invidia keeps her gaze on me, "you were saying?"

"*I'm sorry,*" he says to me.

"For...?"

"For saying you're a moron, Anne."

"Because, in fact, Miss Merchant is...?"

"Very"—he looks like he might choke on this—"smart."

Invidia smiles, releases my lock of hair, and saunters to the door. Casting one last smile at me, she swings the door in and leads the Guardians into Dia's office.

Certain everyone here is crazier than a squirrel in a nuthouse, I zip through the atrium and push open the doors of Goethe Hall, stepping into a rare sunlit morning. I catch a short glimpse of someone just on the other side of the gates. A brown-haired girl. She's not wearing a school uniform. She's simply standing there, looking in, with sunlight through the trees casting shadows over her face.

"Hello?" I call. "Is someone there?"

The girl steps backward and vanishes into the shadows.

"Miss Merchant!" a woman calls.

I whirl to see Garnet Descarteres stomping my way. I've barely had time to gulp when she halts before me, raises her hand, and moves to slap me. I just duck out of the way—to the hoot of that strange, unseen girl outside the gates—but, even still, I feel exactly what Garnet wanted me to: embarrassment, pain, intimidation.

"Take it easy," I say and dodge around her.

That's not gonna happen. She tugs my arm until I can't help but face her again. Anywhere else, a teacher would be fired for touching a student like this; here, it's a dog-eat-dog world, and I'm going to need to bite back to survive.

"What?" I snap at her.

"He's *mine*."

"I'm not going to fight over a guy. Not with anyone, least of all you."

"What does that mean, *least of all me*?"

"It doesn't mean anything! Look, I'm sorry—"

"You're gonna be sorry."

"Shouldn't you be inside with the rest of the Guardians, Garnet?"

"Shouldn't you be making out with *my* boyfriend somewhere? He's not going to fight for the Big V because of you! Do you under-stand that, you selfish cow?"

She pushes her enviably pretty face toward mine, and waves her fist near my face, so close I see the faintest shadow of a shackle on her wrist. It throws me. I've barely had time to process the fact that she surrendered her soul for this time with Ben.

"If you had a heart, you'd force him to be with me, Merchant. Without me, he's dead. You know that. But you sit quietly while he slowly kills himself."

"No one's stopping *you* from helping him! You could be inside right now getting the scoop on whatever Dia's telling all the other Guardians."

She flinches like she hadn't thought I'd see things so clearly. Rather than arguing the point, she pushes me hard in the chest. She might have kept pushing, and that pushing might have led to an actual fight, if we weren't interrupted. Behind us, all at once, a stam-pede of Guardians tramples out the doors and down the steps. Like a herd of wildebeests, they race around us; they envelop me and Garnet. I check to see if they're being chased and hear my name just as I spot Pilot, who's calling for me. Sidestepping the throng, Pilot reaches for me, yanks my arm, and drags me away from Garnet and total pandemonium.

"Anne, it's incredible!" he gasps, his perfectly straight teeth dazzling. Behind me, the last of the Guardians stream out noisily, letting the massive oak doors fall shut behind them. I turn to see them dart onto the path others have stomped into the grass and whiz away—until Pilot tugs me back to him. Garnet has fled with the crowd. "You and me, we're gonna get serious about the Big V now, Annie."

"Don't call me *Annie*. That nickname died when you did."

He tries to catch his breath. "K. Fine. Walk and talk?"

Reluctantly, I turn toward the quad with him. The pack of Guardians has dispersed; a few that have found their students are whispering with them in little pairs next to Valedictorian Hall, in the middle of the quad, near the dorms, by the cafeteria, outside of the Rex Paimonde building and Heorot Hall—everywhere. A conversation finishes and a duo high-fives; another finishes and a Guardian and student actually hug.

"Anne, listen, I know we've had our differences."

I laugh.

"But I want you to know that I've always, deep down inside, been fully committed to seeing you win the Big V. I was just doing what Mephisto told me to."

"Sure."

"Hey, you weren't exactly a good friend to me, either."

"This world is doomed if you're giving lessons on how to treat people."

"I faked a friendship with you—and I was only partly faking, Annie. But I didn't kill you."

"You faked a friendship with me so you could live while I died. You *would have* killed me. I just killed you faster."

"You're in a coma! You wouldn't have died." He can see I'm not buying it. "Look, I'm ready to help you win the Big V now. We can do this. Together."

"What's in it for you?"

"'In it for'—Anne, whatever could you mean?"

Guessing it's something big, I pull back. "Forget it. If you're gonna lie to me—"

"Fine!" He stops me from leaving. And sighs. "I get something, too, if you win."

The only reward that could possibly inspire Pilot hits me. "It's life, isn't it?"

"See? This is why you're going to win! You're razor sharp." He smiles awkwardly as I roll my eyes. "Dia wanted to up the ante for us. The winning Guardian gets one wish granted, and, yes, that could include a new life."

"As long as there's something in it for you, you'll help me."

"Totally!"

"That's not something to be proud of, Pilot."

"I'm helping you!" he defends, throwing his hands out and tracking me as I veer away. "How can you find fault in my motivations? So what if I get something? You'll get something, too. And, Anne, you *can* win this. I happen to know you've got excellent untapped skills. We just have to change your PT, and you're good to go."

"We don't *just have* to do anything. I'm alive, remember? I don't need the Big V."

"But we could win. Easily. Cakewalk."

"I'm done with you, Stone! I wish I had Teddy as my Guardian again."

He stops cold as I march on. "You don't know what you're saying."

"Go to Hell. Again."

"Anne, there's more to winning the Big V than a second life!"

Now I stop cold.

"It's trivial stuff for most of us," he continues. "But it could be big for you."

I turn to him. "Spill it."

"*Riches.*" He drags the word out. "Everything you'd need for a great new life. Valedictorians have gotta set up a new identity, move somewhere no one will recognize them, buy a house, go to school, get a car, all that stuff. Money was nothing for Mephisto, and it's nothing for Dia. These rewards are a little extra perk for the person destined to be a great success in this world. You'd get...a lot. As in *never-worry-about-money-again* a lot."

I could go to Brown.

Buy a New York brownstone.

Open an art gallery.

My dad could start new, too.

"Why is this the first I'm hearing of these 'riches'?"

"Like I said, it's small potatoes to most of us. Life is our big prize." He can see me considering it, and I wish I could pretend I'm not intrigued. "We'd need to change your PT, though, to guarantee your victory. See, I work with Lou Knows—the janitor—and he told me something about you. About your soul. Something I don't think you know, but you really, *really* should."

"What is it?"

"I'm not sure if I'm allowed to tell you. Just lemme find out—I don't wanna piss anyone off. But, Annie, truly, if we change your PT to one that's more like Harper's—"

I should've seen that coming! Harper's PT is to succeed by using her sexual desirability, which is possibly the most offensive PT ever committed in blood. Teddy spent his time as my Guardian trying to convince me that I was predisposed to such a PT, and now Pilot's trying to do the same thing.

"Do you find it hard to look in the mirror?" I snarl.

His smile vanishes, and he grabs me by the arm. "Don't make this worse than it has to be. It's a simple win-win arrangement. You scratch my back—"

"And you'll stab mine?" I free my arm. "Pilot, be real. This 'magical reward' Dia's promised you? It's impossible. You don't have any blood or sources of *Pilot Stone's* DNA. You've only got your soul, which was barely enough to qualify you as a human before."

"He can make me human again."

"Even powerful demons—even devils—even Lucifer—can't *make* a human."

The sunlight slips behind a cloud, and Pilot becomes a still, silent silhouette.

"Look, I'm sorry to rain on your parade." I shove my fists into my cardigan pockets.

"You're missing the obvious." His voice is as cold as the wind blowing down from Canada. "Think of all the long-dead people who've left pieces of themselves behind. Frozen blood. Locks of hair. All perfectly usable DNA samples."

"So you're going to find Einstein's hair and, like, be reborn as Einstein? Good plan."

"I'm talking about sure things, Anne, not fantasy."

"Right. Because you're firmly planted in the real world."

"Actual DNA," he continues to explain. "The stuff you find in mummies. I'm talking about reincarnating as one of the kings who ruled thousands of years ago. Their souls have moved on, so there's plenty of room for me under their skin. Museums are filled with the DNA of ancient royals, and when my dad gets his hands on some"—he steps into the sunlight—"I can and will be born again. My soul. In the body of King Tutankhamen."

"You realize Tut had a super-long head and a cleft palate, right?"

"Don't mock me."

"To mock you, I'd have to entertain the possibility of this actually happening for you, or of me helping you. Let me clear this up for you right now: it'll be a cold day in your neck of the woods before I fight for the Big V." His frustrated glare follows me as I spot Ben and start away. "I don't want your prize, Pilot. I wasn't kidding when I threw your vial over the cliff. You deserve to be exactly where you are."

BEN AND I are on the fourth floor of the library. He is flipping through a massive Latin dictionary, and I'm reading about the celestial rules believed to dictate the creation of human beings.

"See!" I say, smacking the page every time some ancient religious scholar proves me right. "Dia would need a physical human body to put Pilot's dark, ugly little soul in. And to create that body, he'd need the combined DNA, masterfully united, of two humans. He ain't got that. Those are the rules. *Boom.*"

"'Invidia' means *envy*," Ben tells me.

"And," I continue uninterrupted, "although these books are a tad outdated, it seems like every time the underworld has tried to make a human, it's been a disaster. The closest was Jack the Ripper, so"—I meet eyes with Ben—"*clearly* the recipe is still in the test-kitchen phase."

The lights and the heat on this little-visited floor of the library have been off, broken, or flaky for as long as Ben can remember, which is why we're sitting in a circle of candles of all shapes and sizes, some of them scented. We're reading over their dim glow, rubbing our hands every so often over their flickering flames, and starting to get a little hungry from the aroma of melting vanilla and brown sugar. Outside, it's dark already, and sleet hits the windows with flat thuds. If Ben hadn't spazzed about our uberbrief kissing session the other night, I might think something would happen here, in this perfectly romantic setting. But there's room for a whole extra person to sit between us.

"Did you hear what I said?"

"Something about wanting a fresh-baked cookie?" I guess and blow out the vanilla candle. "You *actually* said"—I put my book down—"that *invidia* means *envy*. In Latin."

"And *superbia* means *pride*. And *avaritia* means *greed*. And…"

"And? Am I supposed to be following your train of thought?"

"The seven deadly sins. Pride, greed, envy, and so on. Invidia is one of them."

"Maybe that's, like, her special demon power or something: to inspire envy."

"Or," Ben positions a candle under his chin to cast dramatically eerie shadows over his face, "she *is* envy."

I nod and whisper, "She's *totally* envy. I guessed that she was one of the Seven Sinning Sisters—she left Mephisto for Dia—but I hadn't realized they are the seven deadly sins…personified."

"Where'd you hear all that?"

"Teddy told me."

Oops. I'm supposed to hate Teddy, not reveal our private convos. My easy tone hasn't escaped Ben's attention. Leaning back on his hands, he chews his lip as he observes me.

"Why was Teddy telling you all this?"

Keeping Teddy's secret mission for me from Ben will be about as hard as keeping your heart from knowing what your brain is doing. I don't want to keep secrets. But until I talk to Teddy more, I'm not going to risk anything.

"You know me," I say. "People just love spilling their souls to me."

"I actually *haven't* noticed that."

"Maybe it's just demons then." Time to maneuver back to safer territory. "Mr. Zin, you are a smart dude, figuring out who Invidia is. I guess I know why my ego takes a beating every time I see her. She makes me envy her."

After a beat, he confesses, "She makes me feel inferior."

"Envy."

I scoot next to him and, careful not to knock a big pillar candle over, tug his book until it's half on his lap, half on mine. We read everything we can about the Seven Sinning Sisters.

"Pride, greed, lust, envy, gluttony, wrath, and sloth," Ben reads. "Those would be some powerful demons to have on your side. They were all Mephisto's?"

"That's what Teddy said. But, you know. Who would trust him?" I choke.

He continues reading aloud, but, word by word and line by line, I find myself thinking more about the fact that my left knee is pressed against his right knee, part of his thigh is against mine, and our shoulders brush every time his chest rises with a deep breath. He smells delicious. His hands are very strong looking. And there's no denying that he's most irresistible when he's either reading or talking about books. But he's made it clear that he doesn't want to move too fast, not that I do, either—but I think he may have more self-control than I do. So, to keep from throwing myself at him, I slam his book closed.

"What just happened?" he asks with a smile.

I grab his hand and jump to my feet, tugging him up. "Let's look up Dia Voletto next."

Ben and I dart down to the first floor, where a few Guardians and their students angrily hush our excited whispers, and dash to the card catalog. In our previous lives, we both lived in the library, so we're fine with the Dewey decimal system, which Harper's peon Plum is groaning about near the periodical section. Hurriedly, we find four cards for books that mention or are about Dia Voletto.

"He's the demon of ego," Ben reads on a card as we take the stairs two at a time back to the fourth floor. Only to find the books on Dia Voletto are all gone.

"He took them," I say.

"What more could we expect from the demon of ego?"

"Major faux pas." We settle back to the middle of the ring of candles, which thankfully haven't burned the place down in our absence. "Stealing books from the library."

"Yeah. If he wasn't already condemned to Hell."

I begin closing the books. And Ben stacks them. But we're moving at about half speed. I pray he's killing time for the same reason I am: I don't want a reason to leave. I'll gladly pretend we need to be here as long as possible. I don't want to go yet. I can't imagine ever wanting to go.

When we've made towers of the books we read, books Ben has been reading for years, he starts unfolding dog-ears, and I pull my knees into my chest as I watch him. He's talking absently about the world of demonology, and it's not until he sighs and sits back that I realize I haven't told him about his dad. He notices my face drop, and he comes to my side, wrapping his arm around my shoulders.

"What is it?"

"I saw your dad today."

"Was he sober, by chance?"

I turn to look him in the eyes. "He was burned. On his neck. And he looked...dejected. Like he'd lost all hope."

"He probably has."

"Ben."

He shrugs. "*'Abandon all hope, ye who enter here.'* My dad held out longer than the average man would."

"Hiltop said your dad wanted the burns. As a reminder of your car accident."

"He's doing what he has to do to cope. Y'know, with my decision to die."

"But if you were to fight for the Big V..."

"I'm not going to fake I'm into Garnet. Please, Anne. Drop it."

He lifts my hand and holds it up flat, and we watch as he folds his fingers between mine. The lines distinguishing my skin from his blur, like they're glowing at the edges, like we're melting into one person.

"More spirit than flesh," I whisper.

He brings our hands to his lips. And, when he doesn't let up, I shift until my lips are pressed against the other side of the fist we've made. Our eyes meet. We lower our hands.

"Ben, you're going to have to choose Garnet."

"I hope you mean garnet the gemstone."

"You need to win the Big V."

"Shh." He puts his finger to my lips, and I pretend to bite at it. "I'm with you. Not her. Any plan that keeps me from you is no plan for me."

"But Ben—"

"If I have to choose between death and life without you, I choose death."

"That's very"—I pause—"cheesy."

Because we can't actually stay in the library forever, we make our way outside and, holding hands, meander down the dark island, past the red line that used to mean so much, past the old Zin mansion in which Dia and Invidia now live, past Gigi's old cottage, toward the village. Most of the villagers' homes, which were enormous, are being demoed to make way for the college.

"Why do you think Mr. Watso's here?" I ask Ben. "Everyone else is gone."

"He made a deal with the devil. I assume he's here because he has to be. Maybe if he signs the island over to them, they'll let him go."

"Sign it over?"

"My dad has this idea that Villicus *wanted* you and Molly to break the rules and be friends. He put you at Gigi's so you'd be more likely to run across the only village girl. That way, he'd have some leverage—he could dangle Molly's life in front of Mr. Watso in exchange for the island."

"I don't get it."

"Mr. Watso is a shaman. He's the spiritual owner of this island. Or so the story goes."

"So he can just give the island to the devil if he wants to?"

"If he had to. It'd be a clear gateway in for the underworld. But I doubt he'd do that."

"He's got no reason to now that she's gone." I meet Ben's gaze. "Do you think Mr. Watso will hate me forever because of what happened to Molly?"

"Molly's gone because you guys were friends. She was a part of that friendship."

"She's dead because of that friendship."

"Hey, don't be so hard on yourself," he says.

"I just can't believe how dumb I was."

"Hold on there." We stop walking and he turns me to face him. His hands are on my shoulders, and he's looking quite serious when he says, "That's my girlfriend you're talking smack about."

With that word—*girlfriend*—running through my head and the warmth of his hand on mine, we return to campus and cross the quad. I watch Ben walk to the boys' dorm. He smiles back at me when he opens the door, and we wave again, smile again, say good night, and eventually, with me suppressing dumb giggles that I sort of love, retire indoors.

Harper isn't in my room when I curl up with thoughts of the beautiful Ben Zin, the boy who is, at last, mine. I see bright lights like fireworks behind my eyes. *Ben's my boyfriend.* We'll figure the Big V stuff out. He'll find a way to win. I'll help Teddy—maybe I can find a way to wrestle the Seven Sinning Sisters away from Mephisto and Dia—and then get Teddy to wake me up. And, after that, Ben and I will be together in California. It won't be easy, but we can do it.

It is that gloriously satisfying thought that sends me swiftly into dreams, dreams I'm quite certain will feature a tall, lovely, mint-eyed sculptor.

Except it's not Ben in my dreams.

It's Dia.

At first he and I are arguing, but we swiftly find ourselves in a far more compromising position than I've *ever* been in. I feel the soft ring of his open mouth moving down my neck to my shoulder, leaving a glowing tattoo that looks just like Invidia's. When he leans away from me, his mouth is open—and he's screaming.

My eyelids burst wide to find Harper standing over my bed in the glow of a lamp. She's screaming at me. She reels back as I stagger out of bed, holding my arms out defensively.

"What is it?" I cry, looking for an intruder. "Where? Who?"

"*Y-y-you!*"

I catch a glimpse of myself in Harper's full-length mirror as she staggers backward.

And I do a double take.

Everything about my reflection is exaggerated: my lips and cheekbones are fuller; my eyes are huge and a strange violet color; my curves are inflated like helium balloons; my legs are sinfully long. It's only my big, everywhere hair that looks like me.

"I'm dreaming," I utter. "This must be a dream."

I shift, watching the movement in the mirror to be sure I'm looking at my own reflection. As I do, I see what Harper was screaming about and what she is now, from the furthest corner of her bed, pointing at in dumbfounded silence.

"What on Earth?" I breathe as a shimmering silver tail wraps over my shoulder.

I look at it, and it wags once. Then it disintegrates into a million sparkling fragments that glow, dance, and vanish, taking my larger-than-life exterior with them.

six

INNER DEMONS

IT SMELLS LIKE WET DOG OUTSIDE THE CLOSET IN WHICH Lou Knows and Pilot keep their janitorial supplies. I must have walked by this closet a dozen times in the last month and seen Lou bent over, filling his dingy yellow bucket with soapy water. All along, he's known something about me. Or so Pilot suggested the other day.

Today, I'm going to find out what Lou Knows knows about my soul.

And so restarts my attempts to act on my PT to "look closer" when, in fact, all I really want to do is close my eyes and, like all the other Cania students do, act as if nothing weird is going down. But last night I saw something I'd have to be brain dead—not just in a coma—to forget. I saw something I'd be crazy not to investigate. I saw something that Harper is *so* going to blab to the whole school; even in a land of sworn enemies, Harper has a way of spreading news. So before I have to deal with girls in the bathroom whispering trash about my (I can't believe I'm actually admitting this) *tail*, which has thankfully not reappeared since Harper screamed it away, I need to get a handle on what's up.

So I wait for Lou.

I lean against the wall. I drum my fingers on the cool painted cinder blocks. The clock above me ticks so loudly, it echoes all the way down the hall, bouncing off the lockers. I'm next to the chem lab, inside of which Miss Incitant—one of many new faculty members Dia brought in—is conducting a lesson I can just overhear. Her name is Latin, just like Invidia, though *incitant* isn't one of the seven deadly sins, so Miss Incitant can't be one of the Seven Sinning Sisters; this is a little more proof that my hunch was right: Dia's demons go by Latin names.

"The study of chemistry dates back how far?" Miss Incitant asks her students, who are so quiet, their silence echoes. Evidently none of her students' PTs is to be successful by throwing the teacher a bone. "Thousands of years. To where? Anyone? To the Middle East, where philosophers and scientists engaged in what we now call... anyone? In what we now call *alchemy*. And what is alchemy?" She waits, patiently pulling teeth. "It is the art of freeing parts of the Cosmos from temporal existence. To what end? Yes, Jackson—oh, you're just stretching. Anyone else care to try? Alchemy achieves the goals you seek here: longevity, immortality, and redemption. And thus chemistry is magic."

Magic. Immortality.

Was what I saw last night magic? Was it the work of alchemy? Did someone put a spell on me? Does every student at some point look like I did, thanks to our proximity to demons? Or am I, like, possessed?

I slide to the floor to wait for Lou. I open my sketchbook. Time ticks by. Before I know it, I've filled page after page with hasty renderings of the vision I saw last night: her voluptuous body, her pillowy lips, her commanding stance and impressive height. The movement of her hand as she tugged her nightie to cover herself. Yes, I'm thinking about my own reflection as if it wasn't mine at all. That's because whatever I saw, it was nothing like me.

I tear out a page and absently roll it into a long tube. I stare down the hall through it, like a telescope. Still no Lou. I flip it over and write his name on it.

"Lou knows my soul," I whisper. "Why do you know my soul?" I ask the name on the page.

I tap my pencil over *Lou Knows* and stare ahead. Lou is a demon with a non-Latin name, a demon that was here before Dia arrived. It's probably safe to say he serves Mephisto.

"But why does Lou know something about me? Or why does he think he does?"

Lou suggested the same thing that Teddy did: that I could succeed by using my "feminine wiles." But Teddy only said that after he'd read my soul; I've never even touched Lou, so he couldn't have read my soul. How did he gain special insight into who I am?

A noise up the hall steals my attention. It's just a heater cranking on.

I look at the page again: *Lou Knows.*

And then I see it.

I can't believe I've missed it.

I jot a phrase under his name: know soul. And then, moving between his name and those two words, I strike out letters until I've proven my guess right.

His name is an anagram for 'know soul.'

Wondering if that's just lucky—just a one-time coincidence— I write down the next staff name that pops into my head: Trey Sedmoney, Harper's Guardian, the only teacher I've had the displeasure of seeing in the buck (purely for artistic purposes), and a decidedly creepy dude. He was here before Dia, so he's one of Mephisto's. Do all demons have a special power? Is it possible that all of Mephisto's servants, when they arrive here, get names that are anagrams of their powers? And maybe Dia's followers have kept their underworld names because he was rushed here; I've already seen that Dia needs Hiltop's help with almost everything related to this school, so he definitely wasn't prepared to come here. It's possible...

I stare at *Trey Sedmoney.*

Rearranging that name is a lot harder because I have no idea what Trey's power could be, unlike in the case of Lou Knows. Trey is Harper's Guardian, so maybe something to do with sex? But no matter what I try, those twelve letters don't rearrange to form any sex-type phrases.

I scribble his name out. Maybe I'm wrong about this. But before I discount the whole idea, I remember that, my first day here, the secretary Kate Haem used all sorts of anagrams for my name. I thought it was just an annoying game, but maybe it was more than that. Maybe it was a hint. Was Kate trying to tell me something almost from the moment I stepped foot on this island? But why would she do that?

I write down *Kate Haem.*

That turns into "aka theme," "take me ha," and "meet kaha" until eventually I land on something that just might be right.

"Make hate," I whisper.

Kate Haem's power could be to make hate.

Immediately, I write down *Hiltop P. Shemese*, which rearranges easily into *Mephistopheles*. It's not a single power, but perhaps that's because Mephisto is higher-ranking and, thus, has multiple powers.

I list everyone I can think of. The secretary, Eve Risset; my sculpting teacher, Dr. Weinchler; the music prof, Maestro Insullis; the gym coach, Stealth Vergner; the history teacher, Star Wetpier; the poetry prof, Levi Beemaker. Then my housemoms, Elle Gufy and Shera T. Bond. And Ben's housedad, Finn Kid.

I start with the short names. They're easier.

"Finn Kid might be able to *find kin*," I say as I write it down. "And Elle Gufy could be *feel ugly*. Maybe Shera is *bond hearts*? And I think…Star is…*rewrite past*. Or *trap sweet*." No, that leaves an extra *I* and *R*. "*Rewrite past*. That's what Star can do."

As I'm working on Stealth Vergner's name, Lou finally rounds the corner. He's hunched over his yellow bucket, steering it with the mop and the lever he uses to ring the mop out. Between the gap in his teeth, he is whistling a low tune. Until he spies me. Then he stops in his tracks.

I close my sketchbook and stand.

"If you's looking for Pilot—" he says and starts pushing his bucket again.

"I'm looking for you."

"Some idiot throw up or something?"

"No, I don't need you to clean anything."

Watching me from the corner of his dark purple eye, he pushes the bucket past me, jingles with his keys until he unlocks the door, and shuffles into the cramped space of the janitor's closet. I follow him in, almost pass out from the muggy chemical stench, and close the door behind us. Lou dumps brown water out of the bucket and sticks a hose in it to rinse the remaining grime down the drain.

There's nowhere to sit.

"Cut to the chase," he says over the rush of water.

"Pilot said you know something about my soul. My history. Something that makes him think I'd be successful in life"—*ridiculous*—

"on my back." Old pipes squeal as he shuts the water off. "Were you guys just being pervs, or is there something I need to know? About my soul."

Lou faces me. His blue coveralls are wet with mop water, and a smear of mud or oil crosses his stubbly cheek. With the set of his jaw, if he weren't so thin, he'd almost look like a bulldog.

"Pilot told you that?"

"Tell me what you know, Lou. Please."

"It don't work like that."

"Well what *do* it work like?"

"If a demon's gonna get me to cough up what I know about their soul, they're gonna have to be my master or twist my arm a good deal."

"And if a human wants to know?" I tap my foot.

"I ain't high 'nough ranking to give no human what they want, unless I serve them."

"Demons can serve humans?"

"And humans go 'round serving us, too. Happens lots. Usually don't work out though."

"Your master is…Mephisto?"

He nods fast and taps the pin on his shirt pocket. It's just as I'd suspected.

"Then how come you told Pilot about this secret you're keeping about me? Did he twist your arm?"

"We was just shootin' the shit at work. It came up. Wasn't a favor or special request or nothin'."

"Well, what if *we* were to shoot the shit?" I ask hopefully. "You and I."

His lips curve. His stringy black hair shakes. "It's never been that the likes uh you'd do that with the likes uh me."

The bell rings, and Lou takes that as his cue to limp out of the janitor's closet as if we weren't just in the middle of a conversation. Frustrated, I give the messy closet one last look, hoping to see something I can use, but come up empty-handed.

I boot it to my next class: Exploring the Science of Consciousness. There Mr. Farid—whose first name is Moses and whose power, I spend ten minutes working through, is to *disarm foes*—drones on about anesthesia, cognitive unbinding, and seeing visions. His words remind me of the woman I saw in the mirror last night. That's a vision I'll never, ever tell Ben about.

Which is exactly what I think when I find Ben waiting in the hall for me after class.

As I walk toward him and watch his smile turn into that crinkle-nosed grin I love, I privately will whatever that weird vision was last night to go away and never return. Let me be as normal as Ben is. Please.

"Hungry?" he asks.

"On Wormwood Island?" The upside of vivification is you can't die of anything, including hunger; the downside is that your will to eat virtually vanishes. "We could go for a walk."

"That sounds good."

Our fingers touch, twine, and release in a way that gives me shivers. I know that, eventually, I'm going to have to convince Ben to leave me and tell Garnet he's made a huge mistake in rejecting her. But for now—just for now—I'm going to enjoy it.

Or so I think.

As we push into the cold air, I spy Pilot sprinkling salt on any icy patches of sidewalk. Although Lou may not have opened up about the skeletons in my closet, Pi is going to. Even if I have to force him.

"Gimme a sec?" I ask Ben. "I've gotta talk to my, um, *Guardian*. I'll meet you by the dorms in five."

He suspiciously eyes Pilot, whose back is to us, but finally agrees and turns away. I rush behind Pilot and tip over the broom he's rested against a tree. He stumbles, curses, and scrambles after it. But when he pushes up his woolly cap to see me glowering at him, his eyes light up.

"Anne! You ready to talk about the Big V? Great! We've gotta get prepping for the Scrutiny."

"The what?"

"I'll tell you all about it—don't worry, it's not till Christmastime. Short-list stuff." He hurriedly starts shoving the bucket of salt to the side. "We can meet now—that's cool, let me put this stuff away—but I want a session every single day, got it?"

"Cut the crap, Pilot. I asked your little janitor buddy what he knows about me."

"You did? Even better! So you're ready to change your PT?"

"I might consider it."

"If?"

"If *you* tell me what he wouldn't."

"Lou didn't tell you?"

With my hands on my hips, I shake my head. "So go ahead. I'm listening. What's my story?"

"I—I can't, Anne. Lou outranks me. I'm just a punk. I'm still trying to become a demon. If my superior won't tell you, I sure as hell can't. We get destroyed for breaking rank."

"Get real, Pilot. Your chances of escaping this crappy life of yours hang in the balance."

"I know, but rank is everything. If I knew Lucifer—the leader of Hell—was plotting against Mephisto, I couldn't tell him, even though I serve him. Rules are rules."

"'Rules are—'? What happened to the Machiavellian son of my favorite sex-addict senator? You make up your own rules."

"I wish I could help you, Anne. I really do."

"So Hell has turned a sinner into a saint?"

"I don't know what to tell you."

"The truth! I know that Lou's power is to know my soul."

"How do you know that?"

"I figured it out. And Kate Haem makes people hate each other."

"That's great. See? You could easily win this thing."

"Only if you tell me what Lou knows about my soul."

He shakes his head. No matter what I say, Pilot's adamant that he can't tell me a thing, insisting that the underworld follows a medieval caste system he'd be a fool to ignore.

"So what's your power?" I ask him.

"I'm a punk. I don't have one yet."

"Great. What good are you to me?"

"Don't give up!" He calls as I storm away, "Use your PT, Anne. The one you've got now—use it!"

Look closer. Look bloody closer. It's become code for *You're on your own, sucker.*

seven

DIA VOLETTO

EVERY DAY THAT PASSES BRINGS BEN'S DEMISE CLOSER. And the days are racing by like they've got the devil on their heels.

Ben and I have been dating (yay!) for just over five weeks, but every time we kiss and every time our hands touch, it feels like we're leaping off the cliff again, like no time has passed at all.

But it has.

The countdown to save Ben's life is well under way.

Unfortunately, I'm the only one trying to save him.

Garnet—the woman who's still *technically* Ben's Guardian, the woman who loved him enough to surrender her soul to be with him here, the woman who could easily save him—wants nothing to do with him. Because he's with me. And she won't budge on the matter. No matter how much I suck up to her. No matter how much I try to downplay my relationship with her ex. No matter what I do, Garnet refuses to show up to her meetings with Ben, and she hasn't even talked with him about the upcoming Scrutiny challenge, which, Pilot explained to me weeks ago, is an annual challenge that gives us all chances to get gold stars. When your every move is graded, gold stars can erase all manner of shortcomings. For seniors, they're especially important: they can move you onto Dia's short list of fave Big V contenders.

"Why do you keep hiding our relationship from Garnet?" Ben asks me. "She knows."

76

"Why don't you fight for the Big V?"

"Seriously?"

We've fallen into a pattern of asking the same questions. Always with the same non-committal answers. I refuse to tell Ben the truth: naively, I believe Garnet just might change her mind and help him. Yes, it's naive. Ubernaive. Like doe-eyed, post-lobotomy naive.

But like Ben once said, hope—innocent hope—is the only thing we've got.

It's almost November now, and sleety rain has turned into thick white snow that sticks to the green grass in the quad. (Not even grass dies on Wormwood Island.) This weekend is the Day of the Dead, which gives all our friends and family back home a day to remember the dearly departed. But given that every day is the day of the dead around these parts, the most we're doing to celebrate is presenting an assignment in Garnet's workshop: If we could vivify as anyone from history, who would it be?

I'm already dreading standing in front of Garnet and this classroom of piranhas when Garnet drops a bonus bomb on us.

"Headmaster Voletto will join me in grading your presentations today," Garnet tells us.

On cue, Dia walks in, all swagger, and gives us a wave. Standing side by side, Dia and Garnet look like a gorgeous celebrity couple we should be snapping photos of. Maybe if I could set them up, Garnet would ease up on Ben, and she'd be so grateful to me, she'd stop snapping at me every chance she gets. It's possible. Except Dia's got that *Dia + Gia* tattoo, which I guess means he's already taken.

"Earth to Merchant," Garnet calls.

I realize I've been daydreaming when I hear everyone, but Harper, snickering. Harper has been avoiding me since that weird-ass vixen with the sparkly tail showed herself in our room, but she hasn't spread a word about it, to my relief. It's almost like she wants to pretend I don't exist. Or maybe she's scared of me? I dunno. She addresses me only when I miss a Social Committee meeting, and even then her eyes never meet mine.

"I was calling on you," Garnet tells me. Next to her, Dia is watching me intently.

"Oh." That's my great response.

"Didn't you hear your headmaster's question?"

Obviously not! "No. Sorry. Would you mind repeating—"

Garnet groans. "Honestly. Have you tried cleaning your ears? Miss Merchant, if you would like to remain a student at this school, you're going to need to pull up your socks." She turns to Dia. "I'm so sorry about her. She's always been a problem."

Wow. Nice.

"I'm not surprised by that one bit," Dia says, but he's smiling at me. "Miss Merchant, I was wondering if, given the secrecy that clouded your orientation at Cania Christy back in September, anyone told you about the Scrutiny. It seems you weren't told very much. Secrecy is the name of the game around here."

"Oh, yes, I know. Thanks. My Guardian told me. It's a challenge on New Year's Day."

"If you have any questions about it," he says, "my door is always open."

Annoyed now, Garnet encourages Dia to sit down. Then she turns her scowl on me again.

"Miss Merchant, let's get your presentation over with. Up to the front. Now."

If Ben only knew what I put up with.

I set my painting, covered in a sheet, on the easel at the front of the room. Garnet has very specific rules about how art is to be presented, and she's a major fan of drama. (Surprise, surprise.) She likes us to introduce our piece, do a countdown from three, and whip back the sheet. It's hokey, but I'm hardly in a position to do things my way.

I face the dead glares of my peers and Garnet.

"If I could vivify as anyone," I say dutifully, as an introduction.

Only Dia looks interested. He's turned his chair around so he's straddling the back, with his arms wrapped around it. He's almost likable. Almost. The way bright, twinkling lights are "likable" until you realize they're on the front of a semi-truck that's charging straight at you.

"Well, as I understand," I begin, "to vivify, your blood has to come in contact with Wormwood Island—unless the blood's been touched by the headmaster, in which case you don't have to, like, be touching the ground."

"Exactly," Dia confirms.

"Miss Merchant, we don't have all day."

"I wondered, if you blended a bunch of drops of blood together from a bunch of different people, could you make one new person?" I anticipate the groaning objections, so I rush to add, "I know it's more complex than that. It's about your DNA, not your blood. And I guess our souls have to be in there somehow, so you'd have a bunch of souls fighting for room"—thinking about Damon Smith, I look at Dia and add—"unless that soul has already reincarnated, leaving their body empty."

"Is your PT to bore us to death?" Augusto shouts from the back of the room.

"We're already dead! Bore us into resenting vivification, more like," Plum adds.

"Miss Merchant, *today*." Garnet snaps for emphasis.

I mumble, "Three, two, one." And I "whip" back the sheet, by which I mean I lift it a little faster than normal. There, on the canvas, is a mosaic of all the people I'd want to be. I've used torn pieces of photographs and thick, oil paints and wispy watercolors to blend them into one.

"If I had to vivify as someone other than myself," I explain, "I'd come back as my mom, and Molly Watso, and Gigi Malone—"

Plum's hand shoots up. "Aren't those all people you killed?"

"Not her mom," a girl I barely know says. "Her crazy mom taught her how to kill."

I'm at a loss for words.

"She killed Pilot Stone, too," Emo Boy says, "but he's not up there."

"Who're you gonna kill next, Murdering Merchant?" Augusto adds. "Harper must be scared to death, sleeping in a room with you."

I can't believe my ears. Is that really how they see me?

Dia has shifted on his chair to watch my peers hurl accusations at me. Garnet has, too, but she's watching with a cool smile, which she shines on me before she adds her own indictment.

"Easy students," Garnet says, "Miss Merchant has her sights set on killing Mr. Zin next."

I take my painting from the easel. A thousand dark thoughts are racing through my mind, but I don't dare say anything. They don't need more ammunition. I have my gaze fixed on my workstation when, to my surprise, Dia speaks up.

"Tell me your PTs," Dia says. I look back to see he's standing at the front of the room. "You, boy with the moustache at the back. Or you, boy wearing all that eye makeup. Or you," he points to Plum. "Your PT is to use your desirability to win, isn't it?"

She nods.

"What is desirable about saying such hateful things to Miss Merchant?"

She looks down at her workstation.

"Whose PT is to attack others publicly? Whose PT is to spread rumors and lies?"

Everyone looks down.

"Meanwhile, Miss Otto is perfectly enacting her PT. She couldn't be more desirable in her quiet defense of Miss Merchant."

I glance at Harper. She looks as surprised as I feel.

"Choose your enemies carefully," he warns us as he sits again. "Who's next?"

It's not until after class that I start to recover from hearing the long list of deaths I've been closely tied to. I'm packing up my stuff when I notice Dia standing in front of me, a playful grin teasing the corners of his lips. If he wasn't a demon and Ben wasn't my boyfriend, I could see possibly—maybe—only slightly, of course— having a teensy tiny crush on him.

"Anne, I have a question for you."

I look at where my watch would be if I wore one. "I've gotta get to my next class. Can it wait?"

"You have a spare minute now." He knows my class schedule. Why does he know that? "Look, instead of trying to wriggle your way out of talking privately with me, let me make this easy. Walk with me to Goethe Hall, and I'll let you make a phone call. As a reward."

"I can call my dad?"

An unexpected phone call? He'd freak!

I agree, and we start toward Goethe Hall.

"It sounds like you're close with your parents," Dia guesses.

"Pretty close. I'm an only child."

"Of course you are."

Whatever that means.

"I have a proposition for you," he says.

"I'm not really the propositioning type. You might want to try Harper."

"I'll keep that in mind," he says with a laugh. "Anne, remember a few weeks back when we talked about beauty up on that cliff?"

Vaguely.

"Well, I've been thinking about it since. And today's class gave me an idea." He pauses like he's waiting for me to guess. "I'd like to mentor you."

"Mentor me?" *Quoi?* "In what?"

"I've been a great admirer of art for, well, a long time. You've got potential. Untapped potential. So," he tilts his head bewitchingly, "will you let me coach you?" He leans in close enough that his aroma floats around me, and I'm extremely disappointed to find he is *sans* the brimstone odor most demons skunk up rooms with. "I'd like you to join me every Saturday, starting tomorrow."

"So soon?"

"Yes. You'll paint me. A beautiful painting we can hang in Cania College. Something real. Raw."

"Every Saturday?" *Nooo!* Find a way out! Make up an excuse! "Um, sure, that sounds...great."

Sonuvabitch!

"Great."

We're standing outside the front office, inside of which Kate Haem and Eve Risset are watching us like odd-looking birds.

"I'll see you tomorrow morning. Nine o'clock. In my office. Enjoy chatting with your father."

I do. Even with Kate and Eve obviously eavesdropping on me, I get a kick out of surprising my dad. He picks up on the first ring, and he takes a while to convince that I'm allowed to be talking to him; rule breaking is his biggest fear, understandably.

"Dad, seriously, the new headmaster let me call you."

"Headmaster Voletto? Well, he seems to be a decent guy, punkin'."

"Yeah," I say, turning away from my eavesdroppers, "he's surprisingly great."

THE SUN IS setting. Ben's holding my hand and leading me through the brush on the southwest side of the island, where Mr. Watso lives in an ice-fishing tent in a frozen-over inlet. Because Ben and Dr. Zin lived on the island for so long, they got to know Mr. Watso fairly well, and they weren't punished for their relationship because they weren't technically breaking a rule: Dr. Zin and Mr. Watso often fished together off the island, where Mephisto's rules don't apply. But ever since Ben became a student and Dr. Zin was forced to live off the island—in a yacht just offshore—they haven't seen Mr. Watso much.

So now, according to Ben, Mr. Watso has invited us, *even me*, to join him for some ice fishing this evening. I strongly doubt my name was on the guest list. But Ben insists.

"His ice-fishing tent is probably too far off the shore," I say to Ben. Half-frozen muck keeps sucking my boots into the ivy-spotted forest floor. "We'll get more than a few feet away from the power of Wormwood, and we'll end up on the shore again. Like when we jumped off the cliff and you reappeared on the island."

"His tent is practically on the hillside."

"This isn't gonna work."

"You have to be a good ten feet from land to vanish and reappear on land again."

"More like five feet."

"More like ten. I know what you're doing. And you're not getting out of this that easily."

"*Please* go without me," I say, pushing branches out of my way. I let a branch go too early, and it flings a wet leaf into my mouth. Ben doesn't see it go in or get sputtered out. "Mr. Watso hates me."

"He doesn't hate you. He's dealing remarkably well with Molly's death."

"Her murder, you mean. The murder for which I'm responsible."

"That was between the Watso family and Villicus. You weren't involved."

"Mere technicality."

"Just be nice, and he'll be nice. A bit of time has passed since Molly died. Six weeks. If he held something against you, I think he's forgiven you."

I tug back on his hand. "I don't know, Ben. I feel icky about this. Six weeks is no time at all. I've seen how long it takes people to mourn—"

"*Anne.*" He stops and takes my gloved hands in his. He's lovelier than ever with the cold ocean wind nipping his cheeks and the desperate need to convince me lighting his eyes. "Okay, you got me."

"I what?"

"This was supposed to be a surprise. Tomorrow is our two-month anniversary, and I wanted to celebrate by having a proper dinner with you, me, my dad, and Mr. Watso."

"Wait, it's our…what?"

"*A-a-and* since Dad's here tonight but leaving tomorrow, I thought you wouldn't mind if I shifted the dates a bit."

"You've been keeping track of our anniversary?"

"Well, yeah."

I haven't been keeping track!

"Of course," he says, "we actually met five years ago, but that's not the same."

I watch him in awe. "No wonder Garnet hates me so much."

"What do you mean by that?" But he's blushing. He knows what I mean. He's constantly catching me marveling at his profile, or ogling our blurring, entwined hands as we sit on the beach together, or admiring him when he spouts off some line from a book. He is a wonder. "I'm a cheese muffin, aren't I?"

"You're a romantic, Mr. Zin."

"Is that better or worse than a cheese muffin?"

"It's lower fat."

"Anyway," he says with a small smile and a sigh, "will you come with me now? My dad's dying to get to know you. And Mr. Watso is honestly totally fine with you. He might even like you."

"I can't believe you had this plan all cooked up."

"I love a surprise."

"I'll have to pay you back one day."

He taps his lips. "I'll take an advance payment."

"You are *definitely* a cheese muffin." I kiss him. "Who even says that, 'cheese muffin'?"

"Chalk it up to my old age."

I kiss him again. And, when he doesn't pull away, I take that as an invitation for more. Since the night he told me he wanted to take things slowly, we've been like a nun and her priest. Well, not totally. We hold hands and stuff. In fact, we hold hands so often, we're becoming extensions of one another. But you could set a three-second stopwatch by our kisses. *One, two, three, pull back!* So it's a major step that, at least ten seconds into this kiss—not that I'm counting—Ben's not only failing to pull away, but he's actually leaning into me, and his hands are exploring a little below the "safe zone" of my lower back. I feel his lips part, and I hear my name on his breath, and I dare to tug a little at his hair in response, just enough to raise his chin and expose his throat to my mouth.

But then an owl hoots somewhere in the woods. And Ben, with an awkward laugh, pulls away. His skin is red with heat, and his eyes are luminescent; I know he doesn't want to stop, but hell if I can convince him we can go slow without going at a snail's pace.

"So the thing of it is," he says, taking my hand and turning us back on our path toward the small inlet where Mr. Watso lives, "my dad's yacht is anchored just at the outskirts of the inlet."

"Oh?" As if my head is anywhere near this conversation. If I ever find that damn owl…

"Yeah. He can basically jump off the boat, swim a few strokes, and climb up the shore."

"Not that he would, though."

"No, not that he would."

"'Course not."

"Yeah."

Oh, God, is this how it's going to be for the next six months? The fake chatter to mask what we're really thinking, what we'd rather be doing? I could honestly care less about his dad's boat.

"Here we go," Ben says. "He lives right…about…there."

Ben and I push through the last of the woods and find ourselves on the top of a semi-circular hill surrounding Mr. Watso's small, private enclave. The water is frozen-over here, and pale brown driftwood pops out of snow-dusted ice, creating the sense that we're standing next to the world's largest piece of almond bark, as if the ruler of this island is Willy Wonka and not a devil. A blue tent sits on the ice below, butted up against the snowy hill; it's Mr. Watso's ice-fishing shack—a good one, the kind money buys.

Just beyond the opening of the inlet, the yacht Ben's dad lives on bobs below a layer of fog. It's at least ninety feet long and two stories high, and it can't be more than a year or two old. Written on its side is *Forever Tallulah*. My stomach drops. Tallulah Josey's parents must have surrendered that boat in exchange for her admission to Cania, and now she's expelled, thanks to Harper.

Ben catches me looking at the yacht.

"The whole bottom of it is refrigerated," he says. "To hold hundreds of vials our dads have collected, with plenty of room for more. They renovated it to make it hypothermic. Medical grade. So the blood won't spoil."

"They're storing backups of the vials in Valedictorian Hall?"

"No," he says, staring pensively at the boat. "Have you wondered why Hiltop would stick around if she's not even allowed to run Cania anymore?"

"Of course."

We start inching our way down the steep hill, which is thick with soggy snow; multiple sets of footprints have etched a path for us, a zigzagging line of green down a canvas of white.

"The bottom of that yacht is filling up with the vials of people who haven't died yet."

"Living people's blood."

"Yup."

"So, let me get this straight—let me think with my Demon Hat on. If I were in the business of vivifying the dead, why would I start collecting the vials of living people?"

"And keeping them close to shore," Ben adds.

Why would Dia do that?

Damon Smith is why. I remember his vivification gone wrong. Too much time had passed between his death and their attempts to vivify him.

"Your dad's yacht is just far enough from shore to prevent accidental vivification…"

"…And just close enough to get a vial onto the island without so much as a minute passing."

So the vials containing the blood of the living are like insurance policies. "Kids that haven't died yet get to know their vial is just feet from shore. As soon as they die, they can be vivified here."

"Adults, too."

"Adults, too?"

"If someone pitched you on a new life for your kids, don't you think you'd want one for yourself, too? At least as an option?"

"I wouldn't."

"Well, the rest of the free world would."

"I doubt that."

"You should read 'The River Styx Runs Upstream,'" he says. "The market is *limitless*. Hiltop's here because she—Mephisto—wants to expand. Cania was taken from her, but that's just one small school on one large planet. Mephisto will expand. Cania College is just the beginning."

"But Cania College was Dia's idea, not Mephisto's."

"Are you sure?"

"I've given up feeling sure about anything."

We're standing at the zipped-up door of Mr. Watso's ice tent. Ben takes off his glove and scratches his fingertips over the material in lieu of knocking, calls, "Knock, knock," and we wait.

"If I've learned anything about Mephistopheles in my years under his tyranny," Ben whispers, "it's that he is always a step or two ahead of the rest of us. If you ask me, I think Mephisto wanted Dia here. Sure, he got in trouble Downstairs, but he used that to his advantage. He lured Dia here to babysit us, which is giving him the time and freedom to expand."

"But Mephisto didn't know Dia was coming. He didn't know the disruption you and I would cause."

Ben shrugs. "I'm just saying. I wouldn't be surprised if Mephisto gives Cania College to Dia to placate him, gets his baby, Cania Christy, back, and finds a new island where he can build an elementary school, a retirement home—hell, an entire town. Full-on expansion. In a world brimming with people who are terrified of death. Mephisto's going to take all those vials my dad's living with and, when their owners die, give people life all over the world. For a price, of course."

"Dia sent Teddy away to look for new locations."

"How do you know that?"

"I was there when it happened."

Ben rolls his eyes. "See?" He scratches the tent again. "Where's Watso?"

"Did we get the time wrong?"

"Maybe. My dad's not even here," he says. "Come on. Let's go throw rocks at the yacht. Make some noise. He's gotta be in there—probably passed out drunk."

"*Ben.*" I hate when he makes light of his dad's alcoholism.

"Hey, if you can't save yourself, might as well destroy yourself, right?"

"I'm not much of a fan of your new philosophy. Especially when you *can* save yourself."

"Not tonight, Anne. Please give it a rest. Just once."

The hillside makes a *C* around the inlet, with *Forever Tallulah* anchored at the far right of the opening. We follow a path already etched in the snow until we arrive just at the edge. The island makes a short, rocky cliff here. The yacht is hooked to a huge tree by a 100-foot steel rope that must be a foot thick.

"Speaking of our self-destructive powers." Ben's eyes are fiery with mischief. "Wanna try your trapeze skills out?"

"Walk the rope? Funny."

"What's the harm?" He picks up a small stone and hurls it at the yacht; it falls just short. He tries again. "We can't actually die. If you fall, you'll just end up standing right here again."

Vivified, we can't live beyond the limits of the island.

"*When* I fall." I throw a rock, and it makes a *tink* on the side of the boat.

"What happened to the fearless girl that broke into my house?"

"That was Molly. I was terrified."

He smirks. "I wish you saw what I see in you. Fine, if you won't do it, I will."

My arm stops him. "Challenge accepted, Zin."

I step toward the rope and tug the loop holding it to the tree. A part of what Ben's saying is, I have to admit, interesting. We're unbreakable. When have I let myself enjoy my immortality? Everyone else has an excuse for being on their best behavior: they care about winning the Big V. Ben and I don't. So I hold the tree for balance as I position myself on the taut rope. It's got a little give, but I'm hardly heavy enough to drag a whole yacht back to shore. Ben whistles through his teeth—"*I was kidding, Anne!*"—as I awkwardly turn, face the massive open ocean under the darkening night sky, and pretend I'm on the balance beam in some elementary school gymnastics class. Except this beam is rounded. And it's wet with frosty mist from the Atlantic, over which it droops precariously. So, yeah, I'm doomed. But not to death.

I put my arms out for balance. And take a step. The rope squeals. There's still earth under the rope, though. A dozen small steps separate me from the really freaky part over the water. Those small steps go quickly, and soon the rocky ledge disappears from under me.

"Anne, hun, sweetness, come on. Let's go back and wait at Watso's."

"What if," I begin to distract myself from the icy ocean, over which I'm suspended, "Mr. Watso is just gone?"

"Careful with that—it's swinging a lot—come on—Anne, get down from there."

I take a tiny step. Thirty or so feet down, the white-edged black waves pound thin blocks of ice into a short, jagged, bluish-white ice floor at the base of the cliff. I squint to make out something attached to or stuck in—it's hard to tell which—the ice. It's a blurry object of some kind, and it's about ten feet away from the rocks of the cliff.

I wobble, catch my balance, and place one foot in front of the other.

"What if he moved, Ben? What if his tent's empty?"

"Moved where? Come back right now. Enough."

"Off the island."

Ben growls as the rope swings. I drop to my knees, crossing my ankles over the rope, and I swear he goes into cardiac arrest.

"Why would he move, Anne?"

"Why would he stay?"

"He's the Abenaki shaman."

"Why wouldn't a shaman follow his people? Especially now that the whole village is demoed."

"The island is spiritually his. The underworld is leasing it from him. He needs to invite them here every day. You know all this. Now get back here, or you're going to vanish, and it's not gonna feel great—trust me."

I inch out on my hands and knees. "But he could just—"

All at once, the world goes gray. I hear nothing, see nothing, feel weightless. A woman's voice whispers to me, and a flash of violet eyes disappears in a blink. I open my eyes to find I'm standing next to Ben again, on the hillside, facing the yacht I was crawling toward only moments ago. He shakes his head at me. Watching the movement is dizzying.

"Just had to push it," he says and helps me get my bearings. "You're gonna feel groggy for a minute or two. This is why you should stay on the island."

"You're the one who dared me to go."

"Well, now I'm daring you to come with me to Mr. Watso's. We'll wait there for them."

I glance back at the rope.

He notices and shakes his head.

"I saw something in the ice."

"What did you see?"

"I need another look."

He tries to stop me. But I make my way back onto the rope, balancing again. My head's still spinning from being "reborn." I crouch for stability. This time, Ben's right behind me.

"Anne, you're hardly the most coordinated person I've ever met."

I laugh, but softly, and brace myself against the rope. Inch out. And peer down. The lapping waters are dark below the ice floor, making the gray ice glow white. I can just make out the shape of the object embedded in there.

"If you're trying to give me a heart attack, it's working."

"Yes, Ben, that's what I've been trying to do all along. Kill you."

I lower myself until I'm flat against the rope, and I squint. "It's a box," I tell him. "Small. Square. Maybe metallic. There's something written on it. A short word. Or some kind of jagged line."

"It's probably just debris from an old ship or plane wreck. Mystery solved."

I glance back at him. "Oooh, do you think it might be?"

"Aren't you wondering where my dad and Watso are?"

I have to get closer to the box. But I can't risk getting too far away and vanishing again. Moving fast, I grip the rope. In one fluid movement, I swing down. I'm dangling a good twenty-something feet above sea level before Ben even knows what's happened.

"Did you fall?" he cries, rushing to the edge. I hear him scramble to help me—until he realizes I didn't slip. "Are you nuts?"

"I need—" I gasp "—to see."

"Then let's go get binoculars. Come on."

He reaches to grab my hand, but I don't want to go get binoculars. So I dangle by one hand. Ben swears. I tell myself it'll only hurt for a second. And, counting down from three, I take a deep breath. And let go of the rope.

I free-fall.

I crash into the ice, landing hardest on my right knee.

A fault line cuts through the ice, shooting over the box. The box is just far enough from land that I'd vanish before I got out to see what it is or what's in it. It's maybe eight or nine feet away. I shuffle closer to it, or try to. But I've definitely done a number on my knee. A darkening, growing splotch of red shines through my tights.

"Oh, God, is that blood?" Ben shouts down.

I'll heal, I think as a cold wave washes the icy, breaking floor. I smile up at him—faking the smile, of course, through the intense pain of what may be a dislocated kneecap—and look out at the box. So close, but so far away. It's at the end of a ten-foot-long bar that's bolted to the rock face, just five or so inches below the water line, under the ice.

"It's bolted," I shout.

"Bolted? To the island?"

"Why would someone bolt a box this far off the island?"

"Maybe it's something morbid," Ben suggests, trying to scare me. "Like the vial of an ancient monster. Maybe they're keeping it there in case they want to vivify it one day, like, to punish students that go snooping around."

Now I can see that what appeared to be a sharp, jagged line drawn across it was really two letters: *M* and *W*.

"Well, what does it look like?" Ben calls.

"It looks like there are initials on it."

"Whose?"

That's the question.

eight

UNDERWORLD RISING

"ANNE?" BEN SHOUTS DOWN.

"The initials are *MW*," I tell him.

"What do they stand for?"

"What's Mr. Watso's first name?"

"Jim, I think."

I stare at the box, and I wonder if Ben was onto something when he was joking about a monster's blood being stored in the box. It could be that someone's storing vials in it, but I don't think they're the vials of a monster. Nor do I think it's an accident that Mr. Watso set up his ice-fishing tent so close to this box when he could have set it up anywhere around the island. Nor do I think Mr. Watso is still on Wormwood Island because he's spiritually obligated to be. I think he's here because of this box, because of its contents, because of the initials *MW*.

I glance at Dr. Zin's yacht. It's refrigerated to keep the vials on it cool; the ocean water is just as frigid, perfect for keeping vials cold in this box. His yacht is just far enough from the island to prevent the vials from touching this enchanted (or cursed) land and their owners instantly vivifying; this box is just far enough away, too.

"I'm coming down!" Ben shouts.

I look at him. "The initials are for Molly Watso."

His brow furrows. "What?"

"Mr. Watso is keeping her blood stored near the island. Kept in the freezing water. It's as good as refrigeration."

"You think he's got her vials in there?"

I nod.

"Christ, you don't think Mr. Watso has brought her blood onto the island already. You don't think she's—do you think he's vivified her already?"

That's what I need to find out. I slam my fists into the fault line cutting through the ice, hoping it will give and I'll be able to pop into the water, open the box, and, before I vanish, see if there are containers of blood in it.

In my mind's eye, I glimpse the girl I saw outside the Cania gates weeks ago, back when I was arguing with Garnet. Could that have been a vivified Molly? Could she have been here all this time?

The only conceivable reason Mr. Watso would stay here—when his granddaughter's been murdered and the rest of the Abenaki have left—is if he'd vivified Molly. This is the only place she can live, so this is the only place he would live. But he'd have to keep her vivification secret from everyone at the school because if Mephisto or Dia found out, they'd demand she follow the rules all vivified people must follow here: she'd have to enroll at Cania, compete for the Big V, and surrender something of extreme value as her tuition. This island would be her tuition.

"If Mr. Watso brought her vial to land, she'd vivify immediately," Ben calls down.

"I know!"

"If she's vivified already, Anne, they might have discovered her."

"I know!"

"That could be why Mr. Watso and my dad aren't at his fishing tent. What if they found her today?"

"You think Dia found her?"

"Or Mephisto. If they found her, Mr. Watso could be signing Wormwood Island over as her tuition right this second. That would turn Molly into a Cania student and this place into a gateway to and from Hell."

I bring both my fists down on the line. Nothing.

The ice is too thick. No matter how much weight I put into it— which is admittedly not a lot because a sharp shot of pain zips through me when my knee touches the ground—it doesn't give.

"I think there's still hope," I shout at Ben. "Dia might not care about getting Wormwood, and Mr. Watso might be above all of this. He might have her blood, but maybe he hasn't brought any of it close enough to the island to vivify her. Maybe he and Dr. Zin are just off doing something else. Maybe that's why they're late. It doesn't have to be the worst-case scenario."

Ben's face looks panicked suddenly, so I glance away. I don't want us to overreact when we're really just running on assumptions right now. Mr. Watso might be above playing with fire. I mean, so what if he kept vials of her blood? That doesn't mean he'd use them!

"Anne," Ben shouts, "get up here. Fast."

"No. I've gotta see if her vials are in there."

"Anne, please. Hurry!"

"Ben—"

"I'm not joking. Find a way to get up here! There's something coming!"

I ignore him. He's freaking out for nothing.

Folding my hands together, I raise them high above my head and, with all my strength, and with Ben shouting something I can't hear, I bring them down again. Hard. So hard something in my hand snaps. But it's not my force that cracks the ice—it's Ben's.

He's jumped down. He lands near the box. The ice snaps under his weight and the force of his landing. It shatters into blocky fragments under him, under both of us, and it exposes a deep, dark, and angry pool of icy cold water into which Ben begins sliding, tumbling down. I grasp at his arm. My hands wrap around it, but his momentum is unstoppable. He's halfway in the water at once. And I'm a short, gasping breath behind him.

The ocean tugs us in.

I go under fast, just after Ben. And bob up. And under again, flailing.

Frozen blocks bang against my head and arms. They push me under what's left of the ice floor, which is still attached in places to the island, where it's thickest.

For the longest moment, I can't see anything. Just dark blurs. And light blurs.

I can't see Ben.

A glint near my toes catches my eye.

It's deep in the murk.

It's not one glint but many.

They're rising up. They're swimming toward me.

I swirl, looking for Ben. It's too dark. Too much seaweed. It tugs at me like long fingertips, pulling me in when the force of the tide wants to pull me out. I finally spot Ben. He's way beyond my reach. His gaze meets mine. Bubbles push out of his mouth as he tries to say something. He's pointing at our feet. And then he's gone, vanished, back on the island.

My head hits something. It's the iron bar that's holding Molly's box. The ice floor is solid above me.

I look down again. Where the glints were. But they're not glints at all. They've taken shape—the strangest, eeriest shapes. They are eyes. And they are teeth. And they are swaying, in eel-like motions, up from the murk, up toward me. They are looking at me. And there are dozens of them.

Something has been living under the water. And it's coming up for air.

Or it's worse than that. Much worse.

The gateway to and from Hell, I think.

Desperate now, I pull myself up to the ice that's trapped me. I pound my fists against it. In futility. Bubbles of my breath collect under the grayness I can't break through.

I swivel to see. Far below. Climbing up. Living beings. With legs and arms and heads and eyes. But also horns. And snouts. And tails.

Instinctively, I try to scream. Water fills my throat, touches my lungs. I can't cough. This is how you drown; this is how I drown, if I'm not first killed by whatever's swimming up at me.

But all at once, the world is gray. And the flash of violet eyes. Nothingness and lightness. And then I feel the earth under my feet again. Ben is standing, quivering, on the snowy bank next to me. We are soaked through, drenched in ice water. He grabs me and wraps his arms, his whole body around me, and I cling to him. We're gasping for air. I cough, trying to form words. Our bloodshot eyes meet.

"I tried to warn you," he says, convulsing with cold. "I saw them. From above."

"Are those what I think they are?"

But the woods answer for Ben. The ground beneath our feet, which starts to move and take the shape of a large man's back, is all the answer I need. The quaking ground growls under our boots and throws me off balance. Just before I fall, we grab hands and leap off the rounding, rising lump of snow-dusted cliff. We stagger backward, stagger toward the woods. And when the thing takes full shape, facing away from us—"*What is it?*"—"*Some sort of man-thing*"—we spin on our heels and haul ass. We refuse to look back. We race into the woods, through them, as fast as our wobbly new legs can go, and stop short at the road. I'm fearfully certain more of what we just saw will find us here.

And it does.

The demon-women push through the frozen mud near the road. Ben pulls me back into the shadows just before their heads swivel in our direction. Together, we watch those things, dressed in diamond-printed unitards, faces painted a streaking white, dash forward and scurry up the trees like lizards, a third set of limbs helping them. Lumbering across the road far ahead, an elephantine creature dressed in formal clothes from another time drags a wrecking ball in its trunk and moves slowly into the woods on the other side.

"Either we've just stumbled into the circus from a nightmare," Ben whispers, "or Molly's alive."

"And found."

"And Mr. Watso had to sign over the island to keep her alive."

"So it's a gateway now."

"It's owned by the devil. And his demons are here. They're making it their home."

"It's what Mephisto always wanted."

"But," I pause, "it's Dia's now. Not his."

"Does it matter? We're on the property of the underworld. It's Hell on Earth. Dia's demons or Mephisto's—they're here."

The island is filling with demons—real ones in true form, not semi-palatable human avatars. The tree we're clutching begins to morph, its bark taking the shape of the man in Munch's *The Scream*, which is our cue to get the hell outta there. As if we needed nudging. Keeping low, we scuttle along the road, feeling anything but protected by the starless night. We move fast, stay together, back to back. We look the other way when a fern quivers. We pick up our pace when the earth rumbles.

It seems as if campus will never be in sight. But why should we think things will be better there?

There's a moment, when we're near Dia's mansion, that we talk about darting inside and hiding. But the lights are on within. And huge shadows pass by nearly every window at once.

"It's packed with his demons," Ben says.

Enormous winged creatures—could be bats—could be vultures—sweep up to perch on the rooftop. They are dripping wet, as if they've risen from beneath the water.

"Mephisto's going to flip," Ben whispers to me. "If all the students see these demons running around, it'll be impossible to pretend that this place is anything but evil. That won't be good for enrollment."

"Are you seriously thinking about *admissions* right now?"

"I'm seriously thinking that Dia is reckless. This is bad. In so many ways."

Just as we turn from the mansion, we are faced by a tall, pencil-thin man with bright red skin. He dwarfs the trees.

We stop dead. And stare up. And up.

Fear paralyzes me. Ben yanks me closer to him. Trying to protect me.

With long eyes stacked one above the other, this enormously tall demon is watching us from the middle of the road. The stretched, ribbed horns of a gazelle rise skyward from his soaring forehead, and his legs in red striped pants are those of a painted giraffe: endless, knobbed at the knees. He is too thin to house a heart, too thin for the things that make you human. He watches us with the curious expression of a hunter observing his prey behave most strangely—the dance of death. I know this thing can't kill us. We can't die. We can, however, be brought to the point where we'd beg for death. With no one to hear us. Or help us.

"Back off," Ben warns it. "Leave us alone."

The thing's thin upper lip curls. It's laughing at him.

"I'm not kidding."

I notice the others. All around us. Up in the trees, glaring down with thin eyes. Behind the forest ferns, in heaving rows. Large ones that seem made of rock, and small wiry ones that are all teeth. Some look human, dressed in top hats and tights as if they've raided a demonic dress-up trunk. Others are anything but: webbed feet and scales, beaks and horns, hairless, made of smoke. I don't have to turn around to know there are more at our backs.

My next thought catches me by surprise: *Look closer.*

I hadn't thought I was so indoctrinated in the Cania Christy way of thinking as to use my PT when no one's even grading me. In what precious little time they're allowing us before they pounce or do whatever demons do to vivified kids, I take in the scene and then each of them individually, starting with the tall red man. He is standing exactly where, beneath the snow, a red line is painted across the road. Something about that lessens his power, as if he is made of paint, as if he's nothing to fear after all. Looking even closer, I find that he's not watching Ben anymore. He's fixed that stacked gaze solely on me.

They're all looking at me.

Expectantly.

Curiously.

My heartbeat quickens. As if I have two hearts, and they're racing each other. Adrenaline surges through my veins, rippling under my skin. The rush of fear that froze my legs explodes into waves of energy, straightening my back, lifting my chin, arching my eyebrow. Ben is whispering that he'll find a way to get us out of this, that I shouldn't worry, when I fix an unwavering glower on the tall red thing.

"Get back to Hell," I command it.

The red man looks like he might speak. But, instead, he folds in half, almost as if he's bowing, and then in half again, and again, as Ben and I stare silently, until he disappears beneath the snow. The others crawl and slurk back to where they came from, one by one, sinking into the frozen earth or retreating to the ocean.

I feel Ben's arms stiffen around me. But it's not until we're alone again that his body starts to shake with laughter. My heart, to my surprise, is still thumping hard.

"I don't know where that came from," I confess. Why wasn't I more afraid?

"They obeyed you," Ben says as he pulls back, holding my shoulders and laughing. He kisses me. Hard and full on the lips. I wish I could be in the moment with him—these moments are so rare—but I can't believe what just happened. "What are you?—some kind of demon tamer? Maybe that's why Teddy brought you back here. The underworld's recruiting you."

Easy for him to laugh. He doesn't know what I saw in the mirror.

My heart slows to normal. Finally.

Slush and mud squish inside my boots as we walk back to campus. A hot shower is all we can talk about when we part ways outside his dorm. He tells me to warm up—I'll feel better then, he says. But I can only shrug. I guess five years on this island have normalized interactions with the underworld for him.

"I'll meet you after your mentoring session tomorrow. Okay?" he asks. "We'll celebrate our anniversary in the cafeteria. Nothing better than food we can barely taste to celebrate, right?"

"Sounds good." Can he sense how messed up my head is right now?

"Have sweet dreams. I'm sure there's an explanation for what just happened."

I'm sure there is, too. But I'm not so sure I want to hear it.

I've only just started up the stairs to the second floor of the girls' dorm when I see Harper and Plum. Their arms are full of clothes on hangers, shoe boxes, and hat boxes. I tiptoe up the rest of the way, and they finally notice me when I'm at the top of the stairs; Harper's face pales.

"Spring cleaning?" I ask, my tone flat.

"It's *winter*," Plum says.

"You finally learned your seasons. Congratulations."

"I already knew the seasons."

"All four of them?"

Harper interrupts us: "You've got a new roommate, Anne. I, um, had to move out. Not that I wanted to. I—I really liked living with you."

Gulping so loud I can hear it, Harper casts her eyes down, gestures for Plum to keep moving, and hurries into Plum's bedroom, closing the door and locking it behind them before I can even ask if they saw any of the demons Ben and I saw.

I shuffle into my room—right past my new roommate, who's digging through her closet. And I stop.

It just occurred to me who she is.

I turn back to her. She's standing. A big ol' grin spreads across her pretty face.

"Surprise, roomie!" Molly exclaims.

nine

THE MENTOR

HERE SHE IS, MY BRUNETTE FRIEND WHO'S AT LEAST A foot shorter than I am but is always, even now, *especially* now, larger than life. She tosses down the sweater she was stretching onto a hanger and throws her arms around me, ignoring my owl-like stare and the stiffness of my drenched body as she squeezes me hard.

"You're soaking wet, but I don't care!"

"Oh my gosh. I was totally right about you," I stammer.

"Good to see you, too." Her laugh fills the room as she lets me go. When I don't crack a smile, she shakes my shoulder like she's waking me up. "What, has rigor mortis set in? Look alive, Anne! It's been *sooo* long. Did you forget me already?"

"I was just looking for you. Ben and I. We fell. We fell into the water. Looking for you. And then the demons were there. And then. Gone."

She smiles coyly. "Ben? *Ooo la la.* I want to hear everything!"

She tugs me onto her clothing-covered bed, oblivious to the fact that I'm going to drench all her stuff. She starts flouncing my wet hair over my shoulders.

"Look at you. Look at us! Roommates at Cania Mother-Effing Christy. Who'da thunk it?"

"How long, Mol? How long have you been vivified?"

99

"Since, like, gee, how long since Villie gave me the ultimatum? About a week after that, my grandpa buried a little container of my blood in the ground, and voilà."

"So it *was* you outside the gates that day."

She blushes. "I gravitate toward you—what can I say?"

"Then your grandpa really was keeping vials of your blood out in the water, just beyond the power of the island."

"*Précisément.* The night he got so mad at you—remember?—was the night he took my blood as a precaution. Just in case the worst happened. Which, of course, it did."

"And then he vivified you without Dia or Mephisto knowing?"

"Bingo. Anything that touches this place vivifies—including moi—so The Great Mephisto didn't even know. But enough about all that." She rolls her eyes like her top secret vivification is so boring. "Tell me about Ben. Are you guys, like, making out on a regular basis now?"

"So, wait, back up a sec. Your grandpa waited a week to vivify you?"

She sighs. "This is not the girl talk I was looking forward to."

"It's just that I'm trying to keep ahead of things here, Mol, instead of, like, living in the dark. I saw them try to vivify this kid named Damon Smith, but they'd waited too long, and his soul had already moved on. He'd only been dead, like, three days."

"Well that sucks."

"It's just lucky that your soul was still available to be vivified along with your body. I mean, waiting a week to vivify you sounds risky. You're lucky."

"Oh, yes, I'm the luckiest girl on Earth!" she laughs and starts braiding my hair absently. "I managed to live in secret on this island for, like, five weeks. But today, I was snooping around Cania, just checking things out, and that weird chick with the bangs—Hiltop, right?—she spotted me. Turned me in."

"She's one of Mephisto's avatars."

"Seriously?"

"Seriously." I watch her fiddle with my hair as if nothing's wrong. I can't keep it in any longer, so I whisper, "I'm so sorry, Mol."

"Sorry?"

"You never wanted to go to Cania. You never wanted to compete for the Big V. And now you're doing both. And your island is your tuition. And it, like everything, is all my fault."

"Oh, no, you're not inviting me to a Pity Party, are you?"

"I'm serious."

She smiles. "Well maybe there's a loophole."

"We both know there are no loopholes with these guys. You lost your island for good."

"Anne, stop worrying. Losing Wormwood was bound to happen. Molly's okay with it."

I lean away. "You did not just talk about yourself in the third person."

She clears her throat. "Molly likes to do that sometimes."

I'm laughing when it finally sinks in that my only friend is back in my life. Molly has replaced pain-in-the-ass Harper as my roommate. I throw my arms around her.

"You're here!"

"You're wet!"

We head into the shared bathroom, where Molly shoos a couple sophomores out and sits on the counter as I hop in the shower. She rattles off stories about sneaking around on the island and asks me questions about everything—she seems to care most about my relationship with Ben and my dad's new position here—while I trade chattering teeth and de-thawing hair for a rush of hot water that, after ten minutes, leaves my skin almost as red as the pencil-thin demon's. I wrap myself in a plush towel, push away all the dark thoughts of this evening, and step onto the heated tile floor.

"You look like a sundried tomato—ever heard of turning the cold on, too?"

"You sound like my parents."

"Your hair is a rat's nest. Come here!" Molly shoves me onto a vanity stool and wields a wide-toothed comb. We watch each other in the mirror as she starts working through my knots. "So, exactly how much naughty business have you gotten up to with Mr. Ben Zin?"

I can't help blushing, even though there's not much "naughty business" to relate. "He's…he's amazing. And too good for me. And…amazing."

She smiles. "I guess that dress I loaned you really made an impact."

"So much has changed since that night," I say in a breath.

"*Everything* changed that night," she echoes. Our gazes lock in the reflection, but, to my relief, her smile widens. "Anyway, get this—you'll never guess who my Guardian is."

"Nice topic change. This is so *awful*."

"Go ahead. Guess."

"If you'd just been a cow, Molly, we wouldn't have been friends, and this whole mess—"

"*Guess, bitch!*" Molly's forcing a mean face that doesn't look even remotely scary. Her dark eyes twinkle against her olive skin. "Guess who my Guardian is…or I'll start teasing this big ol' hair of yours." She taps the comb impatiently on my head. I smack it away, but she doesn't give up. "I swear, it'll pick up radio signals by the time I'm through."

I relent. "Well, I've got Pilot for a Guardian, which is the worst possible punk to get stuck with."

"*Pilot?* That pervy sex-senator's son? The one you freakin' dated?"

"And then killed."

"Hold up—" Her eyebrows hit her hair. "You what?"

"It sounds worse than it was. It was this situation when Ben and I jumped off the cliff. Long story."

"You black widow, you."

"I'm not exactly proud of it." I wait for her to make me feel better, but she just keeps combing. "Anyway, Ben's a student now, too, and he's got Garnet as his Guardian. She's the blonde chick I kept seeing with him. They used to go out."

"Remind me?"

I stare in disbelief at her. "The blonde girl. We broke into his house to learn about her."

"Oh!" She shrugs. "I forgot."

"You forgot that?" I laugh it off. "Anyway, it turns out she's a teacher. And she's kinda obsessed with him. And pissed he's not into her."

"Well, gee, mine doesn't seem so bad now." She puts the comb down. "Ready for it? It's Teddy! Wasn't he your old Guardian?— that scrawny little guy? Man, what a puke."

Teddy? "I thought he was off looking at places like Wormwood. Dia sent him away."

"He was here tonight, and he tried to 'read' me. Creepy much? I wouldn't have it."

"You didn't let him read you?"

"I told him any part of him that touches me, he ain't gettin' back."

I silently curse Teddy for being here and not coming to talk to me. It's been six weeks since he told me our so-called mission. The least he could do is check in. For a second, I think about telling Molly the truth about Teddy, but if I didn't tell Ben, I can't tell her. Teddy warned me not to trust anyone.

"So how did he give you your PT?" I ask her.

"I chose my own PT."

"Of course you did."

"I'm going to succeed in life by surprising people."

"You're off to a good start. What did Teddy think about that?"

"As long as I can use it in sinister ways, he's fine with it. What a freak. Made me write it down and sign it with my blood, right in Dia's office. And, can I just say"—she stares dramatically into space—"in another world, I would totally have Dia's babies. Damn, that is one fine devil-dude."

Laughing, we head back to our room. Void of Harper's motivational posters and flush with Molly's carved trunks, golden twinkle lights, and family photos, this rectangle of a room actually feels like it could be home. The lights are dim, and the faint moonlight beyond our windows is reflecting the falling snow outside. For the first time since I moved in, I flick on the little gas fireplace in the corner of the room; Molly smiles, and so do I.

"So Teddy must be sticking around here now. To be your Guardian."

"I don't want him anywhere near me, so I hope not. He said something about traveling the world. Thinks he's a big shot. And who needs him?" She tosses me her fancy body lotion, which smells like cookies, and locks the door. "I have a surprise for you."

"Save it until someone's grading you for it!"

"Uh-uh. Guardians can't see this surprise."

From under her bed, she pulls a shoe box large enough for boots, doing her best not to get lotion all over it. A grin lights her eyes as she lifts the lid and reveals a laptop, a Kindle, a bunch of magazines, and an MP3 player. I rub the rest of the lotion into my hands so I don't smudge the devices.

"Contraband?" I ask, trailing my fingertips over the silver laptop. "Here I thought you'd have a secret vial of, I dunno, Hiltop's blood."

"My gramps saved this stuff for me. Consider it a crash course for the two years of life you slept through." She pushes the Kindle at me. "*Fifty Shades of Grey*—like it or not, a pop culture must-read." Then the MP3 player. "Imagine Dragons. One Direction. Adele." Then the magazines. "The Kardashians. That's all I'm going to say."

For the rest of the night and almost until the sun rises, Molly and I talk breathlessly. We both know I've gotta meet Dia Voletto tomorrow, but neither one of us wants to sleep. She has a thousand questions about my life, though she never actually asks about how I got into a coma or who brought me back here, to my relief; I don't want her to get the wrong idea about my mom, and I don't want to openly lie to her about Teddy. I'm struggling to keep my eyes open by the time her sentences start breaking up and her questions turn into mutterings that finally peter out.

I make sure to wrap my covers tightly around my body, and I wait until I can hear her heavy, slow breaths before I close my eyes. One day I'll tell Molly about the creature I saw in the mirror, but not now. We need time for some friendship rebuilding first, methinks. There will be enough forces trying to pull us apart as the Big V becomes an actual consideration and we find ourselves competing against each other for it. I don't want to lose her now, not to something as foreign and confusing to me as it would be to her.

I'm relieved to make it through the night without any screaming whatsoever. But my relief vanishes when I wake to the first in what is sure to be a dreadful series of Saturday mornings spent in "mentoring" sessions with Dia.

"Why are you dreading seeing Mr. Sex himself?" Molly asks me. "I'd be waxing my lady parts."

"There's just something about him," I say.

"You don't like bad boy types?"

"I don't like devils."

Molly got up early to see her gramps, who's going to live on the ice until spring, and brought back a thermos of coffee for us to share. I sip mine as I watch her put away her insanely gorgeous wardrobe, all of which she's told me I can borrow. Her jeans would be flood pants on me, but the sweaters and dresses will totally work.

"What's he mentoring you in again?" she asks. "The art and science of *luuuv*?"

I throw a balled sock at her. She bats it away and celebrates her awesome instincts.

All sense of levity vanishes twenty minutes later, when Dia opens his office door for me. I've just zipped through the quad and found myself looking both ways for clownish devils. Dia's grinning as I stand before him, but there's nothing funny about any of this. And I won't step foot into his office until I get him to agree to sending those demons back from whence they came.

"Headmaster," I begin, "you've gotta get rid of all those dudes from the underworld, stat."

He looks confused. I can hear Tom Waits' *The Black Rider* on a record player inside. My mom would play that on her darker days.

"The demons," I clarify.

"My staff?"

"No. The ones that, like, infiltrated Wormwood last night. In their scary circus costumes."

"Oh, them. Done. Gone. They went away last night."

"Permanently?" *Please say it's not because I asked them to. Please say I'm not a demon tamer.*

"I traded the island to Mephisto last night. So my little followers had to leave."

I struggle to process what he's just said.

"Mephisto owns the island now?"

"Sure does."

Why does this seem so much worse than Dia owning it? It is. It is worse. I don't know why, but I feel it in my gut. Already I've developed a hunch that Dia isn't quite as clever as Mephisto is, and I wouldn't be surprised if he was just a pawn in Mephisto's larger world-domination strategy.

"Anyway, it's not like they would've harmed you, Anne." Dia tugs me by the sleeve into his office, closing the door behind us. Seven beautiful women are standing behind his desk. I freeze. "And, as you can see, I made out much better than Mephisto did in the exchange."

Before I even know what I'm seeing, I say, "The Seven Sinning Sisters."

Here they are. In the flesh. In the spectacular, mind-numbingly beautiful flesh. Mephisto traded the remaining six goddesses of sin for the island. Which means his legions are at an all-time low, and his power might be zapped with it. If there was ever a time to destroy Mephisto, it's now—but Teddy's nowhere to be found!

"Anne, please meet—"

"Superbia," I say to the first woman, who's taller than the other six and holding her chin haughtily as she looks down her long, straight nose at me. She can only be the sin of pride.

The Seven Sinning Sisters, oozing appeal, arch their well-shaped eyebrows at one another and turn their impressed gazes on me. Each of them has translucent violet eyes edged in thick black lashes. Each has hair at least as wild as mine, but theirs are streaked with jewel tones like amethyst and ruby. Each is tattooed, the mark of their master Dia, and their tattoos reveal their powers. Each is more striking than the other, possibly having to do with their submission to the beauty-obsessed Dia Voletto. Each has afflicted me in my life, and each one has the power to destroy me. But in spite of their destructive power, I'm awestruck by them, trapped in a rapturous enjoyment of the simple act of looking at living dolls. I want to touch them. I want to be them. And it takes me too long to realize what a terrible thought that is.

"Nice work, Anne," Dia says. "Yes, she's Superbia. Of course, you already know Invidia."

"The sin of envy," I say.

"Don't hate me because I'm everything you want to be," she offers, pinpointing exactly how I've felt in her presence for weeks.

"And you're Avaritia," I say to the blonde woman dripping in diamonds and draped in white mink. "The sin of greed."

"I'll be teaching Modern American Economics," she says.

Dia introduces the rest of them. Dressed in fishnet stockings and a tight black dress is Luxuria, the sin of lust, who bats her eyelashes at me while Dia explains that she'll teach biology. Gula, whose heavy curves are barely contained in her tight jeans and tighter blazer, personifies the sin of gluttony and will oversee the cafeteria. As Dia's talking, Acedia abandons her sisters to make herself comfortable on the divan near the fire; there she seems ready to sleep—until Ira, frustrated with her, shoves her off the lounger and to the floor.

"And they," Dia says with an eye roll, "are the goddesses of sloth and wrath. Acedia has informed me she won't have anything resembling the energy to teach a course, but Ira has agreed to manage the school secretaries."

"Am I going to be painting all of you today?" I ask.

They laugh. Deliciously. In unison. Rather than answering me directly, they begin filing around the desk and, one by one, they give Dia a kiss on the cheek on their way to the door. Acedia, too slovenly to make the epic journey to where Dia's seated, blows him a kiss from across the room and drifts slowly to the door, which she waits for Luxuria to open for her.

"I'll see you in class, Miss Merchant," Superbia says to me, pausing to look me up and down. Her tattoo is a tiara, and it sparkles when the light catches it. "I'll be your English Lit instructor in Term Two."

"I can't wait," I stammer. And I'm not even lying. These women draw me to them in the strangest way—not like a moth to a flame, which can only end in misfortune, but like the waves to the shore. Inevitably. And powerfully.

Superbia closes the door behind her, leaving me and Dia alone.

"Aren't they stunning creatures?" he says.

I can't even speak.

"Sorry if that was uncomfortable for you." He shows me to the area he's set up for us. "They asked me if they could meet you."

"They did?"

Of course they did, I think. I'm the girl who outsmarted their former ruler, Mephistopheles, and lived to tell. I'd want to size me up, too.

"Now, take a look at what I did for the artist known as Anne Merchant."

Half of Dia's office has been transformed into an art studio, draped in white sheets, with an easel and backless chair just an arm's length from a black suede chaise longue. A small shelving unit sits next to the easel and displays a rainbow of perfect little ceramic pots of paint. A silver stand meant for icing champagne is on the other side, its glistening vessel filled with a birdbath of warm water to clean my brushes in. Unlit pillar candles are positioned around the chaise; Dia catches me eyeing them up.

"Lighting is everything, isn't it?" he says.

I flick a look from him to the candles. "You're not planning on lighting those."

"Of course I am." He strikes a long match and walks from one to the next, creating a glowing trail.

"It's just—have you noticed that candlelight makes things feel, um, more intimate?"

"Sexy, don't you think?"

Ugh. That word.

"That's kinda the problem, Mr. Voletto."

"*Dia.*"

"*Headmaster,*" I push, hoping he gets my point. "Can we be honest?"

"Only if it scares you. You should always do things that scare you, Anne."

I'm beginning to notice that he calls me *Anne* when we're alone and *Miss Merchant* when others are around.

"I'd just like to be sure everything's… Well, I know that some students here have reputations for doing, um, *favors* for extra credit."

"You mean as Miss Otto does for her Guardian, Mr. Sedmoney?"

I nod.

"They have quite a relationship," he says.

"That might be stretching the meaning of the word *relationship.*"

"He worships her."

"I don't want to be worshipped."

With a dark smile, he waves out the match.

"Listen, Anne, I was serious about mentoring you. And I was serious about you painting me. I come from a world filled with succubae and incubi. If I say something that makes you uncomfortable, simply overlook it. Sex is a non-issue for me."

"Just overlook it? Even though it makes me uncomfortable?"

"It's just for fun. Adult fun, yes, but fun nonetheless."

"I'm sixteen."

"Exactly."

"So not an adult."

"Do you want to become a better artist?"

I cross my arms over my chest. "Please don't give me some song and dance about sexual liberation and artistic liberation."

"Dante Gabriel Rossetti—limited by Victorian morality in his early and forgettable years, but—"

"But revolutionary in his later years. Are you really going there?"

"Why was he so revolutionary, Anne? It's because it was only as he aged that he realized morals were and are created by immoral people so terrified of the lust they feel for their own shadows that they castigate the unwed lovers they envy and label long-haired beauties *witches* simply because they'd like to make love to them but are rejected. When at last Rossetti surrendered to his thirst to paint sensuous women, it was then and only then that his art came alive."

"Are you just pulling convenient examples out of the air?"

"That was a good example," he insists. "I was, in my life, Italian. And, well, Rossetti's subject Saligia is near and dear to my heart. So Rossetti is hardly random."

"Well, I'm an American, so let's not forget Rossetti's friend and fellow artist, Whistler."

"What of him?"

"His work was best when it rallied against eroticism. The model for *The White Girl*—"

"Joanna Hiffernan," he says.

"—also posed for Whistler's friend Courbet—"

"Several times. And it destroyed their friendship. But, hell, what a way to go." Dia's eyes brighten. "On a piece like *L'Origine du monde*. Have you studied it?"

Before I can answer, he darts to a distant bookshelf, which is filled with volumes on De Stijl, American realism, shock art, Ukiyo-e, and aestheticism, and, pulling down two, flips through them. Then, dashing back to me, drops one on a row of paint pots, rocking one until it tips, a mess he doesn't seem to mind. The book is open to *L'Origine du monde*. I have to remind myself that it's art, not pornography, and that no real artist blushes to see a naked subject.

"I can't blame Courbet for painting her, and I can't blame Whistler for being jealous." Holding the other book open, Dia flips back and forth between the two paintings in question, huddling in with me. "If given the choice between the dowdy, reserved Jo in *The Little White Girl*—what is that fan she's holding?—and the challenging statement of that very same woman's spread legs here," he slaps the page with Courbet's painting and turns his sparkling eyes on me, "you must choose Courbet. Anne, you must! If only because your uptight American Whistler thinks of a stunningly sexual creature in such a sexless, childish way. If only for the sake of feminism!"

"Feminism?"

"Yes!"

"Mr. Voletto, both versions of this woman are courtesy of the male gaze."

"Then explore it—her, me, yourself, everything—through the female gaze, Anne, with your own brush. Right here. In this room. With me."

His wild and enthusiastic leer runs over my face, and I know at once that studying under Dia could elevate me to a level of artistry I'd forgotten existed and, perhaps, have never personally known. Art fired by passion. Art that begs and pants and commands unapologetically. Art that is, I hate to admit it but can't help recognizing it as I watch his lip tremble distractingly, the opposite of what I've done in my life. I have painted timid, voiceless works within the confines of a hush-filled funeral home. I have painted flat, soulless works under the weight of competing for the perfection required to win the Big V. I have yet to really, truly express or explore myself on the canvas.

"Your purple is dripping down the back of the shelf," I stammer.

"It's violet, Anne, *violet*. And let it go. Let it all go."

I stagger out of our session weakened by Dia's fervor but—I can't deny it—hungry for more. It's with a ravenous appetite I can't explain that I meet Ben, and, on seeing him, clutch his sweater at the chest, pull him to me, and kiss him, refusing to let him go even when he starts to pull away. It's not until a snowball hits me in the back that I release him.

I turn to find Molly smiling at me as she shapes another snowball.

I turn back to Ben, and he's scooping up snow, too. He stands, tells me to duck, and whips one at her. But she's too fast for him.

"Nice try, California boy!" she shouts. She runs our way and throws a snowball at Ben, catching him just above the belt.

I join in, too. But my next mentoring session is on my mind; it can't arrive soon enough. When it's finally Saturday morning again, I show up ten minutes early and endure Dia vilifying every stroke I paint. But even when he scorches my canvas in the fireplace and tells me to come back when I have a better sense of who I am, I eat it up. I want more. I want to be the person—the artist—Dia sees in me.

Weeks pass.

Saturdays come and go. Ben says little about my rekindled obsession with painting, and I say little about how desperately fast his remaining days on Earth are flying by. It's like we've both agreed that if the other person won't like what we're thinking, we'll keep it to ourselves.

The Scrutiny hangs over our heads as November turns to December and Christmas nears.

The Scrutiny is held every New Year's Day. The entire student body competes in it. It's one of the few events in the year that gives us the chance to set ourselves apart from the others. Dia's been talking about it in our sessions almost every week, though he won't reveal what he has planned. Each year it changes, but it's usually little more than brainteasers and word puzzles you have to solve.

Of course, Pilot is desperate for me to win it. I need to excel at everything if I'm going to stand a chance at the Big V because, although Dia seems pleased that I humiliated Mephisto, the other Guardians against whom Pilot will be debating are sure to spin my escape-plan-gone-wrong as a failure and, by extension, me as unworthy of a second chance.

"So focus," Pilot insists when he sees me sketching Dia's eyes behind my palm. We're in our daily coaching session in the cafeteria. "How are you ever going to win the Scrutiny like this?"

"You don't even know what this year's Scrutiny challenge is," I remind him as he balls up my paper and throws it over his shoulder. Whatever. He'll be the one cleaning it up later, anyway. "We've been going over word puzzles and past challenges so much, I can barely see straight. Everything looks like a puzzle to me. The opening and closing of a door is starting to become a puzzle."

"It should! That means the practice is paying off," he says.

"I can't help but think I'd be better off with Teddy coaching me."

"That twisted shithead would ruin your life, Anne. Avoid him. I'm serious."

I roll my eyes.

"Listen, no one knows what the Scrutiny challenge will be," Pilot says. "But if you win it—hell, if you even rank in the top— you'll get tons of gold stars, Anne. You'll be at the top of the short list, and that is where you want to be even if you're not up for the Big V until next year."

"Yeah, yeah. The short list." The list that Ben's nowhere near topping.

"Yeah, yeah. It's just my life on the line."

"It's actually *my* life on the line," I remind him. "Yours is already gone."

"You'd think you'd feel remorse for having killed me, Anne. This is your chance to give me back the life you stole. I can't make it up to Anastasia. You should count yourself lucky that you've got this chance to clear your conscience."

"Is Anastasia the girl you murdered?"

Dropping his eyes, he nods. "I wish I had the chance to take that night back. I think about it all the time."

A tear drops onto the sheet of paper, ballooning the word *liar* rather poetically. I watch him until he lifts his gaze. There's no mistaking that he's looking up to see if I'm buying his sob story. Which I'm not. *Same old Pilot*, I think as I leave him in the cafeteria and head back to my dorm room.

Night after night, Molly watches me sketch furiously at my desk and marvels at the number of trees that have to die just so I can crumple pages up and start all over again, all in an effort to impress Dia the following Saturday. Morning after morning, Garnet growls in our workshop, nonplussed by Dia's interest in mentoring me, to say nothing of her frustration at Ben's insistence that he doesn't want to be with her—insistence that even I can't help challenging. To no success. All I want is for Ben to have a chance at the Big V, but he refuses to give in to Garnet—he refuses to leave me for her, as if the short-term loss of our relationship isn't worth the long-term gain.

Ben.

It's only when I'm with Ben that I *don't* long for Saturday and *don't* hope the seconds will tick away faster. It's only with Ben that the arrival and passing of another Saturday means something bad: we're getting that much closer to his graduation. I've taken to coaching Ben the way Pilot coaches me, but, for someone as bright as Ben, it seems that nothing sticks like it should. He takes my energy, smiles appreciatively, and then reminds me that he's doomed. As if I should give up the way he has.

And, to be clear, he has given up.

"Maybe you should be flattered," Molly offers as I get ready for bed. "Ben wants to be with you for as long as he can."

Molly has become the girl everyone goes to for illegal gadgets, which her gramps keeps her stocked with. Instead of taking payment, she's been stockpiling favors. She is reading through envelopes of them as I groan about the new year being Ben's last year on Earth.

"No, he wants to be with me for six more months. And then die. And in the meantime? I'm totally getting crazier about him."

"Aww."

"Molly, seriously."

"It's sweet! You have a boyfriend you adore who seems to adore you right back."

I do adore him. I adore him more than I want to admit. I've never really believed in *meant to be*, but the way I feel just thinking about him, I can't help but hope that it's our destiny that we be together. But for how long? Am I supposed to fall in love with him... just to kill that love and live the rest of my life yearning for it? Letting him die would be like condemning myself to a living hell.

I just wish he would put my feelings a tiny bit above his.

My frustration with Ben's stubbornness finds its way into my last session with Dia before Christmas and the Scrutiny. While the fire crackles, he reclines on the chaise and rolls up his sleeves to trace one of his many colorful tattoos with his finger. It's my job to study him as my subject, which leaves me helpless to studying his body and gives me good reason to marvel, even in my frustration, as the blue, pink, and red of his many tattoos glow when his fingertip strokes them. I'm surprised to see him entirely transform a red rose tattoo into a Betty Boop with just the touch of his hand.

"Could you please stop redrawing your tattoos?" I snap. "It's impossible to paint a changing subject."

"Why don't you throw that painting into the fire right now?"

"You haven't even looked at it."

"Yes, well, I can tell it's garbage from here."

Thanks, *mentor*.

"Do you wanna know why I'm so sure that piece of junk isn't worth my time, kid?"

The worst thing is playing along with questions like that. Of course I don't want to know. Especially not when he calls me *kid*.

"It's because," he swings his bare feet down and waits until I return his stare, "you're in a bad mood. You're obviously in a bad mood about something—probably Ben—or it could be Christmas without your dad—and here you are grinding your teeth."

"Mad about Ben?"

He smirks.

"Is something funny?" I ask.

"You don't think that maybe you and Ben are a little poorly matched?"

I swallow. "Why would you say that?"

"Forget it."

"Tell me."

I wait for him to tell me Ben's flawless. And privileged. And meticulous to the point of OCD. While I, in comparison, am too tall, too thick-waisted and thick-legged, too wild-haired, too poor with teeth that are too crooked. But he doesn't say any of that. He says something much worse.

"You're not meant for him."

ten

THE MUSE

I KNOW NOW THAT I'M GETTING TOO CLOSE TO THIS DEVIL called Dia Voletto. I know that because, like a good little devil, he's found my Achilles heel, the gap in my armor, and he's driven his sword into it.

"Come on, Anne," Dia says to me. "You must know you're meant for someone much better than that simple Zin character."

"If you could please. Stop. *Moving.*"

"You're angry."

"I just think you need a better sense of boundaries."

"Then take it out on the canvas."

"Don't act like you're getting under my skin just to motivate me to paint better."

"Take your feelings out on the canvas."

"But I'm painting *you*," I snap. "I'm not painting my feelings."

With a laugh, he claps his hands together and grins behind the temple they form. If he expects better than a glare from me, he's *beyond* out of touch.

"Now I know exactly what you've been missing," he says.

"I'm sure you think you do."

"Narcissism," he says, his eyes twinkling.

"Says the demon version of Narcissus."

"Anne, listen to me carefully." His eyes, already dark, seem to blacken. "Every portrait that is painted with feeling is a portrait

115

of the artist, not of the sitter. The sitter is merely the accident, the occasion. It is not he who is revealed by the painter; it is rather the painter who, on the painted canvas, reveals himself."

"That was eloquently put."

"It should be. It's straight from *The Picture of Dorian Gray*. The beauty of the portrait of Dorian Gray was not his at all, but the desire of Basil, the artist."

"I haven't read that book."

"You ought to. It will help you." He adds, with a smile, "And it's very sexy."

"You talk about sex too much."

"Says the virgin."

He strides over to observe the rendering of his lean, tattooed body on my canvas. As he hunches next to me and pensively taps his finger on his lips, his loose button-up grazes my arm. I shift away.

"You don't know anything about me and Ben," I say.

"About Ben, no. But about you, yes."

"About *relationships*."

He lowers himself elegantly to the floor and crosses his brightly colored arms around his knees, looking up at me as he does.

"You think I haven't had relationships? Look at me, Anne. Do you think I'm unfamiliar with girls falling in love with me?"

"Nice ego."

"A girl like you ought to have my confidence. Or does Ben hold you on too high a pedestal to touch you the way beautiful women deserve to be touched? No, this must be it: you both scrub down with bleach, head to toe, before you can, what's the word? Snuggle."

Exactly the words to make me drop my brush in the birdbath and pull off my smock. He sees me get up to leave, and he laughs a little more. But he doesn't try to stop me. Not physically, at least.

"I had a serious relationship once," he says. "She was lovely. Well, to be honest, she was a tease who tormented me."

I grab my book bag. "I thought we agreed to be … not like that."

"Like what? Personal?"

"Inappropriate."

"I'm not trying to seduce you. I'm trying to talk to you. I forget sometimes that you're so young. Please," he says, tugging my bag from my grip and gesturing to the chair I've just abandoned. "Sit."

Reluctantly, I teeter on the edge of my seat.

"Her name was Gia," he begins. I glance at his *Dia + Gia* tattoo, which is the only one he never changes. "She was the most powerful underworld goddess. The Seven Sinning Sisters served her. Every incubus and succubus in existence served her. As did witches, familiars, all of them. She was particularly good at claiming the souls of men."

"She was a succubus?" I ask.

"She started as one, but she became a goddess. She was at least as powerful as Mephistopheles, and twice as powerful as I."

"Did you leave her behind in the underworld to come here?"

"She left me. Just like Ben will leave you."

"Seriously, I don't want to talk to you about Ben."

"Why not? Because you only want to do what's safe? Even if you did talk to me about him, you'd do it in the safest possible way, wouldn't you?"

"I guess we'll never know."

He shoves his hands through his hair and messes it wildly. He's beaming when he looks at me again.

"The *unsafe* reality is the one you need to explore, Anne!" he proclaims. "The one where humans are darker than Lucifer himself. The one where a demon *is* a human. The one where nothing is black or white and we are more than the places we come from yet inevitably and tragically tied to them."

The unsafe reality. It's a terrifying reality, one I've been avoiding since the day my mother was diagnosed with rapid-cycling bipolar disorder. It's becoming clear to me that I've exchanged my artistry—who I am—for the safety and comfort of a normal life. Is there such a thing? If all life comes in shades of gray and we can be just as evil as demons—I mean, I killed Pilot, and I truly haven't felt a twinge of regret since—then perhaps normalcy is simply an unattainable illusion, a mirage.

The sound of paper tearing interrupts my thoughts.

"I like this," Dia says, pushing against my knee to lift himself. He waves a sketch at me. It's from my sketchbook. He was going through my bag. "I'm taking this. This is passion."

My heart stops when I see the sketch. It's the girl I drew outside of Lou Knows' room. The girl I saw in the mirror.

"No," I say, grabbing but just missing it.

Like a child with an idea, he backs away slowly, grins, and lets his eyes roam the page as I protest.

"You can't have that. It's not yours."

"*This* girl is not in a silly, prudish little uniform," he says. "This is raw."

"Give that to me."

I snatch it, but he tugs it from my grip and catches my fists almost at the same time, then locks them between the fingers of one hand, showcasing his otherworldly strength. I try to free myself. His grip refuses to give, and his gaze feasts on the girl with the tail.

"She's beautiful," he says. "She's your muse?"

Mortified, I shake my head. "I don't know what she is."

"She's an enchantress. A goddess. Just missing her wings."

Thoughtfully, distractedly, he releases my wrists and settles onto the chaise, still looking at the woman in my sketch. He dismisses me without another word, and it's only when I'm in the hallway outside his office that, beneath a disturbingly beautiful Beksinski, I steady myself against the wall and pray that my proximity to demons is not, somehow, transforming me into an underworld goddess.

"I'M SORRY WE don't have a tree," Ben says. "And I wish our dads could be here."

It's Christmas Eve. Ben and I are walking hand in hand under a still, starless, and cold gray sky through what was once the village. On Ben's mind is the sad absence of twinkling lights, green garland, silvery wrapping paper, and all the signs of this time of year, a time he loves with an enthusiasm he reserves for only his favorite things, of which he has few. On my mind is the Scrutiny—it's a few days away, and it's Ben's big opportunity to up his game and elevate his status in the Big V competition. He's asked me to stop thinking about it, stop talking about it, but that's an impossibility. Every moment with Ben is a reminder of how few we might have left.

"We can *pretend* our dads are here," I suggest. "I used to pretend Christmas was different all the time. Didn't you?"

"Different how?"

"Different like—well, Christmas was always busy for my dad. Suicides, post-party car crashes, Christmas tree fires. But his staff would take their holidays. So my mom would have to help him with one funeral after another."

"You spent Christmas alone?"

I smile at him as he lifts our joined hands to kiss mine. We're both wearing mittens, so he presses his lips to wool, not skin. "Don't cry for me, Argentina," I say lightly.

"Now I *really* wish we could celebrate Christmas properly."

Enormous construction spotlights shine on the fully framed Cania College. The hammers are down and the chain saws are off for the first time in months.

"It's starting to look like a real school," Ben says. "I think there'll be more moss than ivy on its walls, though."

"Maybe there's a way for you to go to Cania College after graduation," I suggest. We head back onto the road north. "Or you could *try* to win the Scrutiny. Let's pretend you wanted to try. Just entertain the idea. What would you do next? How could we make that happen?"

"You know what I'd like to pretend?" Ben says.

"That I'm okay with my boyfriend having a death sentence?"

He stares into the puff of white his breath makes. "I'd like to pretend we're in New York City for some Christmas shopping."

"Sounds fun."

"And we just went to see a show on Broadway. Something Christmasy. A ballet." He checks to make sure I'm watching him, which I am, which I always am. "Tomorrow, we'll be flying home to spend the holidays with your dad. You've been talking about how quiet he can be throughout the year but how he seems to come alive as soon as you put that record on for him—that Christmas one by that weird European group."

"Boney M."

"Exactly. And I've been acting like I'm not afraid of offending him somehow and turning the two of you against me forever."

"This is a detailed daydream, Mr. Zin."

"And it's nighttime, of course," he says, refusing to let my reality check pop his expanding bubble, "because New York is *almost* beautiful enough to deserve you when it's all lit up. And we're walking through Times Square—the lights are so garish they'd be offensive if it wasn't Christmastime. People are hurrying around us, running off to see their families, and there are no bad moods."

He looks at me. Expectantly.

"And you and I are on our way back to our hotel room…," he prompts.

I'm silent. Silent girl on a silent night.

"We just saw *The Nutcracker*," he continues when I add nothing. Squeezing our hands together, we meander up the road, and the woods thicken on either side of us. "You, Miss Merchant, liked it a lot more than I did."

"I did?"

"You did, yes. And after the show, we went to this place in the-Theater District that's supposed to have the most amazing flourless chocolate cake. You'd heard about it from an art critic who's been hounding you to let him host a show for you. With maybe a few of my pieces on display, too. Anyway, we took his recommendation and went for dessert."

At last, I decide to play along, to help Ben shape this vision that will never be.

"And, lemme guess, I liked it more than you did?" I ask.

"What can I say? You're all the sweetness I need."

"*Sooo*," I say, laughing off his cheesiness and trying to fit myself into his imaginary world, "we walked back to our hotel. Even though I wanted to catch a cab."

"Because you're in heels."

"You said it was too nice to catch a cab. You insisted we walk."

"You look amazing in those heels, by the way."

"Why, thank you."

"And what do I say when you *reluctantly* agree to walk with me?" he asks me.

"You say…if all else fails, you'll carry me."

He smiles. "Hop on."

I laugh. "Right." But he's serious—he wants me to get on his back. "Ben, I'm heavier than I look." I've never pretended to be petite. But he keeps staring at me like he won't move until I do.

That's when I catch a glimpse of something in his eyes. It's clear—as clear as the green of his irises—that this fantasy is real for him. A normal life for the two of us is real for him. That's what he wants. All his bravado these past months has been for show.

So I nod, and he stoops, and I try not to be too awkward as I wriggle onto his back and pray for a Christmas miracle that makes me about twenty pounds lighter. He tucks his arms under my legs and heaves me up the rest of the way without so much as a grunt. I wrap my arms around his neck, kissing his cheek as I do.

"Where are we staying?" I ask him.

"The Plaza—where else?"

He starts jogging, and I have to love the guy for his solid effort to make me look light as a feather. He's breathless by the time we make it as far as Gigi's house. I expect him to let me down, but he starts trudging through the snow toward the old cottage.

"It looks like the valet has retired for the night," he says.

He lets me down just outside Gigi's front door and, smiling a smile I've never seen before—one that makes me nervous, like he might say the *L word*—tells me to close my eyes. I do. Nervously.

He takes me by the hand.

"What's going on?" I ask in the darkness.

"Step up. And again." The old creaky front door announces that it is swinging in. "Merry Christmas, baby. Open your eyes."

Ben's fantasy, which seemed impromptu when we were walking, is a reality inside Gigi's transformed living room. Strings of golden lights enrobe the dingy wallpapered walls, and rich golden velvet has been draped over and tucked into the old sofa Skippy used to sleep on. The staircase and the entry to the kitchen are strung with lights and evergreen garland that make gap-filled walls, keeping us in this room. My eyes skip from the Christmas tree to the wrapped gifts on the coffee table to the record player spinning none other than Boney M to, at last, the brass bed Ben must've dragged down from Gigi's bedroom and blanketed in beautiful linens from who knows where.

"Molly helped me," he shyly admits. "The two of us had to sneak into Dia's place—all my old furnishings and things are there. Thankfully, it wasn't her first time breaking in." He leads me in. "Look past the flaws, okay? Believe the illusion. Just for tonight."

"What flaws?" I ask.

It's gorgeous. And dazzling. And filled with heart and love.

... Yet I can't keep my gaze from returning to the bed.

The bed.

Oh, God, the *bed*.

"Are you okay?" He's been watching my reaction. "You look like you've seen a ghost." When he finally notices what I'm trying hard not to stare at, he smiles. I do my best to look as cool as Garnet probably looked when they were together. "Aww, honey, it's not what you think."

"It's just—I think you got the wrong idea before, Ben. I'm not..."

"That bed is not what this is about..."

"It's just...I don't think..."

"Baby, I know..."

It's like we're competing to make as little sense as possible.

He gives up first and takes my hands in his, forcing me to look at him. How am I supposed to get out of this? It's really beautiful and everything, and I have been about as desperate to make out with Ben as a person can get without imploding, but. But. *But*.

"Anne," he's trying not to smile at my distress, "I want to wake up and find you next to me, that's all. That's my selfish Christmas wish. Of course, yes, I'd love to do more—"

"You would?" I'm not sure if I knew that before.

His eyebrows hit his hairline. "Are you kidding?"

"But you always stop us."

"Because I want to protect what we have. Not because..." His voice drops, and a smile flickers across his lips. "When it happens—" He half laughs. "Well, let's just say I'm looking forward to it. But I would never pressure you. Ever."

For some reason, I picture him and Garnet together. I squeeze my eyes as tight as they'll go.

He waits for me to open them.

I know I'm being an idiot. Ben just wants to have a sleepover— why am I acting like I've never shared a bed with someone, especially with someone I love? But I know why. It's not just about sex. It's not just about wanting to move from the Hand-Holding Phase to whatever wonders lay in Phases II, III, IV, V—hell, every phase right up to the last one. That's only part of the problem. My real anxiety lays in wondering whether Ben will wake me up with his screams as Harper did months ago.

"If you're not comfortable sleeping next to me," he says, "we can turn around and leave."

To prove there's nowhere I'd rather be than here with him, I sit on the bed. It sags in the middle, but it's otherwise comfortable. I smile at him, and relief lights his gorgeous face.

To my surprise, he turns on the TV.

"*It's a Wonderful Life*," he says, pushing a disc into the Blu-ray player. "A Christmas classic."

It's a wonderful life.

Sure, it is. As long as you're playing pretend. As long as you buy into the illusion.

"It's like we're at the movie theater," I say.

"No—the hotel room."

One fantasy at a time. I get it.

All smiles, Ben joins me on the bed and positions fluffy pillows and blankets around us. I've developed a habit of holding my breath and leaning away from him when he gets near—anything to avoid inhaling his sweet-meets-musky scent, anything to avoid the risk that his arm will brush mine and he'll just apologize. Now I know that he desires more than hand-holding and kissing, but what am I supposed to do with that? As Ben wraps his arm around my shoulders and I clamp my fingertips into my thighs to keep from clawing at him, I realize that the vision Ben sees is quite different from mine. There's no way I'm going to have an actual sexual relationship with a man on Death Row. Why would I? So he gets everything he wants…and I'm left living in the aftermath of his selfish destructive forces?

Remembering something, Ben pops up and swings open a mini-fridge next to Gigi's old hutch. "Can I get you something from the minibar?"

"They always overcharge for those things. Six bucks for a Pepsi."

With a heartbreaking grin, Ben pulls out two cans of soda and shimmies next to me again.

"Money is no object," he says.

I want to smile with him. But this whole charade is actually starting to frustrate me. So while Ben watches George Bailey dance his way into a swimming pool, it occurs to me that, instead of making sacrifices, Ben's PT should be to live selfishly. He'd be a sure thing. He's selfishly choosing the briefest period of time with me and creating these charming illusions of a life we could lead together, a life he's keeping us from.

"I know you mean well," he says out of the blue, "but let's just watch a movie like two normal people."

"We are."

"Your whole body is tense. You're thinking about that damn competition."

"You knew what I was thinking? And you were just letting me sit here and stress out?"

"*Letting you?*" He laughs. "When did I get any say over what you do?"

"This isn't funny, Ben. This is your life."

"I know."

"Then do something!" I spring from the bed. "Fight for it!"

"Anne, just give me tonight. Give that gift to me. For Christmas." Calmly, he pauses the movie. "Just one night of normalcy."

"I've given you three and a half months."

"Do you regret that?"

"None of this is real. How can this be enough for you? Tonight, like every night, is bringing me closer to you when all you're going to do is leave me."

He takes a deep breath. "All roads lead to death. Mine is just shorter."

"It doesn't have to be that way!"

"It already is that way!"

I watch him try to calm down, but that's the last thing I want him to do. I need to see him angry. I need to know he's got fight left in him.

"I can't be the reason you die, Ben. To spend a short time with me. Don't do that to me."

"I'm already dead. Why don't you understand that?"

Leaning back, he stretches out his long legs and looks up at me. The twinkle lights glimmer against his irises, transforming his eyes into bright pools I can see my reflection in.

"For five years," he says, his playful tone long gone as the old Ben, the anguished Ben I first met, makes a surprise appearance, "I've considered myself dead. Because, as hard as it is for you to hear, I am dead. I've been here to help my dad get through his grief. But I've never fooled myself into believing that I'm alive or could be again. I'm here because a devil is selling immortality to fools. A *devil*."

"I know."

"Well, then, you know this isn't a miracle. It's a dark art. And it's been keeping me from reuniting with my mom and Jeannie."

Always the words to shut me up. There's no arguing with Ben when it comes to his mom and sister. I could never ask him to choose a life with me instead of the afterlife with them.

"You've thrown a wrench into things," he says. "But just because I *feel* alive doesn't mean it's my right to expect to live again."

"You never intended to stay with me."

He closes his eyes and drops his head, exasperated. "*A-Anne!* I'd love to spend forever with you."

"Then prove it. Go with Garnet. Break up with me now. Fight for us by fighting for you."

"We all die!" Ben's eyelids snap wide open, and he bounces to his feet. His cool façade slides off, exposing the mere mortal beneath. "Death is permanent. That's the idea! These fleshy bodies of ours are always fighting it. Yet you want me to leave you now, hook up with Garnet, align with her so I *might* become valedictorian."

"It's possible!"

"And risk dying without even memories of you to help me through?" He looks at me like *I'm* the one who's not making sense. "Or, in your vision, you think I'll win the Big V and you'll wake up. Only to what, Anne? Only to spend the rest of our lives worrying about being separated by car accidents, disease, plane crashes, cancer, global epidemics?—an endless list of forces driving us to the grave!"

"Well, that's life!"

"No, that's death. And that's what we're driving toward. So I'm done fighting it! Let's die. Together."

His final words floor me.

"Wait, you want me to die, too?"

He looks guiltily at the floor. "The ethical dilemma of euthanasia." His face, unaccustomed to fury, is still scarlet with the force of his outburst. "I think I should go softly into that good night this May. And you should die next May—"

"The line is '*do* not *go softly into that good night*.'"

"—and I'll wait for you on the other side. And there, only there, we can always be together."

"So much for 'it's a wonderful life.'"

"I know I sound like some suicidal weirdo, but I'm not. I'm being logical about this. It would be great to be alive with you in California. To take you on an actual date. To go for coffee and people-watch. To go back to our little apartment and be the big spoon to your little spoon." He shifts like he's physically trying to disconnect himself from the imaginary life he wanted us to have. "But my odds of winning the Big V are remarkably low, as are yours. You have an escape route, of course, in your coma. So I realize I'm asking for something huge from you, Anne. And I wouldn't do it if I hadn't spent these last months giving my every waking thought to it."

"You think I should pull the plug...on myself."

He sighs and, taking me in his arms, buries his face in my hair. "I just want you forever."

"What if your spirit's gone when I die, Ben? What if you don't wait for me?"

He cups my face in his hands and brings his lips to mine, softly. I am like a starving prisoner; I ravenously consume what little he gives me and wait, hopefully, for a bit more. Which he, as always, withholds.

"I *will* wait for you. Forever," he says, his voice thick with emotion. "But please don't ask me to throw away the time I have left with you. Especially not for the slim chance of winning the Big V."

I let him run his hands over my hair and give me that imploring look of his, and I even let him lay me down on the bed again and spoon me just as he described doing in another life, a real life. It's not until the movie ends and he hands me the flannel pajamas Molly brought for me that I stop letting him get away with making this fantasy whatever he wants it to be. I'll play along, but only if I can make it mine, too.

"I'll give you some privacy to get changed," he says.

He's about to shimmy under the garland to wait in the kitchen. But I take hold of his arm as he's leaving and turn him back to me.

"No," I say.

"Do you need something?"

I nod. And I kiss him. "Come here." I tug him back to the other side of the bed, and there I coerce him into sitting. "Stay right here."

I back away slowly, keeping my gaze fixed on his, which lets me see his intrigued expression pass right by confusion and turn, in a flash, to concern. "I had a great time Christmas shopping with you today, Mr. Zin."

"What are you doing, Anne?"

I flick off all the lights except the twinkle ones. And I stand before him again. In one movement, I take my pullover off.

"I just love Christmas shopping in New York, don't you, baby?"

He swallows. "Anne."

"Don't you?"

Appearing torn, he concedes. And watches my sweater fall to the floor. "FAO Schwarz. It's ... so ... intense."

"It is." I take off my socks, then I unbutton my pants. My eyes don't leave his, not even when I tug my jeans down and lay them over the back of a chair. His gaze flickers, like he wants to look at my exposed skin, skin he's never seen before. "Remember how, years ago, we had that amazing Christmas Eve on Wormwood Island?"

Ben's face pales. "Anne, come on."

"Did you think that was gonna happen?"

His gaze washes over me, standing in my t-shirt and underwear. "Remind me what happened."

"How could you forget, Mr. Zin?"

With that, I lift my t-shirt over my head. I'm about to straighten my hair when, with a choked voice, he asks me not to.

"God, I love your hair," he whispers. His breath is short. "I always picture it down and wild. Covering you. A little." He swallows again. "But not completely."

"It was down that night in Gigi's house. Remember?"

He nods and moves to stand, but I shake my head and wait until he sits again. He arches his eyebrow, and I might think I'd pushed things too far if his approval—his enthusiastic approval—didn't show in other ways. I step toward him. He shifts back on the bed. I'm standing before him, and my hair is covering me when I unhook my bra; as if I do this all the time, I slip it off, letting it fall to the floor. Ben's gaze is a lost cause. I straddle him to reclaim attention on my face.

His eyes have never been so beautiful.

He moves to kiss me, but I lean back.

"That was the night," I say, "that you agreed to fight for the Big V."

He flinches. His breath is audible, so heavy.

"Would you like me to do for you tonight what I did for you *that* night?" I ask him.

"More than anything," he says. And I believe it.

So I whisper into his ear, "Agree to fight, Ben."

He nuzzles his nose against my neck. "Anne, I'd love to."

Would love to…but won't.

I push him back so I can see the resignation on his face. There it is. That unmovable, stubborn resolve to die. No matter what I do, no matter how I try.

So I stand, grab my clothes, and tell him where he can stuff his fantasy. I've barely dressed when I slam the door, cutting off his weak protests, and run through the snow up to campus.

eleven

UNDER SCRUTINY

AMONG THE HUM OF A HUNDRED STUDENTS AND THEIR Guardians on the main floor of what is normally a vacant library, Pilot holds up a flashcard for me and stares me down from the other side of it:

D in F in a L Y [—] T on an O [x] L of a C

"Gimme a sec," I mumble at Pilot as I scratch my calculations on the wood of the little cubby desktop. Cubicles like ours line both walls of the narrow, dark corner in which we're studying.

Molly is sitting at a long table near us. She's the only one in here without a Guardian, and she's piggybacking off my session with Pilot, to his great irritation.

Ben is not among the 100 sweating, fretting students. I don't know where he is.

The Scrutiny is tomorrow morning. We won't know what the challenge is until we're in it, and that's got everyone on edge—except Molly, who never lets anything get to her. The best we can do is to rely on what our Guardians know about past challenges.

"You won't have a freakin' breath to spare tomorrow," Pilot groans.

"The answer is…189."

The flashcard hits the desk. "Did you double up on your idiot pills today, Merchant?"

"That's not right?"

"You might as well just throw in the towel for the Big V now."

"You're an exceptionally motivating coach, Pi—anyone ever tell you that?"

"It's negative forty-three. So obvious."

"Ack! Order of operations—what a dumb thing to mess up on," I say with a laugh. He jabs his tongue into his cheek like I'm really pissing him off. "Oh, come on, Pilot. Don't act like you would've known that if it wasn't written on your side of the card. Can you even translate this calculation?"

His eyes glaze over the flashcard as he glances at it.

"This first part here means 'days in February in a leap year,'" I explain, pointing, "which is twenty-nine. And this is 'tentacles on an octopus,' so eight. So twenty-nine minus eight, but that's where I went wrong because it should have been eight times—"

"Oh, hell, Anne, this isn't about *my* brain!" He throws the card aside and pulls out another one. "You're gonna be on your own. Focus on *your* brain."

It's tough to focus. I haven't talked to Ben since Christmas Eve, and it's New Year's Eve now. I wish he would have learned from my blowup at Gigi's house and reconciled with Garnet, but he didn't. (Garnet chastised me in front of the whole class just this morning.) Ben keeps giving Molly apology notes for me, which she hands me with this sad face that makes me wonder whose side she's on.

"Remind me why on Earth I'd need to do these calculations in the challenge," I say to Pilot.

"Last year, Villicus put us through a geocaching drill. We all started at different points on the island and with different directions. Did he just give us the coordinates? *Hellz* no! He asked us things like 'If each child in a family has at least five brothers and three sisters, move west ten times the minimum number of children in the family.'"

"One hundred degrees west."

"Try ninety."

"Try 100. Each brother needs five brothers—that's six—and each sister needs three sisters—that's four. So ten. Times ten."

"BFD." He rolls his eyes. "Don't be too impressed with yourself, Merchant. There's no pressure on you right now. And the Scrutiny challenges go way beyond logic puzzles. All these demon guys, they *love* screwing with words and sounds to mess your sad little human brain up."

"*My* sad little brain? *L of a C* means *lives of a cat*. Nine lives. Nine times eight is seventy-two—"

"That's just math with a smidgen of word gamery."

"*Gamery* is not a word."

"What about chronograms, mondegreens, sobriquets, and—oh, Jesus—their favorite: anagrams? You ready for those?"

He has no idea I've decoded the names of almost all the school staff. No one knows. Over the past few months, I've been chipping away at my list, and I've discovered that Eve Risset has the power to *sever ties*, Aseat Weinchler can *increase wealth*, and Trey Sedmoney can *destroy enemy*. I'd be unstoppable if I could actually do anything with that knowledge.

"Need I remind you, Pilot, that your hero, Villicus, is gone b'bye? Dia's not gonna make us geocache or rearrange anagrams. He's got more imagination than that." The nearest door swings open, and my heart skips, hoping to see Ben. But Hiltop pokes her irritating little bobbed head in. "Speak of the devil."

Hiltop's leer lands on me and Pilot. She scoffs. She still thinks it's oh-so-funny that I have to endure Pilot as my Guardian. Her head swivels to the table where Molly sits, and she pushes the door open further, revealing her companion.

"Teddy!" Molly exclaims, a relieved smile bursting across her pretty face. "Come. Sit."

I watch in slow motion as Teddy crosses the floor, keeping his gaze fixed on Molly, never looking at me. He warned me once to put on a good show of detesting him so no one guesses that we're allies, and it's never been easier to do as he says. After all, he's not only left me here without checking in, but he's also abandoned my best friend, who deserves better from her Guardian.

I wait for Hiltop to walk, in her stilted way, out of earshot before I address Teddy.

"It's about time," I hiss at him.

Teddy simply opens his book and looks at Molly. "Apologies for my delay."

"Hey! I'm talking to you, Teddy."

Pilot kicks me under the table. "Hello? I'm your Guardian now. Focus. We have work to do."

I can't believe Teddy's just going to ignore me.

A rush of cold sweeps through our far corner of the library. The front doors are wide open, letting whirling gusts of snowflakes in, which are followed by Headmaster Voletto, the Seven Sinning Sisters, and at least 100 snow-dusted students and Guardians.

Dia claps the snow off his gloves and unwraps his scarf as students fan out, looking for a free spot to sit or stand in the crowded library. Just as the front doors are closing, I spy Ben sliding in. Our gazes lock. He looks beautiful. I'm the first to glance away.

"Why's everyone here?" I ask Pilot to keep from looking at Ben.

"A preamble to the Scrutiny," Pilot explains. "Like a pep talk."

Ben is weaving my way. I pretend not to notice.

Dia unzips his Canada Goose parka and hangs it on the back of Plum's chair; she must think nobody's watching because she trails her fingertips longingly along the jacket's furry hood. Ira and Avaritia, dressed like their sisters in white chinchilla and silk scarves that put the Model UN from Hell's wardrobes to shame, close the library doors, sealing us in, as Invidia and Superbia quiet the room.

The library is standing room only. I keep my gaze locked ahead, on nothing at all, as Ben approaches the small desk Pilot and I are at; he pauses next to me and then sidles into the large gap between our cubby and the one next to it, where he leans against the wall.

"Evening, everyone!" Dia calls. "Are you ready for the Scrutiny tomorrow?"

The well-trained student body, constantly seeking the headmaster's approval, hoot their replies. Just like Pilot said, this is starting to feel like a pep rally. I turn my attention on the front of the room, where Dia smiles, rubs his hands together, and begins walking between the tables. Sensing someone watching me, I see Hiltop, who is standing just behind Jack, Agniezska, and Emo Boy, with her eyes on me. She's always watching me. But she never actually does anything. She has more reason than anyone to want to destroy me, but she just stares. Like she's waiting. Not to pounce, but to see what I might do.

And I, as always, ignore her.

"I can feel the excitement in here," Dia says, shaking a senior lightly by the shoulders, "and for good reason! Look at you beautiful souls. Studying up a storm. Turning that gray matter red hot. And everyone that was outside running laps, climbing trees, and whatever else you nuts get up to," he laughs, "good for you! The more prepared you are for what tomorrow brings, the better your chances of winning, naturally. But, my passionate friends, don't forget the most important rule of all. Don't forget the foundation of your success. Who can tell me what I'm referring to?"

Harper's hand flies up. "To live by our PTs."

"Very good," he says, eyeing her approvingly. Then he looks straight at me. "Your PT will get you through this." His gaze skips away.

I hear Ben half cough. I know what he's thinking. Although we never talk about it, I know he's been curious about my weekly mentoring sessions with Dia. I've been careful not to talk too enthusiastically about Dia. Ben would think I was venturing to the dark side if I told him that, in spite of being the devil he is, Dia has been amazing for my growth as an artist.

"Trust in your greatest strengths," Dia says, "however vicious they may be!" Someone claps. Someone follows. "After all, they're not *vicious*. You're not *vicious*. You're *survivors*!" More clapping. Not thunderous, but some. "Your personal strengths and unmatched qualities will see you through. You're only savage in the eyes of people who don't understand you now, people who don't know what it's like to be you. Like your parents. And the friends you left behind. Friends who attended your funerals," Dia pauses and looks sadly at a small freshman, stroking her cheek as he does, "and then moved on. Trust yourselves, students." His gaze skips to mine. "*Trust your PT.*" And away. "Work your butt off in tomorrow's Scrutiny. Because I have a surprise for you."

Dia stops in the center of the room, and the Seven Sinning Sisters make a half circle around him.

"This surprise is really something," he says, turning his captivating smile on us. "Should I tell you what it is, or should I delay the pleasure of knowledge until tomorrow?"

The room begs him to tell us. He obviously relishes their begging. I say nothing.

"The Scrutiny begins first thing in the morning. Most of you will find yourselves in it. But a select few will have something different in store."

Dia walks, veering through the narrow gaps left between chairs and book bags, until he's standing before me. It's so intentional; he made a beeline straight to me. I hear Ben shuffle his feet.

"Would you like to hear the surprise, Miss Merchant?" Dia asks.

The hundreds of eyeballs that turn in my direction are freezing beams. I can't move. Why single me out? Why stand in front of *me*? Why do this now...to me...with Ben watching and with things so shaky between us?

"Um, sure," I mumble.

Dia scoffs and turns to the room. "Miss Merchant doesn't *like* surprises."

Everyone boos. The Model UN from Hell heckles me.

"Okay, I'd *love* to hear the surprise," I say.

"So you say." Taking a deep breath, Dia pushes his hand through his thick hair and *very* suggestively moans, "Now make me feel it, Anne."

Pilot kicks my chair. I hear Molly gasp out a laugh. Teddy's eyes narrow. I glance at Ben, whose jaw has dropped.

Heat rushes into my skin as time—as this exact second, as this long arm on the face of the clock—stops. It stops just for me. Just so I can think. Just so I can look around the room, from face to stupefied face—as Ben's jaw clenches now, Pilot's lips curl up, Molly's eyebrows disappear under her hairline, Teddy's sneer vanishes, Harper's eyes burst, Garnet's gaze slides toward Ben—and determine exactly what they all think I do in my painting sessions each week with Dia. There is no one on Earth who could take that phrase and *the way Dia said it* as anything but provocative. Which means I am about to be labeled a total skank. An easy bitch. A whore. Any number of labels waiting, always waiting, on the tips of tongues. It doesn't matter that *he* said it to *me*; it doesn't matter that I've never let Dia touch me; it doesn't matter that I've got a serious boyfriend with whom, let the record show, I do little more than hold hands, even when we almost spend the night together at a pretend hotel. None of that matters. Because high school whisperings are like Cania students: more spirit than flesh, indestructible, and manipulated by darkness.

The clock ticks.

I've got to say something before anyone else has a chance.

"I think Harper could make you feel it far better than I could, Headmaster," I say.

Spurts of giggles tell me I'm safe. But safe from what? It's not the whispering I care about as much as it is…what? My gaze meets Ben's, and I find myself searching his face to see what he's thinking. I can't bear to face the truth: I don't want Ben to know I may have developed the tiniest crush on Dia. Even worse? The possibility that Dia has similar feelings for me. I mean, it's not like I'd do anything about it! Dia is a freaking devil. And, though I've never said it, I'm in love with Ben.

"Oh, yes, Mr. Voletto," Harper calls from across the room, her voice oozing with sensuality that should make her blush. Dia strides her way. "*Please* tell us the surprise."

"Since assuming the role of your headmaster, my team and I have been reviewing each of your files," Dia announces to the room, "and we've found some truly deserving students among you. Ten of you, in fact, are superior students."

I look at Ben.

He turns away.

"Now," Dia continues, "traditionally, your one and only chance of leaving Wormwood Island alive has been as valedictorian. But ten of you—the Lucky Ten—are going to wake up to a different environment tomorrow."

We're all ears.

"This is the first part of the surprise. Ready? Listen closely." Dia temples his hands under his chin. "Ten students are going home for good *tomorrow*."

One massive gasp fills the room.

Pilot gets up, swears, mumbles that I'd better not be going home, and drags his chair away from me. Typical Pilot, bailing when he thinks he might not get what he wants.

"Tonight, while you sleep," Dia continues, though I'm not sure anyone can hear him over the exclamations of hope clouding our heads, "my team will be transporting the Lucky Ten from this island to a spectacular location. It will be your new home. And you won't find out if you're one of the lucky ones until you wake up."

Normal people fantasize about a lottery win.

This is our equivalent.

"That's not all," Dia says. "I've got *one more* surprise up my sleeve."

twelve

SECOND CHANCES

EVERYONE IS EATING OUT OF DIA'S HAND. BEFORE, WE might have feared him, objectified him, or just put up with him; now, with remarkable skill, he's become a hero, mercifully setting ten prisoners free. Even Ben has his beautiful gaze fixed earnestly on Dia.

Watching Ben long to be part of the Lucky Ten—even though he must know, as I know, that he's not on their list—breaks my heart. Harper could be on the list; Jack could be. But neither Dia nor Mephisto would let Ben go. They've got six months left to use him as the leverage they need to keep Dr. Zin as close to sober as he can get. Ben has no chance of waking to find himself at a new home. None. He knows that. But you could never tell it by the look on his face.

"Now for the second surprise," Dia says. "All years are competing tomorrow, as you know, but instead of simply making your way onto a short list, we've got a much bigger prize in store."

Dia tips back and forth on the heels of his Converse shoes and smiles like he's got the most delicious secret. A girl shifts in her chair, making it squeal, and thirty kids glare, smack at her, tell her to *shut up*. It's like no one has breathed since the moment Dia started talking. I can't imagine what the prize could be. Well, I can imagine, but I'm scared to hope.

"There will be *four* winners. One from each grade. Would you like to know what they'll win?" As if overwhelmed by good news, everyone stays quiet. "The Scrutiny will be a foot race of sorts. And the first freshman, sophomore, junior, and senior to return to campus will get…"

Dia's fingers prance under his chin, and he smiles like the charming little devil he is. The Seven Sinning Sisters are smiling as well, enchantingly. I almost forget I'm dealing with malevolence personified.

"Please tell us!" a sophomore cries out, unable to take the anticipation any longer.

A smiling Dia finishes his speech with such impressiveness, I almost forgive him for embarrassing me moments ago.

"The winners will get to ask me for anything—anything—they want for themselves."

Anything?

"Anything," he repeats, as if reading my mind.

The wheels in my mind start turning in a new direction. And that turns my *head* in a new direction: straight at Ben, who's looking at me. I've got two thoughts: one, *you'd better win this, Ben*; two, *I wish you'd listened to me and at least prepared for the Scrutiny.*

A third thought struggles for my attention: What does Hiltop think about Dia handing out new lives like they're candy? Villicus kept tight reins on new lives. Hiltop's expression is as blank as ever.

"Yes, each victor can ask me for one thing you want for yourself." Dia purses his lips and beams again, loving these revelations. "Ask, and you will get it. Instantly. All you have to do is cross the finish line before your classmates. You've each got a one in fifty chance of winning life tomorrow."

THE NIGHT SKY is gray with swirling snowflakes as the crowd flows out of the library and thins. Dia has called all the Guardians for a pre-Scrutiny meeting, leaving the rest of us to marvel at this turn of events. We head back to the dorms under the pretense of getting ready for tomorrow's Scrutiny, but in actuality, most of us will close our eyes and dream of what it would be like to wake and know we've been selected as one of the Lucky Ten. When that fantasy wears itself out, a more likely one will replace it: win the Scrutiny, and ask Dia to give you the reward a valedictorian gets.

Molly and I walk through the quad together. Ben is quick to catch up with us, but he's smart enough to stay on Molly's other side, not to venture too close to me. Sure, he might be weirded out by Dia, but I'm still angry with him about his moronic decision to die.

"Pretty good news, hey, Ben?" she asks him. I stare ahead.

"It's almost too good to be true," he says. Which annoys me. Was Ben always so doomsday about everything?

Molly notices me tense up. "There's just so much to want," she says, clapping her hands together. "I mean, there's the obvious one: a second life—new name, cash money, all that jazz. But for anyone who stands a chance of winning the Big V, or, hell, for anyone who doesn't actually want to live again, the sky's the limit."

"What do you mean?" Ben asks.

"You could ask for a house made entirely of marshmallows. I mean, that'd be a waste. But kinduv cool." She whirls to grin at us and walks backward. Ben and I are now side by side. "What would you ask for, Ben?—other than a second life."

"Oh, Ben wouldn't ask for a second life," I say.

"I'm not sure," he says. "Maybe to free my dad."

"Well, that's noble," Molly says, filling her cheeks with air and pushing it out. "Boring but noble."

He half smiles. "You want something more exciting?"

I'm not sure who he's talking to.

"Before I fall asleep standing up, yes," Molly laughs. "Please. Dear God, *please*."

"Okay. I'd ask for a month-long trip to Bora Bora. With a hundred thousand bucks to spend."

"Yawn."

"That's not good enough for you, Mol?" His eyes shine. "A year in *Bangkok*. With a *million* bucks…in…in gambling winnings. Without the taxes paid on them—because tax evasion is badass, right? And—hold on, what's that drink that made people hallucinate—oh, the Green Fairy. Lots of that. And, like, six girls from rap videos."

"I will only accept that response if you would actually drink the absinthe."

Ben shrugs.

"I'll take that as a no," she says and turns to me. "Outdo him."

"Outdo him?" I repeat. "What would I do, what would I do…?" I'm not in the mood to play, but I don't want to put a damper on the lightened mood Molly's worked hard to create. "Naturally, I would free Pilot."

She laughs, and even Ben chuckles a little.

As she always does when the three of us get close to the dorms and the say-good-night-and-kiss part steps out from the shadows to stare awkwardly at us, Molly dashes ahead even though I have no intention of kissing Ben tonight. "Don't stay out too late! The Scrutiny starts at eight tomorrow morning." She waves to Ben and wishes him luck—for tomorrow or tonight, I can't be sure—before darting away.

Ben and I are left standing in the dim glow of a sconce outside the boys' dorm. His stare is fixed on the growing mounds of snow at his feet. Snow dusts his hair and settles on his shoulders.

"Did you get my notes?" he asks me.

"You know I did."

He looks up sharply. "Well, gee, Anne, I'm really sorry I can't give you what you want the way Dia Voletto could."

"Are you mocking me?" I snap.

"Are you into him?"

"Have you been drinking from the Crazy Fountain?"

"For someone who doesn't like secrets, you keep a lot of them."

"Dia is not a secret, psycho—"

"Name-calling. Nice."

"He's my *mentor*. I don't know what he was doing in there. Maybe trying to get a rise out of me, make me embarrass myself. I dunno. It's hard to figure out the devil. Scratch that—it's hard to figure out anyone."

"I see the way he looks at you. And I know how much you love your Saturday sessions."

"Why the hell are we even talking about this? You know what the real problem is. It's you. It's your stupid plan to be together in death, which, by the way, did sound *completely psycho* when you brought it up. Certifiably nuts."

His chest is puffed, like he's holding his breath. "Cheating death is just cheating."

"Don't play pious! I saw you in there tonight. I saw your face. Dia gave you hope. Remember *hope*? You told me once it's all we have, and then you took it away from me."

"I've got no hope!" he bellows out of the blue.

A handful of students stare our way. So he tugs me around the side of the dorm and down to the icy shore. I shake him off me.

"Have you ever thought that maybe it wasn't your time to die yet, Ben?"

"Only a million times. But that's just vanity."

"Don't cop out. Maybe you were supposed to go through that accident. And I was supposed to see you at our funeral home. And we were supposed to reconnect here. And this conversation was supposed to be the turning point in our relationship. And you were supposed to win a new life. And I was supposed to join you later in the flesh, *not* in the afterlife."

"That's a lot of steps," he says. "Complicated steps."

"No one ever won a game of chess in a simple move." I wait for him to look at me. "You've been on this island for five years. Did you participate in any Scrutiny challenges at all?"

"Of course not. I was never a proper student here. Not until this year."

"But Garnet did."

"She was in three—as a sophomore, a junior, and a senior. She won in her junior year." He considers my line of thought. "I guess I can work with what she told me about those."

I close my eyes.

"What's wrong?" he asks.

"That's just," I slowly open my eyes and have to blink back the tears, "the best thing you've ever said to me."

He smiles and pulls me into his arms. "I'm sorry I didn't try."

"As long as you try now. Tomorrow."

"I will. I promise."

"Listen, Dia kept looking at me when he said to use our PTs," I confess, hoping it will help him. "So try using your PT and, if that doesn't work, try using mine. It's a long shot, but you never know."

"Look closer," Ben says.

"Yes. Read into everything tomorrow. Accept nothing at face value."

"Thank you." He kisses my nose. "See you in the morning?"

"In the quad. Bright and early."

With the purest hope I've felt in a while, I sneak into our room to find Molly is asleep. As I tuck myself under the covers, I think of all the questions I'll ask Teddy if he's still here tomorrow. And I think of the future Ben and I could actually have if he wins the challenge. I fall asleep thinking of Ben and hoping, as I always do, that I won't wake to Molly's screams.

I don't wake to screams. Not hers, not mine, not any.

No, I wake slowly, leisurely. Not to the beeping of an alarm. I wake in a deep, cushiony bed with my head on the softest pillow known to man and a duvet wrapped around me. It's so comfortable, I want to sleep the day away in it…

…until I realize I'm supposed to be in the quad for the Scrutiny challenge.

What time is it? Why didn't Molly wake me?

Where the hell am I?

I pop up in bed. The room is violet—it looks so much like my Cania Christy dorm—but it's different. Larger. More luxurious.

I'm not in my dorm room. My old bed and friendly roommate are nowhere to be seen.

I don't know where I am. It's nice, though. Too nice.

A thought I hadn't even fathomed rushes at me, flattening me against the pillowtop mattress.

I am one of the Lucky Ten.

thirteen

THE LUCKY TEN

WHEN BAD THINGS HAPPEN, YOU ALMOST ALWAYS ASK, *Why me?* When good things happen, you're just supposed to accept them.

Being selected as one of the Lucky Ten is definitely a good thing. The best thing. It means I'm free. I'm alive again. I can go home to my dad.

But I can't help wondering why I was selected. Of all people, why me? I've only been at Cania four months, and I've managed, in that time, to cause nothing but trouble for the school and its leadership. Is this Dia's way of thanking me for Mephisto's removal as headmaster? Or is he so pleased with our mentoring sessions that he wants me to go be an artist in the real world? But we haven't even finished his portrait yet! And he certainly hasn't suggested that I'm ready to paint without coaching.

How could I possibly have qualified to be one of the Lucky Ten?

I sink into the bed. It's like nothing I've ever felt.

I stare up at the white coffered ceiling with its pale purple accents. It's almost exactly like the ceiling of my dorm, but it's vaster and more detailed, with sparkling chandeliers that catch the sunlight through a long, cream-colored wall of four dormer windows.

I inch up. Look around.

White desk. Velvety drapes. Cream-patterned cushions on the window benches. Smaller lamps that look like chandeliers. Amateurish paintings in gold frames.

The aroma of breakfast sausages and fried potatoes hangs in the air, telling me I'm somewhere new, somewhere wonderful. Just as Dia promised for the Lucky Ten.

A familiar pattern catches my eye: a Hermès scarf draped over a lamp on the other side of the room.

"Just like Harper had," I whisper and flop back in bed.

Harper told me once that she'd decorated our dorm room to look exactly like her bedroom back in Texas. Did Dia give me a new home that looks like Harper's? Why would he do that?

Why am I here?

Did Dia somehow find out that Teddy's a celestial secret agent? Did he connect the dots between me and Teddy? Does the underworld now see me as a threat? Would they actually see me, a comatose artist, as a threat, and send me away? I can't believe that.

Like I've opened Pandora's box, more questions explode in my mind. Hard ones. And easy, obvious ones. Like, what time is it? The sun is shining through the windows. Could be ten or eleven. Did I really sleep until ten? That's not my style. Or did I wake late because Dia's team was transporting me here and it took a while? And where the hell is here? And, really, *truly*, how did I qualify for this? If Dia suspected I was up to something, would he just casually ship me off the island? Seems awfully un-demon-like.

I force myself to sit up again.

I *must* be one of the lucky ones.

It'd be the first time in my life. Feels too impossible to believe.

But it's obvious I'm in a new home, as Dia promised.

But why this home? Why a room like Harper's?

I lie back again, as if compelled by the coziness of this king-sized bed, as if the only answer is to sleep. It's hard to keep my eyelids open.

"Look closer," I tell myself.

I have a brand-new thought: I'm not one of the Lucky Ten. This is part of the Scrutiny challenge.

My eyes pop open. I flip the covers off.

"There is no Lucky Ten."

Maybe that whole Lucky Ten business was just a red herring, a way to keep us from paying attention to the fact that we were each waking in a room that's . . . that's actually part of the challenge. Could it be? Scrutiny challenges are puzzles, games—maybe mind games?

Nothing has felt right until now.

If there is no Lucky Ten, that means I'm in the Scrutiny challenge. I'm in a foot race. And the clock's ticking.

"K, so, if this is a challenge, what do I have to do to beat it?"

We wouldn't all wake in a room like Harper's Texas bedroom. Everybody must have woken in their own version of this. Which means this room is significant to me somehow. Figuring this out has got to be part of it.

"The room's not real," I whisper. "It's just in my head."

Surely Dia and his team wouldn't construct 200 distinct rooms— like movie sets—for 200 students. Unless they aren't making a Cania College at all; unless I'm in the village now. I slowly pull myself out of bed and, with my feet sinking into the area rug, walk to the windows, thinking I'll see Wormwood Island. But that's not what I see at all.

"Horse stables."

Stables, and not an evergreen-covered hillside in sight.

I go to the door. It opens easily. I expected it to be sealed, to be fake. But a long hallway outside it runs toward an ornate staircase in a house that's Texas-sized. I close the door.

"So I'm not on Wormwood Island," I say, returning to the bed, which doesn't seem to want to let me leave it. I curl up under the duvet. "And this room—hell, this house—could be Harper's."

Those words sink in as my eyes close.

This house could be Harper's.

I sit up. Of course it's Harper's! I'm in Harper's house. But it's only in my head.

Unless I *am* one of the Lucky Ten.

"God, Anne, make up your mind," I mutter at myself. I drum my fingertips on the duvet cover. "Okay, if I'm one of the Lucky Ten—if that shit's real—then it won't hurt a bit for me to sit here and imagine that this might actually be part of the Scrutiny. Because I've got nothing but time if I'm free of Wormwood Island and in a new house. *But!* If the Lucky Ten is a red herring, then I've gotta figure out this challenge immediately."

The bed pulls me back. When's the last time I felt this tired, this slothful? I don't even have the energy to figure out what could be a critical challenge.

"That's gotta have something to do with it," I say to Harper's ceiling.

I'm not slothful by nature. But Acedia, goddess of sloth, is. She could be influencing me right now. This whole challenge could be based around her. Or around all the Seven Sinning Sisters.

"This could be one part of a bigger challenge. A seven-part challenge." It hits me what that means. "I've barely even started the challenge! Everyone else might have figured this out already."

But how could they?

You'd have to know about the real identity of Invidia and the other six. Who would know that? Ben and I figured it out on our own; Molly would only know because I told her. Is everyone else screwed? Or are they all in different challenges? Or do they all know what I know?

"Don't worry about anyone else," I say.

But not worrying is just as exhausting as worrying. So I throw the covers over my head, close my eyes, and think of how much I want to stay in bed and waste the day away. I can feel myself nodding off, and it feels delicious. I open my eyes a sliver as I roll away from the sunlight—and I realize I'm not in bed anymore.

I'm sitting at a breakfast nook in a sunny kitchen. A table of breakfast dainties and savories is before me, and none other than Harper, her dad, and her stepmonster are seated with me.

Now I know. I know I was right.

I'm in a challenge. This is it.

But how did I get from Harper's room to her kitchen?

It wasn't until I stopped fighting my laziness that I got here. I had to give in to the lure of the sisters. Not resist, not do the opposite. I have to sin to win. I've already done what Acedia would do—I've preferred sleep over activity—so sloth is satisfied. Six to go.

"Pass the bacon," Harper says to her dad.

She flips her straight red hair, and I feel that familiar twinge of jealousy. Envy, I think. This is Invidia's handiwork; she's put me in the house of the person I envy most. There's a reason *this* Harper doesn't look like she used to, like she did before she was vivified; I wasn't jealous of that girl the way I've been jealous of the vivified Harper.

The Otto family kitchen is at least the size of the second floor of our funeral home, and it could be pulled from the pages of a magazine; beyond the folding deck doors that are wide open, letting in a warm breeze, an Olympic-size pool sparkles crystal blue in the sunlight. Harper has so much; they have so much. How can one family have far more than their fair share while my hard-working dad and deserving mother had so little? It eats me up inside. I look at Harper merrily crunching on bacon, and I want her to be the overweight girl she was before. Because she's not allowed to have everything *and* be beautiful.

Their housekeeper comes out of the butler's pantry carrying a plate of croissants.

I think I've just graduated to gluttony. Because I hit envy out of the park—it was easy.

There's no question in my mind that a solid handful of the top students back at Cania are figuring this out, too. Even if their PT isn't to look closer, and even if the whole school isn't privy to the true identities of Invidia, Superbia, and their five sisters, they'll be working their way through this challenge fast because it only takes doing the sin to move along in the challenge; you don't have to be conscious that you're even participating in the game.

So I attack the plate of croissants. Just tear through them like I'm at an old-school pie-eating contest. One after the other. Barely chewing. Washing the buttery bread down with milk, coffee, juice, everything they have on their table. A stack of pancakes follows. And fruit salad. Everything must go.

Harper and her parents are staring at me. I didn't know they could see me. They're an illusion, of course; obviously, Harper isn't home with her family—she's at Cania with the rest of us, probably sitting in some classroom, motionless, under a spell in which we're only virtually doing all of these things.

"What?" I ask them with my mouth full.

"Are you okay, dear?" Mr. Otto's looking at me over the top of his reading glasses. His newspaper is flipped down.

"You're not real," I tell them. "None of this is real. So zip it and let me get gluttony out of the way."

"Sweetheart, are you"—Mrs. Otto pauses and glances with concern from Harper to me—"are you hungry?"

"Obviously."

Mr. Otto's face softens. "Is it your parents? Your dad doesn't make enough money to feed you, isn't that right?" He puts his paper down as I stop slurping my coffee long enough to pay attention. "Let us help you. We can give you the money you need for food, clothing, an education."

"Help me? I don't need your help."

"It's as if you haven't had a decent meal in months," Mrs. Otto says, tsking in pity.

Even Harper looks concerned for me.

Irritated, I shove away from the table. "I don't need anyone's help. I can do everything myself. I always have. I always will."

Without realizing it, I've passed gluttony and moved swiftly through pride. Back at Cania Christy, if the Seven Sinning Sisters are watching me, Superbia, Invidia, Gula, and Acedia can check me off their lists. There's only Avaritia, Ira, and Luxuria—or greed, wrath, and lust—left.

I waste no time.

As Mr. and Mrs. Otto watch in stunned silence, I clutch the string of pearls encircling Mrs. Otto's neck. I'm about to yank them off. I'm all set to fly through the greed test. But her eyes are so wide with fear, I can't help but utter the faintest apology for what I'm about to do.

Which lands me back in Harper's bed.

"What the hell?" I snap at the ceiling.

How frustrating is this?

I wasn't remorseless with that sin, so I'm back to square one? Just because I was apologetic. Just because I didn't let the Seven Sinning Sisters get the better of me. Just because I let a little humanity shine through, which is a no-no in the land of devils and a surefire way to fail at the Scrutiny.

"Fine!" I shout at the sisters, as if they can hear me. Maybe they can. "Fine, I'll do it your way. I'll be the vilest little excuse for a human that ever walked through this house."

I whip the blankets over my head. Dutifully, I say, "I wish I could spend all day in bed."

I open my eyes expectantly.

But I'm not in the kitchen.

Dammit! I don't have time for this. Which is part of the problem. To pass Acedia's test, I need to be lazy as all hell. Legitimately lazy. I need to *not* think about time; I need to drag my ass through life, languishing away.

With a deep breath, I close my eyes again. And let myself really sink into the pillows, really wrap in the warmth of the duvet. I push out thoughts of moving fast, of winning, of the other kids crossing the finish line, whatever that line looks like, and focus on how tired I am. And I *am* tired. I even yawn. It occurs to me that winning the Scrutiny isn't a big deal. No, it's far better to spend as much time as I can in this bed. It's beyond comfortable.

I am sitting in the kitchen.

I smile. Perfect.

Enviable Harper is next to me. The platter of croissants follows. Mr. Otto looks like he could cry for me, and I am filled with pride, which makes me want to knock them down to size. So I wrap my fingers around Mrs. Otto's necklace and, this time—without even a sense of hesitation—yank hard. It pops, Mrs. Otto yelps, and I race after a handful of loose pearls that get away, collecting them all greedily.

"And nobody touch a bite of this breakfast," I add. "It's mine!"

I glimpse their silver on display in a curio, and I start emptying that as Mrs. Otto whispers to Harper to call the cops.

"Call the cops?" I repeat. "Nobody's calling anybody!"

"You cheap little bitch," Mrs. Otto snaps at me. "Get out of our house!"

"Your house?" I stomp up to Harper's stepmonster. "What did you do to earn this? Marry a man with money? This isn't *your* house. These aren't your pearls, those aren't your horses in the stables, and this isn't even your daughter you pretend to care so goddamn much about. You really care, you Botox-injected bitch? Then why do you let her stay at a school you know damn well is run by 'people' who can't possibly be playing for the good team? Why don't you ask her why she hikes her skirt up and constantly feels the need to display her G-string and bra? Here's why! Because *you don't care*! That's why she's there. Because you *never* cared."

I'm seeing red and can hardly breathe when I find myself back at Cania Christy.

But I haven't done lust yet. Wrath and greed are both done, but what about lust?

Then I realize where I'm standing. Not in a room with a bunch of other entranced Cania kids. But in Dia's office. And Dia's here, too; he's leaning against his desk, and his gaze is fixed on me.

"It's all come so easily to you," he says. "You're light-years ahead of everyone else. Even your little boyfriend Ben isn't this far ahead, and he knows all about the Seven Sinning Sisters, doesn't he?"

I'm winning?

"Are you real?" I ask.

"Do you wonder why it comes so easily to you?"

"You're trying to slow me down, aren't you?"

He smiles. "I want you to be honest with me."

"If you'll be honest with me."

"Ask me anything, Anne, and I will tell you. But I cannot break the code of the underworld. I cannot reveal anything about a superior devil."

"I'm sorry, what?"

"You realize this is a foot race, right?"

"A superior devil?" I wrack my brain. "Do you mean Mephisto?"

"As I said, I can say nothing."

Just like Pilot said! Damn demonic hierarchies. But what does Dia know about Mephisto?

"Why did you tell me to trust my PT yesterday?" I ask him. "I want the truth."

"Because I wanted to give you a chance to win. But not because I want you to leave. Simply because it's not safe for you here. And now," his gaze rolls from my head to my toes and back again, making me want to slap him, "be honest with me."

"About what?"

"How did you feel when I embarrassed you in the library in front of everyone?"

"You mean yesterday?"

He nods.

"Embarrassed. You hit the nail on the head. That's how I felt. Now, can you put me in whatever task will make Luxuria happy so I can finish this race?"

"*Embarrassed?*"

I groan. "Did you hear anything I just said?"

"You said you'd be honest, Anne."

"I am!"

"Then tell me how you felt. When I stood in front of you. And I moaned and told you to make me feel it."

"Em-barr-assed."

"But in fact you felt…?"

And then I realize.

How did I not realize?

"You think I lust for you?" I utter, unable to believe it.

"I know you do. You look at me."

He pushes away from his desk and steps toward me. I back up.

"I look at you? Like when I'm painting you?"

"You're attracted to me."

"I think you're a better looking dude than I'd like you to be, sure—"

"Exactly."

"But I'm into Ben. Completely."

"Then why am I here? Why did Luxuria put me in your challenge? They got Harper and her family right, didn't they? You whipped through the first six parts of this with the greatest of ease. Could they have been wrong to finish with me as the object of your lust, the sin you should give in to?"

He's backed me all the way against the door.

"Do the wrong thing, Anne," he says. "Do what scares you. It's the only way to succeed in life, or at least at Cania Christy. The right thing is usually just a cover for something wrong anyway."

"I don't know what—"

"Just do it. Do anything. Bite my lip. Suck my tongue. Surrender to lust."

In a heartbeat, I grab his hair and kiss him, just cutting off the last of his words as I do. Our mouths are open; I'm stunned by how swiftly he envelopes me. A flash of light explodes behind my eyes, and I see something, feel something I haven't felt since the night Harper screamed. It's overpowering.

The sound of applause forces my eyes open again.

I am in Valedictorian Hall.

And I am breathless in the aftermath of kissing a dark lord, of doing the worst thing I could do just to win a stupid race.

CR&O

MAESTRO INSULLIS BEGINS playing the organ at the front of the hall as Dia and the Seven Sinning Sisters, all of them clapping, glance from me to an enormous projection screen covering the wall of vials. My face, hot with a blush, is showing on the screen. My name and year are at the bottom of it, and my status as winner for the junior class is confirmed in print.

I need to catch my breath.

I look away from Dia. Fast.

I'm surrounded by 200 unmoving students on gleaming pews. Well, 198 of us are unmoving. Hiltop, the fake student, is standing at the back of the room. I am the first actual student to burst, with a jolt, out of the trance. I am the first to escape the illusion. I am the first to wake from the Scrutiny.

"I won," I whisper.

Molly sleeps a few people down from me, and Emo Boy is to my left. I turn to find Ben is with all the other seniors in the three rows behind mine. Their heads are down. I wonder what they're each going through. Who they envy, who they lust after, what inspires their wrath, and if they're going with or against the compulsion to sin in these minor, everyday ways.

Guardians are lined against the walls. Pilot sees me shake off the residual grogginess caused by the spell I just broke and storms out of the building. I spy Teddy, who stares blankly ahead, as if I'm invisible and not the winner for the junior class, as if I don't have the option of leaving now and letting him do what he will without me. But he knows I won't leave. He knows I wouldn't let my mom down.

So what will I do? What will I ask for?

I laugh to myself. It's so obvious. I'm going to give Ben a new life.

Smiling now, I take in the long, narrow, and ornately decorated room I haven't seen in months, the room that's supposed to be locked until graduation day. Candles flicker in sconces and from three massive chandeliers. Portraits of past valedictorians circle the perimeter of the room. At the front, with a new floating stage before it, stands the massive apothecary-style wall I know well; in each of its small locked doors are vials of blood belonging to the students of Cania Christy.

Dia arrives in front of me and takes my hand. It's too soon for him to touch me. The memory of kissing him is too fresh. Does he know about it?

"Congrats," he says casually. Maybe he hasn't got a clue that he was *lust* for me? "I don't think Hiltop's impressed,"—we glance and find her scowling our way—"but it's my school now, right?"

Molly wakes with a start, which Dia takes as his cue to leave.

"Beat you," I say lightly to her.

"Why am I not surprised?"

We both look at Ben. Still no movement. But a boy near him—a senior named Toshio—starts shaking his head, waking. I grimace; why can't Ben win this? He knows about the Seven Sinning Sisters! Toshio's eyes, wet with tears, open.

Harper wakes just after Toshio does. She snorts hard at my picture on the screen.

The first freshman and sophomore to wake shriek uncertainly and then powerfully, getting up to dance little jigs on the spot when they realize they've won. Our photos rotate on the screen.

I'm watching Ben when his head lifts. It takes a moment before his gaze finds mine, and I wave. His face is flush, making me wonder if he finished with Luxuria's challenge, too, and, if so, whether I was his object of lust or not.

"Am I first?" he mouths. Frowning, I shake my head and point to Toshio, who is rubbing his face maniacally and sweating like the devil in a lightning storm. Ben shrugs then adds, "Are you the first junior?"

A smile spreads across my face, and his eyes light up. But darkness replaces whatever initial joy he may have felt. Because the question of the hour is, what will I ask for?

"So," Molly says, nudging me, "you need to ask for unlimited wishes. Totally. If one of you four lunatics doesn't ask for that, I'll lose all faith in humanity."

More people awaken, one after the other, some with shouts, some with tears.

When others block my view of Ben, I turn to Molly.

"Do you think the reward is transferable?" I ask her.

"Girl, you planning on giving me your prize?" She slaps at me. "I love you, but I couldn't possibly! …Oh, all right, twist my arm. I'll take it!"

"Molly."

"Okay, I'll be serious. Well, Dia said the winner can choose something for themselves." She doesn't look hopeful. "Freeing Ben would be, in effect, for you. So maybe."

The teachers tell everyone to return to their seats as Dia and the Seven Sinning Sisters take the stage. The walls seem held up by Guardians, all but three of them expressionless.

Superbia claps her hands, and the twenty or so remaining students who hadn't awoken open their eyes, lift their heads. Emo Boy, seated next to me, stares around like he's in the wrong place and grinds his fists into his eyes until it seems he might rip his retinas right off; his eyes are red when he darts a glare at me.

I hadn't given any thought to those who believed they were among the Lucky Ten. Now I wish I'd never seen Emo Boy wake. You can almost see hope drain like blood from his skin. He thought it was real. I wish I didn't know that. I wish my imagination didn't jump to how long he lay in bed, filled with certainty that he'd been granted a special prize. I wish I couldn't hear his light sobs as everything he almost had vanishes. He innocently, naively hoped, never remembering that the only way to survive Hell is to abandon all hope.

Dia switches on the microphone.

"How was that for a challenge?" he says, panning the room with his arms out like Cristo Redentor. "Pretty cool stuff!"

The three other winners hoot, but Dia will be standing up there a long time if he waits for the rest of the room to warm up. They've all just tasted freedom. Many of them believed they were among the Lucky Ten and this entire ordeal was over.

"All right, all right, so." He rubs his hands. "We've got four smart kids to congratulate, haven't we? Now I know that whole Lucky Ten business is something we created for the challenge, but the reward I told you about yesterday—the prize these four kids are getting—is real." He reads the labels on the vials Dr. Zin hands to him. "Please rise, Miss Shanta Penrose, Miss Jihong Wu, Miss Anne Merchant, and Mr. Toshio Ona, our winners."

Molly whoops once as I join the other three in standing, awkwardly, among a crowd of desperate people who can only see me with hate. They loathed me for killing Pilot and despised me for being alive, and now their jealousy is palpable enough to paint the room green. I've just taken a second life from someone who actually needed it.

"The winners will join me in my office, where I'll reward them with anything they choose."

I keep my gaze fixed on Dia as he leads the crowd in their half-hearted applause. He strides from the stage, trailed by the Seven Sinning Sisters, and motions for the four winners to follow them out of Valedictorian Hall.

Molly pats my arm as I pass her. Plum tries to trip me.

I'm in the center aisle when Ben and I lock eyes, and he nods his encouragement. So positive. So optimistic. Much too good for this place.

A wobbly Dr. Zin takes Dia's place on stage. He is holding his black doctor's bag and a large ring of keys I recognize.

"Wave good-bye," Dia tells the four of us as, at the door, we form a small crowd behind him and the Seven Sinning Sisters. "If you're going to ask for what I think you're going to ask for, this is the last time you'll see any of these people."

I glance at Molly, who gives me a thumbs-up and throws me kisses. I look at Teddy, who has the greatest poker face on the planet and off. At last, as I near the door, I look at my beautiful Ben. He presses his hand to his heart, and I wish I could go to him. Then he mouths the three little words we've never actually said to each other.

That seals it. I thought I was certain before about giving this prize to Ben, but now I know there's no other way: if Ben doesn't get a second life out of this win, I'll have to agree to his love-in-the-afterlife plan. Ben's life or bust.

fourteen

A DEVIL'S GIFT

DIA LEADS ME, TOSHIO, SHANTA, AND JIHONG OUT OF Valedictorian Hall. I hear Dr. Zin begin a speech just as the doors to the massive building close, with a dull snap, behind us. Someone locks it from the other side.

I've only taken four or five steps when I hear the first scream, which comes from inside the hall. But the word "scream" is not big enough. I jump to a stop. The other kids flinch but continue on at the peals of terror. The knell of horror. The chorus of shouts and pleas that the heavy front doors of the hall barely muffle.

Ben, I think. *Molly*, I think.

Dia strides confidently on like the Pied Piper with his short train of children—and seven otherworldly goddesses—in tow.

"Dia!" I shout after him. Uselessly. Only Superbia stops for me. "What's happening in there?"

I dart back to Valedictorian Hall. I jiggle the enormous handles and bang the too-solid door. It's no use. The screaming continues—five, ten, maybe twenty students are shouting—but it soon falters, wanes, and then, obediently, stops.

I bang on the door. But no one comes out, and no one tells me what's happened.

So I race up to Dia and stop dead in front of him. "What was that about?" I demand, shoving him in the chest. "What did you do to them?"

"Me?" He sidesteps me, brushes where I shoved him, and gestures for the others to continue on to his office. "What could I possibly do? I've been here with you."

I plant my boots in the snow.

Dia turns back to me, and the others stop. They all glare my way. The Seven Sinning Sisters appear to be weighing me against Dia, looking us both up and down, wondering who will prove stronger.

"Only the weak ones are screaming," Dia says.

"Who are the weak ones?"

"Miss Merchant, good news always comes with bad news."

"That's not true."

"Can we please *go*?" Shanta insists. Her leg is jittering like she has to pee. "This is—I've waited so long!"

"You're a *freshman*," I fire at her. "You've been here how long? A month?"

That shuts her up.

"Tell me, Mr. Voletto. Tell me now."

"Look, we didn't have a Lucky Ten," Dia explains, tightening his woolly cardigan to block the wind, "but we did have an *Unlucky* Twenty."

Even Shanta, with her impatience for escape, can't ignore that.

"What does that mean, *unlucky*?" I ask.

"Twenty kids who should've been gone long ago," Ira clarifies. "They're gone now."

"Twenty. Expelled." I have to keep saying it to believe it. "Twenty. Dead."

"Whom did you expel?" Toshio asks Dia.

"The ones we had to wake. The ones who *believed*," he says with a smirk. "Their chances of actually being successful in the world are crap, wouldn't you say? I'd be slapping the four of you in the face if I'd let them continue battling for something they don't deserve. And I'd be keeping how many deserving students out of Cania by letting them take up seats?"

"*Twenty*."

"But their parents pay for them," Jihong says softly. "They pay to be here, sir."

"We have contracts, Headmaster," Toshio says. "This isn't fair."

Dia shakes his head, chuckling lightly. Almost all seven of the sisters chuckle, too.

"Is *your prize* in the contracts?" Dia asks. "Is your potential freedom today in your contract, Ona-san? No. Of course it's not. And the idea of the Lucky Ten wasn't in anyone's contract, either. But you're all more than happy to accept the good; you forget that light brings shadows."

"And you forget that expulsion is always an option for a disappointing academic performance," Avaritia adds.

"Now," Dia says, "before I change my mind about your reward."

He starts away. But only Shanta and the Seven Sinning Sisters go with him.

"Come on, you guys," Shanta calls to me, Jihong, and Toshio. "It's done. Besides, it happened to them, not us."

The ones who were still asleep have just been expelled. All of them. They were killed because they believed they were free, because they had hope. They're gone now. Ben's safe. And Molly's safe. Even Harper's safe. But Emo Boy. With his teary eyes. With his hope.

Before I can think, I blurt out, "I want to use my wish to save Emo Boy's life! Give him my second chance!"

Dia turns back. So do the Seven Sinning Sisters, but where Dia looks irritated by my outbursts, they look intrigued.

"Go ahead to the office," Dia commands them. As they glide away, he turns his dark stare on me. "Who exactly is Emo Boy?"

Oh, hell, what's his real name? Is it...Jake? Wally? Alec? Connor?

"It's big of you to offer that," Dia says, "but you can't save anyone else with your wish."

"I can't?"

"You've got one request to make, and it has to impact you directly. No tradezies."

So I can't help Ben at all? That changes everything!

As we trudge to his office, I quickly rethink my plan.

I'm not going home—I refuse to. But I can't send Ben home, either. So what can I use this one wish for?

I've got three things to do, as I see it: save Ben, help my mom (and Teddy), and get off this island. In that order. I think of my list of teachers' names. I think of Ben's Guardian. And I piece together a plan that had better work. Because I'm going to lose a lot today, and it has to be worth it.

CR&O

DIA STANDS BEFORE the fire in his office. The Seven Sinning Sisters are behind him. We face them as he explains that we each get to ask him for one thing, and that one thing has to be for ourselves, not for anyone else. He takes a moment to remind us to word our requests carefully so we get exactly what we want.

My easy plan to free Ben has slipped through my fingers and crashed like a vial on the floor. I think about exactly how to word my request so I'll get the most out of it.

Superbia hands Dia a silver bag, which he sets in the middle of the fire. The flames lick at it, and smoke swirls around it, but it glistens as if untouched. He takes our labeled vials—all twelve of them—from his sweater pocket and lays them in a row on the carpet.

"Freshman first," Dia says.

Shanta, shaking with anticipation, carefully says, "I'd like to be my living self again. Just as I was before I came here."

"Very well."

Dia double-checks her name on the labels of the three vials closest to him. He dangles them over the silver sack in the fire. He whispers a charm, or what sounds like one, in fluid, elegant Italian.

We hold our breath and watch. Waiting. Shanta whines to see her vials so near the destructive fire. Dia, silent now, slowly lowers them into the sack. His palms circle the opening of the bag, wiping through the fire painlessly; the fire is his element.

Shanta's unmoving, unchanging. She looks like she might start tearing the place up if nothing happens soon.

Seconds turn into a minute.

At the very moment it seems there's no point in paying attention to her anymore, a shimmer of silver passes down her body. It moves like a searchlight in the fog, shining under her hair, then in whispers over her stomach, her knees, her toes—and rolls back up again. Shanta gasps and, as if in the richest ecstasy, closes her eyes to take the experience in. Pearlescent strands of color circle her in magnificent swirls, dazzling the three of us and even, it seems, Dia. At last, the color diffuses, twinkling about the room like light through a prism, and vanishes.

Shanta vanishes with it.

"Enjoy your glimmer of life, Shanta," Dia says as the Seven Sinning Sisters giggle. "Sophomore next. That's you, Jihong."

Jihong nervously wrings her hands.

"Wait," I say to Dia. "What did you mean, her 'glimmer' of life?"

"She asked to be *just as she was before she came here*." He waves Jihong forward. "Shanta's gone back in time to just before she came here." He lifts Jihong's vials, checking the names. "So she's in the moment before she died. She'll relive her death, unless she can escape it, but this time I don't think I'll let her into Cania. Been there, done that, right?"

"So Shanta's...dead?" Toshio asks.

I think everyone's starting to see who we're really playing with.

"Not yet," Dia says. "But soon. She should be riding her bike now. The car that hits her won't be along for at least a minute."

Jihong, a little thing that could be toppled over by a cough, looks nervously at me, certain now, as I am, that the only way to get what we want, not some demonic version of it, is to ask for it precisely. Great. Not like language is open to interpretation or anything...

"I am request," Jihong says carefully in her second language, but Dia stops her. She can*not* be expected to ask for the right thing if she's not even speaking her language! In fluent Mandarin, Dia says God knows what to Jihong, who, with the most earnest expression, makes her request of him in her native tongue.

I hold my breath. I hope she got the wording just right.

The transformation we witnessed in Shanta repeats on Jihong. Except she doesn't disappear at the end of it. She just stands there, looking as flawless as any Cania student. I wait to hear her fate.

"You won't be your mortal self again until you leave the island," Dia explains. "Now, go pack and head to the village. Some of the construction guys are boating to Kennebunkport in an hour, so they'll probably give you a ride. Just remember: you'll need a new name."

It looks like that worked. She got through it. A skip in her step, Jihong waves good-bye to us and leaves the office.

"Doesn't she get a new name?" I ask. "Pilot told me winners get the whole package. Money, a new identity, documentation."

"Jihong asked for a second life like that which winners of the Big V get," Dia says. "Not for the riches. Naturally, she'll have to change her name; that's part of our contract. But we won't help financially or otherwise."

Tricky, tricky stuff. I take a deep breath, stand straighter, mentally will myself to get this right, and try not to think about the craziness of what I'm about to request—something that will probably make Toshio pass out with shock.

"Okay," I say to Dia and step forward, feeling the weight of the stares of seven intimidating underworld goddesses on me. "Let me phrase this just right."

"Actually," he says, "would you mind if Toshio goes next?"

"Toshio?" I look at the senior; he's nodding like a bobblehead on an ATV dashboard. "Why?"

"God, you're inquisitive." Dia's smile is smooth and beautiful. If I had half a brain in my head, I'd ask to wake up in California and be free of that smile. "Well, we've spent a few Saturdays together now, and I'd like to say good-bye to you. Properly. I think we all would." He gestures to the sisters, who agree. "Is that okay?"

Just the thing to make my stomach sink. After all, I just sat through a lust challenge with this guy, which he may or may not be aware of. I don't want this to get awkward.

"Murdering Merchant can wait." Toshio bellows. "I'm ready!"

It happens even faster for Toshio, now that he's seen it done twice and knows what to do. He asks for the prize he would have received had he won the Big V, which seems to be just the ticket. When it's over, he bows to Dia and proceeds to back all the way to the door, bowing as he goes and fumbling to grab the door handle without looking. It's only because he takes so long opening the door and bowing his way out that I catch a glimpse of Ben standing in the hallway, trying to peek in. Our eyes meet, and he leaps forward, catching the door before it closes after Toshio.

"I'm sorry, Headmaster," Ben says. "Anne, I just wanted to say good-bye."

"Anne's about to take her turn, Mr. Zin. We were going to have a private discussion. I, too, would like to say good-bye."

"Wait," I say, holding my hands out to both of them. "Nobody has to say good-bye. I'm"—Ben's not gonna like this—"not leaving."

Like they're both ducking from an unexpected blow, they lean away. The sisters gasp and whisper among themselves.

"You're not?" Dia asks.

"Yes, she is," Ben says, marching into the office.

"No, I'm not."

I let Ben turn me toward him. This is the last time for a long time—maybe forever—I'll see him look at me with those beautiful green eyes, with his heart beating somewhere deep inside them, behind the flecks of gold and the few but lovely dark stipples. This is the last time he'll touch me like he wants to keep me near him. If anyone wants to say good-bye, it's me.

"Ben, my plans are different from yours."

He shakes his head. As if he has any say. "Don't do anything you'll regret. Please."

Surely, at some point, I'll regret what I'm about to do. I'll lie in bed at night, feeling martyred, wondering if I'm always going to destroy my chances at love, wondering if I took a gamble and lost. I wish I could have warned Ben, but I wasn't entirely sure what I'd do until he mouthed that he loved me. I smile at the memory, which he misreads as a lunatic's grin.

"Dia," he rushes to stand before our headmaster, "I refuse to let her give me this gift. I don't want the new life. She needs to take it."

"She couldn't give it to you if she wanted to," Dia tells him. "But I'm not sure she wanted to."

Dia has been leaning against his chaise, observing us with interest. Now he moves to pace before the fireplace. My vials are the only ones that remain on the carpet, and he sweeps them up.

"I would, of course, love to know what she wants," Dia finishes. "I thought you'd want to get away from Teddy."

"Teddy?" Ben asks.

I'm thinking exactly the same thing as Ben. "My ex-Guardian?"

What does Dia know? But he reveals nothing. And he shrugs like it's none of his business.

Ben returns to my side. He grips my hands, arms, shoulders, anything he can, maniacally, as he begs me not to do whatever I've got planned.

"So Miss Merchant," Dia coos, "what *do* you want from me?"

This is it. This is the last chance I'll have.

Knowing that, I clasp Ben's too-perfect face and, holding my breath, press my lips to his. It's a replica of our first kiss, our falling moment, with all the breathlessness of wanting him and the agony of knowing that, in moments, he is going to be torn from me, and I'll be thrust into a life I can't imagine. By choice.

I hold him as long as I can, careless to Dia's stony gaze and the sisters' *ahhh*s.

Only when I've had my fill—and even then, *even then* I kiss him one more time—do I release Ben, pray I'll never forget what it's like to be loved by him, and turn to Dia.

"I want you to bring me to Eve Risset." I take a breath. "And let me watch you use her to sever Ben's ties to me."

fifteen

SPIRIT AND FLESH

MOLLY IS IN THE HALLWAY WHEN THE THREE OF US—ME, Dia, and a white-faced Ben—leave the sisters behind and dash out of the office. We make a beeline for the stairway to the second floor, where the secretaries' lounge is. Molly's smile fades when she sees Ben's wide eyes.

"What's she doing?" Molly asks him. "Isn't she going home?"

Dia opens the door to the stairwell, and I follow him through, with Ben and Molly close behind us. I hear them talking back and forth, the metal staircase clattering under eight stomping feet, but I refuse to give in or say anything about my decision. My throat is so tight, I can hardly breathe, let alone speak.

"She asked Dia to get Eve to break us up," Ben says in exasperation. "Sever ties. That's what she said."

"Break you up?"

"She won't listen to reason."

"What's Eve got to do with it?"

"I dunno. Anne seems to know. Molly, help me stop her. Please."

"But she's crazy about you, Ben. Why would she—?" Molly's voice drops. "Oh, God."

Six footsteps on the stairs. Then four.

Dia and I keep marching up, leaving the two people I care about most behind. I hear their voices, Molly's soft and Ben's high with panic.

"What?" Ben asks her. "Mol, tell me before it's too late and she ruins everything."

"She couldn't transfer her prize to you, could she?"

"I don't think she wanted to!"

"She did. But evidently she couldn't. So she has to do this, Ben. For you."

"She has to break up with me *for* me?"

"For you ... and Garnet."

Dia swings open the door to the second floor.

I glance back to see, half a flight down, Molly's face softening and Ben looking about as desperate as a person can. Her gaze catches mine as I pause in the doorway, and, to my relief, she nods at me. Ben sees her look, sees me, and abandons her to chase me up the stairs and out. He bolts at us just as Dia and I enter the dimly lit wood-paneled staff lounge, where Eve is drinking scotch with Kate at a dirty-looking old card table.

Ben flies into the lounge. He grips my arms in his hands. The unruffled Ben is gone; the fighting Ben, the one I so rarely see, is here. Finally. But too late.

"I know you want to be with me. I know it!" he says wildly. "So stop this now. We'll figure something else out."

"There's no other way," I tell him. "You have to be with Garnet."

"Ending you and me won't start me and Garnet."

I don't tell Ben that this is only the beginning of my plan. I know things I haven't told him; I know the powers of most of the staff; and, thanks to Lou, I know demons can serve humans. I might—I just *might*—be able to convince Pilot to serve me, if there's something in it for him. (Long shot, but worth a try!) And if I can do that, I'll gain a little power, possibly enough to charm a demon into using their powers for me ... and, in turn, for Ben. Because I've seen how hurt Garnet is. So I know it's going to take more than severing my ties with Ben to soften Garnet's hardened heart; it's going to take a spell.

First things first: separate Ben from me.

Second: see how to charm a demon. Which is why I'm standing here, why I need to watch.

Third: watch Ben win the Big V at the end of May.

Detaching myself from Ben in more ways than one, I calmly remove his hands and turn back to Dia, who is looking impatiently at me as Eve and Kate sit, waiting for something to happen.

"Sorry, yes, this is what I want, Mr. Voletto," I say. "Please proceed."

Dia eyes Ben. "You gonna stick around and watch your own heartbreak, kid?"

"I'm staying if she is."

"Will he remember this?" I ask Dia.

"No."

"But I will?"

"Would you like to?"

"Yes," I say. "Sever his ties to me, but I don't want to forget anything. Not even this moment."

"Anne!" Ben begs. "Stop. This is *insanity*."

Dia sets his gaze on Eve. "You. Stand up."

Exchanging a glance with Kate, Eve rises. She is as crazy-looking as ever, with a windswept hairdo straight out of the eighties, smeared neon-pink lipstick, and bleached eyebrows like sun-drenched tumbleweeds. She is wearing the brooch of Mephisto; she is his servant, which is just as I'd thought, given that Eve was here before Dia arrived. I want to see how to get a demon that doesn't serve you to use their powers for you.

"Come to me," Dia commands Eve.

Hesitantly, she steps within arm's reach of Dia. As she does, he grabs the bottle of scotch from the table and smashes it hard against the edge, creating an explosion of shards, sending alcohol flying.

Ben and I jump; he pulls me into his arms protectively. His breath is warm in my hair as he whispers his last pleas to me. I sink into him, already regretting my decision.

"Dia Voletto," Eve murmurs, "show me mercy."

Sneering, Dia tosses the bottleneck aside and lifts a long, thin sliver of glass from the chair. He yanks Eve's arm and pins it behind her back, pulling up hard enough that she doubles over and cries out. He wrenches her arm violently, so much that Ben and I both flinch—though neither of us can keep from looking—and jerks her hand around until it looks like her whole arm might snap off. She pleads. But he's relentless. He tugs on her fingers; joints pop. He brings the six-inch-long glass shard to her fingertip.

I have to watch every step. I have to make this worth it.

Eve yelps as, pitilessly and with a low growl, Dia pushes the sharp shard under her fingernail, into its tender bed. She squeals and gasps. At the table, Kate looks on helplessly. Squirming.

Molly walks in and stops short. I hear her sharp gasp. She rushes to me and Ben.

"Get out of here, you guys," Molly says to us. "Why would you want to see this?"

"Stop!" Eve pleads. Her voice is raw, like burning acid. The more she cries, the deeper Dia pushes the thick, sharp shard—well past the nail, all the way under her skin. I look away when I see it tear through layers and pull the nail up. "*Mercy!* Please. I'll do anything! Just stop!"

But he doesn't stop.

He cranks her arm like a winch. I hear first a snap and then a wail. Ben and Molly have turned away. I have to look. To take mental notes.

"What—what is your command?" Eve asks at last.

"Sever ties between Anne Merchant and Ben Zin," he says. "Disconnect Ben from her."

This is it. This is where my life with Ben ends.

When Eve pants her agreement, saying it is done, Dia throws her to the floor, letting her writhe and struggle for breath. Her arm is broken. Her hand is mangled.

Ben's arms loosen around me. I find him staring in blank confusion at me, as if trying to figure out why he was standing so close to me.

Molly puts her hands on my shoulders and whispers, "You can still be friends."

But Dia's not done. He turns his dark, glistening eyes on Kate, who gulps. To our surprise, he slips across the tabletop, gliding easily, and lands in a straddle on Kate, who is white with fear. He pins her in her chair.

"Dia? What are you doing?" I ask.

Dia's on a mission I can't understand. He seizes the bottleneck with one hand and, with the other, clasps Kate's hair at the roots and yanks her head down, cracking her neck. Unlike Eve, Kate suffers in silence, biting back the screams, though I can't say the same for

Molly, who's muttering about lunacy as she tries to tug me and Ben to the door. But I can't stop watching.

Kate's neck is exposed to Dia. The race of her pulse in her throat is audible. He slashes the sharp fragment up her neck, up her jaw, all the way to her eye, where he stops just long enough to watch her thrash in pain, to feel her body wriggle under him. Dark red blood oozes from the gash he's made as a sob leaks from her lips.

"You," Dia commands Kate, "you will make Ben Zin *hate* Anne Merchant."

"Wait," I stammer. Molly steps forward, looking as concerned as I am. *Wait, wait, wait.* I didn't ask for hate.

"It's done!" Kate cries.

Dia leans back, spent. Scarlet drips down Kate's long, gnarly hands, which clutch at her bleeding neck and face.

On a slow pivot, like Damon Smith, like my soul has been removed and left me with the emptiest possible shell, I turn to Ben. His blank expression changes, like he's put on a mask for the Cupid and Death Dance—but he's playing the part of Death and playing it well: his sneer is deep and disgusted when our eyes meet, and he recoils, taking my heart with him.

This is the worst, by far, of all the times Ben has rejected me. Not only because I brought it on but also because, unlike the other times, there is no hope that it will ever change to acceptance. No friendship in store for us. The spells have been cast; the deed is done. And I am left, motionless in Molly's embrace, to watch Ben excuse himself from the room like the overly polite, too-formal boy he is and dart away, past Elle Gufy, who is just coming into the lounge.

Ben.

"Now it's your turn, Anne," Dia says.

I'd forgotten anyone else was here. Molly shakes me back into reality—a reality I'd like to avoid—and I glance, gape-mouthed, at Dia. He's left Kate to clean her gashed face, and he's stepped casually over a moaning Eve. Now his gaze jumps from me to Elle to Molly.

"You wanted to see how it's done, right?" Dia asks me.

"You knew that?" I stutter. Molly whispers for us to go. "How did you know?"

"Because you've put the pieces together."

"What pieces?"

"You know why I came here. Surely you know everything. And you wanted to know how to use your powers without telling anyone."

"I what?"

"So do it. Use Elle here to make Molly feel ugly."

I look at Molly, who is motionless with confusion.

He yanks Elle closer and nods for me to grab a shard of glass. "I'll submit to you temporarily, if you'd like, just to loan you my powers. So you can be who you are."

Molly looks as lost as I feel.

"Dia, put that down and let her go," I say. "I'm not doing anything. I don't know what you're talking about."

His smile fades. He thrusts Elle away. To my surprise, Elle's face drops as if she's crestfallen to have escaped a torture that's left Kate and Eve bloody, broken, and agonized. As if she wanted it.

"Then why did you give me that picture?" he calls after me as Molly leads me out.

Molly utters an awkward *thank you* to the demons we leave behind—all of them surprised to see me go—as she tugs me into the hall, drags me to the stairwell, guides me down to the first floor, and, without a word from me, wrenches me into the wintery air, where she stands me up like a dummy against the cold stone wall of the back of Goethe Hall.

"That was brave of you, Anne," she says. I think she's been saying other things, too, but that's the first line that makes it through. Her teeth are chattering with the cold when I finally look at her. "Now Ben is free to be with Garnet, and he might actually win. Was that your plan?"

I nod.

I haven't breathed in a while.

I take a slow gulp of air.

"It's a good plan. But why did you have to watch it happen? Why didn't you just get Dia to break you guys up? He must have the power to."

I stare at her.

"Is it true, what Dia said?" she asks patiently. "Did you want to see how to do it?"

My reasoning runs through my head in perfectly plotted form: make it so Ben will be with Garnet, and then eliminate all the obstacles from his path to a new life. But my mouth just hangs open. Snowflakes land on my lip and melt.

"I think you're in shock or something."

I don't want to move. I don't want to take a step because that means it's all real, everything. And I don't want to move until I understand what Dia meant.

"Who does he think I am?" I utter.

Molly looks relieved to hear me speak. "If you don't know, why would he think you do?"

"The drawing. He asked why I gave him the picture. But he took it."

"What was it?"

"A sketch I did. Months ago. He took it from me."

"A drawing of him?"

"The girl I saw in the mirror. I drew her. He said she was an underworld goddess."

"I don't understand. What girl?"

"She had…a tail. And she was *me*. I was her. Harper saw. She screamed."

"Were you tripping on acid by chance?"

"Mol."

Our eyes meet.

In a moment of clarity I realize that she is watching me with thinly veiled judgment—and why should I expect anything else? It was only because I was afraid of this moment, of this look in her eyes, that I kept my secret from her, waiting night after night until she was asleep before I'd even close my eyes.

Now I've lost Ben. And maybe even Molly. Never has a life fallen apart so swiftly. Even Faust had twenty-four years before his life came crashing down. And he had the pleasure of a life-altering exchange to indulge in before things fell apart. I've had nothing; I've had three months with a guy I love, two months with a forgiving friend, and as good as those things have been, I hardly feel like I've had enough to make losing it all worth it.

"I need to be alone," I choke.

She doesn't stop me when I turn to the iron gates of Cania Christy and stand before them. She is gone when I look back. Instead of heading to the road, I retreat and veer toward the south end of campus, toward the woods that lead down to the old Zin mansion, taking the path I used to take to Gigi's every day. Frosted leaves are frozen into the hardened mud at my feet as I step into the forest, feel the darkness cloak me, and stop. I inhale deeply through my nose, and exhale through my mouth. And close my eyes.

Wormwood Island has never been this silent. Not a drumbeat, not a drill, not a demon to be heard. The stillness is heavy and light at once. The calm is unmovable.

And there, in the perfect silence, I yell. I scream. I roar as loud and as hard as I can. I roar to shatter windows and make birds drop from the sky. I roar to chase Ben away and bring him back to me. I roar to fight who I am, whatever that may be, and invite it in. I roar in one long, clear, uninterrupted streak, with my eyes squeezed tight and my body arched, forcing all my air and sound and hate and love up and out.

My roar wanes into a holler, and my holler into a groan, and my groan into a whimper.

But there is so much more where it came from. It will never be done; it's just muted. It's always happening. It will never stop.

When I open my eyes, Teddy is standing not ten feet away.

"You decided to stay," he says to me. Calmly. As if he hasn't just witnessed the manic cry of a girl on the edge.

"*You.*"

Shaking with rage, I storm at the asshole who brought me back here. I crush my forearm into his throat. I push him hard, with a crunching thud, against a tree. Even as he tries to form words, I grab a branch. Back a step away. And, with all my strength, bring the cold, jagged hunk of wood down on his shoulder. As hard as I can. He doubles over. I bring it down on his other side and catch him just across the face.

"What don't I know?" I scream as I hit him, feeling Ira herself awakening inside of me. "Who am I?"

I smash it on top of his head, bringing him to his knees. I could kill him; it's like nothing I've ever felt before—the desire to destroy and the wild itch in my arms to feel his body collapse and stop moving, surrounded by all the fluids a mortician would drain away. That he can't be killed by blunt force means nothing to me. His immortality is a subject for a logical person, and that's not me right now.

Why can't I be with Ben?

Why am I here?

Why does he want me to play this horrible game, a game with no prize but the possibility of one day waking only to find that everyone I love is gone?

"Why did you choose me?" I throw the branch down. "Why?" I repeat, spent and weakened. In a final whimper, *"Mom."* As if she can hear me.

Once I'm unarmed, Teddy bolts at me. Hard. Just as I did to him, he does to me: his elbow nearly breaks my windpipe as he sends me stumbling like a rag doll onto the forest floor and then drags me up, propping me against a wet, mossy tree.

I don't care. Hurt me. Kill me, if you can.

His arm is hard under my chin, pressing harder at his wrist, hard enough to snap my neck, when he sneers into my face, his eyes glowing in the dark of the woods, and his gray skin broken and bleeding.

"Just because I'm playing for the good side," he snaps, bits of his smoky spittle flying onto my face, "doesn't mean violence is off-limits, kid!"

"Tell me the truth," I choke, though I'm barely able to force a sound out of my throat. "Why do you believe I'm the one to help you? Why me?"

"I was waiting to tell you this." He knows better than to loosen his hold, even as I'm gasping for air. "I couldn't say it until I knew you were committed. And now that you've saved Ben instead of going home—"

"I haven't saved Ben." I couldn't save him. I could only push him away. Maybe they're one and the same when it comes to me.

"—I can tell you more. A dark secret, Miss Merchant. But if you think your heart hurts now, prepare yourself."

"Tell me, Teddy."

My chest is heaving, and I might pass out any second. It's only adrenaline and his arm that keep me upright. He relaxes his hold on me just enough that I can speak without choking.

"How old was your mom when she had you?" he asks.

"Get to the point."

"How old?"

"Forty-something. Forty-four. What does that matter?"

"How many miscarriages had they had?"

It's something my parents rarely talked about and something I've always tried not to think about. My mom used to blame the funeral home for her losing so many pregnancies—said a person can't profit from death and hope to bring life into the world. And then she would smile at me, mess my hair more than it already was, and say I was her perfect exception.

"Lots."

"They even tried in vitro, but your mom couldn't carry babies naturally, Anne. She worked in a library, right?"

"She was smart. Even when she got sick," I cough, "she was smart."

"Ben gave you a copy of Faust, but you didn't have to read it to know it. So tell me, why did you know the story of Mephistopheles and Faust?"

"She told it to me. It was one of her favorites."

"Your mother knew it well. She knew Mephisto was someone you could go to in your most desperate hour, and he would come through for you. For a price."

My jaw tightens.

"Your mother did what no sane person has done before."

"Teddy, don't you dare say something that's not true."

"This is no lie. She crossed a line to get you."

No. I can't stop shaking my head. *No.*

"Anne, your mother asked Mephisto for a baby."

sixteen

IN THE SHADOWS OF ANGELS

I'M NOT HERE. I'M NOT IN THE WOODS WITH A GRAY-FACED demon telling me things no one should ever hear. I'm back home, back in California, and I'm six years old, and my mom is braiding my hair as she tells me she'd give up everything she has and then some for me. I'm four years old with my parents in a small LA playhouse, watching a performance of *The Black Rider*, listening to my mom whisper an explanation of what I'm seeing: the hunter traded his soul to the devil for bullets that couldn't miss. I'm eleven years old, a year before my mom was diagnosed bipolar, and sitting in the car with her outside a church, watching her wring her hands, and then I'm biting my tongue as the rear wheels skid on the gravel and we speed away. I'm twelve, and she is at the kitchen table, her face wet with tears; she smiles at me through them, and she says, *No matter what, it was worth it.*

I'm there.

I'm not here.

"But," Teddy continues, bringing me back to these cold, damp woods, "you and I both know that demons can't create humans."

I look into his eyes, which are swirling with a mix of dark and light emotions, sorrow shining through the strongest. He's just told me Mephisto helped make me. But maybe it's not true?

"So it didn't work?" I ask, clinging desperately to this shred of hope. But it's slippery. It's a cliff I've slipped off; it's a branch I've

caught just in time, but I can't hold on much longer. I know, without
Teddy saying it, that this story doesn't end well.

"It worked," he says.

"Impossible."

"Mephisto cannot *create* humans. What does he need in order to
vivify kids here?"

I try to swallow. "Their DNA."

"Your mom had a fertilized egg from in vitro."

I've stopped breathing.

"All Mephistopheles needed was a soul," he says. "Where do
you think he got that soul?"

"I—I don't know."

But I do know.

The underworld is filled with souls. Dark, damaged, writhing
souls. The souls of the Seven Sinning Sisters and the demons, punks,
dark witches, succubae, and incubi under them and alongside them.

Releasing me, Teddy watches my reaction as he backs away.

I've fallen into my own grave. Anne Merchant has been shoved
into a six-foot hole, and every new realization is a shovelful of earth
that's been thrust onto me, burying me alive. The unearthly woman
I saw in the mirror and sketched; Dia said she was an underworld
goddess. Invidia touching my hair, and the sense of power that filled
me. Mephisto's tolerance for me in spite of the trouble I've brought
on him. Even the reason Mephisto wants me here at all. To say
nothing of how easily today's challenge came to me, as if the seven
deadly sins are second nature for me.

"Am I possessed?" I stammer.

"You are a soul reincarnated."

It takes me a while to actually utter these words: "Not just any
soul?"

"Not just any soul."

My voice is tiny. "Is it very bad, my soul's history? The person
I am?"

"Not in my books. I proudly served you."

"You what?"

"Don't you remember anything?" He sighs. "You took me under
your wing when I was first cast into the underworld. You trained me,
you coached me, and when it came time for you to trade your many

legions for this opportunity, you freed me. I was able to retire my powers so I might never be made to do wrong again."

"Hold on," I say, holding my hand up and trying to keep it together.

But he charges on. This is a secret he's been keeping since the day Villicus introduced me to him, back when I thought he was just my apprentice Guardian. He's known who I am all along. Unfortunately for me, every word he says tears me further from the person I thought I was, from Anne Merchant, daughter of Nicolette and Stanley Merchant, high school sweethearts. Every word he says condemns me to Hell.

"I served a powerful goddess named Miss Saligia," he says. "*Your* name was Saligia. Miss Saligia, the goddess overseeing the Seven Sinning Sisters," Teddy clarifies at last, draining the blood from my whole body as he does. "And you, my dear, were spectacular. A rare symbol of hope in a dark world. Where Mephistopheles and Dia Voletto built their legions with fear and intimidation, you compelled yours to love you, which is, to be sure, as rare and as powerful as…as eternal youth. Or perfect beauty. Your followers' love for you would make Romeo jealous."

"Love…"

"Do you understand, Miss Merchant?" He searches my face. "Miss Saligia was the soul put into the body of a girl born Anne Elizabeth Merchant. You were Miss Saligia."

I know. I know. But I don't want to know.

My heart thumps harder. I breathe through it, quieting it.

"Saligia started as a succubus. And she—you—worked your way up until your powers neared those of Mephisto himself. Under your leadership, the Seven Sinning Sisters came to conquer the human world and win countless souls for the underworld."

"Not exactly news worth writing home about, Ted."

"But think of what it means about who you are, about the power you had…and could have again." I feel him watching me. "Miss Merchant, don't be so hard on yourself. Each of us has Heaven and Hell in him. And as a wise man once said, 'I like men who have a future and women who have a past.' Be proud of your past. You were amazing as Gia."

"Gia?"

Oh, shit. That's Dia's girlfriend's name.

"*Gia* is short for *Saligia*?"

So this past I'm supposed to be proud of started with me as a mother-effing succubus and then landed me in the arms of Dia Voletto. No wonder Teddy once suggested I'd be successful in life by using sex to get ahead. Little wonder Pilot, after Lou told him about me, insisted I change my PT to match Harper's. They both knew I started as a succubus. Hell, years ago a boy said he had a naughty dream about me. Even then. Even then I was part Saligia.

And then there's Dia.

Luxuria put me in a lust challenge with him. Because of our past.

He said he came back here for a purpose. He wasn't sent here; he came here intentionally. Was I that purpose? Did he come to win me back?

Was Ben never meant to be mine?

I slide down the tree and slump on a mossy stump.

"I'm a demon."

"To define is to limit." Teddy sits opposite me. "You gave up everything you had in the underworld to help me. And, along the way, to seek revenge on Dia."

"Revenge?"

"Dia hurt you. Embarrassed you. Betrayed you."

Daylight turns to night as I sit in silence, my hands on my mouth, my eyes skyward, and let it all sink in. With the calming tone of a friend, which makes me wonder why I've always felt such tension with Teddy, he explains that he and Gia were close friends almost from the moment he feigned a fall from grace and landed in her command. She showed him that even condemned souls were not entirely black.

I listen, but all I can think is, *This is how it feels to die.* You're just going about your business, on your way to an appointment, thinking about what's for dinner tonight, and then a bus hits you. You're just swimming laps, wondering why you don't do this more often, and a clot loosens to find its way into your heart. You're just looking for stronger pills to fight your migraines, and the doctor says it's cancer. And me? I was just trying to help Ben win the Big V, and Anne Merchant died.

"There was a reason you came here, Anne. A purpose."

I stare at him. I can't speak.

"Gia wanted to destroy Dia. And I need to destroy Mephisto, though admittedly I can wait."

"But Dia has a tattoo of her name. And he speaks so fondly of her."

"Trust me on this."

"Gia became *me* so she could kill Dia? But how would she know Dia would come to Earth?"

"It's destiny."

"And what does that have to do with you and my mom's plan?"

"We want Dia gone as badly as we want Mephisto gone. You were on board with this, too, when we were friends in the underworld."

I grip my hair at the roots and groan. "Mephisto *made me* Anne Merchant," I say. I must be in shock to voice the words without getting sick. "Why would he agree to let me come here if I was only going to destroy him?"

"He didn't know. He was your mentor, you see. You loved him like a father."

Now I *am* gonna be sick.

"Haven't you wondered why your punishment for breaking the rules left Molly Watso dead and you barely bruised? Haven't you wondered why he hasn't killed you yet? He knew you as Gia. He loved you as Gia. If he didn't love himself and his Earthly activities more, he might have found himself serving you. But Anne, never forget this: when he made you into his first proper, real, functioning human being—when you agreed to be part of his experiment—he became, in his mind, your father."

"But he tortured me in Valedictorian Hall," I say. "Why would a so-called father do that?"

He smiles. "It's so nice to hear you ask questions Gia never would have."

"Teddy, why?"

"Miss Merchant, isn't it clear? That was a show of love."

"Oh, please."

"Demons seek pain. Pain is pleasure. It's how we operate."

Kate, Eve, and Elle didn't run from the lounge when Dia entered the room. And Elle looked disappointed when she realized Dia wasn't going to hurt her.

"That's twisted," I say.

"The combination of your distaste for the underworld and mastery of the darkest arts—"

"Mastery of what? I'm not a master of anything!"

"You will find that you are. And you will see that the two parts of you, Anne and Gia, make you perfectly suited to execute Dia Voletto. Start with him. He's the easy one," he says. "It will help earn Mephisto's trust. And it will be easy to do without me."

"Wait, wait, *wait*. You want me to destroy Dia...on my own?" I leap to my feet. "Forget this. I'm out! I don't care who I was. I'm someone else now."

He shouts after me, "I'll do my best to return to help you. And Anne, don't forget that your mother is party to this." He had to play that card. The Dead, Angelic Mom Card. "You wouldn't have agreed to become Anne Merchant if we hadn't talked through all of this and you hadn't agreed."

Slowly, I turn to face him again. "To destroy Dia."

"Destroy him first. Build up your courage. And then face the one you're scared of."

"I'm only *afraid* of Mephisto because I got my ass handed to me when I went up against him in Valedictorian Hall!"

"The bravest amongst us is afraid of himself."

"What? Are you, like, quoting someone? God, just talk normal."

"Miss Merchant, you ultimately won against Villicus."

"Barely. And only because of Ben, who's out of the picture now. And let's not forget that I was trying to save myself then, not destroy a devil."

"Imagine if you were to *try* to end the simpler of the two."

After the casual way Dia executed twenty students today, I'm not averse to returning the favor. "Fine. But you'd better have a plan."

"I have a strategy, yes. Many of Dia's servants were once yours. Take them back."

"Get them to serve me?"

"Yes. Start with the lesser demons. Don't begin with the Seven Sinning Sisters, or Dia and Mephisto will see you as a threat."

Finally, decent advice. Crazy, but something I can busy myself with.

"You will find yourself at least as powerful as Dia in little time— because although he has beauty on his side, you have brains."

"Thanks. I think."

"Never underestimate genius! I've seen with my own eyes that genius lasts longer than beauty."

"I'm hardly in the realm of genius."

I'm starting—slowly—to come to terms with this. It's as if I've always known my life would be a short one and my fate something to run from. There's a reason my paintings are never of rainbows and honeybees.

"So I try to get demonic followers, and then you come back, and we, like, somehow, I dunno, battle Dia?"

"That's fine. But I'll need a reason to return," he says. "Dia continually rejects my requests to return here. I know I'll be allowed to return for graduation day when all Guardians are here. Do you think you can re-establish Saligia by then?"

I throw my hands up. "It's my first time re-establishing demonic powers, Teddy. I'll do my best."

"Very well, Gia."

"I'm Anne!"

"Listen, you may not like the idea of being Saligia, Miss Merchant, but that is who you are. And my gut tells me that, once you start exploring Gia, you'll have a hard time wanting to be Anne Merchant again."

I glare up at him. "I'm *Anne*."

A small smile colored gray and black cracks a line through his face. He presses his finger to his lips, reminding me that we must keep all of this on the DL. I wonder for a second why he didn't use the Silencer to erase this conversation. We're not so far from campus that we couldn't be overheard.

"Remember: Many adored you once. Love doesn't die. Nothing dies. It just shape-shifts."

"You're a real poet, Ted."

"And you thought I was just a pretty face."

The sun has set on the longest day of my life, the day in which I lost Ben, lost Molly, and even lost my parents—I am not their creation as much as I am Mephistopheles'. It is also the day I gained something I've never wanted and still don't: a spiritual connection with the underworld.

I leave Teddy in the woods and stagger, in a cold daze, back to the still, gray campus. I pass the boys' dorm, inside of which Ben is preparing for a new life with his old love. I have to numb myself. Immortality is a curse; it would be a relief to die of sadness right now.

I climb the stairs to the second floor of the girls' dorm.

I walk into the bathroom, stumble past a group of sophomore girls who look surprised to see me still here, and turn on the hot water in the shower. Under the scalding rush of water, I strip off my uniform and stand like someone anesthetized. Like the walking dead. Like a girl in a coma.

I am joined by Hiltop. She observes me silently. My "father."

I wrap a towel around my body and leave my uniform behind on the shower floor, under the still-running water, where Hiltop continues to stand.

Molly is asleep when I go to our room.

I sit on the edge of my bed and know I do not need to worry about falling asleep first. Molly will not scream if and when she sees my tail. She heard who I am. What I am.

I get under my covers.

I sleep.

I wake. Molly is gone.

I get ready. I go to my art workshop. My classmates look at me like I'm a spoiled brat, like I have so much life I can afford to throw second chances away. Augusto comments on the amount of time I have been spending under the mentorship of Dia.

The bell rings. I pack my bag.

I walk into the hallway.

Ben is standing in the hallway.

He does not look directly at me. He hands a note to me. He takes care not to touch my fingers.

Garnet joins him. She takes his hand. They walk. Garnet tosses her hair and looks over her shoulder at me. She giggles.

I open the note. I fold it again.

I go to study hall.

Molly looks at me, and I feel like a dog that has had two legs amputated. Like it would be humane to put me down. I sit at the desk in front of Molly.

Mr. Italy tells everyone to be quiet. Fisher T. Italy. Power? To shift reality. Could I make him serve me? If he served me, could I leverage his power to change my new reality back to my old, naive, loved-by-Ben one?

It is a blizzard outside. The windowsills are stacked high with snow.

I unfold Ben's note.

Molly kicks the leg of my chair.

I read Ben's words.

Anne—

Garnet has informed me you are harboring feelings for me, and it is disrupting her work as your teacher. I appreciate your interest, but there is no world in which you and I could be together. Please leave us be.

Ben

I turn the note over. The blank page stares at me. It wants to blind me. I want to let it.

It is good that Ben is gone. If he knew the truth about me, he would be revolted.

I pick up my pencil. I tap the end of it on the paper. The beat is slow. It keeps time with the memories I shared with Ben. Ben behind the village bench. Ben on the cliff, saving me, holding me. Ben in the twinkle lights of Gigi's house, deep in a fantasy.

Maybe I, too, could play pretend for a while. Pretend I'm normal, not a girl with the worst case of inner demons known to mankind.

I stop drumming.

I hold my pencil in both hands.

Molly kicks the leg of my chair again.

I snap the pencil in two.

And, with that, a tsunami-sized wave of relief washes over me. The release of hearing the thin wood and lead snap, even as half my classmates swivel to scowl and even as Mr. Italy stares over the top of his narrow reading glasses at me.

Like I've been holding my breath for a day, I sigh and relax my neck, my shoulders. I just wish I had another pencil to snap. Just one more—no, maybe 100 more—to give me the push I need to cry, which I have yet to do.

I rest my head on my desk. I pull the note closer to me and, with the working half of the pencil, begin sketching Ben and Garnet's intertwined fingers in the top corner. The stroke of my pencil lulls my mind back into my conversation with Teddy last night, back to everything he told me in the stillness of the woods. I know now why I was allowed to step foot in this school. It had nothing to do with my dad's position as a funeral director to the wealthy, although surely that's been a perk for Mephisto. I'm here because I'm one of the bad guys.

Molly kicks my chair again. I jerk my head but don't look at her.

I draw a heart around Ben and Garnet's hands.

I catch a glimpse of my reflection in the window and squint to try to make out Gia, but I see only a wild-haired blonde with her dad's eyes. Surely the reason I was able to see Gia that night in the mirror was because we are more spirit than flesh here, and something—what, I'm not sure—triggered it; I would never see her in California, and I might never have known about my soul's past had I not been thrust into a coma at the hand of my mother.

Will I ever see Gia again?

Will I see her soon?

If I'm more spirit than flesh here, am I more Gia than Anne?

Do the demons here know who I am? Dia knows. Mephisto obviously does. And if the Seven Sinning Sisters served me, surely they've known my secret all along. That's why they wanted to meet me in Dia's office. I told myself they wanted to see the girl who'd outsmarted Mephisto, but they really wanted to see their former leader.

I glance at Harper and Agniezska, who are sitting on the opposite side of the room swapping lip glosses, kissing their compact mirrors, and blotting their lips clean to start again. All this time, I've accused Harper of profiting from her own objectification; I've never let the image of her on her knees before Trey Sedmoney, exchanging sexual favors like they're some sort of currency, leave my mind. And yet she's got nothing on Gia. I started as a succubus. I traded sex for souls.

I close my eyes.

I can't bear the thought.

I can't bear any of this. Especially not if I have to bear it alone.

So I scribble a note on the back of Ben's and, stretching like I'm yawning, drop it on Molly's desk. I listen for the familiar sounds— unfolding, pen scratching, refolding, fake scratch of her leg so she can drop the note and kick it my way—and scoop it up. We spend the rest of study hall feigning deep studying while writing back and forth.

U freaked out by me?

Totes. U r terrifying.

Still mad?

I was never mad at you! U OK?

Meh. U talked 2 Teddy?

Not since I saw him in VH. Hope u don't mind but I read Ben's note. Pretty rough.

I'm over it. Pause not. (Borat)

Why didn't Eve's spell work on u?

U mean cuz I'm obv still in love w/Ben?

Yep. Shouldn't u be over him?

I wanted 2 stay connected 2 him. I want the memories of Ben + me when we were in ... u know. I worded my Q so I'd keep Ben-cheese-ball alert—in my heart.

Because u r a masochist?

Crazy, right?

Certifiable. That heartbreak's gonna hurt.

Well evidently I do my best work when I'm in pain.

U r not a demon goddess, gf.

Do u think all demons r bad?

That's NOT who u r.

What if it is?

Even if it WAS, u don't have to be a bad chick NOW.
Don't u think we all get to choose who we r? Didn't u
come here 4 a fresh start???

I *did* come here for a fresh start. A second chance for me—not for Gia.

Molly said I had a choice. If she's right, then I choose me.

Sorry, Teddy. Sorry, Mom. Sorry, Gia. But I choose Anne Merchant.

And that is how I find myself, that afternoon, back in my old room in Gigi's attic. I am staring down the staircase. Its sharp wooden edges. Its narrow width.

It was at the bottom of these steps that I woke last. Things were different then. If this much has changed in four months, perhaps by the time May rolls around, I'll have forgotten all about Ben and Garnet, Dia and Gia, Teddy, and Molly—and I'll be living it up in California. So I take a deep breath. Close my eyes. And let myself fall. I tumble hard, feeling every wooden corner, every jutting nail, every thick sliver jabbing my skin. I land in a heap at the bottom.

But it's not like it was so many months ago. Nothing happens.

"Damn pentobarbital," I say to the ceiling.

The tears begin. With my hair all over my face, wet with sweat and blood, and splayed out on the landing of a house they're bound to demo any day, I cry. In short sobs, I imagine what it would be like if I'd woken now. Would it be any better? I'd be livin' it up at the ol' Fair Oaks Funeral Home. Spending my weekdays shoegazing as I walk through Menlo-Atherton High—*Go Bears!*—and my weekends nerding out back at the library my mom used to work at. Living in a house with dead people, being ignored by rich high-schoolers, painting morbid drawings in my ample spare time, torturing myself with ideas of Ben and Garnet's date-night activities. My dad would be free of this place, thanks to the arrangement I made so long ago, but then what?

It'd be just like life here.

Except I wouldn't have Molly.

I'd escape my crazy responsibilities and crazier spiritual history. But would I be any better off in my old life? And if I go home, would I stand even the *remotest*, smallest, fleeting-est chance of seeing Ben again? At least here I've got that. I can see Ben in the halls and remind myself that *there was a time when*. I can tell myself that he had to be put under a spell to be separated from me. I can tell myself that I loved him enough to do this for him.

"Waking up is always an option," I tell the emptiness and get to my knees, crawling back up the steps. "I *choose* to stay. At least until Ben's safe."

I hunch on the top step and wrap my coat around myself. If things get awful—if I catch Ben and Garnet kissing or something equally nightmarish—I can always do a thousand swan-dives from this very step until I wake in sunny C-A.

I recall the goals I listed just yesterday as I walked to Dia's office.

One, save Ben.

Two, help my mom by helping Teddy.

Three, get off this godforsaken island.

I glance at the chair Ben sat in so many nights ago. He was soaking wet and stunningly beautiful. I can almost see his glowing silhouette now in the shadows. There's no question in my mind. I need to guarantee that Ben gets the Big V. And I need to use the resources at my disposal to do so.

"Be Saligia," I whisper.

The house shudders with a gust of wind.

I know what I have to do. I know I'll have to start with Pilot, a punk so low ranking Mephisto won't notice his absence from his ranks. I just need to find the right moment to go for it—and hope the slippery slope I'm about to walk doesn't send me flying back to Hell.

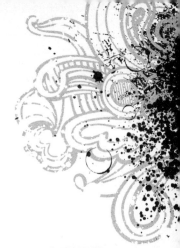

SEMESTER
TWO

seventeen

THE ROAD TO HELL

MOLLY AND I ARE SITTING BEHIND HARPER AND HER NEWEST recruit, a girl named Jasmina, who enrolled at Cania days after Emo Boy and the other Unlucky Twenty were expelled. That was a little over a month ago. All twenty of the empty seats have been filled; it makes you wonder if Dia didn't expel a tenth of the population just to cash in on a bunch of new tuition fees.

The second semester of our junior year starts today, bringing with it A Critical Exploration of the Supernatural in Literature and Society, known in normal schools as English class.

Superbia is our instructor. She elegantly sets stacks of novels on the first table of each row. She doesn't tell us to take one and pass it back; there is little the goddess of pride would deign to do. Harper, a goddess in her own right, waits for Jasmina to hand a copy of Oscar Wilde's *The Picture of Dorian Gray* to her and lets her do the work of passing the remaining four hardcovers back to us. Because, like Superbia, Harper doesn't do grunt work.

Superbia stands, looking down her nose at us, at the front of the classroom. Her hair is pinned in a bun high on her head. She makes everything look small and futile. Especially her cowering students.

"Morality. Immorality. Meaning," Superbia says. Her commanding voice silences us. "Mortality. Immortality. *Art*," she adds, raising a copy of *The Picture of Dorian Gray*.

She flips open the book to exactly the page she wants, and as everyone scrambles to find where she is, she reads: "We are punished for our refusals. Every impulse that we strive to strangle broods in the mind and poisons us." She glances up at us, her violet eyes piercing, before continuing: "Resist it, and your soul grows sick with longing for the things it has forbidden itself."

She places the book down.

You can feel a question coming.

The whole room tenses.

"The movement that Mr. Wilde, through Lord Henry, was referring to here," Superbia begins, eying us. "What is it?"

I glance around as, one by one, my classmates drop their heads, pretend to read or, in Molly's case, simply wait for someone else to answer.

I raise my hand.

"Miss Merchant," Superbia says. She drags out the s and snaps her teeth together on the t. To her, my name is just a cover for my darker identity, the way *Superbia* is just a cover for *pride*.

"He was referring to aestheticism," I say.

"Which is what?"

Dia and I discussed the most popular aesthetes, Whistler and Rossetti, in our first session. Spending all those Saturdays with him, even if I've skipped them since the Scrutiny, drove into my head his love for beauty and his own position as an aesthete.

"It's a movement that holds that there's no purpose for art outside of creating or representing beauty," I say. "Art for art's sake."

"Very good. Thank you, Miss Merchant."

She slowly paces the front of the room.

Molly writes on the top of her page, *Smarty pants*. I add a smiley face under it.

"Oscar Wilde is perhaps the best-known aesthete of his time in the literary world," Superbia says, "though the debate continues as to whether he was promoting or condemning the intensity and, dare I say, meaningless gluttony in the novel you'll read, dissect, and know by heart before the end of this term."

When Superbia turns to write on the board, Harper scowls over her shoulder at me. Jasmina, realizing she must support her great leader, copies her. Molly rubs her cheek with her middle finger until they get the picture.

"Now what," Superbia turns back to us, "might be problematic about pegging Mr. Wilde as an aesthete?"

When no one else raises their hand, Jasmina inches hers up. Like she's scared Harper might flip out on her for having a brain. Superbia nods for Jasmina to speak.

"Well, Wilde's the one that said, 'To define is to limit,' right?"

"In this very book. Chapter seventeen. To define is to limit," Superbia says as pages flip. It occurs to me that I've heard that line before. Must be popular. "Who says it?"

Without having read the book, it's almost impossible to know. Quotations in this scene are sparsely attributed, and the scene goes on forever. I don't know who says that line—either this Lord Henry dude, or this Gladys chick, or Dorian Gray himself. I grimace at Molly, and she shrugs.

"Nobody knows?" Superbia asks.

Everyone's madly skimming the lines.

"It's Dorian!" Harper calls out at last.

"Try Lord Henry." Superbia tsks at Harper. "Dorian rarely says anything interesting; he tends to quote others. Dorian is beauty; he is never wit. His existence both challenges and *is* the foundation of aestheticism." I feel like she's speaking directly to me when she adds, "Any artist would be wise to steer clear of Dorian."

I can't help but wonder if she's talking about Dia, who's as beautiful as Wilde might have imagined Dorian to be. Is she trying to warn me to stay away from him? From somebody, certainly. But whom?

For the rest of the hour, Superbia reads snippets of the book and asks questions few dare to answer. Harper tries to define art, at Superbia's request, but fails so miserably Superbia bans her from speaking again. By the time class lets out, I understand that this is the story of a beautiful dude named Dorian Gray who trades his soul for eternal youth and beauty and winds up trapped in a painting that—spoiler alert—gets destroyed, killing him. I'm pleasantly surprised to know we're going to be discussing art. It'll be a nice reprieve from what these next few weeks have in store for me.

Life as I know it is about to change.

It has to.

Even if I don't want to think about doing what Teddy said about getting demons to follow me somehow, I can't put it off any longer.

And, if Ben's going to win the Big V this May, I need to get moving on my plan. Stat.

"Everything okay?" Molly asks as we leave class.

"Peachy keen."

Molly can't know what I'm plotting. She'd never speak to me again.

That Friday afternoon, as drips of melting icicles rain down on campus, I put my plan in action. I find Pilot kicking back espressos in the cafeteria after school. He's looking about as pissed as one punk can look. But it gets even worse when he spies me. His face scrunches up into a little knot.

"You've missed more of our meetings than I can count," he snaps.

"Um, lest you forget, you totally bailed on me the second the Scrutiny gave me an out." I pull out a chair. "You realized you couldn't use me anymore, and you took off. And then when I won!"

"Hi, my name's Pilot Stone. I'm selfish," he growls. "Nice to meet you."

"Whatever. I'm over it. Actually, that's why I'm here. To help you. And me."

"That'll be the day."

"I'm serious."

"Seriously playing me."

"You can keep going like this," I tell him, "but you're wasting precious time."

Scoffing, he heads off to make a second espresso, looking over his shoulder at me every so often, like he's not sure if I'm kidding or not. Like he's indecisive. There's no way he's indecisive; I'm his only hope. And he's not demon enough yet to have abandoned all hope. That said, he's pretty angry. He starts rattling off his frustrations with me—and he's got a lot of them—and the rumors before he's even back at our table. I strain to hear the end of his tirade.

"They're saying that, after the Scrutiny, Ben admitted he'd never been into you, like who didn't see that coming, and he dropped that on you just as you were about to give him your second life."

"Who's saying that?"

"Only everyone. And, instead of asking for something that would help *you*, jealous little chick you are, you asked Dia to deform

Ben and Garnet's babies." He shoves the demitasse into my hands. "Here. You like coffee, and I've spent so many afternoons here wait- ing for you, I've learned to make it like a prize barista."

I take the tiny cup and saucer.

"Well, the rumor mill's turning out some real crap." I watch Pilot sit again. "People actually believe Ben dumped me just as I was about to save his life—because *that* would be super-smart of him— and my oh-so brilliant response was to . . . curse his future kids?"

"It's not true?"

I roll my eyes.

"Likely story, Merchant. So now Ben's back with Garnet, where he belongs," he says, "and Little Miss Artsy-Fartsy realizes she's pissed away her *Get Out of Jail Free* card on the boy who broke her heart. And comes crawling back to me. Is that it?" He watches me sip my espresso. "And now you wanna get serious about the Big V so you don't have to watch them anymore, right?"

His assumptions are starting to irritate me. So I cut to the chase.

"Pi, I know who I am."

"You know you're a loser death chick who got her ass dumped."

"No." I try to stare into his head, as if that might help him focus. "I know who I am. Who I was."

We sit in silence. He blinks.

"I was Gia. Miss Saligia. The underworld goddess."

Wheezing through his teeth, like he's torn between smiling and wondering if he's got even more to worry about now, Pilot eyes me up. I swirl the black liquid through its perfectly brown crema in the porcelain demitasse. He's taking a while to process this.

"Look, before you start making BS jokes," I begin.

He leans in, closer this time, conspiratorially. "Anne, as much as I want out of the underworld, I'm not a moron. I know my rank here. And I know you've got—" he lowers his voice until it's little more than a rumble. "Anne, you've still got a lot of demons who dig you around this place. And in other places. You saw how Invidia bitched me out when I blinked wrong at you. I'm not gonna talk smack."

I was hoping to hear how the demons feel about me. But Pilot doesn't need to know that. I act stupid so he'll keep talking.

"Are you saying demons here know who I used to be?" I ask him.

"Not who you were. Who you are."

"But I'm not her."

"Yes, you are. You just don't have any servants. I mean, Harper has more followers than you do."

I was thinking the same thing. Dia said it himself: Trey Sedmoney worships Harper. And then there's the Model UN from Hell—slaves if I ever saw them.

"The people who know Anne Merchant think she's the girl in a coma," Pilot continues. "The people who know Miss Saligia think she's on, like, a vacation. Both sides are waiting for you to come back. Wake up. Be your old self again. Question for you: Which side will you choose?"

I focus on the warmth of the cup against my fingertips.

He sips his coffee, and I sip mine.

"You should change your PT," he says at last. "Embrace who you were. Use it. You were a succubus in the beginning, and then you led thousands of them."

"What would I do with a different PT? Bat my eyelashes and host a kissing booth…on the off chance that Dia or Hiltop agree to let me, with my history, leave this island? You honestly think that's the best plan? You think I'm going anywhere the old-fashioned way?"

"Well, if you're not gonna win it," he says, "then why are we even talking?"

"I'm wondering the same thing." I shake my head, disappointed in him. "I would've thought you'd have something more creative worked out by now, Stone. Instead, you spent the last month perfecting espresso."

He rests his chin on his fist and goes quiet for a bit. Thinking, thinking.

"You *had* powers and legions and all that amazing stuff—stuff I'd sell my soul for, if it was worth anything," he says. "Do you have any powers now?"

"Only the power to drive people away from me."

"Depending on the person, that can be useful."

"Ha."

He looks caught between jumping ship and taking the wheel. I can only wait for him to come up with the idea I need him to. I can't suggest it or he might not go for it—but if he starts thinking what I'm thinking, this could get interesting fast.

"What if…?" Pilot begins. He's tapping his lip and looking at Vale Tuefurre, a cafeteria lady. I can almost hear the wheels turning in his head. At once, his gaze hops back to me. "I've got an idea."

"I thought you might."

"I can help you."

"How?"

"I could serve you. That would immediately give you a boost of underworld cred."

Bingo.

"But no powers," I remind him. "You don't have any. You're a punk."

"Thanks for the reminder."

"Mephisto wouldn't notice you've left him to serve me?"

"I'm a punk, like you said. I barely register. And with whatever island Teddy finds for him, he'll have bigger things on the go for the next few months."

"If you barely register," I counter, "how could you help me?"

Thinking fast, he darts to the cutlery stand, where he grabs a steak knife. He runs back and, with a single swift motion, raises the knife until it's just above my ear. A flash of him torturing me the way Dia tortured Eve and Kate makes me recoil. I fall off my chair with a cry. But he straddles me and, in one stroke, swipes at my head.

I squeeze my eyes shut, squeal, and wait for pain.

But there is no pain. Wet blood doesn't flood my cheek or ooze into my mouth.

I open my eyes to find Pilot holding a large chunk of my hair; blonde strands glisten in his fist. I feel around my head and find a good inch-wide lock missing.

"My hair!"

"Gia's calling card was her hair. It was her thing. Hey, maybe that's why you've got such crazy-ass hair."

"What're you doing with my hair?"

"I'll help you rebuild your army," he says, tucking my lock of hair into his pocket. "I bunk with a shit-ton of demons that could serve you again, if they knew Saligia was seriously back. I'd have to tell them in secret. Can't let Dia or Mephisto hear."

I consider it with wide, innocent eyes, as if this entire idea isn't something I've been trying to steer the conversation toward.

"If punks, demons, 'n' shizzle are gonna serve you," he says, "they're gonna need a token from you. Hence the hair. I'll get my dad to send a butt-load of lockets pronto. We'll clip your hair in the lockets, give 'em out to newbies, and build you up."

I didn't know about the hair, but everything else about this meeting is going pretty perfectly. It took me a month to nail down the starting point of my plan: get Pilot to serve me, and then get him to recruit for me. Of course, I know he won't do it without getting something in return. But I think I might be able to give him what he wants. I'm just waiting for him to get to that part of the conversation.

"You'll help bring, um, your *kind* on board?"

"My kind and better. I'll put the word out! I'll be your mother-effing right-hand punk. Your recruiter."

"In exchange for?"

He beams, almost looking as genuine as he did when we first met. "The ultimate, Anne-a-bam. I want to live again."

"You want me to…give you life?"

"Let's circumvent the Big V. We'll build you a big army with the right recruits to give you the powers to hand out your own version of the Big V."

"Do you know who gives out life?" I ask him. I've got a list filled with the powers of the demons on staff here, but none of them seem in control of vivification.

"No, but we'll figure that out." Then something dawns on him. "Oh, shit, you're not doing all this just so you'll be able to, like, put a spell on Ben so he'll fall for you?"

"After cursing his kids?"

"I totally hate the dude, but he looks really happy with Garnet. He always looked so tortured around you."

"I don't want to break up Ben and Garnet," I promise.

But inside I'm smiling. I can almost feel my heart grow inside my chest. Pilot's so wrong about Ben. My hard-to-reach Ben, tormented by demons far different from the Cania variety. For the first time in a long while, my soul feels lightened. Ben was his deep-as-the-Atlantic self with me; with Garnet, he's just playing the game his life depends on. Exactly as I'd hoped he would.

But I know better than anyone that hope isn't enough.

Hoping Ben will win isn't going to guarantee that he will. And I need a *guarantee*. I need to know that there's no one else in the running. With Pilot helping me rebuild the strength of Gia, I'm going to do exactly that—even if a few demons have to get hurt in the process.

And so begins part one: Operation Save Ben.

I have a follower now. Soon, I'll have more. With their allegiance, I'll be able to remove obstacles from Ben's path to the Big V. When that's all done, I'll be strong enough to help Teddy destroy Dia.

"Wait," I say to Pilot. "How will you convince the others that I'm, as you say, seriously back?"

"They know you're Gia. They just need to see something from you. Put on a bit of a show. Get them talking about you."

"Show them I'm her."

"*Wow* them. And," he lowers his voice as a sophomore passes our table, "humans can serve Gia, too. Human witches serve demon witches all the time. Is there anyone you might be able to coerce into serving you? In exchange for, say, the same thing you're giving me?" He taps his lip, thinking. "Someone capable of venturing to the dark side."

"Someone to tiptoe through Hell with me? A Virgil to my Dante?"

He stares at me. "Literary references? Really?"

I stand to leave. I know exactly whom to ask—the only person who's proven to me she's capable of doing anything to get what she wants, and the only person here with followers of her own.

I move to shake Pilot's hand. But, with a quick look to be sure no one's watching, he bows instead.

And my heart thumps faster.

The heart I share with Gia, a goddess regaining her followers one by one, thumps at double time.

eighteen

GOOD INTENTIONS

HARPER IS CLAPPING CHALK BRUSHES TOGETHER IN THE empty parking lot when I sneak up behind her and give her a scare: I flick her ponytail, and she jumps. She nearly punches me as she whirls, but I duck.

"You!" she cries. "Comin' up on me like an outhouse breeze. What's the matter with you?"

"I've got a proposition for you."

She rolls her eyes. I'm sure she's not only heard that before but said it herself. And it never comes to any good.

"A real one," I tell her.

"You planning to turn into a scary devil child on me again? Steal my soul this time?"

"No, but I want to talk to you about that night. Sort of."

She smacks the brushes together.

"Look, I know you don't trust me," I say, "but I didn't kill Gigi. She committed suicide. And I wouldn't have ended Pilot's second life if it hadn't come down to me and him that night."

"I ain't judging."

"Sure you aren't. Listen, you once said we should both sleep with one eye open. Remember?"

She drops the brushes in a bucket. Stares me straight in the eyes. And starts screaming bloody murder.

I muzzle her with my hand, but she pushes my arm away and screams for help even louder. So I grab her by the hair—it's the best I can think of—and start tugging and shoving her toward the path leading up to the cliff-top. Her screams turn to short, choppy cries for me to let go of her. I shove her against the hill's steep incline. She shouts as she stumbles. I can't see any other option, so I gently—okay, a tad more than *gently*—butt the back of her head against the hillside. She growls at me but quiets down.

Gripping her chin, I get close enough to her face that our noses touch.

"I'm not going to hurt you," I say.

"You're going to *wish* you'd *killed* me. Let me go."

"Harper, you saw who I am. You and I both know you're powerless to me." With her pinned, I glance over my shoulder, but no one's here, no one came when Harper cried. Of course they didn't. Caring about others isn't the Cania way. "But you're not totally powerless."

She's breathing heavily. Her straight, white teeth are clenched like a growling dog's.

"Calm down," I say. "If you want to live again, I can help."

"You'd better sleep with one eye open now, Murdering Merchant!"

"You've done worse. Admit it." I wait for her to say something; she blinks. "The real reason you don't like me is because I'm still alive."

"That's just one item on a long list."

"I'm about to give you a chance to live, too. If you trust me."

"I'd be a damn fool."

"No, you'd be free."

Slowly, I release her chin and lift myself away from her. She shakes her hair until it's straight again and pushes my hand away when I try to help her get upright.

"Trust *you*?" she snaps as she dusts her uniform off. "In what world?"

Her glare doesn't leave me, and mine doesn't leave her. But she doesn't scream. And she walks when I do. We watch each other closely as she follows me into the Rex Paimonde building, to our workshop. No one's here. I close the door behind us.

"Spill it, Merchant. How can you help me? And why the hell would either one of us agree to help the other?"

I start at the beginning. My beginning as Miss Saligia, and my incarnation as Anne Merchant. She listens impatiently, more patiently, solemnly, and then with wide eyes. I tell her everything I need to, leaving out only the details that will hurt others and, as always, avoiding any mention of destroying Dia in order to ultimately destroy Mephisto. Teddy doesn't even come up. Harper doesn't need to know the whole truth; she just needs to know enough to trust me. And join me.

"So Hiltop's actually Villicus, and Villicus was actually Mephistopheles, and Dia's from Hell, too, and our teachers are the creators of sin?" she asks. "I knew some sicko-type stuff was up 'round here, but I didn't know the place was crooked as a barrel of fish hooks."

"No one knows, although I think some have a hunch. I was sworn to secrecy. But, well…"

"You've got Hell's dust on your boots, Merchant. If anyone's allowed to break an oath, it's you." She leans back. "But what's all this got to do with me and the Big V?"

"I'm not talking about the Big V. I'm talking about a second life sooner than next May. You have followers," I explain. "Trey Sedmoney worships you. And then you've got your, um, friends."

"I know you call us the Model UN from Hell."

"In all fairness, Pilot taught me that."

"Alls I know is you must need my help awful *ba-a-ad* to come nosin' around me. So what's up your sleeve?"

I hand her one of my mom's glued-together barrettes. She recognizes it. Months ago, she snapped it in two.

"*Ew*, there's hair in this," she says as she holds it far from her, between two pinching fingernails.

"That's my hair."

"Grody." She hands it back to me.

I don't take it. "I need you to serve me, Harper."

She laughs. "You're about two sandwiches short of a picnic, Merchant."

"Look, Gia was powerful. Super-powerful."

"I ain't surprised you're a monster underneath."

"If I can build up the fanbase she once had," I continue, "I can gain the power Dia and Villicus have. I can attract demons with the power to vivify, and we can give you—and your whole clan, if you want—what you've been looking for."

"*Life*," she says in a breath. She's looking at the barrette.

"Life off this island. But I need you to help me get started. I need you to serve me and grow your own fanbase, which will, in turn, serve me by serving you. Get it?"

"Are you seriously asking if *I* get how hierarchy works? I invented it." She turns the barrette over. And eyes me carefully in the orange glow of the setting sun through the windows. "Prove it."

"Sorry?" I say.

"Prove. It."

"You saw Gia with your own two eyes. What more proof do you need?"

"Wait, am I the first soul that'd be serving you?"

"No, Pilot's on board, too. He's also going to get a new life out of helping me."

"Then bring him to me right now. He can tell me it's all possible. And that'll prove it."

"Fine. We'll go to the staff quarters."

"Uh-uh." She wags her finger in my face. "If you've got this power, if you're this big shot in a dummy's body, then bring him to me now. He can tell me in person, right here. Or, what, can't you even communicate with your own servants telepathically?"

"That's not how it works."

"Why not? Because you're lying like a sidewalk? I knew it!"

"I'm not lying. I just...don't know."

"You're slippery as a pocketful of pudding. What a whopper."

No matter how I beg and try to convince her, I can't get Harper to listen. She shoves my barrette at me and disappears out the doorway, muttering as she goes. If I'd just been able to summon Gia somehow, I might've been able to call Pilot like Harper said.

I know now I'm never going to be able to do this if I can't start proving who's under my skin. So that night, while Molly sleeps, I lie in bed and try to recreate the scenario in which Gia last appeared to me. I'd gone to sleep thinking of Ben, hoping to see him in my dreams—but I hadn't dreamt of him at all. It was Dia in my dreams. Dia and me. In a compromising position.

Dia, the ex-lover of the woman I once was, awakened her.

"Oh, damn," I groan, knowing what I've gotta do.

CRECO

SATURDAY MORNING FINDS me at Dia's office door for a meeting I've avoided as long as I've known about my inner demon's history with him. But he's not here. He's left a note taped to his door, as if he knew I was coming—that, or he tapes the same note to his door every Saturday:

Miss Merchant, I'm at my house. Come on over.

Double damn! His house. His private home. The former home of Ben and Dr. Zin. I make my way down the island to his mansion. The last time I was here, I snuck in through the back window with Molly. I'm at least as anxious now as I was then, and I'm not even breaking in.

"Do this for Ben," I coach myself. "Do it for Mom. You can't help either of them if you don't wake up Saligia."

I ring the bell. No one answers. I try again.

Then, amid the sound of melting ice trickling from the gutters into basins, I hear footsteps around the side of the house, just beyond the porte cochere. Footsteps crunching through the hard shell of snow. I look to my right just as Harper, Agniezska, Plum, and Jasmina—all of whom must have been inside Dia's only moments ago and snuck out the back when I rang the bell—stop dead and, in unison, look at me. The girls stack up behind Harper like they're a living version of dominos.

The girls clutch most of their clothes to their chests. You don't need to look closer to know what they've been up to. The messiness of their normally stick-straight hair. Their matching lacy undergarments: garters and fishnets. It's a no-brainer for four girls who share the same PT: to use their desirability to win.

"We've tuckered him out," Plum tells me proudly. Harper pretends to inspect the snow at her boots. "So good luck."

"Well, I don't do sloppy seconds."

"*Seconds?* More like *twentieths*, Murdering Merchant."

Everyone but Harper breaks into giggles.

"She's paintin' a picture of him, you numbskulls, not screwin' him," Harper says, cutting through their laughter. She marches up to the road, stomping the snow. "Honestly, y'all get me so *agger-vated*."

"Hey, Harper!" I shout. Her shoulders jerk, but she doesn't turn back. "Great call choosing this option instead of mine. Genius decision. Good luck with the whole Big V thing, if Plum doesn't beat you to it."

I ring the bell again. I'd feel kinda bad for Harper if I wasn't jealous of the souls she's got under her command. Lucky bitch. How long is it going to take for Pilot to get *me* some followers?

The door swings open. Dia is sans shirt. "Anne!"

I frown as I look him up and down. "I can come back another time."

"Hang on."

He darts away. Moments later, he slides back into view wearing a tuxedo shirt and grinning. He is still far too casually dressed—light pants that look like they're about to fall off his narrow hips, most of the buttons undone on his shirt, his sleeves rolled up to reveal his tattoos, as always. I see *Dia + Gia* on his arm; it's a reminder that I *need* to be here right now.

"Better?" he asks me.

"Is there a reason you wanted to meet at your house instead of your office today, Mr. Voletto?"

"I got tired of waiting in my office every weekend. Now come in, come in. Superbia and her crew have gone home for the weekend, so it's just us."

"They live with you?"

He smiles. "We all have our own bedrooms."

I step inside, silently marveling at how different it feels compared to when Ben lived here. Comparing now and then will torture me, so I try not to. As I tug off my boots, Dia hangs my coat, takes my bag, and gestures for me to follow him.

"You've been avoiding me," he says. He's astute. "If I didn't know better, I'd think you wanted me to chase you."

"Chasing me and luring me to your house are two different things."

He laughs. "We can be more comfortable here. No nasty secretaries knocking on the door every ten seconds. Come, come. Are you thirsty? I'm chilling a pinot grigio."

"Even if I wasn't underage, it's ten in the morning."

"I can add OJ."

The house smells like body heat. Plum's comment about *twentieths* sticks in my head as I leave the marble foyer, walk through a hall lined in actual fur—which must be one of Dia's "upgrades"—and find myself in the library Molly and I once broke into. But it, like the hallway, has been transformed. Most of the books are gone, and erotic statues have taken their places on the shelves, with undermount lights drawing the eye to them.

He's holding a bottle of wine, two glasses, and a corkscrew when he joins me in the library.

"So why do you stay here on the weekends?" I ask him. "Don't you want to go back to the underworld?"

"Do you think I want to go back there?" He pops the cork. "Downstairs has its charms, but this is where beauty lives. Little wonder the heavens have kept this place so greedily for themselves. You forget how lovely this world is until you return to it. But when you do,"—he smiles wistfully—"you can forgive a soul for choosing life here."

Oh, God, is he talking about Saligia? The way he's looking at me, there can be no denying it. But he doesn't know I know. The last time I spoke with him, I had no clue about Saligia, a fact that seemed to stun and disappoint him.

"How long will you stay?" I ask with a choked voice.

"How long would you like me to?"

If he only knew my and Teddy's plan.

"I'm asking because, if Wormwood Island is Mephisto's now, why hasn't he sent you home?"

"You honestly think I was *sent* here? I chose to come. I've told you that."

I can't believe Mephisto would just let him stay. But perhaps it's as Ben said months ago; perhaps Mephisto wants Dia to babysit us while he works out a larger world-domination plan.

He pours a glass. "Do you want to know why I chose this life?"

Fearing he's about to tell me about my past as Saligia and our connection in the underworld, I wuss out. I know I came here so he'd help me awaken Saligia. But now that that's actually an option, I'm not sure I can handle it.

"I actually don't," I say and, to take the edge off, accept a glass of wine from him, "because I'd like to keep your intentions a mystery. It might make for a better painting."

"Ah, yes, the matter of the portrait."

"But there is something I'd like to know."

"Your wish is my command."

"Do you remember the...lust challenge? In the Scrutiny?"

"I do."

"Were you aware it was happening?"

He sets his glass down and nods. "Shall we recreate it?"

Eventually we might have to, if that's what it takes to wake Saligia. But not yet.

"I was actually just wondering about what you said," I stammer, "about not being able to 'reveal anything' to me about a superior devil. I assume you meant Mephisto."

"Yes?"

"Well, what can't you reveal about him?"

He laughs. "Why, Anne, how could I answer that? I can't reveal it. That's the whole point."

"But there's something to reveal?"

"Isn't there always?"

"Something with Mephisto? Is it why I'm here?"

"You tell me why you're here."

I sit before the easel he's put out for me. He's reorganized the library to look like the artist's studio he set up for me in his office. The leather chaise, the white drop-sheets, the easel and stool, even the champagne stand filled with warm water. He sits across from me, watching me with his too dark, too large eyes. His irises are dark purple and big, as if his eyes are all pupil.

The better to see you with, I think.

His smile is too broad, and his lips are too full.

The better to eat you with.

I can't help but look at him now and see someone buried deeper inside. Someone my soul once loved, even if I have no conscious recollection of our relationship. There's definitely a connection.

"I'd like to present the portrait to the whole school on graduation day, which will be the opening day of Cania College," he tells me. "If we work exceptionally hard between now and then, we just might meet that deadline."

"Great. But before we begin," I say, taking a deep breath and hoping this all works as I need it to, "you took a sketch of mine a few months ago."

He thinks about it. Then he flips through a large hard-cover scrapbook and pulls one out. "This?"

My breath catches when I see that the sketch is not of Saligia; it's my old sketch of Ben in his casket. His beautiful eyes are closed—I had no idea then how lovely they could be—and his face is peaceful in a seemingly endless sleep. I take a second to collect myself and, feeling protective of the ties that were only severed for Ben, roll the sketch up. I tuck it into my bag. That one's going in the vault.

"Where did you get that?" I ask.

"Library. Top floor."

For a half second, joy rushes like heroin through my veins. Joy at the possibility that Dia found this sketch recently, which could only mean that Ben had brought it into the library, which could possibly mean that he's been thinking of me in spite of Kate and Eve's curses.

No sooner has joy raced through my system than a dull surge of dread replaces it. Ben shouldn't be thinking of me. He needs to be with Garnet so he'll win the Big V. And I need to help him win it, even if it means playing dirty—because, for everything I've promised Pilot and Harper, I'm not sure I can actually give anyone a new life. Pilot and Harper don't need to know that; they just need to hope.

"When?"

"Dunno." He shrugs. "Maybe around Christmas."

Relief is the final drug to sweep into and out of my system. He found the sketch when Ben and I were still together.

"I was actually asking about the other sketch," I say. "The one of Miss Saligia."

"You know her name?" He tilts his head. "How much do you know?"

"That's the thing around here. Just when I think I know something, I find out there are about a thousand other secrets hidden behind the first one."

"So you know you're...?"

"I know that, in another life, I was Gia. The girl you used to... date."

A delicious smile spreads across his face. Oh, I know why I dated him once. It's never been a question of why anyone would be attracted to Dia. It's only been a question of why I decided to give up everything to leave him and the underworld, and that question has been, thus far, not fully answered. Teddy said Gia wanted to kill Dia, but surely there had to be an easier way than reincarnating as some human chick.

"So you know why I chose this life, too," he says.

Wait, he's here for *me*?

"You are Gia even now." He pulls up another stool and sits across from me. I lean away. "I see her in everything you do. In the way you move like you're gliding across a dance floor. In the way your hair can't be tamed. In the shape of your beautiful curves. You're back, aren't you?"

"Are you talking to me...or to Gia?"

"When you left, Gia, I felt like my soul departed with you."

His gaze pushes into my chest, making my heart quicken. But it doesn't feel like it did with Ben; I still lose focus and break out in a cold sweat when I glimpse Ben on campus. That's not this. This quickening heartbeat can only be Gia awakening. Sticking with this plan is harder than it looks. So much energy is whirling inside my skin, behind my eyes, through my veins.

"So you never really liked Ben, is that it?" he asks. "Did you miss me, Gia?"

"You're the one who said Ben and I were poorly matched."

"I didn't want him in your life. And that worked out."

"Whatever. I hope he and Garnet enjoy their last months of life together."

"So you don't think he'll win the Big V?" he asks. When I shrug, he adds, "From what I hear, Garnet's concerned that he's so adamantly opposed to you. Evidently he gets angry whenever she mentions you."

"Why the hell would she mention me?"

"To test him, obviously."

I swirl a brush on my palm to loosen the bristles. Acting natural. Being natural. Not snooping. Not fishing for details. Not trying to figure out how I can change Garnet's mind so she feels totally secure in Ben's attraction to her. If Garnet doesn't trust Ben's love for her, she won't fight for him the way I need her to.

I need Garnet to trust Ben.

I need to make her forget Ben and I were ever together.

"Perhaps I'll make the feats of strength harder than ever," he says. "That should guarantee Ben won't make it onto my short list. If destroying Ben will make you happy, I'll do it."

Oh, crap. "What feats of strength?"

"I've got about twenty seniors on my short list, and I seriously don't know who's got the chops to win. So I want to use some challenges to whittle the list down. Smart, right?"

"Smart."

Smart? Not smart at all! Now Ben has to endure feats of strength? Like there's not enough standing between him and life.

"You know Ben well enough," Dia says. "What is a feat of strength he couldn't possibly overcome?"

I tap the brush handle to my lips. "Reading," I lie. "He's a terrible reader."

"Oh, Gia, you haven't lost your edge."

"That's not my name."

"Miss *Saligia*."

He stands. His thighs press against my leg.

Just as I'm about to resist, I remind myself that *this is the point*. This is why I'm here. I need Dia to wake Gia up. If I can just think of Dia touching me the way I think of throwing myself down the stairs—an unpleasant means to a necessary end—then I can get through this. Not that he's hard to take, visually. Not that his touch isn't completely…well, it's little wonder Luxuria made him the object of my lust.

He takes my hand, wrestles the brush from it, and pulls it flat against his chest, just under the opening of his shirt.

I can feel his heartbeat. He has a heartbeat. I wasn't sure.

"Look at me, Gia," he says.

My head feels light, like it's filled with cotton. Aches have started coursing through my legs. My arms tingle. And a heat is rising in my chest, a fullness that makes my breath heavy. It's working. It's going to happen.

"Gia," he insists, "look at me."

"Wait."

"Miss Saligia, my love, I know you're in there. I need to see you. I need to talk to you."

He lifts my other hand to his mouth, kisses my palm. Our eyes meet. His breath is as heavy as mine.

"Good," he says. "Yes. A little of Anne. A lot of Gia."

I refuse to tear myself away. Because it's working. I let my hands roam his chest and up his neck, over his jaw, to his partly open, waiting mouth. He lightly bites the tip of my finger.

Something's about to happen. The thing I wanted to happen.

"Show yourself to me, sweet Saligia."

I can feel her rising under my skin, tightening everything. I can feel her like I never have before. But I never expected her to feel so...hostile.

"Gia, come back to me."

Everything goes dark until, all at once, a cyclone of color whips around me. It sends my head into swirls. It's just color, and it's just light, I tell myself. He groans. His sound triggers a reaction in my body that I've long been turned away from, the reaction Ben forced me to quash. He bites harder on my finger. Just as Teddy hinted: agony is an aphrodisiac.

He presses my hand to his face and pulls me to standing. "Make me feel it."

With that, the whirlwind of light explodes like a star, bringing darkness like a black hole.

I have no idea what happens. But something does. Instantly. And I find myself standing in a room that is quaking. In darkness that is slow to relight. In the aftermath of the fierce awakening of Miss Saligia.

nineteen

GIA

THE WALLS ARE SHAKING, CONFLATING, AND I AM STANDING in the old Zin library with my hand still out, my arm straight as an arrow. I am standing in an eddy of broken easels, shredded canvas, sprayed paint, bent champagne stands, tattered drop cloths. I am vibrating with the power I once possessed and have just made real again. And I am looking at Dia, who is lying in a heap at the opposite end of the room.

I pushed him there. I thrust him away.

With strength greater than any I've ever felt.

Turning in terror—no, in heart-thumping anticipation—I see Gia in the reflection of the pulsating windowpane behind me. She is looking over her shoulder, looking at me just as I am looking at her. At her tempestuous hair. At the tattered school uniform that clings for life to her ample form. And at the silvery, spectacular tail that swivels up and dances toward me; I reach for it, and it hurries into the curve of my hand. Like Skippy used to rush at Gigi. Like my own little pet.

"Velvety," I breathe as I stroke my tail.

A dull itch runs over her back—my back—and I have only thought of taking my school blazer off when my tail does the job for me, pulling my collar back and down, sliding the jacket off.

I expect to see two of them. But I see only one.

"*A wing,*" I breathe.

210

Though unpaired, this wing unfurls spectacularly. It is eight feet wide and beautifully detailed. It could be painted by beams of light that curve and radiate shimmers like sunlight in the reflection of a forest pool. As I breathe, it rises, flits, falls, and rises again over my right arm. Azure blue feathers ripple through it. Ribbons of silver glimmer in it.

"Told you," Dia groans. "Dia and Gia. Forever."

He is a distant profile on the windowpane. His clothes are torn, and he is grinning through a trickle of blood as he tries to get to his feet again.

Trails of white light glide high above as the chandelier, which was swinging wildly, slows to a sway in the middle of the ceiling, from which it has dropped by at least ten feet.

"More spirit than flesh," I utter.

I drink up the reflection of the woman I once was, the woman I could be. She is all things exaggerated. Her physical presence is too overpowering. Her curves are too sexy. The pierce of her fiery violet-colored stare is too stabbing. Her violent anger, directed at Dia, was too furious.

And, as I quietly observe her—marvel at her and eventually condemn her for being, in fact, a demon—Gia vanishes in a soft whirl of purple sparkle, leaving me staring at the void she's left. I've never been a dainty girl, but I suddenly feel small, deflated, frail. I long to see the majestic wing again, to see its pair; I long to hold my velvety tail. Her power is undeniable.

Dia is tiptoeing through the tangled chaos toward me.

Quickly, I mentally note the circumstances of her awakening so I can try to reproduce it later. I touched him, and he touched me, and he said that he wanted to see her and he wanted her to make him *feel it*—that classic line of his. But she didn't waken gently; she exploded into the room. She shoved him as far away as she could. It's as if she came not to love him but to fight him. As if the story of *Dia + Gia Forever* is a demon's lie.

So then it's true what Teddy said. Gia wants to destroy Dia.

"Why does she hate you?" I utter, still not looking away from the window, still hoping she'll reappear.

"That's just the way you are. You're a tease, and you know I like to play rough."

But it didn't feel like that at all. In the brief moment in which I was one part Gia again, I felt her emotions, and they hardly endeared him to me.

"She's mad at you."

"I'd love her to return," he says and turns my chin to look at him, "but I hate the idea of you leaving. I love seeing you, Anne."

I follow his gaze down. The buttons of my blouse and cardigan popped off when Gia appeared. I clutch my top closed.

"I'm going to Gigi's. I know where she left a bunch of her old sweaters."

Dia, still dazed by the reappearance of the underworld goddess he once loved, instead sends me to a storage room in the north wing of the house.

"The Zins left a bunch of stuff here. Surely you can find something suitable," he says. "Head upstairs, take a left, follow the hall to the end. I'll be waiting down here for you."

"I should probably just go." I got what I came for. Sort of.

"Anne, this painting won't paint itself."

So I dash up the curved staircase and drift left. And stop. I lean against the wall to catch my breath and marvel. I have to force myself to stand and walk again, to stop obsessing over the beautiful creature that had such astonishing strength. The beautiful creature I could be.

"Get a sweater," I remind myself.

Walking through this house is like walking through my own home, not because it is familiar or warm but because it seems filled with spirits—those of two worlds: the underworld I am struggling to recall, and the one in which Ben and Dr. Zin were a relatively normal family. Spirits cling to the intricate fixtures; they whisper to me from behind potted aconite and hemlock plants; their unseen gazes follow me down the hall filled with Ben's sculptures on plinths. And they are waiting for me outside the dark storage room at the end of the hall.

"*Abandon all hope*," they seem to whisper, "*ye who enter here.*"

Am I a fool for playing with fire like this?

No, I think. *I need to do this. To help Ben, and then to help my mom.*

I open the door and flick on the light. I find boxes, crates, and small containers at the front of a vast room filled to breaking with the Zins' furnishings, artwork, books, everything. I breathe in the musky scent of the space, knowing it's nothing like Ben's fragrance but loving the closeness I feel to him here, with his belongings under my trailing fingertips. Fingertips that were, only minutes ago, long, vicious, and relentless.

In a box marked *Ben's Winter Sweaters*, I find the familiar candy-and-musk-scented clothing Ben would have worn on the weekends or after school. Delicately, I lift a gray wool cardigan with patches on the elbows; I set it aside and pull out a beautiful black turtleneck that *is* Ben Zin. Each layer of sweater reveals a better layer below it. I slide on a green cashmere sweater, inhaling deeply as the soft material passes over my face. Delicious. But I can't put the rest back—I can't leave them all here. So the black turtleneck goes over the cashmere. A thickly ribbed sweater over that. I am fat with five layers when I button the gray cardigan over it all and, at last, hug myself, breathing in Ben as I do.

The spirits are waiting for me outside the storage room as I click the door closed. But rather than letting me go, they turn my attention to a room at the exact opposite end of the hall, down in the dimness of the south wing.

Checking for Dia, I tiptoe past the staircase and soon find my hand resting on the doorknob of this room. It could be any room. Could be empty.

So I turn the knob.

Before I flick on the light, I hear groans and breaths and sighs. Then a flick. A sterile fluorescent glow floods the large, bare space—four plain walls, with a closet at the far end, and two shaded windows.

The light confuses the four beings ambling in circles within: a girl, two boys, and some unimaginable creation that barely passes for human. The girl is chattering about the magic of moving pictures. The first boy is blank. The other thing is…unmentionable; its three arms clutch at each other, and that is the least of the horror. And the final creature is none other than Damon Smith.

I freeze. They turn their vacuous stares on me.

"Interesting, aren't they?"

I jump at Dia's voice behind me. He pulls me, in all my stiff shock, closer. The beings start toward us, and I back up, even with Dia's arm holding me tight. He lifts his free hand, and the creatures stop like they've run into an invisible wall. Their knees keep bending, their arms keep swinging, but they move no closer toward us. He drops his hand; they walk forward. He lifts his hand again; they stop.

"What is that? A spell?" I ask.

"There's always plenty of magic at my house," Dia says. Then he drops his hand one more time—this time to flick off the light, close the door, and trap the beings within again. In the safety of the hall, he eyes me up. "Were you freezing? You've got about a hundred sweaters on."

"You kept Damon Smith?" I ask, unable to budge. Dia has to manually move me away from the door and back to the staircase.

"Who's Damon Smith?"

"That boy in there. You vivified him in front of me. He had no soul. You don't remember?"

He looks like he's about to shrug until he catches my confounded expression. He scratches his chin instead. "Oh, sure, that kid."

"He stood like a zombie in the middle of your office. His parents were crushed. How can you not remember?"

"Sure. The boy in there."

"Hello? His dad's building your college in exchange for seeing that heartbreaking display."

"Oh, the *Smith* kid. Yeah, he was my first vivification, so I only destroyed one of his vials. Get this, though: he's reincarnated as an impoverished girl in Brazil. Smith's wife already moved there to keep tabs on the baby as she grows up." He nods like it's cool, like this is all perfectly acceptable.

"You're keeping zombies, you know."

"Nah, they're not brain-eaters or anything. They're just interesting creatures."

I storm downstairs. Dia follows, rattling off facts about those beings as if he doesn't realize how upsetting they are.

"The soul that's coming through for the girl," he says, "is one of her past ones, from the 1920s."

"Leave me alone!"

"And that really odd-looking one? I made it myself. Just blended drops of blood. That was based on your idea."

I glare up at him from the foyer. "I was talking about making art. Painting!"

"*That* was art," he says, pointing upstairs. "Why are you putting on your boots?"

"I'm leaving."

"But why? We haven't even painted."

"Are you serious?" I grab my coat. "Y'know, I wondered why Gia would leave the underworld, and I wondered why she would react so violently to you. But now I know."

"You think you know."

"It's because, as beautiful and appealing as you are, you're ultimately the darkest and coldest of all the demons and devils in history."

After a pause, he says, "You think I'm beautiful and appealing?"

Growling, I turn to go.

"Gia—Anne, stop! Please stay. Don't be angry with me."

I look at him, at his earnest expression and his pleading eyes. "Those were real people once," I say.

"I'm sorry."

"I thought you loved beauty. Not monsters."

"They're beautiful to me. They would be beautiful to Gia. You're tainting them with your morality."

"Spare me the lesson in aestheticism."

"Anne, deep down inside, you're just like I am. You're an artist. You blend paint to see what colors you can make. That's all I'm doing."

He tries to brush my hair away from my face. I smack his hand. He mouths, *"Ouch,"* but grins through it.

"See you next Saturday," he says.

"Not if you've got those monstrosities up there."

"You know how I love threats."

When he closes the door behind me, I have to stop and catch my breath. I hope he's not right about the way Gia would have seen his experiments, about the dark areas she easily navigated. I need to use who she was to help me, but the last thing I want is to start looking at people like test subjects.

That's when I hear voices.

"Garnet, I said I'm sorry!"

I flatten against the wall at the sound of Ben's voice. He and Garnet are on the road, heading toward the college. She is storm-

ing ahead of him. I hide behind a column. If they saw me here...
oh God. I'm wearing six of his sweaters! Can you say *stalker*? I close
my eyes. Even when a melting icicle starts dripping on my head, I
don't budge.

"You know damn well that sculpture looked nothing like me,"
she snaps at him. "And stop calling me Garnet. I'm Lizzy to you—I
always have been."

"Of course, Lizzy. Please hear me out. I think my sculpture does
look like you."

She whirls to face him. They're stopped directly across from me,
up on the road. *No*, I think, *move along. Go.* Dia could open the door
at any moment and reveal me here.

"Look at me." Garnet motions up and down her body. "Am I
some sort of Amazon woman? Is my hair huge and crazy?"

"I swear, I was thinking of you. It's not... her."

"It's not your ex-girlfriend."

OMG, they're talking about me. If they see me now... I shift
closer to the column. I accidentally step onto a slick mound of ice.
My foot slips. Biting my lip, I grab hold of the column and rebalance.

"I have no idea what I ever saw in her," Ben says. "It wasn't her.
I swear."

A spell made him say that, I tell my heart.

"Here's a tip, Ben: girls don't want to hear about other girls.
Like, *ever*. And we sure as hell don't want our idiot boyfriends to say
they're going to make a birthday sculpture for us only to show up
with some dumb-ass statue of their *ex*!"

"It wasn't her!"

"Especially," she insists, "when your life hangs in the balance.
Got it?"

twenty

A LEGION OF THREE

MOLLY IS READING *THE MANY LIVES OF THE GIRLS OF CANIA
Christy*—the book that told me the truth about this school months
ago—when I open the door to our room. To my surprise, tears are
streaming down her cheeks. I've never seen Molly anything but
cheery.

She wipes her face when she looks up at me.

"Are you okay?" I ask her.

"Are you doing a Michelin Man impersonation?"

I glance down at my sweaters. "These are Ben's. I got them at
Dia's. Don't ask."

"Don't ask what you were doing at *Dia's* house? K. I'll just jump
to conclusions."

I start pulling off Ben's cardigan. "What are you doing with that
book?"

"Harper brought it to me this morning. Said I have to add my
page to it. Then she took your hairbrush and left."

"She what?" I glance at my dresser-top. My brush is gone. It had
strands of my hair in it.

Does this mean what I think it means?

Has Harper come around to my idea?

"I was gonna stop her," Molly says, tossing the book aside, "but
I kinduv couldn't believe what I was seeing. Why did she take your
brush?"

I decided long ago that I wouldn't tell Molly about my plan to help Ben and my mom. She wouldn't understand. Every time I've suggested, even jokingly, that I've got a demon-lady under my skin, she gets so upset, so adamant that I couldn't possibly be a demon goddess, no matter what my mother asked Mephisto for. She's left me no choice; I have to lie to her.

"Maybe she secretly digs my puffy hair," I say with a short laugh. Molly arches an eyebrow. "Anyway, what are you gonna write on your page?" *That you were murdered by Mephisto? That I was partly responsible for your death?*

"I'm not sure," she says. "It's such a morbid book."

We've never talked about her murder. Or her life before Cania. We barely even talk about our memories together. It's always felt like too sensitive a topic to broach. But now, with Molly wiping her tears away, it feels like the perfect—maybe the only—time to bring it up.

"Hey, Mol?" I begin. "I've wondered for a while… How did Mephisto do it?"

"Do it?"

"How did he…kill you?"

Her face pales. "Um, it doesn't really matter."

"Of course it matters." I sit next to her and take her hand.

"The memories are blurry. A lot of my memories are. Must be a vivification glitch or something."

I don't mention that my memories aren't spotty.

"Well, what about your gramps? I don't imagine he just sat there and let Villicus, like, poison you? Was it poison? Or something worse? Something faster? It's just so—"

"I don't really like talking about that, okay? I'm here now, so that's what matters."

"I know, but—"

"Anne! Drop the interrogation."

"Interrogation?"

Someone knocks at the door. Molly, looking relieved at the distraction, tosses my hand aside and bounds to her feet as a senior boy pokes his head into our room. She darts to his side. Her expression has totally shifted back to cheery—her mischievous brand of cheeriness.

"Anne, you know Paul? Paul, Anne."

"The girl who chose to stay," Paul says with a half smile and small wave.

"Paul's a chemistry major," Molly explains.

"I'm sure he is," I say. It's clear that Molly doesn't want to continue the convo we were having. So I sigh and offer, "Well, Paul, what's in your shopping cart? Must be something pretty sweet for you to risk coming into the girls' dorm."

"It is," he says as Molly yanks her box of contraband out from under her bed. She holds up a smartphone, and he hands her a folded slip of paper in exchange for it.

I watch the exchange, fascinated as always by Molly's take on trading. It's the opposite of Mephisto's. Molly has become the go-to person around here for forbidden technology. For a long time, I thought she was trading tech for favors, mostly IOUs. But it turns out she's been asking students to commit to being nice to just one person. That's all the payment she takes. They write the name of the person they'll be kind to on a slip of paper, and that's it. I once thought that Molly should be sainted, and every day she gets more and more likely to earn a halo.

"Come on," Molly tells Paul. "I'll show you where to stand on this island to get a signal."

Before I can say anything more, they're gone. I listen to them chatter on their way to the staircase, and I lower myself to her bed. The book of death is open next to me. I flip through it until I land on the page reserved for Molly Lynn Watso. It's empty. Just her name at the top. And something tells me she's never going to add anything to it. Her death is a topic she clearly wants to hide from, which is odd. After all, she practically ran toward it when she befriended me.

I glance up to find Pilot and Lou standing in my doorway.

"Where's the security around this place?" I ask. "You guys can't be here. Girls only."

Lou nudges Pilot. "I told you!"

That's when I glimpse the lockets around their necks. My hair is in them. I scan their faces for an explanation, but they both keep their eyes averted. Which is explanation enough.

I stand.

"Master," Lou says, "our apologies."

"It's my fault," Pilot adds. "Lou asked if he could see you. Rumor has it you appeared to Dia today. From the sound of it, you put on exactly the sort of wow-worthy show we were talking about."

"Word travels fast." I look at Lou's locket. "Is that what I think it is?"

"I serve Miss Saligia," Lou says with a deep bow. I check to make sure no one in the hall saw that. "Master, I have long awaited your return."

"So I've got two followers now? And maybe Harper, too?"

Pilot and Lou exchange a look. I don't care if I sound like a sad excuse for a would-be underworld goddess. Two followers is awesome! It might even be enough to give me what I need to turn the tables in Ben's favor. At least, I'm gonna try.

I don't know how to dismiss Pilot and Lou, but I need to go. So, short of a better idea, I pat them each on the head, grab my sheet of notes on teachers' powers out of my desk, and dart by them. As I hurry down the stairs and out the door, I unfold the paper and search for the first power I need to use. The sheet shakes in my hands. I have to stop, catch my breath, slow my heart.

"Take it easy, Saligia," I whisper. I look at the list. "I need to rewrite history," I say as I scan the names and their powers.

After what Dia told me about Garnet's fear that Ben's not over me, and after what I heard Garnet say to Ben just this afternoon, I need to change Garnet's mind about Ben's feelings for me; that's my first order of business. If Mephisto or Dia find out that I'm secretly collecting followers—that Gia's gaining power—at least I can die or be sent home knowing I did the best thing I could to secure Ben's win: I made Garnet *believe* he loved her. I need to remove my relationship with Ben from their memories.

"Of course!" I kiss the paper and tuck it away. "Star Wetpier, history teacher extraordinaire and the woman who rewrote *my* memories, you're first on my list."

Star Wetpier is an anagram for *rewrite past*. I'm on my way to the staff quarters at the far end of Goethe Hall, hoping to track her down, when, passing the photocopy room near the front office, I glimpse none other than Star staring my way. I backtrack. Star is watching the archway with her big blue eyes when I step under it. As if she's been expecting me, she bows her curly, silvery head and holds up the locket she wears around her neck. I squint to see strands of my hair poking out of its smooth silver edges.

"I am already yours," she says, "Master." Her gaze stays below my eyes.

Holy crap. I've got *three* of them? Why didn't Pilot say so? Are there *more*?

"How did you know?" I ask her.

"Pilot said you were back. I have been waiting. So many of us have been waiting for you. He's working to spread the word."

"Waiting for Miss Saligia."

At the mention of Saligia's name, Star inhales deeply through her nose and slowly exhales.

"Even when you left to become this lovely girl and gave me to Mephistopheles," Star says, "I stayed yours at heart. Where the love lives. Like you taught me." She gets on her knees. "My powers are yours. You needn't twist my arm to access them, although you are welcome to."

"Star, listen." I glance over my shoulder to make sure no one's watching this. "Can you get up?"

Obediently, she stands. Like Lou, she never meets my eyes. I get that it's a sign of respect, but it's really unsettling. Like talking to a wall.

"Look," I say, "I need your help. I want to rewrite the past. How can I do that?"

"Rewrite the past?"

"Yeah, I mean, your power is to rewrite history for people, right?"

She nods. "Of course. Thank you for acknowledging me, Master."

"So how do I do it?"

"You don't know?"

I got tired of hearing that question long ago. "No, I don't."

"Is it *your* history you wish to alter, Master?"

"No. The history of two others."

"Are they of rank?"

"I don't think so. A human. And a girl whose soul is Mephisto's."

"If I weren't yours, you would need to harm me to put my skills to work for you."

I was worried about that. "But since you are?" I ask, hopeful that I won't have to hurt this poor little thing with her cute, curly hair.

"Since I am," she says, curtseying, "and I'm awfully proud to be yours, Master. So pleased at your return." Wow, these people waste a lot of time being subservient. "Simply do as I do when I'm using my powers."

"You mean when you're not under duress?"

"Yes. I rewrite moments in one's history on a sheet of paper and, chanting my incantation, burn it."

"What's your incantation?"

She blushes. "But, Master, you would use *your* incantation. Not mine."

"I have my own?"

Dammit. I don't know my freakin' incantation! Am I gonna have to try to wake Gia up and ask her what it is? She only ever stays for a few seconds. And she's never spoken.

"Rather than trouble yourself, please, allow me." Star hands a hole-punch to me. "Perhaps you might clobber me with this? Then I'll do as you wish."

I look at the hole-punch. There's no way I'm going to beat anyone! I shake my head.

With a small sigh, Star sets it back on the table next to the printer. "Then, if you'll permit me," she says, "I recall your incantation from our years together. I can share it with you."

"That would be a lifesaver."

She sees me smile, and she beams. Her teeth make sharp little points and her eyes crinkle into thin slivers that glow yellow. But, that aside, she looks happy. A happy demon.

"I heard you say it a thousand times, Master. But I mustn't utter it," she says. "Don't want to turn to stone."

Holy crap, turn to stone? Even if Gia was a decently humane underworld leader, she seemed to have a few screws loose. No sooner do I think that than my head starts to throb. That's the downside of empowering Gia: I've found myself sharing more and more of my private thoughts with her.

Star grabs a sheet of paper, scribbles on it, and, with the deepest bow, offers it to me. Thanking her, I take it and leave her with her eyes still downcast.

Feeling closer than ever to saving Ben, I dash up to the fourth floor of the library, the only place I can be alone to think. Problem is, I'm not alone. No sooner have I opened the door to the chilliest place on campus than I see Ben and Garnet walking toward the stairwell where I stand, dopily squinting at them. On instinct, I whip my incantation behind my back.

"Stalking your ex, Miss Merchant?" Garnet asks me.

I can't help but look at Ben even though everything in my mind screams not to let on that I have feelings for him. My little plan is not so flawless that Garnet, on looking closer, couldn't figure it all out. She would only have to ask Kate Haem and Eve Risset if they know why Ben Zin hates me so much, and that would be that. But even still. *Even still.* I look at him, and in doing so I risk blowing everything. It's just that I so rarely get to see Ben up close like this. I need to soak this moment up, to capture it mentally so that, later, I can close my eyes and remember him. Rapidly, like a camera shutter on overdrive, I memorize his face. I don't need to memorize his eyes. I already know them down to the lightest, smallest fleck.

"Not exactly." I step aside for them to leave.

She doesn't budge, even as Ben hurriedly walks by. I want to breathe him in.

"That's a beautiful cashmere sweater," she says to me.

My stomach knots. Oh, shit. It's Ben's! I glance between Garnet and Ben.

"Um, yeah, it's old," I say.

"I know it is." Garnet's face is red as, catching me off guard, she shoves me against the door. "Take it off. Now."

"She's not worth it," Ben tells her.

"Yeah, but she needs to know that," Garnet says and pushes my shoulder again. "Do you know that, Merchant? Do you know that you're nothing and no one? Have you got a clue, you poor little screw-hard?"

My skin tightens. I can feel Gia rising, but I push her down. This will all be over soon enough. Stopping behavior like this is the reason I'm here.

"I'm not sure what a screw-hard is," I say.

Realizing I'm not going to fight her, Garnet scoffs, flips her hair, and joins Ben by the stairs.

"Come on, baby," she says as she takes Ben's arm. "I never liked that sweater."

"Don't worry about her," Ben says. I just catch the last words he utters before they disappear around the bend: "I don't know why you're insecure about her at all. She's not even pretty."

I close my eyes.

And breathe.

And almost abort this whole mission. But I push past my wounded ego and step into the cold library.

Rewriting Ben's history and Garnet's history takes longer than I'd expected. There are so many moments I need to erase and replace. My hand is cramped and it's dark out when, at last, I light one of the many matches Ben and I have stored up here over time and, watching a flame consume their rewritten histories, recite my incantation:

Omnia peccata in saligia
Cum omnibus vitam saligia

The paper burns until its glowing blackness reaches my fingertips. I place what little is left in my palm, give it a little blow to reignite the flame, and watch the significant moments in my history with Ben and with Garnet get reduced to ashes.

"Done," I say to myself. "Ben will forget me now. And Garnet will forget Ben and I were ever together. Everything we had and did never happened. They've been together all this time."

I walk to the window overlooking the quad and see, far below, Ben and Garnet kissing deeply. He kissed me like that on a few occasions, but he'll never remember it.

I press my palm to the window.

"I'm not done yet, Ben. But it's a good start."

THAT MONDAY MORNING, an unusually happy Garnet greets us in our morning workshop. Everyone seems to notice the improvement in her disposition, but none of them can attribute it to me. I wait for Harper to clue in—to realize I'm behind this—but how could she know? I also wait for her to mention my hairbrush, but she doesn't.

The day passes slowly. I'm anxious to see Pilot, get a tally on how many people he's convinced to serve Gia, and move on with visiting the next staff member on my list. I just want to get this all over with, but classes and acting normal keep getting in my way.

"You haven't asked about Paul," Molly says to me as we pack up after Superbia's most recent discussion of *The Picture of Dorian Gray*.

"The guy you gave the smartphone to?"

"We went for a long walk together."

"Oh. Cool," I say, my mind elsewhere.

"Nice, Anne. Your interest in my life astounds me."

Ugh! Acting normal when I have so much on the go! If only I could tell Molly. If only I wasn't 190 percent positive she'd flip on me and judge me into the ground for exploring my inner demon.

"That sounded bad," I say and put my book bag down, giving her my full attention. She's quick to forgive. "So, you and Paul."

"Not really."

"But you just said!"

"He's cute. But I don't think there's anything serious there. I'm just having fun. You should try it."

"Well, he's a senior with four months left to live," I remind her. "You might not want to get too attached."

She zips her bag. "And you might want to read a book on sensitivity."

"I'm *sorry*," I say in exasperation.

She ignores me and leaves the classroom just as Superbia calls my name. I reluctantly meander to the front of the room.

"Did you get a haircut?" Superbia asks me. "It's a bit of a botch job."

My hand goes straight to the spot Pilot cut. For the briefest moment, I wonder if this is Superbia's way of telling me she's on my side now. My gaze darts to her clavicle, exposed in her boatneck sweater. But she's still wearing Dia's tattoo; she's not mine.

"If I were you," she says, "I'd make sure no one important notices."

"I'll try."

"Are you enjoying the Wilde book?"

I nod.

"What's your favorite line?"

In the corner of my eye, I watch Molly walk away with a freshman just as Pilot and Harper appear at the doorway. They're waiting to talk to me.

"Miss Merchant?" Superbia repeats. "Your favorite line."

"I—I don't have one."

"But there are so many!" She tsks. "For example, 'Sin is a thing that writes itself across a man's face. It cannot be concealed. People talk sometimes of secret vices. There are no such things. If a wretched man has a vice, it shows itself in the lines of his mouth.' Do you like that one?"

"I guess, sure."

"Do you understand what it means? Do you see how, perhaps, it could apply in your life?"

Pilot is coughing to get my attention.

"Not really."

"Your PT is to look closer, is it not, Miss Merchant?"

"It is. I will. I'll look closer. I'll read that whole scene again tonight and look really, really close. Now, I'm sorry," I say, excusing myself from Superbia. "I've gotta go."

Harper and Pilot loop their arms through mine the moment I enter the hallway.

"What was that about?" Pilot asks me, flicking a glance back at Superbia.

"My PT, I think. And something about sin showing on a man's face. Not sure."

They walk me to the cafeteria, where we find a quiet table overlooking the gray ocean. I set my book on the table.

"Why're you reading that?" Pilot asks.

"For English class," Harper answers on my behalf. "Superbia assigned it."

"Interesting." He turns the book over in his hands while I rummage through my backpack. "She was always your biggest supporter. Rumor is she wept when you left the underworld."

"Superbia did? What's that got to do with this book?" I ask.

"Not up to me to say."

"You're my follower, Pilot. Can't I, like, command you to tell me?"

"Superbia ranks above you *and* me. I can't tell you shit about her or that book she's making you read."

"Wait," Harper says. "Pi, did you or did you not tell me that this Saligia chick ruled the seven deadly sin ladies?"

"Yes, but Saligia gave Superbia and her sisters to Mephisto when she left the underworld. Now they're Dia's. It doesn't matter who they serve, though. All that matters is that they don't serve Anne now and they're higher ranking than most of the demons here combined."

"Then let's build my followers already and see if we can't change that." I find my mom's barrette, the very one I tried giving Harper the other day, and set it on the book. "Let's start with this."

Harper looks at the barrette. "I've given your proposition some thought." She glances at me. "Does your offer still stand?"

"You'd have to serve me, Otto. You couldn't act like you're helping me. You'd have to see it as me helping you."

"I know."

"Then my offer stands."

"I've got one condition before I stuff this ugly-ass comb-thing in my hair," she says, holding the barrette. "If you've got so many followers, and they're demon-types, summon one now."

She and Pilot sit back in their chairs.

"You want me to dance for you. That's not how it works."

"Because you can't do it?"

"This isn't the movies, Harper. This is real."

"Summon. Someone."

"Harper, I wouldn't know where to start."

She crosses her arms. "I don't want to serve a chick who can't even get creative when the time comes."

"Well, what would you do if you were me?"

"I'd use detangler, for starters."

Pilot chuckles. Some servant.

"Do you want a life or don't you, Otto?"

"Try—try drawing someone," Pilot suggests. "That's your thing, right? Drawing?"

"Well, she *thinks* that's her thing," Harper says.

"This is exactly the sort of BS talk you'll have to give up."

"Only if you summon someone. Now."

"Draw someone," Pilot says. "Try it. And say your incantation."

If I screw this up, Harper's gone and my hope for an instant human fanbase is gone with her. But if I get it right, she'll buy into the plan *and* I'll have a new uber-useful skill under my belt.

So I unscrew the lid from the salt shaker and empty it onto the table. I push the salt around until I can see an outline of the face of my soft-hearted follower Star Wetpier. When Harper and Pilot both guess who it is, I decide it's time to try. I mutter my incantation under my breath. Harper clears her throat, and even Pilot can't sit quite still.

A wisp of white smoke snakes between the tables. We notice it just as it nears ours.

"Either the deep-fryer's overheated," Harper says.

"Or this is working," Pilot finishes.

The smoke weaves our way and stops in front of me. It slowly takes the form of a human. In moments Star is kneeling before me, her head bowed. She asks how she may serve me.

Harper's mouth drops open.

"I'm in," Harper says. She pushes the barrette under her hair and arranges it so you can't see any of my blonde under her ginger. "Let's begin, *Master*."

twenty-one

'T AIN'T NO SIN

IN THE WEEKS AFTER HARPER AGREES TO HELP ME, I FEEL stronger and more like Gia, like the opposite of the timid girl raised in a funeral home. My heart is racing almost constantly now, my mind is more focused, and I feel like I could run thirty-minute marathons from dawn to dusk.

When I'm in Dia's office for our Saturday session, I feel more in control of our interactions than I ever have.

Last night, I just lay in bed the whole night, plotting what I'd do today, watching Molly snooze across the room, and feeling like I might never need to sleep again. I'm getting my energy from all the students who've committed themselves to Harper and all the underworlders that Pilot, who's remotivated by each new addition to our team, has brought on board. Still no Seven Sinning Sisters, but that's for the best anyway. At lease I've got a solid collection of the more common demon-types around here.

The only thing is that I haven't actually done what I know I need to do.

I've been putting off the acts that I don't think I've got the stomach to do. The cruel stuff. Like walking into a room and torturing a demon. Star Wetpier was easy—no cruelty required. I've got a sinking feeling the others won't go quite so smoothly. I'm actually going to have to hurt some people to get them to use their powers for me.

The torture starts now.

Like, right now.

I can't put it off another day.

It's April already—Ben's only got so much time before he's on the chopping block. Time for me to twist a few arms, and then some. To work up the courage, I down a half-dozen espressos. Pilot pats my back like he's the coach to my boxer. We're sitting in the cafeteria, with sunlight flooding the room through the enormous windows overlooking the shoreline, where the seniors are enduring the first of Dia's feats of strength: very simply, balancing on one foot on a pole in the water. Last man standing gets the gold star.

"Think of it as a feat of strength," Pilot says. "You need to win more followers. Bend them to your will."

Pilot doesn't know that I'm currently stalking Miss Vale Tuefurre—a Dia follower—because I need her to help me with Ben. He can't know that. I sit next to him. Watch Vale chop vegetables in the cafeteria. Chew my nails. Shake away my nerves. Glance out at the water, at Ben balancing uncertainly on a post. And stand.

Pilot locks the door to the cafeteria.

I march toward her.

There's no turning back now.

I'm here to torture her to get her to do what I need her to. *Vale Tuefurre: reveal future.*

Vale doesn't even see us coming. One second, she's chopping carrots into coins; the next, Pilot is muzzling her, and I'm on her back, wrestling her. I do it all without apology. The Scrutiny challenge taught me not to apologize.

Vale is no small lady, so the struggle is ugly and anything but dignified. She's slippery. She almost darts away, but Pilot catches her arm and tugs her back. She reminds him that he's crossing a line because he's lower-ranking than she is. But I'm not. So I take her from Pilot. I scramble to tug her arms behind her and shove her against the counter, and I command Pilot to help me lift her onto it. He pins her long enough to let me crawl up and over her.

"Commit to it, Anne," he demands when he sees me blanch.

"I am."

But I'm not. It's just so twisted. I can feel all her bones shifting under me as she writhes around. And she keeps snapping her sharp little teeth at me. It hits me that I might not be built to pin demons and force them to work for me.

"This is how things get done in the underworld," Pilot reminds me. "She *likes* pain."

Windows wrap the kitchen and sit flush with the countertop. The window behind Vale's head is open. So I tell Pilot to help me shift her, and soon she's crying out with her head dangling out the window. Her neck sits on the windowsill.

She stops cursing me and instead stares in terror as I grasp the window sash high above her throat. I don't apologize, but I do close my eyes when I bring the window down on her throat. Her cries garble. Oh, God, I can't bear the sound. I have to force myself to stay on her, to keep the window down, and not run off freaking out. I dare to open my eyes again.

Her eyes are bulging.

I can't look.

"Yes, Anne, exactly," Pilot encourages. "But really put some muscle into it next time."

"I don't think I can, Pi."

"You can. Even if you have to think about something else the whole time. Even if you have to think about, like, art or something."

Vale's fleshy throat is constricting beneath the window sash. I lift it just enough that she can scream, but that draws the eyes of a dozen Cania seniors, including Ben, balancing on ever-shrinking perches in the ocean not far from us. They see me straddle the screeching chef, and they watch me tug down the sash until it pushes divots into her neck. Her scream is cut short. Her throat can't move. Everyone who was watching looks away one by one. Even Ben, out on the water, looks away. Because looking closer is a fool's errand.

I remind myself that this is all for Ben. And, suddenly, I can manage the task. Putting a demon through hell is practically easy when I think of it that way.

"Pilot," I say, "go watch the front door."

"It's locked. Don't worry about it."

I swivel to glare at him. Saligia must be starting to come through because I don't even need to say another word. He leaves us to do as I commanded. And I turn back to Vale, who's shaking like the bacon she fries every morning.

Think about art, Pilot said. So I do. But I think aloud.

"*The Scream* is so overrated, isn't it?" I'm not even sure Vale can hear me from that side of the window. "It's too literal. *The man is screaming.*"

She sputters. I shove a tad harder on the window. Her body jerks under my thighs. A boy walking by claps his hands to his mouth. I drag my annoyed gaze to him and the new crop of gape-faced onlookers. They do what everyone here has been so beautifully trained to do: pretend it's not happening.

Vale punches and flails her arms. I tuck each one under my knees, rendering her all but motionless. Her head wiggles as much as it can, which is not much, and her feet kick.

I lift the window.

She gasps for air and shoots a fiery glare at me.

"I prefer something more like *The Fountain*, by Mark Ryden," I say. "Do you know it? No? It's this picture of a doll-like child holding her own head as blood spurts from her neck." I begin lowering the window again. "How do you think she lost her head?"

"No, please." Her eyes are wide as she watches the window frame lower.

"*Va-a-ale*," I half sing. "Tell me, which seniors are going to be at the top of Dia's short list for the Big V this year?"

I ease the sash up just enough for her to gasp, "How could I know?"

I inch the window down again. Her eyes bulge.

"Don't play dumb. You think I stumbled in here and did this on a whim? I've been planning this for weeks." When she shakes her head in confusion, I bring the sash down again, cutting off her air. I hear her windpipe crunch. "Your power is to reveal the future. So reveal it."

She curses me voicelessly.

"Do it. Or things are going to get much worse incredibly fast."

When I dig my knees into her arms, she gasps her concession. I lift the window.

She sputters, "Jack Wesson. Joie Wannabe. Ebenezer Zin."

"Perfect." Effortlessly, I hop down and give her leg a slap for good measure. "I invite you to follow me."

She frees herself and, to my surprise, tearfully accepts my invitation. As I leave the cafeteria, I instruct Pilot to get her a locket. He bows.

Okay, that wasn't so bad. The art thing helped.

Now that I know who Ben's primary competition is, I can move easily along to destroying their chances of beating Ben. I figure that if I can get the other top students out of the running, Ben will be the absolute best of the remaining students. To destroy Jack and Joie's chances of taking the Big V from Ben, I need to know what their PTs are. It's only by proving they're not living and breathing their PTs that I can remove them both from the top spots.

A crowd has gathered around the seniors, balancing on their poles in the water. I slip behind them and see that those still standing are none other than Jack, Joie, and Ben. If only I knew of a demon whose power was to shove people from posts, I'd take Jack and Joie out now. Instead, I head to the gymnasium, where Stealth Vergner, whose power is to *reveal strength*, seems to be expecting me. That's not good. If he knows about me, it won't be long before Dia or Mephisto calls me on what I'm up to.

Stealth lets me shove him down and pin him under a stack of dumbbells. He lets me stomp my foot into his throat. He winces in pain, but I think I catch him looking up my skirt as he does. I drop a stinky gym towel over his face.

"Their PTs," I demand. "Tell me. Jack Wesson and Joie Wannabe."

"Jack's PT," he coughs behind the towel, "is to be dependably levelheaded."

"And Joie's?" I ask Stealth.

"It's a shitty one."

"I didn't ask for your opinion." I grind my foot in deeper, then release it so he can speak.

"She's supposed to…it's like…it goes, *love thy neighbor*. That's hers."

This is the part where I know I ought to have a crisis of conscience. Jack's been nothing but kind to me from the first day I met him. And Joie—how am I supposed to take out someone with such a positive PT?

I should have a crisis of conscience.

But I don't.

Jack's gotta go, and so does Joie. Because Ben needs to win. The ends justify the means.

CRED

Dr. Naysi, whose power is to drain sanity, surrenders eagerly to me. After I've nearly broken her arm, she asks for a lock of my hair, pledges her undying love for Miss Saligia, and gives me assurance that Jack will no longer be a contender for the Big V.

"He'll be about as mentally unstable as a kid can be," she says.

Sure enough, later that day, I hear freshmen girls whispering in the dorm common area about "the Goth dude who tried to set fire to the Rex Paimonde building and got suspended." When Pilot sits in stunned silence at our next meeting, torn over the pain his friend and former roommate might now be enduring on "suspension"—which probably isn't good in a world where expulsion is death—I marvel that he has no idea I was behind it. It's so clean, so elegant. I mean, sad for Jack, but that's not the point.

Kate Haem doesn't give in to me quite so easily when I seek her out to destroy Joie.

For hours, I wait for Kate in a bathroom stall in Goethe Hall, listening to every secretary but her come in, do her business, check herself out in the mirror, and prance out. Kate finally takes a seat in a stall. She's got her skirt hiked up around her waist, and her ankles are practically tied together by her pantyhose when I use my library card to twist open the lock of her stall door.

"Surely you've been expecting me," I say to her.

Kate leaps to her feet and smacks at the air around me. I step back and let her waddle past me out of the stall as fast as her locked ankles will move. But she doesn't get far. She trips, smacks her head against the countertop, and falls to the floor.

I watch her crawl away from me.

"Honestly," I say, "who still wears *pantyhose*?"

Having run-of-the-mill physical pain inflicted by yours truly does little for Kate. She's a freak; that much is clear. So I put on the kind of show only she can respond to: I smash the mirror with my fist and, from the heap of shards, select the thinnest one, the one most likely to slice her flesh like a hot knife through butter. The gashes on my knuckles are already healing as I stalk Kate, trapping her in the far corner, near the paper towel dispenser. The splinter glints in her eyes, and I wonder just how much damage she'll need me to do before she gives.

"Are you at all familiar with Andy Warhol?" I ask Kate as I kneel and tug her ankle my way.

She chews her nails in anticipation. I tear her stockings and shoes off. She doesn't make a sound, but she hungrily watches everything I do. What a freak.

"He was, perhaps, *the* pop artist," I say. "He painted shoes often, and he even kept a mummified human foot in his bedroom." Her bare, callous-covered foot is wiggling in my left hand. "I don't understand it, but a lot of semi-normal people have the most unusual fascination with feet."

Holding the shard in my right hand, I jab the end of it deep into her foot's flesh. She bites her fist but doesn't make a sound. I draw a long line from her curled-up big toe, through her arch, and down to her heel. As she wheezes and sucks back another cry, blood begins to trickle out.

"Maybe it's because there are so many nerve endings in our feet," I offer, watching her response. I release her. "Now, Kate, are you ready to do as I say?"

She clambers into a sitting position and draws her foot up, cradling it. She's flexible. She kisses her foot better.

"I'll take that as a no," I say.

I wrestle her foot away from her again and, using all my weight to pin down her writhing body, stab the splinter under her big toenail. At last, she screams wildly, like I'm murdering her.

"Take the writer Goethe," I grunt, pushing the splinter even deeper. "You know him—this building is named after him."

"Get off me!"

"He was one of a handful of writers to tell the story of your oh-so-noble master, Meph. Is the name ringing a bell?" Her whole leg quivers under me. "Goethe had a mistress named Christiane—"

"Someone help!"

"—who, on his request, would mail her worn shoes to him. Freaky, right?"

I glance at her face and find it twisted to the point that she must only be seconds from passing out. She's gasping for air, spent by the pain and her efforts to free herself. The door opens a little, and I glare at a student as she enters; she backs out.

"Kate, do as I say."

"Never."

But she seems unable to tear her gaze from me. A rush of energy surges through me. And, as it does, I catch a glimpse of my hands, gripping her ankles, mid-transformation. For the first time, without even trying, I'm morphing into Miss Saligia. The faint lines across the skin of my hands go smooth; the bulging blue veins flatten and fade away; my fingers and nails extend. Up my arm, a shiver travels, leaving behind the faintest blue trail of vines, a trail that gleams when the light hits it. My wild curls stretch into lengthy blonde waves that brush Kate's bare legs.

"*Gia*," she gasps.

As I withdraw the shard, part of it snaps off under her nail. I leave it there and pound my fist against it. Hard. She gasps and wails, at last, writhing like she might die.

"Turn Joie Wannabe against her Guardian," I command her, feeling invincible. "Fill her with hatred for her Guardian."

"It's done!" she cries.

I let her foot go and get up. Gia looks at me in the reflection. I smile, and she slowly vanishes. Most of the buttons on my blouse and cardigan have survived her appearance, but it takes a while to adjust until I look like myself again.

"You've got blood on your shirt," Kate stammers, "Saligia."

There's a spot on my collar. "So I do."

I turn on the water, run a paper towel under it, and start dabbing away Kate's blood as she hobbles up to what passes for standing. She and I meet eyes in the shattered remains of the mirror. Her gaze is the first to drop.

"I will serve you again," she says. "You need more followers than Mephisto has if this is going to work."

"If what's going to work?" I ask. "What?"

"Build your legions, Master. It's the only way."

"The only way to *what*?"

"To protect yourself."

"From whom?"

"Just be careful."

"From the person with 'sin written on their face'?" I ask, recalling Superbia when she quoted *The Picture of Dorian Gray*. "Is that it?"

She staggers silently out of the bathroom, leaving me wondering what she means. I've been so preoccupied with my own goals, I haven't stopped to think about what people have been hinting at. Superbia knows something; Pilot knows she knows something; and now Kate seems to know something. That I need protection. From someone. But as I look in the mirror and dab at the blood, I realize I need protection from everyone—even, perhaps, myself.

When I'm cleaned up, I leave Goethe Hall and walk into a misty April afternoon to find, in the quad, an angry-looking Joie Wannabe storming away from a rather confused Mr. Farid. It's only a matter of time before her refusal to do anything that pleases him will make it impossible for Mr. Farid to report well on her activities; it will be very hard for her to be short-listed. Others will make their way onto the short list, but Ben's already ahead of them.

I did it, I think as I sit in class the next morning. Ben's going to be safe. One goal down.

Garnet is standing at the front of our workshop. She has my half-finished painting of Dia on an easel next to her, and she is pointing out all the parts that she loves about it. Yes, loves. Because she's forgotten everything. This moment would not have happened if I hadn't rewritten her history. The class claps half-heartedly as Garnet congratulates me on a job well done.

"I think I speak for everyone," she says to me, "when I say we are very much looking forward to seeing your completed portrait of Headmaster Voletto. I understand you'll present it to the school on graduation day?"

I nod, and she says how splendid that is.

"I don't think it's splendid at all," Harper sneers at me as, after class, she pulls me aside. "Was this your plan all along, *master*? To get back in the teacher's good books so you can beat me?"

"What? You think I went to these lengths to get Garnet to like me?"

"This was just one big manipulation, wasn't it?"

"Harper, be reasonable."

"I should never have helped you. I can't believe I was so blind."

"Wait, hold on. I admit I've used the strength you've helped me rebuild to, well, further my plans."

"Your plans to get Garnet to score you higher than me and beat me to the Big V."

"No!" I tug her out of Garnet's earshot. The room is almost empty, and the last thing I need is for Garnet to overhear and get suspicious. That would undo all my hard work. "I *promise*, Harper."

"A promise from a demon."

I've never heard anyone call me that. "I'm not a demon."

Harper points to the barrette under her hair. "Then why am I wearing this and calling you my freakin' master? Speaking of which." She takes it out and shoves it at me.

"Fine. Want the truth?"

"Only the whole truth, Murdering Merchant."

"I wanted to make sure Ben would get the Big V, so I've been doing some ... *things* to make that happen."

"All this for a boy? The boy that left you for Garnet?"

I don't have time to get into the specifics with her. "Yes, Harper. And all this praise from Garnet is just a side effect. But, listen, she can't know about Ben. So keep it down. Please. I'm trusting you in the hopes you'll trust me back."

"When are you going to get me the life you promised?" she demands.

"I'm working on it. I just need the right people to follow me. People with the power to vivify."

"Well, I want to be home for July fourth."

"*This* July fourth?"

"My dad hosts a real big celebration. I want to be there."

Harper's so wired with anger, I don't dare remind her that she's never going to be Harper Otto again. She's not going to attend back-yard barbeques as Harper again. Her family and friends all know she's dead.

"I'll do my best," I tell her.

She sneers. "You promise me I'll be *real* independent as of Independence Day, and I'll serve you again. Until then, my follow-ers and I are no longer yours."

I can almost feel the energy leaving me, like I've had the wind knocked out of me, as I pick up the barrette she's abandoned and watch her go. She's easily cut my follower-base in half.

What follows can only be described as an act of desperation.

twenty-two

THINGS FALL APART

I STORM UP THE STAIRS TO THE SECOND FLOOR OF THE girls' dorm and race to my room, desperate to rebuild my followers now that Harper's taken hers from me.

I throw the door open. Molly, who is sitting on the floor with Joie Wannabe, shoves her box of contraband under her bed. When she sees it's just me, she takes it out again.

I don't know how to ask her for what I need—or to convince her that it's right to help me. She doesn't know anything about what I've been up to. Will she help? Will she see the purity of my intentions, evil though they may seem?

She hands Joie a camcorder. "You know how to work this, right?"

"I can figure it out," Joie says and gives Molly a slip of paper.

"Wait!" I cry and snatch the paper. I turn to Molly. "Before you take this as payment, I need to talk to you."

Molly and Joie exchange a look.

"Please," I whisper to Molly, as if Joie can't hear, "ask her for something else."

"For what else?"

I don't want to say in front of Joie.

Without so much as a flinch, Molly takes the paper from my hand and helps Joie to the door. She agrees to make sure Joie's parents get whatever sad-sap good-bye video she's going to make for them—because the Big V is basically off the table for Joie now—and closes the door after her.

"She's very upset," Molly says to me.

I know she is. And I had everything to do with that. But I can't let those thoughts in. Because of Ben. It's because of Ben I'm going to such lengths. Only for him.

"So," Molly glances at me as she tucks the slip of paper into her envelope—all those favors, all that goodwill, wasted, "my gramps said he thinks he saw Gigi wandering around. Can you believe it? Her bones must have washed up on shore. Like, seriously, we should put walls around the perimeter of this island. She doesn't even have a soul. It's just her vivified body roaming around."

"Molly, I was serious about asking for something else. Not these do-gooder favors you've been collecting."

"Try not to be so upset about Gigi," she says coldly. "I've gotta say, if your mom were alive, she'd be really, really disappointed in you."

"Well, my mom's not alive."

She winces a little. Our gazes meet. Unable to wait another second, I swipe the envelope from her hand and begin flipping through each slip of paper.

"Such a waste," I say. "I need your help, Molly, but you don't even care. You just keep wasting everything. This person has to be nice to some kid named Carson. And this one's for Jack. And Plum. And Toshio—he's not even here anymore!"

She watches as I read one name after the other, and then she calmly takes the envelope from my hands.

"Snoopy called," she says and drops the envelope in the box. "He wants his shtick back."

I square my fists on my hips. "I need your help, Molly."

She mimics me with a mocking smile. "With what, Anne?"

"I need you to stop asking people to be nice to someone in exchange for the devices you give them."

She arches an eyebrow.

"I need you to ask them to serve you, Mol. And then you need to serve me."

For a second, she just looks at me. Then the laughter starts. To my great annoyance.

"Is this some sort of skit?" she asks. "A performance art piece?"

"I'm serious. Lives depend on it."

"Let me check your head for a bump."

I shove her away. "Molly, this is hard enough without you joking about it!"

"Wait, aren't *you* joking?"

"You know what we're dealing with here. You've been under Mephisto's reign longer than any of us."

"'Mephisto's reign'?" She looks like something's occurring to her. "Is this about that stupid demon-chick nonsense Dia mentioned months ago?"

"You're not listening," I say and kick the box. She watches me like she's just realized her patient has flown over the cuckoo's nest. "Harper was serving me. And she had all these followers. But now she left me. And I need followers. But you've been so caught up in your little life, you've hardly even noticed what I'm going through. But I need you now. And if you could just start trading your devices for loyal followers—just have them agree to submit to you, and then you submit to me—I'm a nice leader—then I can rebuild my power and help..."—I hesitate to reveal Teddy's mission for me—"...people."

She stares at me. "Followers?"

"Yes."

"Like on Twitter?"

"Molly, come on!"

"I think you might need a Xanax. Or, like, a psychotherapist."

"And you call *me* insensitive?"

"What's that got to do with—" She realizes I'm talking about my mom. "I didn't mean that. Honestly. You have no idea how much I didn't mean that."

"There's no point in pretending we can be the lightest versions of ourselves and survive here, Mol. Being nice to other students? That's the best you're getting as an exchange? To what end?"

"End? To no end. To, like, being-a-good-person end."

"It's so naive! We're living in Hell, and you're singing *kumbaya* around the fire."

"This isn't Hell. It's Wormwood Island."

"Which your stupid family traded to known devils. Voilà! Hell."

She flinches. "Watch your mouth."

"Don't warn me like you're morally superior."

"'*Like*' I'm morally superior? There's no doubt about it. I'm Gandhi compared to you. Mother Teresa. The pope. Look at yourself! You're running around torturing teachers for God knows why."

I didn't know she knew that. But I guess everyone does. So many people saw me attack Vale in the cafeteria.

"Don't think I don't know why you're acting so nuts," she says.

"Seriously, with the insults?"

She darts to my desk, where she yanks open a drawer, shuffles through stuff, and finds the paper with the teachers' names and their powers worked out. She wags the folded square at me.

"You're using them all to make Ben win the Big V. Hello? Anne, I was there with you the day you watched Eve and Kate get tortured. I saw you drinking it up like it was a lesson you'd be quizzed on. You've just destroyed Joie, and I'm sure you were behind Jack's little breakdown, too."

She throws the note at me—and to both our surprise, it flies well. Its edge catches me in the eye. I fall to my bed, clutching at my face. She groans with what I guess is remorse.

"I knew I shouldn't have asked you to help me," I mutter. "I knew you'd judge me."

"*Anne.*"

"I don't judge you for going through boyfriends like water."

"Um, you *just* judged me for it. And I'm hardly going through boyfriends! I'm just doing what anybody does. Just exploring. And experimenting. Maybe you should try it instead of fixating on Ben effing Zin as if he's the only guy that could possibly be right for you."

"Why won't you help me, Molly?"

"Help you? With what?"

"With building my legions."

She stomps to her side of the room and throws herself on her bed. Her voice is muffled when she growls, "*You're not a demon-chick!*"

"Except I am. I haven't told you this because you're so damn pious you'd never let me live it down, but I was a woman named Miss Saligia in another life."

"Oh, please."

"She's the leader of the Seven Sinning Sisters, or she was before she agreed to come here for ... well, the jury's out on why she's here. But she is. Inside of me. My soul *is* hers."

Slowly, inch by inch, Molly rolls to face me. Her face is ghost-white when she looks my way.

"That's where your soul comes from?" she asks. "Hell?"

"Where I was a powerful goddess evidently."

"Hold on. Did Mephistopheles tell you that?"

"Teddy told me. Dia confirmed it."

For a moment, she looks lost for words. Her face falls, and I think she might cry or throw up. Instead, she finds her voice—and her optimism.

"But you're Anne now!" she exclaims.

"Barely."

"You are. You need to be Anne. The Anne I met in September; the Anne that dated Ben and came crying back to our room on Christmas Eve, after he refused to fight. Be her again. Who you are."

With my one good eye, I stare out the window. The Anne she's describing feels too far away.

"Anne, search your soul."

My soul is where the problem is.

"You're actively destroying real people. Joie. Jack. Who knows who else?"

"Only one person can win, Molly. So what if some dead kids have to die twice?"

"You're killing them."

"Hardly!"

"Classic. Trust you to act like you're not the biggest part of every single problem you create, Anne."

"And what is *that* supposed to mean?"

Someone knocks on the door and asks us to keep it down. We shout at her to butt out.

Molly's teeth are clenched as she stares me down. "You know what it means."

"You blame me for your murder."

"Is there anyone else to blame?" she asks.

"How about *yourself*? *You* pursued a friendship with me," I remind her, pushing my finger into her chest. She smacks my hand. "Even knowing everything you knew—things I didn't have a clue about—*you* came to *my* house. And, seriously, who writes their name in their shoes? Are you, like, four years old? Will the kids at preschool steal

them? You didn't even know anyone, so who exactly was going to
steal your shoes?" Her eyes are cold as she takes in my rant. "And, my
God, who would steal *shoes*? You're on an island filled with the richest
kids on Earth. They don't want your hand-me-down sweat-boxes."

I am trying hard to keep Saligia down but wondering if I shouldn't
just let her out, just unleash her on Molly, with her smug little face.

"Your grandpa served the devil just to make bank," I fire. "And
you won't even help me now."

She plants her feet and takes a deep breath. I'm surprised she
doesn't come back at me with the obvious truth: my dad is serving
the devil. Maybe not for money. But he's doing the devil's bidding.

But instead she says, "You'd better leave before we say things
you can't come back from."

"This was my room first," I state. "You leave."

She's halfway down the hall, muttering about demons, scrunch-
ing a hastily packed duffel under her arm, when I lean out the doorway and shout after her.

"Thanks for being such a *great friend*! Where do you think you're
going anyway? Your gramps doesn't live here anymore!" I slam the
door just as everyone else opens theirs. Then I open it again. "Oh,
and the word is 'grandpa'! What're you, two? Grand. Pa."

I slam the door three times. Four times. Once more for good measure. And then I leave, too. I'm not sure if I'm going after Molly. I'm not
sure what I'm doing. But I find myself, around twilight, sitting, shaking,
in the chemistry lab. Of all places. I've been here for God knows how
long when I glance out the windows to see the black night sky.

It's just as dark in here.

For light, I turn on the Bunsen burner in front of me and try not
to spook myself with its eerie glow and the long shadows it casts.

I run my fingers through the flames. The last time I played with
fire, Ben Zin showed up. So I keep doing it even though I know he
won't come. Only when it starts to really hurt do I start to pull my
hand away from the flame. But I stop myself.

If demons are coaxed out by pain—or at least their powers
are—then perhaps I can wake Gia by inflicting pain on this body we
share. Perhaps she can help me understand how to give Harper and
Pilot new lives. Then Harper will follow me again. And I'll build my
legions without Molly, who'd only judge me anyway.

I slip my hand over the flame. And hold it in place.

It takes a while, but I eventually feel it. The hurt. The sizzling of my own flesh. I grip my wrist to keep my hand in the fire, nearly biting half my tongue off the more my hand throbs.

Okay, that's the pain I needed.

When Gia last surfaced, I felt anger. So behind my eyelids, I force myself to think of Ben and Garnet eating together. To remember his angry glare when he caught me watching them the other day. That works. Fury swells in my chest.

Next, a little verbal coaxing: "Come," I mimic Dia, "show yourself, Miss Saligia."

I squeeze my eyelids tighter. All I see is bright red throbbing behind my eyelids.

"Come, Gia. Let's work together. Help me."

But my burning, blistering hand won't be ignored anymore. I yank it out of the flame and clasp it against my chest, biting hard on my lip to keep from crying out and steadying myself against the station table. I curl my whole body around my pulsating hand. I don't dare look at the mess I've made of my skin; I just beg for it to heal fast. When low waves of relief start coursing through me, and my breath slows, I prepare to start again.

I reach for the Bunsen burner—and that's when I see her.

Standing in the shadows no more than a foot from me, Hiltop watches me.

I scream at the sight of her.

Her normally lifeless eyes burn an unnaturally bright gold in the light of the Bunsen's flame. Without shifting her glare away, she shuts off the gas, and the flame goes out, turning her eyes dark again. Her long face is lit only by silvery moonlight through the windows.

"Always playing with fire." Her voice trails out of her like hot smoke blowing between her clenched teeth. "So you want to bring *her* here? You want to shed this skin that is Anne Merchant and have a glimpse of what lies beneath?"

"I've already seen—"

Hiltop strikes me with the back of her hand, leaving my words dangling in the air. The blow sends me reeling into a wall of test tubes. The top shelves collapse over me, and glass rains down, shattering against the travertine floor. I brace myself to keep from falling into it. I taste blood on my lip, trickling from my nose. I shake off the shock and, my chest heaving, stare my tiny tormenter down.

"I guess that wasn't enough," she says, clenching and unclench-ing the fist she struck me with. "Come on, Gia. *Come out, come out, wherever you are!*"

She raises her hand, hooked like a claw, and stretches it toward me, bringing the points of her fingertips together. I gasp when I look down: my shirt is bunched as if it's in her grip, but she's still feet away. My heels slide out from under me. I clamber at the shelves; she yanks me out of reach. My feet leave the floor. Without even touch-ing me, Hiltop lifts me until I could stand on the countertops. And here she suspends me, watching in simple pleasure as I try to snarl down at her but can barely muster more than a terrified grimace.

"Tough girl," she says mockingly. "You used to be so impressive, Gia. You could do this without a thought." She wags her hand, and I fly back and forth. "And now you are reduced to this *thing* I could snap in two."

"But you won't," I retaliate. Desperate. Clutching at straws. "You won't because I'm the child you *almost* had. I'm your creation."

Her expression softens, and, in her distraction, she lets me drop—but catches me a half foot above the floor.

"Dia told you, did he? Dare I ask what you did to wrangle it out of him?" She lowers me the rest of the way to the floor. "Never mind. Don't tell me. I've never been interested in your sexual exploits."

"There's nothing to tell."

"You might think that. I couldn't possibly comment."

Her tone sends shivers down my spine—not because it is threat-ening but because it is *not*. It's protective. It's the sort of tone my dad and mom used countless times.

"You are my creation," she confirms. She folds her hands on the countertop and, with the most placid expression, watches me straighten up. "You were my muse in the underworld. And you are my muse in this world. You are, have been, and always will be my one true creation."

"I'm not *yours*," I say, feeling my parents slipping away from me.

Now I wish I'd let her throw me down, pummel me, do whatever she wants to. Just to keep my parents close to me, to keep her from saying things that will separate me from them.

"You wouldn't be here were it not for me. When that is the case, that makes me your creator, does it not? Put in your terms, Miss

Merchant: your mother was the paint, your father was the brush, your soul was the canvas—and I was the artist who pulled it all together. Thus, I am your creator."

"I'm Anne Merchant. That's all I care about. Who I am now, in this life."

"*That's* all you care about?" Hiltop's knowing gaze drops to the Bunsen burner. "Seems to me you're curious about the hundreds and hundreds of years you spent in the underworld. Those years in which you adored me. I turned you from a mere succubus to the most feared of all women. A true goddess of the dark."

I busy myself with my bleeding nose, with the glass at my feet, with anything but her.

"You were and are my masterpiece," she says.

"You're nothing to me. I don't even know you."

"But you did. You loved me, and I let you go. I let you run along and find yourself in this world, a world you've loved as much as I have."

"You didn't *let* me do anything."

"Just as a parent lets her daughter go off to college to find herself, I let you go. All in. No memories of your past life. Human, through and through. I let you come here, Saligia, and choose your path. I let you be a blank slate, knowing, all the while, that all roads would naturally lead you back to me. And they did."

The open door is beyond her. I'm not sure she'll let me leave this lab without a fight, and, unless Gia appears, I won't survive a battle with her.

"I gave to you in ways I've never done before or since. I gave unconditionally to you, without asking anything in return, and elevated you to a standing no lost soul had ever achieved."

"Do you expect gratitude?"

"Just respect. I, the Great Exchanger, asked for nothing when it came to you. I always knew you were special, Gia."

"I'm Anne."

"Don't sell yourself short."

I back toward another station and stand behind it, shifting ever closer to the far edge of the room, to the empty aisle that will lead me straight to the door in six, maybe seven strides. The station protects me from Hiltop, although, without question, she could reach me before I'm halfway out the door. She doesn't have to touch me to seize me. And the bitch can fly.

She observes me like I'm a lab rat acting most peculiarly.

"You are free to run away," she says.

Holding my breath, certain she's lying and about to pounce, I inch into the aisle and creep forward, my eyes on her.

"But don't think you can run from who you really are and who I am to you. You will come back to me. All roads lead to me."

"Dream on."

"Why do you think you left the underworld?" she asks. "Your lover had scorned you, making love to Invidia behind your back. You rushed to me when you learned of his betrayal, and you begged me to help you through it. I found a solution for you: this girl you pretend to be. And you loved me even more for it."

"I could never love you." I turn away, dead-set on the door now. "I love my parents—my real parents, no matter who 'created' me."

"You love them?" she shouts. "Perhaps you think you do now … but that wasn't always the case."

I've always *loved them.*

"After all, Gia, you were the one who condemned Nicolette to die."

twenty-three

OUT OF BODY EXPERIENCES

"NICOLETTE MERCHANT WAS THE FIRST WOMAN IN HER right mind to ask me for a child," Hiltop says.

Her voice nears, making my skin itch like it's shrinking, like I might burst out of it. The hallway begins to pulse with shades of red.

"I was floored. And little surprises me, so that's saying something," she continues. "I needed time to think through exactly how it would work and what to request in exchange. You, Miss Saligia, helped me make sense of what to do and what to demand."

"I did not."

"You jumped at the chance to toy with a silly woman who needed to be taught a lesson."

"My mother was a saint. She was just desperate."

I hear the soles of her boots squeal against the tile behind me.

"Aren't they all? But, my, how you and I laughed to think what it would be like for these humans—*Nic and Stan, high school sweethearts*—to discover their miracle baby, spawned nearly thirty years after our lovebirds first met, was not so much an angel as a demon."

"Stop it."

My shoulders are tensing, my hands cramping, my calves tightening. My beating heart pummels my ribcage. I know what that means, but if Gia appears now, will she be able to stand up to Hiltop?

"A witch's baby," Hiltop pushes.

"*Shut your mouth.*"

"And when it came time for me to go to The Land Above," she says, "and settle the terms with Nicolette, you said—why, Gia, perhaps you recall what you said to me?"

I can feel her demonic gaze on my back, searing raw holes.

"Is that a *no*?" Her breath prickles my hair. "You said I should give this foolish woman *half* the time I gave Faust—just twelve years—to spend with her daughter. And then I should seize the two things she deserved to lose for making such a request. Do you know what those two things are?"

Before my eyes, the hallway has started to transform. Patchwork shimmers clap together, replacing the wall of lockers, into misty woods thick with knotty trees, each of which moves like it's alive. A damp chill runs over me. A shadowy figure sways next to me.

"The first?" Hiltop says. "Her sanity. The second? Her daughter. You said, and I quote—"

I know the words before she says them.

Not because I can anticipate them.

But because I can remember them. Because I am in the memory. She is feeding the memory to me.

"—*Make her kill her child, Master, in her lunacy. And I shall join you on Earth to help you expand your reign over these beings.*"

The shadowy figure vanishes, exiting the memory. But I, Gia, am left behind. I feel myself sink to my knees. I feel my palms on the muck of the forest floor. I dig my nails into the powdery ash, the permafrost of the underworld. Arms wrap around me, comforting me, and I find they are not arms but the roots and branches of the shadowy trees that live and breathe in the underworld forest I'm recalling.

Hiltop steps into the hallway. She is an obscure, shape-shifting silhouette in the woods of my memory—now schoolgirl, now lurching man, now animal, now hooved beast.

"You will come around to me," she says, her voice a thousand miles away. "Because you are my child. You will find your way back to me. We will expand our hold together."

Could it be true? Could Gia have agreed to come to Earth, to be me, just to help her mentor? Could she have lied to Teddy? Is she playing Teddy somehow? If it's true that she condemned Nicolette to such a fate, could she, in fact, be as evil as I'd expect an underworld goddess to be? I'd be a fool to believe Hiltop, but I'd be a fool to ignore her, too.

"I've given you the illusion of freedom," she finishes. "Don't make me regret it."

I glance up as Hiltop's nefarious spectre drifts off. She rounds the corner just as the roots untangle, the chill lifts, and my vision fades.

The school hallway is as it was. Hiltop is gone. But I am here. And I am different.

I fight the urge to lower my head, to close my eyes as I might have done in the past. I battle the pity party that would celebrate my penetrating shame—my furious regret—at being the reason my mother degraded through a dehumanizing mental illness, the reason she tried to kill me. And instead, I let my breath come faster, harder. I welcome bright pulsing pain as it rushes through my veins, lighting my skin on fire. I stoke the flames deep within my soul that are brimming up, up, up to my throat, that are surfacing in my mouth, and that explode, at last, with a cry that changes everything.

The overhead lights sizzle on and pop off with bright sparks. The windows flex. The walls shake just as they did at Dia's. Everything is just as it was in the Zin mansion, but stronger.

In the midst of the pandemonium, I keep my head, though I feel weaker than I have in a long time. I force myself to stay present, not to black out, not to run from Saligia. Because I need to know if she's good or bad, and to do that I need to connect with her. I watch the teacher's desk slide away from me and the framed periodic table behind it clatter from the walls to smash on the floor. I watch the stools shove away and I hear the beakers near me rattle together. I refuse to be overwhelmed by my own power—by Saligia.

I am filled with great expectations when I look down at myself. Equally so when I grab for my velvety tail and wait for the itch of light-filled wings, both of which I hope are with me now.

But there is nothing.

No tail. No wings. I pat my hands over my body.

Nothing.

What happened? Why didn't it work? And why am I so sapped of energy? I feel like I could fall asleep standing up.

A glint of silver in the far corner of the room catches my eye. I jerk to look, and there I see her.

She is not a reflection in the window. She is real, here with me in the flesh. She is standing near the collapsed shelves. With her magnificent cat eyes, she watches me, but she is as listless as I am. Two frail wings flit and fall behind her shoulders. I can't even see her tail. She is leaning against the broken shelves, spent.

"Gia," I breathe.

I have, somehow, projected her. Split my spirit. Disassociated. Cast her straight out of me, as if from my mouth. And it's left us both weak. "How did...that happen?"

"Our. Gift." Her body sags into the wall. "Cast. Souls."

Gia and I have a gift. All demons do. Ours hadn't occurred to me. I'd ask more, but I have bigger questions. I don't want to believe that there's a part of me—old or not—that would do what Hiltop said I did to my mother. Or to anyone.

"Did you...condemn Nicolette...like Meph said?" I ask her.

Her lips move. But she's listless and drifting.

"Are we evil?" I ask.

This time I hear her: "Leave. Me. Be."

"I can't do that. I need your help."

"Be. *Anne.*"

Spent, she vanishes. And my heart thumps hard again. My back straightens, my shoulders square; I am my whole self. But a different self than I've been these past few months. Because the underworld goddess I was trying to be has asked me to stop using her, to be who I am.

"I'm not ready to," I say, knowing she can hear me. "Not yet."

No, not yet. I've made too many promises. Too many people are depending on me to help them. Harper and Pilot aside, Teddy and my mom need me to help them take down two underworld leaders. That Gia knows about that but doesn't want to help makes me think maybe Mephisto was right, maybe she's a bad soul. My head throbs at the thought, but it must be true.

"You'd rather back out on the woman you condemned to insanity and ultimately to death," I say to myself, to Gia, "than do the right thing and help her. You'd rather cower. But I wouldn't. Anne wouldn't. So you won't, either."

THE NEXT DAY, I feel renewed. Like I've fought with my inner demon and won.

Until I see Harper.

I'm near the water, where a feat of strength exercise has just ended, leaving Ben victorious with his clapping girlfriend and a decidedly sober-looking Dr. Zin. A small crew of freshmen are taking down what was evidently an obstacle course, with the Seven Sinning Sisters overseeing them, when Harper plants herself in front of me, crosses her arms, and taps her foot.

"I'll take that barrette back, ugly as it is," she says. "I've figured out what we can do to get me a new life. So I'm gonna give you some power by serving you, and then you're gonna do exactly what I say."

Now I cross my arms. "Why would I do that? So you can serve me and leave?"

She chews on her lip. "I'll serve you for a fixed amount of time. Then bail."

"How long?"

"We'll go to Voletto's office right now. Find out what demon gives second lives. Figure out how to get that demon servin' you. And then I'll serve you until, say, the end of the school year, at which time you'll liberate me."

"Why would Dia tell us anything?"

Flipping her hair, she poses suggestively. "You stick to your knitting. I'll stick to mine."

Superbia is watching us. When our eyes meet, she lowers her chin for the first time in the many months I've known her. Oh, God. I know what that look means. Superbia's mine? She begins walking our way, her head down the whole time.

"Let's go to his office," Harper says to me.

"Now?"

"No, next Christmas."

"Do you need me there? I think you're better at that stuff than I am."

"I sure am! But what kinduv master would you be, lettin' me hog all the glory?"

Superbia sidles up next to me, and Harper, never one to miss a chance to suck up to a teacher, comments on how lovely she looks today. Superbia rolls her eyes.

"I have to talk to Miss Merchant, Miss Otto," she says. "If you'll excuse us."

Harper slides her narrow gaze my way. "Half an hour. Be there. I'm not kidding."

As she darts up to Goethe Hall, I turn to Superbia. Sunlight glints off the locket around her neck. Her tattoo is gone.

"Master," Superbia says, "I understand you split your soul last night."

"How could you know that?"

"Good news travels fast. Until now, I couldn't be sure if your return was sincere. But now I know. The others are sure to follow you. Even Invidia will come around. We all will. If your choice is to return."

"Look at me," I insist. "You can't follow me. Dia will notice you've left him."

"So you *don't* choose the life of Saligia?"

As the Existentialism Club takes over our spot in the quad, I pull Superbia aside. For privacy.

"Tell me," I whisper to her, "why did I leave the underworld? Was it because of Dia? Or Mephisto? Or… was it to help Teddy? Do you remember my friendship with him?"

"Ted Rier?"

I nod.

"We cannot be too careful with our choice of enemies."

Shit, that's not very helpful. I realize, at once, that she's quoting *Dorian Gray*. I'm about to push for more, but she is slipping my locket from her neck. She hands it to me.

"Did you just stop following me?" I ask.

"Your question proves to me you are not the Saligia I once served."

That was fast.

I watch in confusion as she saunters away, all eyes on her.

Then the impact of what I've just said hits me. I told her I was helping Teddy! That's the worst possible thing I could have told anyone, especially one of Dia's followers.

Without another thought, I race hard and soon burst into the office shared by the two people who can help me now: the Cania Christy counselors. Scout Colenns, the career counselor, and Lance Crenmost, the grief counselor. I've gotta talk to Teddy. Their powers will connect me with him. The office is empty when I slam the door behind me, startling them. Scout and Lance roll out from behind their desks, swiveling in their squealing old chairs to stare up at me.

"Are you back, Miss Saligia?" they ask in unison.

"Essentially."

"May we"—Lance looks hopefully at me—"see you?"

"I didn't come here to put on a show," I say hurriedly. "And I didn't come here to talk."

"Please?" Scout begs.

"I said no."

A typewriter sits on one of the desks. I march to it, lift it, and stomp back to the guys. Gripping the typewriter by its platen knobs, I raise it above my head. I don't want to waste a second. Lance's heavy brow is curled up like a massive crouching caterpillar, but Scout looks intrigued, like something amazing might happen any second.

And it does.

I slam the typewriter down on Scout's knees. He howls and leaps up. I push him back down and do it again, then let the typewriter fall to the ground. Lance is staring at me like he's not sure if he should be impressed or call the cavalry. I shoot a glare at him, and his brow-terpillar jumps for the roof.

In my mind's eye, I can see Molly wagging her finger at me, and I can see Saligia, exhausted, asking me to leave her. But what else can I do? Superbia knows about me and Teddy. I have to talk to Teddy.

Scout is doubled over when I pull him up by the scruff of his collar.

"Scout, look at me," I insist and wait for his eyes to stop rolling like bingo balls. I think he might cry. Doesn't matter. I need him to use his power for me: connect souls.

"You broke my femurs!"

"Connect me to the soul of Ted Rier."

"That really *hurt*."

"Scout!" I slap him across the face like I'm focusing someone hysterical.

Lance writhes a little in his chair. "Do it again."

I hit Lance. "Was I talking to you?" Back to Scout. "Now, do as I commanded." Grasping Scout's hair, I yank his head hard, like I'm trying to rip it from his neck, and hear a series of cracks. "I told you to connect me with Ted—"

I'm here. At least, my spirit is here; my body is back in their dingy little office, awaiting my return. I turn in circles, temporarily forgetting why I'm in this new place with the surprise of actually *being* here. I can feel the ground beneath my feet. I can. It all feels as real as it looks—and it looks like the beginning and the end of the world.

I'm on a litter-strewn rocky ledge overlooking a vast bluish-gray sea, with a decrepit concrete building seven stories high looming next to me. Two similar buildings, abandoned and dilapidated, are next to it. Garbage everywhere. Broken bicycles and dead things.

"I know this place."

It's Battleship Island, an abandoned island I read about years ago, during a particularly morose period in which I only wanted to paint dead things that had never had a true heartbeat: dreams, rock and roll, education, Latin, and *this* deserted Japanese island. It would not surprise me in the least to find Teddy here. It's dark and awful enough to be an ideal location for the next Cania.

"Teddy?" I test my voice. It works.

I stomp over a stained doll with its dirty stuffing puffing out and creep from the breakwater deeper into the remains of an island long deserted. There's no one living here, but I can almost hear the laughter of kids some twenty stories up. I think I glimpse them darting around corners and looking up from the dark shadows, where their bicycles lay. I follow a shadow around the side of an apartment complex and find Teddy standing not ten feet away.

"Anne." He looks me up and down. "What are you doing here? How are you doing this?"

"With Scout's help."

I hear a giggle, but it falls over us like wind. Scout's laughing. That means Scout can hear us, and we can hear him. It hadn't occurred to me that he'd be able to eavesdrop. If I'd known that, I would never have come looking for Teddy.

There's only one way we can talk in private now.

As I gesture for him to draw the Silencer, I say, "I just wanted to see you because I'm working on a painting of, um, sheer evil. And I thought you'd make a good model."

He shakes his head. I hope he knows that I'm not actually here for an art project.

"Please. Just stand silently there, Mr. Rier. And I'll stand silently here. And I'll memorize your face. Very briefly. And then leave. *Silently.*"

With a deep sigh, he swirls his hands down, just like he did last time, and seals the two of us in a vacuum.

Make it quick, he thinks.

Superbia knows that you and I are ... connected.

What does that mean?

I asked her if Gia came back here to help you.

Christ, Anne!

I'm sorry!

And she said?

Almost nothing. She just stopped following me.

She was following you?

Yes, and now I'm worried. I mean, you haven't been my Guardian during her time at Cania, so she'll be suspicious. I shouldn't have mentioned you!

Just steer clear of her.

You're not worried? What if they figure out our plan?

Stay away from her. Ignore her. In fact, ignore the Seven Sinning Sisters. They've always been hateful to me. He dusts his hands like this is over. *Now, if that's everything.*

It's not!

He groans.

Ted, Hiltop told me something about my mom.

That you condemned her to insanity?

It feels like I've been punched.

Can you give my mom a message for me?

Yes. But wait for me to come to you with her response. Don't pull a stunt like this again.

I nod.

Tell her, I begin, *that I'm sorry I had anything to do with her illness. And I love her. And I'm only doing this for her. Oh, and if she feels bad about how I got into a coma, she shouldn't. I love her.*

If that's everything.

I am back in my body in the office, where Lance and Scout are watching me. It's a huge relief that he's not worried about what I told Superbia. And as a side perk, Teddy's going to be talking to my mom. If only I could talk to her directly.

"All that for a stupid drawing?" Scout asks me.

"You're spot-on painting that Ted Rier guy," Lance says. "Sheer evil."

That's when I notice Lance holding a chunk of my hair. I pat around my head and quickly find my newest bald spot—right up front. I scowl at them. Guess I'll need to cut bangs now.

"You couldn't even do it in an inconspicuous place?"

"The others will be so pleased to know you've returned, Master," Scout says, taking a lock of hair from Lance and rubbing it over Dia's tattoo on his wrist. The tattoo vanishes. "We'll divide your hair among those who wish to serve you. Pilot ran out of yours a couple days ago."

They bow to me as I leave the room.

But I turn back.

"You guys are both serving me now?" I ask to clarify. They nod. "So I can use your powers without hurting you?" Again they nod. "Show me how you do what you do."

"But then you'll do it on your own!"

"Without coming to see us!" Scout whines, echoing his roommate.

"I promise I'll come back. Really."

Reluctantly, they show me what I need to see. And I leave their office knowing that, without waiting on Teddy and without worrying about someone eavesdropping, I can now connect directly with my mom. With *anyone* who's crossed over.

So, because I've got no interest in returning to my dorm room— not after fighting with Molly—I go to the library, to my favorite spot, where I whip through my very own short list of people with whom I'm going to reconnect. Scout's power is to connect souls on Earth, and Lance's power is to connect realms, like Heaven and Earth. I want to connect with Heaven, where my mom is, where Ben's mom is, and where his sister Jeannie is.

Or, where I assume they all are. I know my mom's there, thanks to what Teddy's told me—plus, I saw her angelic spirit when I was in my hospital bed. But as for Ben's mom and sister, perhaps they're not. Perhaps they're reincarnated, something I'd never before believed in but can't help believing now.

CR&O

THE FOURTH FLOOR of the library is empty, cold, and dark when I start lighting candles. I pull out my incantation and read it briefly, trying to commit it to memory. Then I do as Lance said he does: I hook my hands together, close my eyes, and visualize myself floating to a beautiful, pure space—what I imagine Heaven to be—to see my mother. I think her name: *Nicolette Merchant.*

I recite my incantation.

And wait.

But all I see behind my eyelids is empty, vast whiteness. She doesn't appear. Could I be doing it wrong? Or could I be so bad now as to be forced out of anything as good as Heaven?

I think on her harder. To no avail.

But I need to talk to her! I need to tell her I'm sorry about what Gia did. I need to tell her she'll always be my mom. And her husband will always be my dad. And we'll always be a family, no matter what happens here or how I was created. And I need her to say I'm still her good daughter, not this girl using her inner demon to hurt people.

Unfortunately, my need to see my mom does not materialize her. Nothing does.

"I must be doing it wrong."

I open my eyes, shake it off, and decide to try again. With Jeannie Zin this time. If this doesn't work, I'll have no choice but to go back down to Lance and Scout's office and use force. But I don't want to do that. Because, well, I think I'm done doing that. Because stupid Molly with her stupid emotional logic has made me feel like some sort of underworld deviant—and I hate her for being right.

I close my eyes.

Do something good, I think. *Use this power for good.*

The floor by the door squeaks. I check. Find I'm alone. And close my eyes again. I hook my hands together. And recite. And wait to see Jeannie, a girl I've only seen in photos. I nearly pull my hair out when nothing happens. Bloody Lance Crenmost! His little trick hasn't worked at all.

There's always the chance that Jeannie has reincarnated. Maybe my mom has, too. I'll start with Jeannie and then look for my mom.

The idea of either of them being reincarnated as some sweet girl or boy makes me giddy with excitement.

So I press my hands against either side of my head, which is what Scout said he does to trigger his *connect souls* power. I repeat my incantation. I want to connect with the soul of Jeannie Zin, wherever she is, if only to tell Ben one day, should we ever be together again, who his sister's become. Perhaps we can even visit her and watch her from afar, the way Damon Smith's parents will watch over whomever he's become.

I hope this works.

All at once, I am standing at the back of a library, between two huge shelves of books.

Guys in Harvard sweaters are crowded around a book a few steps away from me. They don't seem to notice my arrival.

Why am I here? What would Jeannie be doing at Harvard? If she's reincarnated, she wouldn't be much more than five years old now. I'd expected to arrive in the frilly pink bedroom of some little girl. I must have connected with the wrong Jeannie Zin.

But I'm curious. So I creep down the aisle behind the shelves of books and nearly run into a student.

"Sorry," she says, turning to me and smiling. "Wow, dig your hair."

I recognize her smile. I know that smile. I know the crinkled nose above it.

But just as I'm about to say something to her—to this girl who is not dead and not reincarnated—to this girl who, with bright green eyes, can only be the living, breathing Jeannie Zin—she glances behind me. And staggers back. Like she's seen a ghost.

I turn.

Ben is standing behind us.

twenty-four

CROSSROADS

JEANNIE ZIN ISN'T DEAD. SHE'S NINETEEN AND A HARVARD sophomore.

I'm standing in a library I've never seen before, and I'm looking from her to her brother, Ben Zin. Jeannie is clearly at a loss for words. So I speak to Ben first, though he hardly looks like he's going to be able to keep himself together.

"You're in the library, aren't you?" I ask. "The library at Cania. You're why the floor squeaked."

He keeps staring at his sister. And she keeps staring at him.

"Ben?" I say.

At the mention of the name of her brother—her only brother, her long-dead brother—Jeannie's shocked expression shifts to a whole new level. I think she might pass out; she's definitely stopped breathing. The crowd of guys is looking at us, so I drag Jeannie and Ben, like the frozen statues they could pass for, to a quiet table in a distant corner. We sit down.

I have a thousand things I'd like to say. But I know that *my* point is not the point right now. So I sit quietly. And pray no one else comes into the Cania library to find me and Ben sitting together.

"You look so much like my brother," Jeannie says to Ben.

"You look so much like my sister," he replies.

Their hands are flat on the table. They are seated across from each other. And they are soaking each other up like they've been blind all

261

their lives and, at last, can see. Ben is the first to tear up. But Jeannie follows fast. Their hands find each other, grab each other, pull each other up from their chairs and bring them into an embrace neither could have possibly expected a mere five minutes earlier. I watch, wishing I could be a part of this experience with them but not daring to move, and I think about how, months ago, I sat with Teddy and felt Anne Merchant dying; I thought about the unexpected nature of death, of how it comes so randomly and changes everything. But it's not only death that has the power to change us, to interrupt us, to get in the way of mundane day-to-day nothingness and routine. Jeannie thought she was just going to the library to read or research a paper; instead she found her brother. Life is constantly getting in the way.

"They said you were dead," Ben says.

"They said the same thing about you! What about Mom?" Jeannie asks excitedly, still in disbelief, still clutching her brother to her. "Is she with you? Where have you been?"

But before Ben can utter a word, we are yanked from Harvard.

We're back in Cania's library, where we started. A raging Garnet is tugging Ben away from me. His hands were wrapped around my wrists; I can still feel the warmth of his touch as I lower my hands.

"What's going on here?" she demands, hollering and appearing torn between crying and killing someone. "What are the two of you doing together?"

"I'm sorry!" I cry.

Ben, dazed, gets to his feet and stands obediently next to his Guardian-girlfriend. She and I look at him as he reorients himself. For one glorious moment, I can see the weight of years of guilt and sadness lift from his shoulders. But then he sees Garnet again. And his face darkens. Thank God I rewrote history for them, removing me from it fully and completely, or this could get ugly.

"It's my fault," I say and leap up. I've gotta fix this fast, or Ben will never see Jeannie again. "I've been dabbling in the dark arts. It's bad; I shouldn't do it. And Ben came up here and saw me, and he tried to wake me from my trance."

Pursing her lips, Garnet looks at Ben. "Is this true?"

He's still too dumbfounded to speak. But he manages to nod.

"And when he tried—well, being in a trance is like sleepwalking," I lie. "You're not supposed to wake a person up. So when he did, I grabbed him and pulled him into the trance with me."

"It looked like he was grabbing your wrists."

I nod vehemently. "Oh, yes. He was trying to break me out of it. But as soon as he touched me, he entered the trance. It was one of those dark, empty trances. Not much happens in it. Just kind of… zone out. So he probably won't remember much. He'll look a little, like, void for a while. And if he acts strangely, please don't think anything of it."

"I don't like my boyfriend touching other girls."

"Of course not. And don't tell Pilot, okay? It was just part of the trance."

The prettiest smile lights her face. "You and Pilot Stone? I guess the rumors about you being anything but a standard Cania kid are true."

Satisfied, she takes Ben by the hand and leads him out of the library. And I let out the longest breath imaginable. Because she bought it. She really bought it. And because if Ben didn't have anything more than Garnet to live for before, he does now. He's got his sister back! I'm tempted to pop back into Jeannie's world and tell her everything, but I want to wait until Ben's ready. Even if he hates me, he'll come find me when he's sorted out what he wants to do about Jeannie.

Right now, there's only one person I want to share this moment with. It's because of her that I even had the idea to do something good with the gifts I now have.

Unfortunately, the last time I saw her, I screamed bloody murder at her.

Molly keeps her eyes on her Kindle when I knock lightly on our door, poke my head in, and raise my eyebrows like white flags of surrender. I ask how she's doing, and she rolls onto her side, facing the wall, away from me. I offer her a chocolate chip cookie I swiped from the cafeteria, and I pull out a can of Mountain Dew for good measure, dangling my peace offering before her eyes, but she looks only mildly interested. She pops her headphones on and exaggerates the act of turning up the volume. I sit on my bed and wait, but that gets me about as far as waiting ever has: nowhere. So I take out a notepad and begin scratching out an apology letter.

A knock on the door interrupts me. Molly doesn't notice because her music's so loud.

I swing it open, and Harper storms in. With all her strength, she shoves me back. Again. And again. Until I fall onto my bed.

"What the hell, Harper?"

Molly tosses her headset aside and watches us. So does the crowd that's forming at our open door.

"You left me at Dia's office by myself," Harper fires at me.

I totally forgot I was supposed to meet her there!

She straddles me, pinning my wrists back. I rail against her, but she's tough. Gia could snap her like a twig, but I won't force Gia awake anymore, not when I know she doesn't want it, and not just to fend off Harper.

"Do you think I *like* being this? Do you think I wanted to be this person, to have this PT?" Harper cries. "It was chosen for me! I don't want to do those *things* with those *beings*. But I do them! I keep doing what I'm supposed to! And you used me. You used me worse than any of them ever did."

"Harper, wait, listen."

"No! I've listened and listened to you. But you're evil. You're *awful*."

"I'm not! I was on my way to Dia's, but I got sidetracked by something really important."

"By what? Your seven evil bitches that serve you?"

"What do you mean by that?"

"I know why Superbia wanted to talk to you in private. She serves you now!"

Everyone gasps. Girls are pushing each other and spilling into the room to get answers to what's going on with Murdering Merchant, the girl who wanted to leave so badly, was given the chance, decided to stay, and has since been beating up half the staff. Molly, perhaps waiting for my confession or just enjoying seeing me in agony, quietly observes us.

"I promise, it's not like that."

More gasps. More onlookers.

"Why didn't you come to Dia's?" she demands. "What sidetracked you?"

"It's personal," I say. I'm watching Molly as I say, "I'm really, really sorry."

Molly shrugs but looks slightly softened.

Harper, on the other hand, might tear my head off. "You're gonna be sorry. Because if you don't give me what you promised, I'll have a nice long talk with Garnet."

At that, Molly jumps up and shoos everyone out of the room, telling them the show's over as they groan. She closes the door behind them, locks it, and pounds on it to back them away. Then turns to us.

"Please don't," I beg Harper. "You don't know what you're playing with."

"You don't know *who* you're playing with," Harper shouts.

Molly tugs Harper off me. The angry redhead is panting as she watches me sit up. Molly and I position her between us. And that's when the cracking begins. The façade Harper shows the world breaks. Tears well in her eyes.

"I just want to go *home*," she says, and her whole body slumps. Her deep Texan drawl vanishes. "I've been playing this idiotic, over-dramatic part for so long—the so-called mean girl, the most obvious trope, the shallow empty little tease—and I've given up so much. Everything. Don't I deserve a second chance?" Molly and I look uncomfortably at each other. "I didn't mean to die! That wasn't supposed to happen! It was an accident. Stupid horse."

Together, we comfort Harper, who's full-on crying. Molly hands her the Mountain Dew, snapping it open, and I offer her the cookie. She takes both. And we sit together. The three of us. With a box of tissues on Harper's lap.

"You saw pictures of me the way I used to be," Harper says to me. "In that stupid scrapbook, which reminds me, Molly, you need to fill out your page still. Murdering Merchant isn't dead yet, so she doesn't get one."

"I'll get to that, sure," Molly says, tossing me a look.

"I wasn't always like this," Harper continues, taking a bite of the cookie. She chews once then with surprising force whips the cookie across the room. It breaks on the wall above Molly's bed, covering her bed with crumbs. "God, I used to *love* cookies. Now I can't even taste them." She gulps down some soda. Molly grabs the can from her before she can chuck it, too.

"I used to be a lot like you, Anne," Harper continues. "I read a lot. I kept to myself. People never—they never really warmed to me. The only reason I wanted that stupid pink Hummer was because I thought it would make people like me."

"People do like you," Molly says.

"They don't. They don't." She wipes her arm across her nose. "Girls would invite me to their birthday parties because I'd get them big presents. But then they'd talk trash about me at school on Monday."

"We all know how that feels," I say. "They called me Death Chick." I leave out the fact that she's been calling me Murdering Merchant for most of the year.

"I was Heifer Otto. Harper Fat as an Auto. Harpooned Whale. And the constant questions about whether the carpet matches the drapes." She sniffles. "I never even had a boyfriend before I came here. Never kissed a guy. Wanted to marry Prince Harry. When they assigned me Trey for a Guardian, he took one look at me, and I swear he didn't even read my soul. He just said what he wanted my PT to be. So he could use me." The tears flow again. "I should've known then they were all demonic freaks."

"It doesn't take a demon to objectify a girl," Molly says.

Collecting herself, Harper finally gets to her feet again. She finger-combs her hair until it falls perfectly again. You can almost see her mask of cool perfection dropping over her. She pulls a scrap of paper from her pocket and hands it to me, then walks to the door, where she turns back to us. She zeroes in on me. The vulnerable expression Molly and I nurtured only moments ago is gone.

"'Course, this don't change a damn thing," she says. Her thick drawl is back. "If you don't help me get a life off this island, I'll make sure Garnet knows that you did all of this for Ben…and he never really wanted a thing to do with her."

Molly and I stare at Harper. She *just* sat here and cried with us. And now this.

"No, I wasn't always this way," she says, "but I am now. So do us all a favor: don't underestimate the lengths I'll go to for what I want. Life." With a snap, Harper struts out the door. "Make it happen."

Molly locks the door as I unfold the scrap of paper.

"This is what happens when you make deals with the devil," she says and throws herself down next to me.

"The Seven Sinning Sisters," I read.

"What about them?"

"Harper went to Dia's office to find out who has the power to give new life. Turns out, they do," I say. "But they'd have to leave Dia to follow me, and he's bound to notice that. In our painting sessions, I've been watching the little tick marks that represent his followers disappear. If the sisters go, I'm screwed. I'd get my ass kicked by him or even Mephisto—whoever feels most threatened. Maybe both of them."

I groan and flop back on the bed.

"You know," Molly begins, rolling to look down at me, "you could just give up this whole Saligia thing. Your problems would vanish with her. It looks like Ben's a sure thing for the Big V, if the rumors are right."

"But I told Teddy I'd help him, too."

"Teddy?"

"And then there are the lives I promised." I clamp a pillow over my head. "Wake me up when we get to the happy ending, please."

She lifts the pillow. "What did you tell Teddy you'd help him with?"

"Just destroying Dia Voletto. Y'know, easy stuff."

She tilts her head. "What have you got to do with what Teddy wants?"

"Evidently Saligia wanted to destroy Dia because he cheated on her." I sigh.

"Girl, you don't know how badly I wish you'd gone home when you won the Scrutiny. What a mess."

"I know. But I told Teddy I'd destroy Dia. And he's a devil, after all, so destroying him is a good thing."

"Anne, come on!" she says, shoving me. "You don't have to do anything for that little weasel. He's kept you in a coma, for crying out loud. Why would you help him?"

"For my mom."

She looks taken aback. "More information, please."

I tell her everything, all the way back to when I woke to find Teddy over my hospital bed. It feels so good to get the truth off my chest, like there might actually be a way out of this now that I'm sharing it with Molly.

"Why didn't you come to me sooner?" She gets to her knees and peers down at me. "What do you want to do about all this?"

"I want to help my mom."

"What if your mom came down from Heaven, sat here, and said for you to do whatever makes you happy? To forget Teddy?"

I think about it. "I'd want Ben to have a new life. And then, well, I guess I'd want us all to have one. And for my dad to be free. And for Dr. Zin to be free. And for you to have your island back."

She sighs.

"It's a lot, right?" I say.

"Yeah, but let's look for a theme. What do all of those things have in common?"

"Well, they're all connected to Dia and Mephisto."

"So…?"

"So I guess I'd get everything I want if Dia and Mephisto were out of the way."

"If you want to do it, that's one thing. But don't do this because you gave Teddy your word. And *definitely* don't do it for your mom."

"She's *the* reason to do it, Mol. She wants me to."

"I don't think your mom would put you in that kind of danger."

"You don't know my mom."

She flinches. "You think she'd try to hurt you? Is this because of how you got in your coma? Anne, I'm sure she's incredibly sorry for hurting you that day."

I shrug. "It's not that. I just want to do right by her."

"Then do right by yourself." She smiles, lightening the life-lesson vibe in the room. "So, you need to get those devils out of the way to save Ben and, like, the world. That's the plan?"

I nod. But then something occurs to me. "I don't remember telling you about what my mom did to me."

Her smile falters. "You talk in your sleep, girl."

"I do?"

"A lot. But it's not all sad. Sometimes you mention someone named Dr. Jones."

"That's the name of my doctor back in Atherton."

"See? How else could I know about Dr. Jones? So, back on topic: if you're going to take down Mephisto and Dia, you should start with the easier of the two. Got a sense for which one might be easier to off?"

We lock eyes. In unison: "Dia."

"Then we've got work to do. But not because of Teddy or your mom," Molly says. "We're going to have to think of something a lot better, and a lot less violent, than simply, like, battling Dia."

"Did you have something in mind?"

She bounds to her feet, rummages through her backpack, and holds up a book.

"*Dorian Gray*?" I ask her. "What's that got to do with it?"

"Isn't it obvious? You're a painter, Anne. Paint."

twenty-five

THE PICTURE

ALTHOUGH BEN'S FUTURE ALWAYS SITS IN THE BACK OF MY mind, and although my demon fellowship continues to grow even without Gia appearing or torturing anyone, regular life must go on. My plan—my real plan, the one Molly helped me work out—must go on.

And so it has.

For weeks, I've patiently executed each step Molly and I laid out. And now that it's May and there's less than a week until graduation day, I'm closing in on the end. Our plan to destroy Dia depends on two things: my painting of him and Gia's ability to cast souls. Dia's agreed not to look at the portrait until I say so, which is why I've been dragging it back and forth from my dorm to his office. The closer we get to the unveiling of the portrait, the more frequent our sessions have become. The energy my followers lend me has kept me up night after night; Molly's kindly started sleeping with a mask over her eyes to let me work on Dia's painting from dusk till dawn.

"Let me see it!" Dia commands as he playfully but weakly tries to dart around the side of the canvas.

"You know you can't." I slap him away.

"I'll see it in a week anyway."

"And not a moment sooner."

"I must see it, Anne!"

"You've been mentoring me for nearly eight months," I remind him. "Don't you trust your own instruction?"

He flings himself back on the chaise. "Then distract me. Occupy my mind. I'd ask you to occupy my body, but I've been feeling so weak lately."

"Why don't you talk to me about beauty? What's the most beautiful thing you saw today?"

"I'd like it to be my painting!"

I calmly dip a thin brush in violet.

"You are quite maddening, Anne, do you know that?"

I dab the canvas with the brush.

"All right, fine. Have it your way," he says.

"Why don't you tell me why Saligia was so angry at you?"

"Are you still angry, sweetheart?"

"Is it because you cheated on her with Invidia?"

He turns to face me. "I always loved you. It's why I'm here. For you. To protect you."

"I don't need protection."

"Everyone needs protection from Mephisto and his scheming little men."

"Face sideways, please. I'm working on your profile."

"I can't take this! You must let me see it."

"*Sideways.*" When he hesitates, I add, "Do you want this painting to be your most beautiful self, or would you rather waste time on tiny tantrums?"

He lies back again. I blow on the last strokes of paint to dry them.

"When I'm done with this," I say, "it will be the most beautiful thing you've ever seen."

"I can hope, but I know that's not true."

"Why not?"

"Because I have seen pure beauty. I've beheld it. And I've loved it so deeply, I've decided to make it the one and only form of tuition for Cania College."

"What is it?" I ask him.

"It looks like light."

"Tuition fees are going to be *light?*"

"Not any light. A soul's light. A clean soul's light."

The brush falls from my hand. He looks at me, and I scramble to pick it up again, to act natural.

"Everything okay?" he asks.

"Fine," I lie. "Our time is just coming to a close."

He glances at the clock. "So it is."

Hurriedly, I throw a sheet over the canvas. I'm coated in a cold sweat. I can't believe I didn't see this coming. I can't believe it's taken so long for the underworld to get what it really wants from mankind. Mephisto has been so in love with our world that he's taken our possessions as tuition for his school; but Dia Voletto is infatuated with beauty—he would only take the very source of beauty as tuition for his school. He's come for our souls.

I'll have to take his first.

"I'll see you tomorrow," he says.

"And every day this week. Until Saturday's reveal."

That night, for the first time in weeks, I fall into a deep enough sleep that I actually dream on and off. I catch glimpses of Ben in my dreams—small glimpses packed with me running toward him and telling him I love him, telling him to wait for me—but, more clearly than anything, I see Teddy. He comes through so vividly, I realize it's not a dream but rather that Teddy is entering my mind, like an incubus might. Thankfully, though, he doesn't try anything funky with me. He just wants to talk.

"Why didn't you try this earlier?" I ask him. "I could have used a little coaching along the way."

"Are you ready to destroy Dia?"

Typical Teddy, skipping the niceties. "Everything's in place, yes." I don't mention that I'm not doing it entirely for him and my mom anymore; I'm doing it for a greater purpose, one I've worked out with Molly.

"Excellent. This weekend, I'll be there. For graduation day. And I'll support you in bringing down Dia—and then we'll work on Mephisto."

He's about to leave my dream when I stop him.

"My mom," I say. "What did she tell you?"

"That you should help me."

"No, I mean when you told her I was sorry for my involvement in her mental illness."

"Oh, that. Yes, she said you're forgiven."

"She did?"

"Anne, I've got to go."

"Did you tell her she shouldn't feel bad for hurting me when she was sick?"

But instead of answering me, he's gone.

THE LAST WEEK before grad has turned the entire Cania Christy campus into Death Row, with slightly more room and moderately better amenities. The graduating class is now facing the last days of their death sentence. All but one as-yet-undetermined senior have mere days to live, with graduation this Saturday. If they'd been given a week anywhere else, they might indulge in being alive: swim with manta rays, fly a helicopter, have a massive party with their family and friends, eat anything they'd like, apologize to those they've hurt, forgive those who've hurt them, tell the guy they've crushed on exactly how they've felt—and go in for the kiss. But landlocked here, their options are limited.

It's Thursday now. Just two days until graduation.

I'm awkwardly carrying Dia's painting, wrapped in a bedsheet, from my dorm to his office, and I can't help but pause every so often to listen to seniors softly crying or violently raging in the quad, or to see them attempting death-defying stunts, which they could have done all this time but were too focused on being graded well to bother with. A girl named Verily is trying parkour against the wall of Valedictorian Hall and slamming her body into the ground on repeat, as a boy named Justin watches her, clapping at her attempts, laughing off her failures, and obviously waiting for the right moment to confess to Verily that he loves her dark brown hair and her deep brown eyes and that he wishes they could have met under better circumstances. Maybe by the time the Graduation Eve party rolls around tomorrow night—hosted by Dia at his mansion—Justin will have worked up the courage to hold Verily's hand. Only to die.

I hoist the painting up again—its width and height are uncooperative—and silently curse Molly for not helping me with this. But she's been working overtime with seniors trying to record final good-bye videos for their friends and family, which Mr. Watso will mail away after graduation. The girl is seriously racking up karma points.

"Need a hand?" someone asks from the other side of the painting.

My heart thumps to hear the voice I'd recognize whispering in a thunderstorm. But it's not until I see Ben peer around the canvas and take one end, freeing me to focus on the other, that I think I might go into cardiac arrest.

"Thanks," I say. *You shouldn't be around me*, I think.

"I've got selfish reasons for helping you."

In silence, we pass Valedictorian Hall and approach Goethe Hall. But even as I try to steer toward the back entrance, Ben keeps moving to the empty parking lot. I glare at him, but he mouths, "*We need to talk.*"

In the quiet of the parking lot, Ben takes the painting from me, leans it against the Rex Paimonde building, and gestures for me to come closer, to a spot where we'll see onlookers before they see us. It is a very good thing that, during our three and a half months together, I became an expert at keeping my cool when in close proximity to Ben; even now, even with five months of heartache under my belt and with the panicked mood on campus, I want nothing more than to wrap my arms around him and twist my hands in his hair. If anything, my feelings for him are stronger than ever.

But I can't let him know that.

"Why were you with my sister?" he asks. His gaze is piercing.

"It was a random accident. It just...happened."

"An accident? You transported your spirit—or whatever you were doing—to an Ivy League library where my sister, who should be in the ground, just happened to be standing?"

I'm at a loss for words. I can't even dream up a lie. Yes, I knew Ben would have to come after me at some point to ask about Jeannie, but whatever lies I cooked up in my head to feed him have abandoned me now, leaving me only with a truth I have to hide.

"I hate you," he says. Not to hurt me. Just to tell me.

"I know you do."

"But I have dreams of you. Why?"

"I didn't know you did." It could be because I have legions of succubae serving me.

"You hurt teachers and cafeteria ladies all the time. I've seen you do it. They're saying you're some sort of devil."

"I am. In a human body."

A laughing stampede of seniors charges across the parking lot and to the hillside, to the cliff, where they'll jump, splash into the water, disappear, and reappear on top of the cliff, to start all over again. We lean out of their view as they go by.

"Do I hate you because you're a devil?"

"You just…hate me," I tell him.

"But why? You must know why."

He's not supposed to ask why. He's not supposed to look closer. That's my job, not his.

"Why do I hate you," he continues, "when until now I didn't know you were a devil? And why do I hate you when you never do anything but look at me as if you love me?" I step away but he grabs my arm. "And why do I hate you when you sat with me and my sister, and you looked so happy to see us together?" He presses on as my throat tightens. "And why do I hate you, Anne, when standing here with you now makes me feel, somehow, full and complete?"

"Ben…"

"And why do I hate you when every time you visit my dreams, you wrap your arms around me, and I wrap mine around you, and you tell me you love me?"

I'm stricken. "That's what happens when I visit you?"

"Every. Single. Time."

"You mean…it's not some sort of naughty, dirty dream?"

"No, of course not."

Ben's dreams are not induced by Gia's history as a succubus. They've got nothing to do with the underworld. I'm in Ben's dreams because he dreams of me. Because no spell could undo the truth of how he feels about me.

I look at him now, so close to his freedom, so close to being the older brother to a sister who needs him.

"Tell me why, Anne."

This is no time to slip up. We're too close to success.

"I don't know," I say flatly. "But I hate you. *I* hate *you*. So stop bothering me, got it?"

I pick up the canvas and, without glancing back, head to Goethe Hall. My hands are shaking hard enough that the canvas might fall. I just make it to Dia's office without dropping it.

Dia and Hiltop are waiting for me.

I've just leapt from the frying pan into the fire.

CR&O

I SET THE canvas down and adjust the sheet over it. I know what's going on. I know why Dia and Hiltop are both here. It's the moment I've been dreading since half the school staff started wearing my locket and bowing to me when I walk by.

"This is about Saligia?" I ask as I take a seat.

Their arms are crossed over their chests. They are standing on either side of the fireplace and leaning against the pale marble surround. Dia coughs; he looks feeble enough to blow over. Hiltop, of course, is her typical nothing-looking self.

"Why are you rebuilding your legions?" Dia asks me. "Is it to destroy us?"

"Is that even a possibility?"

"Don't be smart with us," Hiltop snaps. "You've been running around here all semester getting so-and-so to succumb to your will. They're talking about it in the underworld. So it stops now. I'm not about to let you tarnish my reputation again."

"I thought you loved me, G," Dia says. "You've taken four of my Seven Sinning Sisters."

Four? Three more, and I could give new life to everyone on this godforsaken island. Without a thought, I leap to my feet and bolt to the door. I just need to get the other three on my side, and this whole thing will be over!

But Hiltop flies to the door. She throws her body against it, blocking me. I shove her with all my might, and she budges, but not enough. Not even close to enough.

"Why haven't you stopped me before now?" I ask her.

Hiltop smirks. "It's been mildly entertaining to watch you return, Saligia, but the fun has been had. Surrender your legions."

"Surrender them?"

That's not how this is supposed to go. I'm not done! I need the remaining three sisters to help me give Harper and Pilot the lives I promised.

"Surrender them to us. Today." Hiltop glowers. She pushes me back toward the fireplace. "Now."

If I lose my followers now, I lose everything. I break every promise. And everyone I know and love suffers, fails, even dies.

I can't stop now.

I can't surrender now. Not yet. Not when everything is so close!

"We'll remove Ben from the running for the Big V if you don't," Hiltop threatens.

I could break into Valedictorian Hall tonight. Get Ben's vials. But then what? I'd need the Seven Sinning Sisters to help me give Ben a new life off the island. But they're not all mine yet.

Hiltop and Dia are watching my wheels spin.

Dia coughs. He looks like he has the flu. Good.

"And then there's the matter of Jeannie Zin," Hiltop adds. She paces before the fire. "She's alive, you know. Thanks to me. It's always a good idea to have a little leverage—a card up your sleeve."

"What's your point?"

"I will kill her," Hiltop says matter-of-factly.

"You can't kill humans," I remind her. "It's against the rules."

Dia and Hiltop snicker.

"The only clearly drawn lines run across the center of this island, Miss Merchant," Hiltop says. "In matters of spirits, demons, and divine beings, lines blur. I will, quite easily, remove Jeannie Zin from this life. After all, I gave her life to her, much like I gave yours to you, much like I give life to one student every year. I can take that life away. Perhaps not directly. But never question, when Jeannie is gone—locked away in a nuthouse or after succumbing to the inner voices that tell her to cut herself until the pain goes away—that it will be your doing. I'll be sure to let Dr. Zin and Ebenezer know she died because a girl who fancies herself the great Saligia chose her demon followers over pure, innocent Jeannie."

That's not true.

But it will sound like the truth.

"So what do you want me to do?" I ask. "How do I get them to stop following me?"

Dia sighs with relief. I'm sure he thinks the reason he's weak is because I've taken so many of his followers. But I know better. His strength won't return when they do.

"They are connected to you by your hair," Dia says faintly. "It's what I've always loved most about you."

Hiltop lifts a pair of shears from the mantel. They glint.

"Cut it off. Now. All of it."

twenty-six

SAMSON

THE SMELL OF BURNING HAIR SEEMS LIKE IT MIGHT HAUNT me forever as I balance myself against the front doors of Goethe Hall and tell myself that what I feel now, this listless and faint energy I have, is normal; it's what everyone feels; it's what I used to feel; I'll get used to it again.

Behind my eyelids, I see myself standing in Dia's office, before one of his many mirrors, and holding Mephistopheles' shears. They made me do the cutting. Mounds and mounds of my blonde curls fell to the ground. Dia called Invidia into his office and had her shovel my hair into the fire. I felt the powers of my followers leave me immediately, like Samson must have felt after Delilah cut his hair.

Hiltop was pleased.

Invidia did not look displeased. I always sensed she'd be the hard nut to crack of the Seven Sinning Sisters, given her history with Gia and Dia.

Dia looked healthier after my hair-chopping, but not by much. When Hiltop and Invidia left, Dia seemed surprised that I'd have the willingness to sit and work more on his portrait, but with the unveiling in two days, I had little choice. I told him he still wasn't allowed to see the painting. But recognizing my new weakness and the futility of my commands, he tore the sheet off it. At the sight of his own beauty, captured in ways only Oscar Wilde, Molly, and I could imagine, he staggered backward and clutched at his chest.

"It's as if you've seen every side of me," he said, wistfully letting his fingertips hover over the oil smears, the coal smudges, the faint watercolor, the raw edges of torn photos, and the lines of my thick pencil. "It's genius."

"But don't you think..." I let my voice trail.

"Don't I think what?"

"That it's not wholly you. It needs to be the greatest version of you ever made, something even better than your real self. Something even more beautiful to you than the purest soul."

"But how?"

I gave it some thought. Or pretended to.

"Leave it with me," he said, still transfixed by his own image. "And then you must meet me tomorrow—"

"You'll be busy getting ready for the party tomorrow."

"Ah, yes! Right. Okay, then meet me Saturday, just before the unveiling, for the final strokes."

I agreed and left him to spend the night wishing he could be as beautiful as the sight he saw in the painting. He knows that beauty is impermanent. But he forgets that my gift has always been to cast souls from one object to another. I can only imagine that Superbia has been trying to tell me how to destroy him since the day she held up a copy of *The Picture of Dorian Gray* for our class.

As I walk across the quad now, I expect people to point and laugh at my newly shorn hair. My wild, enormous hair and the strength I felt, the prideful ways I used to strut, are gone, hobbled.

But nobody points and nobody laughs.

Yes, they stop and notice my jagged haircut, the longest pieces of which are no more than an inch in length. But it's as if they know why I did it, that it wasn't by choice, that everything here is an act of sacrifice. Seniors, juniors, sophomores, and freshmen alike see me, drop their eyes, and raise them again to shrug or half smile or do whatever gesture it is that best expresses in that moment just how powerless we are here.

Molly says, "Oh, girl," when I swing open our door.

The news of my changed appearance spreads fast. Harper comes storming in just minutes later and stops short. Plum is right behind her. I am sitting on my bed, rereading *Faust*—my eyes are on the line *"Des Chaos wunderlicher tochter,"* which Teddy quoted to me back in September—as they stare at my shorn head and abruptly leave.

Molly says everything she can to convince me I'll rock this look. It'll grow on everyone. Short hair is totally in. And it suits my face.

"My mom used to braid my hair," I say to her.

"Well, I'm sure your mom would do awesome stuff with your short hair, too." She snoops through her makeup bag until she finds a pair of eyebrow scissors. She sits me on a chair in the middle of the room, throws a towel down, and starts flipping through some of her celebrity magazines for inspiration. The snipping begins. "You're gonna rock this look—trust me."

"They did this to take away my followers."

"I remember a time when severing ties seemed like a crazy idea," she says, "but it was for the best."

"You mean with Ben." I want to believe this is for the best, like severing Ben's ties to me was, but I can't see the light at the end of the tunnel like I did then. "We were so close. I almost got Dia, you know? You should've seen him today—he was so weak looking. And he told me I already had four of the Seven Sinning Sisters serving me. Four."

"Who's to say they don't serve you now?"

"They need to be adorned with a marker of mine. That was my hair. When I used Meph's shears to cut it off—well, I felt the energy leave my body, Mol, so I think that's that."

"But if they love you, they'll want to serve you."

"They can't love me now that I've let two devils get the better of me. I've shown weakness." The collateral damage of this battle: "I won't be able to help Harper or Pilot get a new life."

"They'll be fine."

"They'll hate me."

"So it'll be like it used to be," she says as she searches for pomade.

"I can't end Dia now," I say. "Not without Saligia's ability to cast souls around."

"Who said you don't have that power anymore?"

She's right. I'm still Saligia inside, even if my followers are gone.

"Look," she says, "you're almost done with Dia's painting, right?" She waits for me to nod. "Then you can do what you told

Teddy you'd do. But, Anne, before you try to take down an under-world leader, can I say something?"

Her pretty, fiery gaze magnetizes mine. I nod.

"Are you *sure* you want to destroy Dia?" she asks me. "You don't have to. You don't have to do any of this. Trust me."

I'm about to answer when, behind her, Harper and Plum appear in the doorway. They wield a selection of scissors, a nylon stocking, and a box of hair dye. They're not smiling, but they don't look like they've come to stab me, either.

Molly turns to see where I'm staring.

"We got a common enemy," Harper drawls. "*They* do that to your hair?"

"They said I had to get rid of my followers. This was how."

"We felt it happen," Harper admits. "Knew something was wrong."

"What's all that stuff for?" Molly asks them.

"If we stay up all night, we can make a wig," Plum says.

"A gnarly-colored one, unfortunately," Harper explains. "My red hair and y'all's dark hair. We'll dye it afterward."

"Jet black," Plum adds, waving the box of hair color. "So edgy."

Molly's fist goes straight to her mouth; she swivels away. When she looks back again, her eyelashes are wet with tears.

"That's really nice of you," I tell Harper and Plum. "But I couldn't possibly take any of your hair."

"Bobbed hair is the next big thing, Merchant," Plum says.

"It's so generous, but I'm going to wear this short cut," I say with a small grin, which vanishes when I give Harper my full attention. This is not going to be easy. Better just to say it, which I do: "Harper, I'm sorry, but I won't be able to give you a new life." I watch her swallow, unblinking. "I know that you'll tell Garnet the truth now. I'd ask you not to, but I'm not in any position to ask you for any-thing, least of all mercy on Ben Zin."

It's so still in the room, I'm sure they can hear my heart beating. Thump, thump. Thump, thump. One thump for me, one for Saligia. The fainter one for Saligia.

"I'm sorry," I repeat.

Harper sticks her hand out, and Plum puts a tube of lip gloss in it. Still watching me, Harper drags the gloss across her lips and hands it back to Plum, who does the same.

Without a word, she and Plum leave.

"They'll be fine," Molly says. She's never sounded less convincing.

It's three in the morning before I finally fall asleep. Tomorrow, Harper or Plum will tell Garnet that I fixed and manipulated things to get a second life for Ben. That I used her, and she didn't even know. That Ben's feelings for her, if they exist at all, are based on a demon's spell. I wake a half hour later. And stay awake until dawn, when I drag my butt out of bed and hope to see Harper in the bathroom, getting ready, so I can plead with her to protect Ben.

But she's not there.

Stiff with dread, I stumble to our morning workshop, the last of the year. Garnet is standing at the front of the room with Augusto; they both notice my pixie cut and drop their chins. My whole body clenches when I see, standing behind Augusto and waiting for their chance to talk to Garnet, Harper and Plum. What are they gonna say to Garnet? Are they going to do this now, right in front of me?

I sit at my easel. Just on the edge of the stool. Put my bag down. And stare at them intently, willing them to be kind.

Harper's face is blank, but Plum's eyes are narrow little slits, glaring at me.

Just make it quick, I think and bury my face in my hands. How did this all fall apart so completely?

Augusto huffs away from Garnet, who turns to Harper and Plum. It looks like Garnet asks them what's going on with my hair, because she speaks first, and tries to be subtle when she points, and they all turn to me.

I hear Garnet say, "Gosh, what would possess her to do that?"

Harper and Plum turn their backs to me. And then it happens: they begin talking to Garnet. I watch it like a car crash in slow motion. I watch Garnet lean in to hear better. I watch her head tilt, her eyes narrow. She glances over Plum's shoulder at me, and then back at them. She nods. Raises her eyebrows. Puts her hands on her hips.

This is it. *Sorry, Ben. Sorry, Zin family. I tried. I really tried.*

At once, Garnet claps her hands to settle the room. As we quiet down, she settles her gaze on me.

"Harper, Plum," Garnet says, "tell the class what you just told me."

Are they gonna announce to everyone what I did? Why can't anything bad at Cania just happen quickly? Why does it have to be dragged out like torture?

"We wanna let y'all know," Harper begins, "that Anne's portrait of Headmaster Voletto will be unveiled this weekend at the Cania College grand opening celebration, hosted by your very own Social Committee."

"Which is led by us," Plum tacks on.

"Well, it's led by me, but Plum's a fine-and-dandy vice president."

"We're co-chairs."

"Anyway," Harper says irritably, "let's put our differences aside and cheer on one of our own, okay? This Saturday. After the Big V ceremony."

A small, perfunctory round of clapping takes Harper and Plum to their seats.

I'm not sure what just happened.

Did that really happen?

I don't think I breathe again until, as I'm cleaning up my work-station after class, Harper saunters by and elbows me in the side.

"I should hurt you for lying to me," she says. "But, y'see, you actually did help me. Not the way you promised to, no. Not even close." She flares her nostrils. "That said, I've gotten pretty good at collecting followers."

"You have."

"And I've got a hunch Superbia and her crew don't like serving Dia Voletto much, do they?"

"I don't know."

"So they're ripe for the plucking."

"Hold on." I stop to figure out how to put this. "Are you planning on seeing this through on your own?"

"I've learned to do what I need to in order to survive. This is no different."

"This is playing with fire, Harper. Not just any fire. The kind that comes from Hell."

"I can play the game. Just keep out of my way, Merchant, and I won't make you or your boyfriend pay."

PILOT IS NOT quite as forgiving—if you can call it that—as Harper. Luckily, Pilot doesn't know that I've been twisting things to help Ben, so he doesn't know he's got a card to play. He only knows anger and hate and stomping around like a spoiled brat. Which I silently endure.

"Why did you give us all up?" he asks. "*Why?*"

He's wearing Mephisto's pin again. A punk or demon in the underworld is asking for trouble without the help and protection of a master. I wonder if my other followers went back to Dia, Mephisto, or any of the underworld leaders. I've been avoiding them all, especially the Seven Sinning Sisters, who keep showing up everywhere and just *looking* at me. I suppose I could take four of them back and, when Saturday comes and goes—when I prove I'm not weak after all—add the remaining three to my ranks, even though Teddy said to avoid them. I could give my followers a new token of my dominance, do the whole thing all over again, maybe even start doling out lives. But for what? To start a war I don't want any part of? To risk Mephistopheles hurting my dad this time or going after the Zins or destroying every vial in Valedictorian Hall and on the yacht just to punish me for challenging his position?

I can't.

I won't.

I'm not ready for that.

"They were threatening my family," I tell Pilot. In a way, they were.

"But now we're back to square one! Except for my dumb promotion."

"Your what?"

He shrugs. "I'm a demon now. Yippee. Sammie M. Firestone—that's my new name."

"Well, you got to keep 'Stone,' sort of. That's good."

"Even got a power," he grumbles.

"It's not the power to vivify, by chance?"

"That's not even funny."

"Hey, there's still the chance we can win the Big V."

"Even if we changed your PT to the skanky one, you'd never pull it off with that haircut."

I leave him slamming doors and hitting walls. And I run, in the dusk, back to my room, where Molly has laid out options for what we can wear to the graduation party at Dia's tonight. Everyone's going to be there. I don't even care that it's at Dia's—he can't keep me from enjoying myself anymore. He and Mephisto have had enough power over me.

Molly has laid out three pairs of shoes on my bed. Her name is written in all of them.

"My feet are the same size as my mom's," she says with a laugh. "Get over it."

"What goes better with super-short blonde hair?" I ask and hold up a sparkly, long black camisole and a silvery dress that's fitted like a corset. She points to the silver dress. "Own my badassness, right?"

She tosses me a pair of strappy heels. "Exactly."

The road to Dia's is filled with so many people, you'd hardly believe there are only 200 students at Cania. Molly swivels her arm through mine, keeping us locked together. Around us, most of the seniors are resigned to their fate, and now they're ready for the last— in some cases the first—party of their lives. We're going to do what it takes to give it to them.

The crowd spreads out across the Zin lawn, flows in and out of the front door, trickles through the porte cochere, and wraps around the back, where the first of many fireworks displays are well under-way, brightening the sky and shedding light on the dramatically changed southern half of Wormwood Island. Gigi's cottage is gone. It's been replaced by a thin patch of green grass and animal-shaped shrubs that wall off Dia's lands, creating a fence, on the other side of which is the vast, seemingly endless campus of Cania College.

Molly tugs me toward the gated entryway of the new school.

"It's really something, isn't it?" Molly whispers to me. She's seen it already in her many visits to her gramps' inlet. "Better than Cania Christy."

"Way better," I agree.

I press my face between the bars of the wrought-iron gate, which is flanked by red brick pillars and topped by a decorative iron sym-bol. It could be the entrance to Brown University. Pavestone walk-ways connect a series of stone buildings, some columned, all of them timeless, that lead to a cathedral-esque main hall. The lights are on in a building made just for visiting parents; in classic Cania form, not even the mothers and fathers of graduating seniors are allowed to connect with their kids until the morning.

I stare at the too-familiar campus.

"I've seen it all before, Mol," I say. "I memorized these buildings on an admissions pamphlet my mom got me."

"Yeah, I know."

"You know?"

"It's obviously a replica of Brown."

It is. And something tells me it's designed like this not to torture, and not to tempt me, but as a message to me: *this* is my destiny. Mephisto won't let me escape; he thinks I'll always come back to him. It seems I'll never be free until Mephisto is gone—so why did I agree to kill Dia first? As I stare at the college Dia will lead, I know he's got darkness in his heart, but I can't help but wonder why I narrowed my focus so quickly from Mephisto and Dia to just Dia. Now that I think about it, it seems sortuv nuts to destroy Dia alone tomorrow. When he goes, a whole slew of demons are going to be looking for new masters fast. I should be ready to swoop in and destroy Mephisto before he takes every lost demon and becomes entirely unstoppable. Why didn't Teddy and I think of that?

"Come on," Molly says, stunting my mounting concerns. "My first high school party awaits. If I haven't made out with three guys by the end of the night, it will not be due to a lack of effort."

We make our way into the mansion, where the walls are vibrating as Pilot plays DJ Who Wants to Deafen Us. I see the Model UN from Hell early on, and Harper and Plum nod my way, but nothing more.

Venturing further in, I find a corner in the kitchen, near the wide-open backdoors that lead to the crowded deck, while Molly grabs us something to drink. I catch a glimpse of my pixie cut in the window's reflection and have to smile; from Miss Saligia to *this*. Frankly, I prefer this.

"It's growing on me," Dia says as he comes to stand at my side. I see him in the reflection next to me. He doesn't look like his old self, either; his broad shoulders slump now, and there's a wheeziness in his breath. "You haven't been here in so long. Not since the day you freaked out about my experiments."

He's got a lot of nerve talking to me after what he did. Of course, I've had some nerve looking him in the eye for the past few weeks even as I slowly enacted my plot. I guess you can't expect much more from a couple of underworld leaders.

"Did you destroy those morbid beings?" I ask him.

"'Course I did."

I glare at him.

"I'm not as bad as you think I am," he says.

"Saligia hated you."

"Well, hate is love in the underworld."

"And cheating on her was...adoring her?"

"I don't know if I should take credit for mentoring you now," he says, "or stand humbly in the shadow of what you were able to accomplish when you weren't under my tutelage."

"Nice topic change."

"I can't stop thinking about that painting."

"Me neither." And I mean it. That painting consumes my every thought.

Molly swoops in and hands me a can of soda. She's shoving chips into her mouth as she smiles at Dia, excuses us, and pulls me into the dancing crowd, where no one can keep their hands off my short hair, which is especially short at the back.

When the music starts to get lame, we venture out back, where the most tormented of seniors have gathered to slice knives across their wrists and stab each other just to see how it feels. That gets old—and creepy—fast, so Molly and I move along, like we're exploring side-shows. A prayer vigil is underway in the porte cochere. A dozen kids hold candles and pray for the souls of the seniors we're about to lose.

"I think we promised to enjoy tonight," Molly says, tugging me away. "Not that...I mean... We can sit and pray here if you want to."

"I never took you for guilty, Mol."

Verily and Justin bolt our way and hand Molly flash drives containing their good-bye speeches, meant for family, and then dash off, holding hands, with a final call of thanks. Molly tucks the drives into her pocket and shoves me when I look at her like she couldn't be a bigger softie.

Around the next corner, to my heart-stopping dismay *and* delight, are Ben and Garnet. Molly tries to steer me away, but I won't let her.

"You are such a masochist."

I hush her.

Ben has his back against the house, and Garnet is standing an inch or two from him, bringing her lips to his, then pulling back, then smiling and kissing him again—on the nose, on his eyelids, on his forehead, and eventually on his lips—bobbing like one of those bird toys that sips from a cup of water.

When she notices us, she calls us over. I try not to look at Ben, even though I can feel his gaze moving through me like fire through dry wood. Last we spoke, I told him I hated him. If he wins tomorrow, will there be time for me to tell him the truth? Or will I have to use Mr. Watso to send notes to Ben in his new life?

"Anne, my prize student with the bold new look!" Garnet is all smiles. "And her friend—I forget your name, sweetheart."

"It's Molly." She throws me a glance that says what I'm thinking: Garnet's barely older than we are, so why is she calling Mol *sweetheart?*

"Yes!" Garnet exclaims. "Such a cute name."

"That's me," Molly says. "Little cutie."

I have to look away to keep from laughing.

"So, are you girls enjoying the party?" Garnet asks us.

"I'm thirsty, actually," Molly says.

Ben's face lights up. "Me, too. Let's go grab a drink, Mol."

"I'll take a chardonnay," Garnet calls after them. She drapes her arm over my shoulders. It smells like she's already had a glass or two.

I drive a glare into Molly's back, but she doesn't turn to see.

"So, Anne, how *exciting* is the unveiling tomorrow? I just wish we could be around to see it."

"You won't be?"

"The unveiling happens after the Big V. If Ben loses, well, let's not go there. But if—no, *when*—he wins, we'll be leaving the island immediately."

So that seals it. I won't be able to talk to him.

"Oh, but it's been so fantastic being your teacher," she says. "Ben and I are planning to move to San Francisco until we can sort out our story. It'll be like living in the Witness Protection Program, but we'll be rich, of course. Beautiful, young, and rich. And in love."

I look awkwardly around, desperate for a change of subject. Which is when Dia heads our way.

"Where's my Saligia?" he asks me.

Ugh, he's been drinking too.

"No, this is Anne," Garnet corrects him. She looks at me like, *Duh, he's been sitting for you for months.*

"No, this is Saligia, the underworld goddess. All full of trickery, this one."

Oh, shit. I can't believe I didn't see this coming. Dia's about three seconds from destroying everything.

"Tell me more about you and Ben in San Fran," I say to Garnet and block Dia with my back.

"What do you mean?" Garnet asks Dia, forcing me to let him back into our space. "You mean she looks like the goddess Saligia? Didn't she have long hair? I seem to remember a Rossetti painting of her with long, wavy hair."

Panic sets in in five, four, three, two—

"No, no, she's *really* Saligia," Dia slurs. "Anne's soul. Mephisto made her. She's been running around here getting demons to follow her," he hiccups, "and do bad shit."

Realizing he'll never stop talking, I slam my lips against his. Hard. To shut him up before he can utter another word. Dia grunts in pain but responds fast. I hear Garnet's laughter transition from fast and surprised, to slow and confused. She gasps when I pin Dia to the wall exactly as she'd pinned Ben. Except I'm not light and kind and sweet when I kiss Dia. I'm rough. I'm openmouthed. I'm coming on as strong as I've got to if I want to shut him up and fill her mind with something new.

I think it works.

Except it works so well, Gia responds. Just like last time, I can feel her rising. My head has started swirling. Bright lights begin flashing. *Fuuuck.* She's going to explode here like she did in Dia's library, and she's going to send everyone flying, and then it will be all over. Secret revealed. All lost.

I tear myself away from Dia, who collapses breathlessly into the wall. He had so little energy as it was; I've sapped him of what was left.

"Anne Merchant!" Garnet says with admiration. "I'm impressed. Role-playing—I never would have guessed you had such a wild side. And with Dia!"

"I—I—"

I can still feel Gia. She's still here, close to the surface, because I'm still near Dia. So I bolt.

I dart away from him, from Garnet. Like I'm on fire and need water, I shove through the throngs that seem to move slower and thicken the more I need to get through them. I race to the nearby woods, praying I'll make it into the cover of the first trees before Saligia appears. *Stay away*, I command her, but then I recall Dia's kiss, and she's here again, she's with me again, right under my skin.

I leap over a fern. Collapse on the earth. In a whirl of leaves and branches and mud. In a tornado of violent energy.

I glance at my hands, clenching the ground. But where I expected long, slender, claw-like hands—her hands—I see mine, chipped black nail polish and all.

"You didn't come," I whisper and think, *Once we do what we have to tomorrow, I won't ever bother you again.*

With my dress destroyed by forest-floor muck, I glance back at the party. Dia has wandered away. Good. As long as he doesn't say anything else to Garnet, we should be okay. With that, I inch my way, crawling, through the woods and back to campus. I can't return to the party covered in mud.

As I get ready for bed, I wonder if Molly's going to kill me for abandoning her at the party. Probably not. She's got three dudes to score with, and I would have cramped her style.

Like so many others will do tonight, I lie back and dream of really living again. Surrounded by sunshine and the warmth of the people I love. I let myself, for the first time in a long time, imagine Ben in that life, too. With me. I imagine the Christmas he'd envisioned for us, with his dad, with my dad—and with Jeannie.

In small groups, girls start returning to the dorms. I listen through my partly open door to them talking quietly about what the seniors are going through, about what it would be like to be so lucky as to win the Big V.

To live again, I think. Did we live before? Who here lived enough in their first thirteen, fourteen, fifteen years to even get to die? We'd barely started.

I'm half-asleep when I hear Molly sneak in, shuffle by my desk in the darkness, and scurry back out. I'm half-asleep when she returns, moments later, and whispers that she thinks I'm sleeping, which means she's with someone. I'm half-asleep when I try my damnedest to hold in a big ol' smile at the idea of Molly hooking up with some senior guy—I mean, what single person wouldn't hook up a little on their last night on Earth? I'm half-asleep when she flicks her lamp on and excuses herself, leaving her friend behind.

I hope they don't make a lot of noise.

I pretend to sleep.

But not for long.

"Anne?" Ben says. "Please, wake up."

twenty-seven

BREAKING SPELLS

I ROLL IN SLOW MOTION ONTO MY BACK, AND THEN TO my side, to find Ben standing above me. He is gazing down at me with the strangest expression. In one hand, he holds a rolled up sheet of craft paper—my sketch of him in his casket—and in the other, a folded piece of paper, writing on both sides. It takes a moment, but I realize that it's the breakup note Ben gave me; on one side is his cold good-bye, and on the other is my conversation with Molly, in which I explained to her that, for masochistic reasons, I'd kept my ties to him while severing his to me.

"I don't mean to wake you," he says, "but I don't have a lot of time."

For a moment, he looks like he might throw himself at the bed, at me. But he's Ben. So he starts to move, and then he stops himself, always letting his reserved demeanor rule.

I sit up and pull my knees to me.

He moves tentatively, watching me watch him in the dim light, to sit where my feet just were.

He's holding his breath.

So am I.

"This was all your doing," he says. His eyes are glistening when he looks at me. He looks older than ever, like Dante must have looked after walking through Hell. "I think about breaking up with Garnet all the time, you know. I lie in my bed and wonder how I could have dated her for years when I've never been in love with her. But she and I have all these memories, so there's no denying our history. Maybe I would have just accepted it," he says, dropping his gaze, "if the spottiest memories of another girl hadn't kept interjecting. A blonde girl. With wild hair."

I absently stroke the velvety back of my head.

"It was you. She was you. Before you cut your hair."

I wait.

"I have these random memories, you see. Memories of seeing you leave Gigi's house and throw a jacket into the bushes."

He saw that? Back on my first day here?

"I remember you and Pilot Stone walking down to the water one afternoon. I remember you washing the dishes in Gigi's kitchen, talking or singing to yourself, as I sat in the shadows of my back deck. That was in September. That was when my dad and I still lived where Voletto is now. All these memories, Anne, of me watching you. But those conflict with this belief in my mind that I hate you, for reasons I can't possibly identify. And then…"

He's going through what I went through. A secret to unravel, all on his own, without more than glimpses of the truth to guide him. I know a secret that is protecting his life, just as he knew a secret that, in his eyes, protected my life and kept him and his father safe. As he didn't tell me that I was in a coma and the entire student body was deceased, I won't tell him the truth now. Not because I'm cruel, but because I know he'll figure it out. I can see him figuring it out. Just as he once saw me figuring it out.

"And then there's the Scrutiny challenge. Anne, you were everywhere in it. You were the lust I had to conquer." He stares at his hands. "To finish the challenge, I had to give into that lust. My lust for you."

I hold my breath. As he exhales.

"I remember feeling," he says, his eyes bright with the memory, "like I had a hall pass. Like I never wanted the Scrutiny to end because this was my chance to have you as I'd wanted to, with no repercussions and no harm done. When I woke only moments after I started kissing you"—he stops like he's holding back details—"I was more upset that it was over than I was that Toshio had beaten me.

"And then there's my enrollment as a student," he rushes on. "I couldn't remember why. Something told me not to ask around, especially not to ask my dad, who's been on the hard road back to sobriety. I thought asking wouldn't help me in the here and now, so why do it? But tonight, I asked Dia. I asked him why I was a student."

"Oh, Ben." I temple my hands on my lips. "Not in front of Garnet."

"There! Why would you say that? Why not in front of her?" His eyes flash. "It's like you're protecting me from her."

I swallow.

"Well, it wasn't in front of her," he says. "Dia told me I was punished for helping *you* run from Mephistopheles. But I don't have any memory of helping you. No, Anne, my few memories of you are memories you couldn't possibly have known because they were happening only for me. And because you couldn't know them," he says, takes a breath, and runs his fingers under mine, "you couldn't erase them. Could you? Using those powers you hinted at the other day?"

I close my eyes for a moment. In defeat.

He knows.

"What does Garnet know?" I ask him.

"I don't have a clue."

"What have you told her?"

"Nothing at all. Look, just tell me. Did you—did you do this all for me?"

He shifts to wrap his hands around mine. My pulse soars. And, for the first time in a long time, I feel like it's my heart beating, not Saligia's. I come to life when Ben's near me, just as Gia came to life when Dia was near her.

"Did you love me?"

"Ben."

"Did I love you? Or am I going crazy, trying to connect dots that are only coincidentally located near each other?"

"I didn't do it for you," I say at last. "I did it for me. I used this dark history of mine to make you win the Big V when you told me you'd never fight for it. I needed you to fight for it. Because I needed *you*. I did it because I selfishly want a life with you, Ben...even if you'll have to battle feelings of hating me each day."

"The hatred is strong," he admits with a light laugh. "But not insurmountable."

To my surprise, he pulls me into his arms. I'm back in his embrace, a place I'd worried I'd never again be. We lean back in bed, and I adjust my quilt around us. If we were to die now, with my head on Ben's chest and his hand gently stroking my arm, I would be totally okay with that. My eyelids are heavy when I hear him whisper.

"If I win tomorrow…"

"*When* you win."

"Promise me you'll do everything you can to join me."

Yawning, I nod. "I'm way ahead of you."

"Because Anne?"

"Yes?"

"I love you."

I smile to myself. "I love you, Ben."

We're fast asleep when Molly nudges us.

"Ben has to get back to his room," she whispers. "Someone will notice. People will talk. Assumptions and all that."

Groggily, Ben and I stand. I am counting my lucky stars when he looks into my eyes and takes my face in his hands. But I pull away before he can kiss me.

"Not when you're with Garnet," I say. "Not until we're both back—Molly, too—in the real world."

"What if I don't win?"

It's a thought I haven't let enter my mind. But it's a possibility, to be sure. As hard as I've tried, nothing's guaranteed. I've never been through graduation day, and I have no idea what to expect.

"Positive thinking," Molly offers.

"Positive thinking."

It's not until Ben slips out of our room that I start shaking. Molly rushes to me, and we fall into my bed, curling up just like Ben and I did. I'm floored by what's happened. I can't believe Ben put it all together.

"Did you ask him to come here?" I ask her. "Was this your plan?"

"He pulled me aside when we went to get drinks for you and Garnet. He asked for the truth. Said Dia had told him something about why he's a student here."

"And you told him about us?"

"I told him he might want to see a drawing you'd done. And a note he'd written."

We smile in the dark, but only faintly. Because tomorrow will tell everything. Tomorrow will decide our fate. Wrapped up together, Molly and I fall asleep.

We wake to the sounding of trumpets heralding the last day of forty-nine lives and the new beginning of just one. It's all been building up to this.

twenty-eight

GRADUATION DAY

DECISION TIME.

The campus is alive, as if the souls about to depart us are expending decades of unspent energy. The sun is shining, birds are chirping, and the ocean's roar is low and pleasant, almost as if we're not preparing for a mass execution.

Harper has insisted I help the Social Committee set up for the graduation ceremonies, so I'm trying to be helpful, even with my mind a million miles away. When I showed up at Valedictorian Hall this morning and started unfolding white wooden chairs, she shook her head, crossed her arms, and stomped her foot.

"No, Anne, *a hand's space* between each chair!" she said in a huff. "If your hands weren't so damn big. Pretend they're small and dainty like mine, and start again." If she's serious about playing the devil's game to get her life back, she's going to make a fine demon.

The graduation ceremony will take place inside Valedictorian Hall, with only the senior class, their parents, their Guardians, and Headmaster Voletto in attendance. (Ben and Garnet are already inside. I didn't even get a chance to see him.) The doors to the *hallenkirche* will be locked. The rest of us will sit outside with our parents and Guardians and watch the events unfold on two large shaded screens. The school band, which has been practicing all morning, will play for us throughout the ceremony, creating a soundtrack that Harper says will build tension and keep an air of excitement in "the

296

boring parts" of the ceremony. There will be popcorn, cotton candy, and soda. After all but one senior is offed, we survivors will dine on lemonade and cucumber sandwiches down at the Cania College opening ceremonies. How charming.

With our Guardians grading us, Plum and I weave long-stem flowers into the gates of Cania Christy as the first of a line of parents come up the road. They are all dressed rather optimistically in shades of white, with bright colors every so often. Linen suits. Summery dresses. As if this is a typical graduation ceremony. Harper and Agniezska stand on either side of the open gates and offer event programs to the guests as they enter, while Augusto and Jasmina usher the parents of graduates into Valedictorian Hall and show the others to their seats around back. Jasmina openly stares at those who surrendered parts of their physical selves to get their child into Cania Christy.

Like the man without a nose, who looks like a snake.

Like the cat-faced woman. At a glance, you'd think she's just a victim of too many plastic surgery procedures. But then you see the whiskers. And the reshaped teeth, when she smiles.

Like Mark Norbussman's 520-pound—exactly, weighed on a nearly hourly basis—mother. Like Alistair Bloomberg's *I Love Porno*–tattooed dad. Like Joie Wannabe's mom and dad, who'd divorced before Joie died but agreed to have their hands sutured together for twenty years, for Joie.

"The graduates will join you in Valedictorian Hall," Harper tells senior parents.

When Harper's dad and stepmom arrive, she gladly accepts their embraces but, always conscious of being graded, shoos them away. She glares at her little followers and even at Augusto when their parents arrive and they let them fawn too long.

But when I see my dad, I don't give a damn what anyone says or what Pilot scribbles on his clipboard. The moment I see his silhouette and that silhouette turns into him, with his twinkling brown eyes and big, bushy beard, I abandon my spot at the front gates and haul ass down the road, throwing myself into his arms. He staggers back, but steadies us and gives me a bear hug that could easily crack my spine. Others are looking, but I don't care. When I lean back, I see him looking at my hair. Or lack thereof.

"Do you like it?" I ask.

"What happened?" He looks worried. Really worried. "Was there a lice breakout? Or have you been listening to your mom's old punk records?"

"I'm just experimenting," I lie. Though it's partly true. "We artists must always be reinventing ourselves."

"Did Picasso ever cut off all his hair?"

"I'm not trying to be Picasso. Just me."

Taking my hand, he walks me, with the last of the parents, to the gates. But he doesn't step through with me. He just stops.

"I'm an employee of Cania, sweetie. I've gotta keep a sense of professionalism."

"So?"

He unhooks our hands. "Pumpkin, go ahead first. I'll meet you at the hall."

"Where are you going?"

He smiles, but it's a mortician's smile, so you have to squint to see it. I notice Dr. Zin walking our way. My dad nods at him, at his scarred face. Between my shorn head, Dr. Zin's scars, and the rest of the weirdos around here, surely my dad has figured out that Cania isn't quite the paradise he's selling.

"Dr. Zin is going to take me to meet Headmaster Villicus," he says.

Dr. Zin joins us and nods at me, "Miss Merchant."

"You're meeting Villicus?"

"Of course," my dad says. "He's my boss, hunny."

Not for long, I hope.

"Villicus has returned to oversee Cania Christy when Headmaster Voletto moves on to the college," Dr. Zin explains, filling in the gaps. "And, naturally, he'll be judging today's debates with Headmaster Voletto."

A cold sweat bursts under my uniform. Garnet has to convince *both* Mephistopheles *and* Dia Voletto that Ben—my Ben—deserves to win the Big V. As my dad and Dr. Zin head to Goethe Hall, my mind races through my interactions with Hiltop. Did I do anything that will absolutely guarantee Ben won't win today? The last I spoke to Hiltop, she was telling me to cut my hair, and I did. I did what she said. I barely put up a fight.

But she knows I did it for Ben.

She knows what Ben means to me. And she cares in ways that Dia doesn't.

With only Dia judging, Ben stood a chance. A solid chance. But with Dia *and* Villicus...

Molly and Mr. Watso find me talking to myself as I close the gates. We walk to the seats she's saved for me and my dad.

"Villicus is judging today, too," I tell her. "As in, Mephisto. As in, Will Do Whatever It Takes to Torture Me."

Molly blanches. I half-heartedly introduce her to my dad—they look at each other in the strangest way—and she and I sit, gripping hands and waiting for Ben to walk the plank. Images of the inside of Valedictorian Hall fill the screens.

"The Seven Sinning Sisters," I whisper to Molly as I spy the dazzling, sinful sisters standing near the screens. "They're Ben's only hope. They can give him life."

"No, Anne. You can't go back to being that person. It's not the way to win."

But my mind has already started working on this problem. I've gotta save Ben. Once and for all.

Pilot takes the seat on the other side of my dad. My dad nods at him, thinking he's just some kid, not a punk. Invidia commands us to be quiet. As always, everyone obeys her. Well, everyone but Pilot.

I hear Pilot whisper to my dad, "I think you know my dad. Senator Dave Stone."

"He's your father?" my dad whispers. "Well, nice to meet you. Annie and I owe a lot to him."

"Sure, he helped get her in."

"Where is Dave today?"

I stiffen. Dave Stone wouldn't be here because Pilot's not a student anymore. But my dad doesn't know that.

"In California."

"He couldn't make it?"

"He wasn't invited."

Invidia zeroes in on Pilot, who sees her and stops talking, to my relief. Is he planning on telling my dad I destroyed his vial? Is he going to expose my secret past, and the way I've terrorized so many staff members, to my dad?—here and now? I fire him a warning glare.

On the left screen is a close-up of Dia's face, which looks dark and hollow. On the right screen, a close-up of Villicus. Dia is the first to speak. Barely. Molly squeezes my hand at the almost inaudible squeak of Dia's voice. It looks like our plan is working. Today is the day I end Dia Voletto for good. What will happen to Mephisto after that remains to be seen. I've searched the crowd for Teddy, who promised to be here, but I can't find him.

"Welcome," he says, "to the sixty-fifth annual graduation ceremony for the Cania Christy Preparatory Academy."

He gestures to the graduates. The camera pans to the first five rows in the hall, where fifty graduates are sitting in cap and gown next to their Guardians. Students whisper names to their parents, pointing out those they know and the front-runners for the Big V. I see Jack, Joie, a half-dozen others—and, at the end of the fifth row, Ben.

On one side of me, Molly whispers, "He'll be okay."

On the other side, Pilot whispers to my dad, "Annie hasn't mentioned me?"

I scowl at him. "Pilot, quiet." And jab my finger at the screens. "This is important."

"So's this," he sneers.

"Is something the matter?" my dad asks. His deep voice hardly registers in a whisper.

"No, it's nothing, Dad."

"Actually, it *is*," Pilot insists.

The Seven Sinning Sisters are watching us curiously. I shrug at them, like I'm not sure how someone like Pilot can exist, and Superbia starts our way. Pilot notices.

"You siccing your thug on me?" he asks me.

I'm as amazed as he is to see Superbia coming over. And so quickly.

"Kids, hush," my dad says.

Pilot hurriedly whispers, "She had me killed. Your little girl. She's not a girl. She's a bad chick. In her soul."

"*Pilot!*" I hiss.

Superbia arrives at the end of the row and gestures for Pilot to go with her.

"Mr. Stone," she says. "To your feet. You should not be bothering the students and their parents."

"Is he not a student?" my dad asks.

"He was expelled," Superbia says. "And we'll see to it that he is sent away once again."

Heads turn as Superbia, apologizing for the commotion, takes Pilot away by the arm.

"Dave Stone's child was expelled?" my dad asks.

I'm getting so tired of the lies. The secrecy. It's always a matter of one more lie, one more half truth, one more cover-up, but they just keep stacking up, and there's always a reason for another one. With a heavy sigh, I look at my dad. I'm ready to confess it all.

But he just rubs my neck and pulls my cheek to him. "I think Pilot has a crush on you."

What?

That's *it*? A kid tells my dad I had him killed and I'm totally bad, and that's the best he can say?

"Dad, he wasn't lying."

"*Shhh.*" He points to the screen. "They're about to read the short list."

"I threw Pilot's vial into the water back in September. I killed him."

"Annie, please. Hush."

"But there's more. Mom made an exchange—"

Molly kicks me hard in the shin. I double over, and everyone around us looks again. Molly shakes her head sharply at me. Like she doesn't think I should come clean.

Invidia asks for our silence. Rubbing my shin, I return my attention to the screens just as Teddy inches out from behind the one on the right.

He nods at me.

Teddy's here! This is going to happen. I'm going to destroy Dia Voletto today, which he knew about, but what he hasn't expected is that Mephisto will surely need to be battled shortly thereafter. It's the only way to keep Mephisto from gaining all Dia's strength. Teddy's going to need to call for some sort of celestial, angelic support.

I mouth *We need to talk* to him. He shakes his head like he doesn't understand. It'll have to wait, but for how long?

"I have in my hands," Dia reads to his captive audience, and we see a paper shaking in his grip, "the names of the ten members of the graduating class who have been short-listed."

Molly whispers to me, "Dia looks awful."

Yeah, awful. Ripe for the killing. Only to unleash a hellish battle that might make all this work for nothing. If Dia's demons just move along to follow Mephisto, what will we have achieved?

I struggle to focus on the screens.

"If your name is not called," Dia says wearily, "please remain seated. You will have… Where was I? Sorry, you'll have thirty seconds at the end of the ceremony to bid your parents good-bye."

A woman behind me mumbles, "Oh, those poor people."

But she keeps sitting. Her child, who will be going through this experience in a few years, sits next to her, yet neither of them seems to appreciate that they, too, are "those poor people." They comment on the mass slaughtering, but no one actually does anything to stop it. Death is both the worst game to play and the ultimate spectator sport.

"But first," Dia says, "as you all know, this year has been a rather exciting one. I've taken over as headmaster, and I've made a few changes. You'll recall the new reward of the Scrutiny challenge. The winning student from each grade was given anything they'd like. And most chose life."

As people clap, my dad whispers, "Who was the lucky winner in your grade?"

"I was."

"You? But… what did you ask for? Why didn't you wake up?"

"This is what I've been trying to tell you."

Shaking his head, he says, "That's enough. I don't know what's gotten into you, Anne."

"Dad—"

"Three years now, Anne. Three years I've waited." He stares ahead at the screen. "We'll talk about this later. But you'd better have a good explanation for your behavior."

I do, I think, *but will you listen?*

"I've decided to switch up the graduation ceremony, as well," Dia says to a hushed audience. Molly grabs my hand. "More about that after we name the valedictorian."

"Oh, how exciting," the woman behind me says.

Molly and I exchange an annoyed stare.

"And now, to the short list and the ten students who have made the cut."

Dia reads the names. Alphabetically.

When he gets to number nine, Jack Wesson, Molly squeezes my hand. Because there aren't many names other than Zin that come after Wesson. Joie Wannabe preceded him.

"And, number ten," Dia reads, "Mr. Ebenezer Zin."

Then he slumps back into his chair.

Molly and I gasp with relief. I want to hug her, but there's a room of graduates and their parents that are facing the worst right now. The audio cuts out. In the moments before the screens go black, mothers fall to their knees and fathers throw back their heads.

Invidia offers a voice-over. "Next," she explains, "the Guardians of the short listed will make a single one-minute statement about their student. It will be timed. The rest of the Guardians will then vote to determine the three students whose Guardians will debate their case before Headmasters Villicus and Voletto."

The screens light up and the audio kicks in again.

The battle for the Big V begins.

Finn Kid introduces us, quite passionately, to his student, Veronica Brass as her PT appears in a banner on the screen. A minute later, Dr. Tina Naysi tells the Guardians why we should care about Corey Dewitt, and we learn his PT. One by one, Guardians present short pitches meant not only to save their students but also to save themselves.

If I had the Seven Sinning Sisters serving me, I could save everyone. None of this would be happening. If only that were the mission Teddy and my mom had in store for me. Instead of destruction, life.

I glance at Teddy.

"Nervous?" Molly whispers to me. "You're shaking. Don't worry. Garnet can do this."

No sooner has she uttered those words than Garnet's beautiful face appears on screen. Written below her face: *Ebenezer Zin. To succeed in life by making sacrifices.*

I can't watch.

I close my eyes. And listen.

"What if your entire future rested on your actions during a mere nine-month period?" Garnet begins. "Whilst your competitors have as many as two full years to prove themselves, you must prove your worth in the blink of an eye. That is the reality my student Ben Zin faced."

So far, fine—but not great. Finn Kid opened with Veronica's death at the age of thirteen, when she was volunteering at an orphanage. That was a good opener. This? I hope for a miracle.

"Yet here Ben is," Garnet continues. "He is at the top of his class, a valiant competitor who has applied himself to his *prosperitas thema*, which is to make sacrifices, the way only a great man does. In fact, he is so giving to those less fortunate," she says, "that he has made the ultimate sacrifice."

I hold my breath.

"Ben Zin has offered his spot on this short list to one other deserving but overlooked student. Yes, he has surrendered this opportunity and wishes to offer it to one of the forty who did not make the Top Ten."

twenty-nine

THE VALEDICTORIAN

I JUMP OUT OF MY SEAT. I WANT TO SCREAM "NO!" BUT MY heart is thumping in my throat.

Molly tugs me down, and my dad gives me a look that says he's sure I've lost it.

"Why's Ben doing this?" I whisper to Molly, panicking. "All the work. Everything I did."

"*Shhh,*" she says, stroking my arm as she pulls me to her. "There's gotta be a reason."

What reason? He knows Jeannie is alive! He knows what I've done to help him! He knows we wanted a life together, that this was all part of my plan for us. Could he have betrayed me? Could he have been the equivalent of Pilot Stone all along? But, no, that's not possible! Why would he give up his chance now?

My eyes are glued to the screen. Everyone's are.

"Last year," Garnet says, with just fifteen agonizing seconds left to speak, "I graduated as valedictorian, at a time when Guardians saw no reward for their efforts. This year, we Guardians too get a prize should our student win. My PT, some of you will recall, was to act *selfishly.*" She looks from Guardian to Guardian. "And so, all things considered, I have overturned Ben's request." The crowd is one big collective sigh. "His sacrificial behavior matched with my selfishness is sure to render us a power-couple like no other. And so I ask you to consider him a top candidate for the Big V because, when you vote for him, you vote for *us*."

Molly whispers, "Your heart beating again?"

I look at her. We're both thinking the same thing: well played. Little wonder Garnet won last year. She's got a knack for working a crowd.

After that pitch, it surprises no one when Ben's name is called as one of the top three candidates, along with Veronica Brass and Joie Wannabe. The camera cuts to the faces of the parents whose children didn't get through. I look away when they show Jack's dad, who looks like he's about to punch something. *I'm sorry*, I think. But my weak apology is not enough. Not nearly enough.

"Joie made it," Molly whispers to me.

"But Jack didn't."

The debate that follows will be swift, Invidia explains.

"First," she says, "former Headmaster Villicus will present a challenging life scenario. Each Guardian will be given the chance to explain how their student's PT would help them succeed in that scenario. They must then support their hypothesis with an example from their life to date. They will have thirty seconds to present their argument. The countdown will show on the screen."

It's the real-life examples that present the most trouble for Ben, who's got just nine months of graded experience to pull from, three months of which were spent *not* trying.

"When all three Guardians have made their arguments," Invidia says, "the Guardians may then challenge each other."

"These challenges," Superbia interjects, "are by far the most important component of the debate. Some Guardians will look closer to find the truth, and others will stop inspecting and simply accept the surface for the truth it reveals." Her gaze lands on me. Something inside me flutters. "Because there is no fiction. And you needn't always read between the lines or look closer. Sometimes the truth is plainly written on one's face."

Is she talking to *me*?

I glance at Teddy, but he's vanished. He was just standing there a moment ago.

I half expect Molly to nudge me with some little joke, like *I guess I Love Porno guy really does love porno*. But she doesn't. She is looking at me, though, out of the corner of her eye. I catch her just before she glances away.

Invidia continues her speech as if Superbia hadn't interrupted. "Villicus and Dia will then assign A, B, or C to each candidate, with A being the most desirable grade. The candidates and crowd within the hall will not be able to see the grades, but you'll look no further than the right-hand screen, where they'll be displayed. Five rounds of questions. This will be followed by our judges' assessment and ultimate ruling. You will then have your valedictorian."

We all hold our breath as Villicus begins.

"Your student," he says to Finn, Mr. Farid, and Garnet, "is guilty of a hit-and-run. The laws of man would send them to prison for life. With the goal of true success in mind, what do they do? Mr. Kid, begin."

Finn says, "Veronica's PT is to lie. A very clean, very elegant *prosperitas thema*. She intends to become a lawyer, which will give her the skills and the network to defend herself effectively and bend the truth to her will. As we all know, the truth, like beauty, is in the eye of the beholder. It is easy enough to convince someone that an utter lie is the truth. So, knowing people are more prone to believe what they're told than to question it," he pauses to think about an example from Veronica's recent history, "Veronica promised a student named Molly Watso that, in exchange for an MP3 player, she would be kind to a boy named John. But Veronica swiftly planted the player in John's book bag and told Headmaster Dia what John possessed. Following this event, John was expelled."

I glance at Molly to see tears in her eyes. Her gramps kisses her on the hair.

"Time," Villicus calls. "Mr. Farid, you're next. Same scenario and question."

"Joie's PT is to love her neighbor," Mr. Farid says. "You may think that such a PT condemns her to a life of do-gooding, but I assure you it does not, for Joie's brand of love is one often referred to as *tough love*. She is a master of drawing strong, often brutal lines to protect herself and 'help' others. Earlier this year, a junior named Tallulah Josey broke a rule. The girl entered the front office when the secretaries were preoccupied elsewhere and called her boyfriend. Joie witnessed this. She promptly told another girl named Harper

Otto, whom she was certain would turn Tallulah in. That's exactly what happened. Tallulah needed to learn a lesson, and Joie applied tough love to teach it."

"That's a whole lotta tough," I whisper to Molly.

"And not much love," she finishes.

"In the hit-and-run scenario, Joie would do the same." With an eye for time, he rushes to finish. "She'd dig up dirt on the person she killed, and she'd use that to weave together a story of righteousness in which she was merely a vessel for a cosmic, justice-seeking power."

"Time," Villicus says.

When it's her turn, Garnet takes a moment.

Molly and I shift on our chairs.

"Dr. Zin's son," my dad whispers to me.

"Yeah, I know him." I never told my dad about the two of us.

"Dr. Zin mentioned that you and Ben don't get along well."

I'd laugh if I wasn't so damn nervous.

The clock starts ticking away the seconds.

We watch Garnet smile and take a sip of water. I hear her swallow. She pats the corners of her mouth with a cloth napkin. Behind her, Ben sits tensely, his hands folded on the table. The woman behind me starts whispering about whether Garnet knows she's up or not. Just when I think Garnet might say nothing at all—might throw in the towel and declare that she knows Ben and I are in love—she sets down her napkin and faces the audience, not the judges.

"When we hear that Ben is to be 'sacrificial' to succeed in life," she begins at last, "we think he will sacrifice his own wants for those of another. We fool ourselves into believing he is magnanimous. But that is not Ben Zin."

The camera zooms in. On one screen, Ben's face. On the other, Garnet's.

"What would you sacrifice to save your life?" she asks the audience. "To whom would *you* go to make such a sacrifice?" She turns back to Villicus and Dia, who looks half-asleep. "Although Joie and—what's that other girl's name?—Veronica might spin their little wheels in search of a way to outsmart the laws of man, they would, in fact, be playing by those very laws, which, let's be honest, we all know are the laws of fools. Ben Zin has spent nearly six years on this island. Six. And he's learned what each successful mother and father here knows well: that the truly successful do not face such obstacles alone. We do not show up for a gunfight armed with a gun; we show up with Mephistopheles at our side."

My breath catches. Around me, most of the students look taken aback, but the only parent that seems surprised by what Garnet's revealed is my dad.

"Ben would sacrifice whatever you tell him to, Headmaster, to escape prison."

Just five seconds left.

"So know this," she looks pointedly at Villicus, "you will not lose Ben Zin, or his father, when you make him valedictorian today. They will always be yours."

Garnet's either clever, or she's just cheated.

I watch the screens for Villicus's reaction. His expression reveals nothing.

"The floor is open to the candidates," Villicus says. "Debate."

Garnet seizes the moment.

"Finn Kid," she begins, "you've just told us that Veronica is a liar. How could any human being trust a known liar? It would take little, in the real world, to expose her. She would have been wise to have a PT to be an escape artist, for that is the only way she'll get out of jail."

Villicus smirks, and Dia smiles weakly.

Veronica's dad boos from the audience.

"And Mr. Farid," Garnet adds, "what if there was no dirt on the person Joie killed? What if she'd killed Gandhi? Any decent lawyer—hell, even Veronica—could dig up just as much dirt on Joie, especially given that she'd have a rather black period on her record. Remember that if she were to win the Big V today, she'd need a new identity. The first eighteen years of her life would be unknown… and suspect."

Finn and Farid have little to say to her. How can they argue that Ben couldn't use Mephisto? How can they say, to Mephisto's face, that he wouldn't be able to protect Ben from prison?

The scores are revealed: C for Finn, B for Dr. Farid, and A for Garnet.

Molly and I smile in relief.

The next question comes and goes just as successfully, with the audience falling for a beautiful and witty Garnet, who fawns over Ben the way only someone in love would do. The crowd eats it up. Garnet is doing a spectacular job of convincing the world that, should they make it through, the world will benefit from such a beautiful and well-matched couple. Even I have to wonder if they don't belong together.

"Don't be jealous," Molly reminds me when Ben and Garnet kiss. "This is all part of the game. It'll be over soon. And Ben will be free. After you destroy Dia, maybe, like, we should try to wake you up? Send you home?"

"But what about Meph? And what about all the lives here?"

"None of that is your responsibility."

"Well what about *you*?"

She smiles and holds her hand to her heart, then says mockingly, "I'll always be in your heart."

The show goes on. It's so hard to watch. Question after question. Kiss after kiss. The applause on the lawn from people who are actually entertained by Garnet. It would be unbearable if we didn't see so many *A*s stacking up for Ben and Garnet.

They turn off the screen with the scores before the last question is asked, but it's a done deal now. Nothing but *A*s for Team Ben. Impossible to beat.

I turn to Molly, whose eyes are bright with hope. "Done," I say. "Ben's safe. He'll be paying Jeannie a visit at Harvard this time tomorrow."

"You've saved him. Will you save yourself?"

Villicus stands, while Dia sleeps peacefully. Doesn't Villicus care that Dia is so weak? Doesn't he know that that must mean something?

"It is time to declare," Villicus begins boldly, "the sixty-fifth valedictorian from the Cania Christy Preparatory Academy."

Molly and I jump to our feet, unable to sit a second longer. Together, clutching each other's hands, we stare wide-eyed at the screens, which are divided now into eight blocks featuring close-ups of Villicus, Dia, the competitors, and their Guardians and parents. Everyone looks terrified except Garnet, who is gripping Ben's hands to her chest and beaming. She has it in the bag.

It's a no-brainer.

We saw the scores.

The Big V is undeniably Ben's.

"This year's valedictorian and the winner of a second life off this island, complete with cash winnings and a relocation package is," Villicus sets his gaze firmly on the camera as Molly and I prepare to hug each other, "Joie Wannabe."

My breath catches.

I hear Molly moan.

The grounds spin. Everything spins. And I don't even feel my head hit a chair, my fingers loosen from Molly's, or my body collapse, in a slump, to the ground.

I WAKE WITH Teddy standing over my bed. At first I don't know what happened. I was feeling elated, like the world was full of hope and wonder. And then.

I sit up fast.

I'm in my dorm.

Thank God I'm not in my California hospital bed.

"Ben lost."

"Easy," Teddy says. "You passed out."

"How long has it been? Is Ben...is he already gone?"

I whip the covers off, jump up, and start for the door, but Teddy grabs me.

"Teddy!" I slap his hands to free myself, but he's unyielding. He tugs me to sit next to him, but I don't have the time or patience. I slap and then punch and then kick, and eventually I get free. "He can't be gone. He can't!"

I bolt out of my room. Down the hall. Round the corner. Down the stairs, my heels skidding. Teddy's behind me—I can hear him calling for me. I push through the doors. Sunlight blinds me. I scramble forward. The quad focuses before me.

"No," I utter when I see the worst: the chairs outside Valedictorian Hall have been put away. I whirl back to Teddy. "What the hell time is it?"

"You've been out for a half hour."

A half hour. *No.* Only parents and the valedictorian leave Valedictorian Hall—those who fail have their vials incinerated within the hall.

I look up at the sky. A thin trail of smoke still twists out of the chimney.

Ben's already gone. Ben's already gone. Ben's already gone.

"Is it over? Is it done?" I ask.

Teddy nods. "But our plan to end Dia lives on. Tell me, what did you have in mind?"

I'm sweating and shaking.

This isn't happening.

All this work—it can't be for nothing.

"I'm sorry Ben didn't win, Anne," Teddy says. Sealing my fate. Until he spoke those words, I still had a little hope. I slump to the ground, and he stands over me. "Your hair. Who made you do that?"

"Who do you think?"

"Why?"

For Ben. For Jeannie. For a vain, stupid hope. I should have known Villicus would never let Ben off this island. Never. Not in a million years.

Like my body is filled with ants, I jump to my feet and shake out my limbs. I just want to scream. Or hit something. I tear away from Teddy. I run as fast as I can to Cania College, to the grand opening. I sail through the campus gates and follow the sound of Cania's brass band, short its seniors, playing in front of the stone cathedral, which is surrounded by brightly colored streamers. Parents are mulling about with their kids. I dart around them all and burst into the cathedral. I stop short. Look up at the painted ceilings. Around at the stained-glass windows. And start madly searching aisles of seats for the Seven Sinning Sisters. Maybe there's still time. Maybe Dr. Zin has another vial of Ben's blood; surely he couldn't have left it all in Villicus's possession! The sisters can create a new life for Ben. I need to convince all seven of them to serve me.

No, I think. *I need to kill off Dia. As planned. Then the sisters will be without a master. They'll choose me—I'll make sure they do.*

"And then I'll ask them to vivify Ben," I say, careless to how crazy I look talking to myself.

The Seven Sinning Sisters will serve me. Superbia will be easy enough to win back; she was trying to say something to me earlier today, to warn me of God knows what. I know she'll serve me. Invidia, the one I'd have the hardest time winning over under normal circumstances, was the first to leave Mephisto. She's unlikely to want to return to him, and I'll be her only other option. The missing link is a vial of Ben's blood. Dare I hope Dr. Zin has more?

I spy Lou and Pilot carrying my painting of Dia. They disappear behind a set of curtains behind the podium on stage. I chase after them.

"Get your hands off that," I shout, shoving them away from the precious painting, the only thing standing between me and reclaiming the Seven Sinning Sisters. "Get out of here!"

Pilot swears at me. But, to my surprise, Lou bows. I grab his arm.

"You still serve me, Lou?" I need a little power to finish the painting.

"If I had a token of your leadership," he says softly, "I would."

I tug off my cardigan and hand it to him. "Serve me. Tell others."

"With pleasure, Master," he says and takes Pilot with him.

When they're gone, I whip off the sheet. I'm taken aback by my work, which radiates an energy unlike anything I've captured before or ever will again. I peek out from behind the curtains, looking for Dia. Where the hell is that guy? I need to put the finishing touches on this, but I can't without him.

My blood is still racing through my body when I see, across the vast room, Molly enter.

I almost call out her name.

I almost don't notice the boy at her side.

She waves with her free hand.

Her other hand is on Ben's arm.

"Ben," I utter.

But how?

Together, Molly and Ben run past the rapidly filling rows of seats and right to me.

Ben doesn't say a word. He just wraps his arms around me and kisses my face in spite of the curse that would make him hate me. He kisses my eyelids and my forehead and my nose—everything. I can't even understand what's happening. As he kisses me, Molly explains: Dia had mentioned there'd be a small change to the Big V this year. I passed out before I could hear it.

"That change," she says as Ben wipes away my tears, tears I didn't even realize I was crying, "was that the two other short-listed graduates would get the chance to enroll at Cania College. Ben and Veronica are the first members of the freshman class here. Dia's gonna fill the rest of the school this summer, and classes will officially begin in September."

This should be good news.

It almost is. Almost.

"The tuition," I say, wild-eyed as I look at them both.

"Villicus said we'll sort that out after this ceremony," Ben says, "when everything calms down."

"They're taking souls," I blurt. "No. We can't let this happen."

"What are you talking about?" Ben asks.

"Dia. He told me what he's going to take as college tuition. Pure, clean souls. Souls the underworld would never otherwise see. 'The most beautiful thing' he's ever seen. Does your dad have more of your blood?" I ask Ben hurriedly. The ceremony's bound to start any second; nearly all the seats are taken in here now. "On the yacht? Did he keep, like, backups?"

"Um, yeah, I think so."

"Do you *know*?"

"I can find out."

"Do! Go now!" I insist, but he stands uncertainly.

"Anne, calm down," Molly says, gesturing at the people watching us. Under her breath, she reminds me, "Dia won't be here after the ceremony. Remember? Ben and Dr. Zin can sort tuition out with Villicus. We'll figure this out."

"I've already figured it out." Just as I say the words, the Seven Sinning Sisters enter the room.

Superbia is followed by an eye-drawing Invidia; by Gula, who's eating a handful of chocolate; by Avaritia, who swipes the Rolex off a man as she shakes his hand, with Luxuria distracting him; and by Ira, who is angrily dragging Acedia inside and forcing her to stand when she just wants to sit. There they are. Ben's solution. I'll just have to be Saligia again, and that's simply the way it is.

Ben turns my face away from the Seven Sinning Sisters.

"Everything's going to be okay," he says.

When I shake my head, he lowers his lips to mine. I pray I can make this work without terrifying him and pushing him away. I would do anything, go to any lengths, sacrifice anything to be in a moment like this with Ben forever.

Molly says something. I don't hear her. She has to manually push us apart before we see what she was trying to warn us about.

"Garnet," she says, pointing to the end of the aisle.

Garnet is staring at us. I can almost see her pale skin filling with blood. When Ben stays at my side, her eyes bulge. I have to look away; she fought so hard for Ben, she deserves better than this.

"He'll use you, Anne," Garnet hollers at us, her voice icy. Half the room looks. "Mark my words."

With that, she storms out.

"She'll get over it," Ben says.

I'm not so sure. I don't let on, though, as Ben and Molly, who wishes me good luck, join Dr. Zin, Mr. Watso, and my dad at the back of the room. I promise to meet them once the painting has been unveiled, but that might not happen if things go as Molly and I have planned. A shitstorm is likely to erupt if things go as Molly and I have planned.

Behind the curtains again, I wait anxiously for Dia and wonder if he deserves what he's about to get. A sophomore pops his head in.

"Sorry, I thought Headmaster Voletto was in here," he says. "Have you seen him?"

"I'm waiting for him, too."

"Well, if you see him, can you tell him we got those things corralled and put them back in the little room upstairs, where he told us to?"

"Sure. Upstairs here?"

"No, at his house." He's about to leave when he adds, "That old lady in the big, ugly sweater was a real bitch to catch, but we managed to lock her up. Oh, never mind. Here he is—he just walked in." The boy darts out.

There's only one lady on this island who wears big, ugly sweaters. I lived with her once. She wanted her body to be thrown into the ocean on the off chance it would float back to shore and she would vivify. Did Dia find Gigi, vivified without her soul, and lock her up?

Dia staggers down the center aisle, past gasping onlookers, and joins me behind the curtain. He crashes against the wall.

"You...ready?" he asks.

"You didn't get rid of those monsters. You added to your collection. You added Gigi."

"I what?"

This is what he gets for lying to me.

This is what he gets for tampering with human lives.

This is what he gets for treating a soulless Gigi like just another human experiment.

"Never mind. Yes," I say. "I'm ready."

On the other side of the curtains, the crowd is quieting. I hear Villicus, who's taken his place behind the podium steps away from where Dia and I are waiting for the unveiling.

"Care for one last look before they pull back the curtains?" I whisper to Dia.

He totters toward me and looks at it. He smiles.

"Do you love it?"

"If only I could be it," he says. "So beautiful. Forever."

"Touch it."

Tentatively, he reaches out to it. When his fingertips graze the portrait, I whisper my incantation, and his whole appearance changes. He stands straighter, lifts his chin like he used to. His eyes reclaim their sparkle. Even his tattoos glow brighter.

He looks at me.

He knows I've trapped his soul within it.

"Your gift is to cast souls," he utters.

"Cutting my hair didn't take my own power from me."

"Hell hath no fury like a woman scorned."

My heart races, and I watch his eyes widen. I'm certain Gia has risen to the surface. Just briefly. Just to say good-bye. And then she is gone, and my pulse returns to normal.

"This isn't revenge for you cheating on Saligia," I explain.

"Then why?"

"I need the Seven Sinning Sisters."

"I'll give them to you."

"I need you gone. Teddy and I do. It's been our plan all along."

He looks confused by the name *Teddy*, as if he doesn't know who that is.

Before he can say anything to reclaim his soul, I shove his hand away from the painting. His soul, captured entirely now, stays in the painting as he crumples and falls to the floor. I hear the crowd gasp at the noise from their side of the curtain.

Through a gap in the curtains, I see Villicus take the stage.

"Good afternoon," Villicus says to the crowd. "As you may know, this college will be run by my esteemed colleague, Dean Dia Voletto. In a moment, he'll join me on this stage to welcome you to Cania College."

The crowd applauds. Dia, who's listlessly shaking his head, groans. I hush him and pull the sheet back over the painting. I try to tug him up, but he's dead weight.

"Just like Dorian," I whisper to him. "You're the one who said I should read it."

Villicus's voice interrupts me. "Dean Voletto has commissioned a portrait by one of our very own students. Please join me in welcoming Dean Voletto and Miss Anne Merchant, the artist behind his portrait, to the stage."

The audience applauds as the curtains are drawn back.

But when they see Dia lying on the ground at my feet, their clapping fades. Villicus looks from me to his hobbled, empty counterpart. He hasn't seen the painting yet. No one has. To see it, you'd know you're in the presence of a soul, dark and tortured though it is.

I step forward.

"I'm pleased to present," I say to the crowd and, after a pause, tug the sheet down, "*Dia Voletto*."

The audience is a single gasp.

Most people look away. Others cover their eyes. Only Villicus can look at the soul of a devil captured, like Dorian Gray's was, in a portrait. But Villicus isn't looking at the portrait; he's looking at me. And I at him. As if we're in the Silencer, I can hear his every thought— or what I hope to be his thoughts, his fear at having allowed me to become a destructive force—and I hope he can hear mine. Because I'm not afraid of him. He should take this as the warning it is.

No one is looking directly at the portrait of Dia Voletto.

And so no one notices when Garnet clambers onto the stage and slips right by the podium. Not even Villicus or I see her. I wouldn't notice her at all if it were not for the shadow that falls over me as she raises the enormous portrait over my head. I duck. Villicus flinches. She brings the painting sailing down on me with all her might, cracking its heavy frame on my spine.

I cry out.

There are more cries from the audience. At first I think they're screaming at Garnet. But then I hear them. I hear what they're saying.

"Something's burning."

It's true. It smells like something's on fire. Outside.

I look up to meet Villicus's gaze as Garnet lifts the painting off me. She's made a hole in it. She loops her arm through it and hoists it up. Then bolts between me and Villicus. Neither of us stop her. She races down the aisle and out of the building, taking that painting—something she must see as a sign of my achievements and her failures—as she goes.

Dia's body is at my feet, soullessly shifting toward the mounting cries of the crowd.

I hear Molly and my dad call for me. Ben shouts my name.

"Was this always your plan, Saligia?" Villicus asks me.

"Not Saligia," I say. "Anne."

All at once, the room goes silent. As if we're all trying to decide what to do now.

I turn to look for Ben, Molly, my dad.

That's when the first student disappears.

She is a freshman. She disappears soundlessly from inside her father's arm. It's not her father who screams but the woman sitting behind them; first she points at the empty spot, then stammers, then screams.

Across the room, another student vanishes. And another, sitting near where I stand.

They're there, and then they're gone.

Parents grab at their children. But it's no use.

Someone else vanishes. I look in time to see a red-haired man and a woman—I've seen them both before. I saw them hug their daughter this morning, and they were in my Scrutiny challenge—cry out when she vanishes.

"*Harper*," I gasp. Harper just disappeared.

Villicus grabs me by the arm. "And this, Anne? Was this your plan, too?"

No, I think. *No*. The plan was to destroy Dia by casting his soul into the portrait and burning it and only it. Molly has the lighter and everything. I search the crowd for her, but she's gone. Everyone's rushing out of the room, as if the cathedral is cursed by a lamia, doomed to take the lives of all the children who enter.

Harper can't be gone. She can't be.

I hear "Fire" and I try to free myself from Villicus, but he won't have it. Villicus tugs me with him up to the second floor of the cathedral, where he thrusts open a window facing north. Below us, hundreds of people pour out of the cathedral, through the gates of Cania College, and onto the road that will take them to the Cania Christy campus, from the center of which an enormous, ominous black cloud of smoke rises. I watch my dad, Mr. Watso, and Dr. Zin lead the pack. I can't see Ben or Molly. As one student after another disappears from the crowd, to great cries, I pray Ben and Molly are still here.

There are a handful of buildings on campus, and any one of them could be burning right now. But I know which one it is. The only one Garnet would burn, hoping to destroy Ben's vials, careless to all the other lives she'd end.

"Valedictorian Hall," I whisper.

Villicus scowls. "Did you expect Garnet to allow you to have the one thing she wanted most?" Abandoning me, Villicus shape-shifts into a broad-winged hawk. He sails over the crowd, over the woods that are filling with frantic parents and students, swiftly to campus. As he goes, I spot Teddy near Dia's mansion, entering the woods...with Pilot following him at a safe distance.

"Pilot?"

Does he know that Teddy and I are working together?

I race back downstairs. Dia is groaning on the floor.

"Garnet's going to burn your painting," I say to him.

"Why?"

"Teddy told me why Saligia came here. To escape you. And to destroy you."

"Don't...believe him."

"You came back to win me back. But that was never going to happen. Saligia hates you."

"I told you. I came back... to protect you."

"You should have protected yourself!"

That's when Dia vanishes. If Garnet took his painting to the fire she set, it seems she's made it there now. Which means Dia's soul is destroyed. And his legions are without a leader.

I flee the cathedral. I find myself at the back of the pack.

Out of nowhere, the chemistry teacher Miss Incitant flies at me. She grabs my shirtsleeve and tugs hard at it. She was one of Dia's followers, and now she's without a master.

"Let me serve you, Miss Saligia," she begs as, finally, she strips the fabric off me.

Before I can speak, the woods come alive—and its new inhabitants, dressed in their freakish circus gear, charge at me. Guardians that were only moments earlier running toward the Cania Christy campus have turned and are now, to my horror, running toward me. They grab at the sleeve Miss Incitant is holding and yank the other one off me. They tear both to pieces, taking threads and fighting over the buttons. More hands grasp at my clothes. My collar is torn off. My shirt hem. The tab of the zippers on my boots. I might be swallowed up by this horde of master-less demons or trampled to death.

But then their energy begins to grow inside me.

And, one by one, they fall to their knees, bowing before me.

But their servitude is no good without vials. If the Seven Sinning Sisters are or will be mine, I'm going to need vials. And so I command them to help me.

"Put out the fire at Valedictorian Hall," I say. "Hurry!"

They obediently turn and charge up to campus. My heart is going on overdrive. Dia's dead, kids are dying, but I'm so close to being able to grant new lives for everyone. If I could just get to campus and find the Seven Sinning Sisters!

I race forward, too. Up the road. Past the mothers and fathers who've just seen their child pop out of their embrace, forever gone, his or her vial destroyed irrevocably. These parents stand like zombies. Or cling in desperation to the ground. Or slow from racing breathlessly to barely holding themselves upright. I run past them all. Past empty rings of arms that were, only a blink earlier, clinging to a beloved child.

I run harder, calling for Ben. And Molly.

I stumble and have to scramble back to my feet as I dart through the gates of Cania.

Valedictorian Hall is engulfed in flames when I skid to a stop in a crowd of people and demons stripping to pat away whatever flames they can. Some are running up from the water. Their arms hold sloshing buckets, bowls, large fronds, bins, anything they could swipe from the nearby dorms and fill with seawater.

Men carrying a massive fallen tree heave it—one, two, three—against the locked door of the hall. Flames gust out as the doors swing in. The men fly back with the force. Students race by them, stripping off their clothes as they sprint into the hall, knowing their burns will heal but their vials, once gone, are irretrievable.

A woman shouts that they've got to put the far wall out.

"Forget the rest of it!" she hollers. "Just get the wall with the vials!"

I join one of many chains of people swinging buckets of water up from the ocean. And that's when I see Ben. He's right across from me.

"Ben!"

He turns. His face is covered in soot.

"I'm safe!" he shouts. "My dad kept an extra vial on the yacht."

Just as he says that, he vanishes. The bucket he was swinging drops to the ground, and the guy who was swinging another one his way cries out.

I haven't even had a chance to get my head straight—to tell myself it'll be okay, Ben said he has more vials, don't worry—when someone grabs me from behind. I collide with Superbia's slapping hand. I reel back. She's slapping me? I thought she'd serve me!

"You killed him!" she screams wildly. "He loved you and you killed him!"

"Killed who?"

"You stuffed his soul in that painting. And you let her burn it. And he's destroyed now."

"Dia Voletto?" I say in astonishment. "But I thought you wanted me to end him. He's a devil! You were warning me all along about him."

"He loved you! He tried to free you on the day of the Scrutiny. He built the whole challenge around your PT, you idiot! So you'd go free. Live again."

"But," I search for words, stunned, "you made me read *Dorian Gray*. To give me the idea!"

"Not to kill *Dia*! He was harmless."

The flames are hot against my back. They're shooting off Valedictorian Hall in all directions, catching nearby trees on fire, slashing by the arms, legs, and faces of parents and students, who cry out.

"Then why?" I cry, confused, worried that I've actually made a terrible mistake. "Why *The Picture of Dorian Gray*?"

"Because of Dorian."

"Dorian? Dorian Gray?" I'm about to say, *He's fiction*, but I know better than that. "He's real?"

"You know him well. We've been trying to separate you from him."

"Who is he?"

All at once, Villicus yanks me out of the line, away from Superbia. She's yelling through tears after me. I struggle to hear her as I shove at Villicus.

"Dorian made a pact!" Superbia shouts.

"Who is he?" I holler.

"Don't trust them!"

"Who?"

"Shut up!" Villicus commands. Unwilling to let me hear another word, he risks full discovery and lifts me off the ground. We're suddenly flying past the heat of the inferno and heading straight for Goethe Hall. "I'm gravely disappointed in you."

Everything is a whir. A blur. I know I hit him, and I know I call for my dad, and I can't help but call for my mom. I call for Superbia, too, but she doesn't follow.

Dorian Gray is real. And I know him well. They've been trying to separate us.

I wrack my brain. Superbia's been giving me hints all year, but I didn't know what to make of them, and I was too busy with my own agenda to care about hers. What has she said to me? I can't remember! I can't think straight, not like this, not flying in Mephisto's hold.

Who is Dorian? The real Dorian Gray?

Superbia said something this afternoon. Something about the truth being plain as day—or, no, she said *plainly written on one's face*.

Dorian Gray was impossibly beautiful. Could that be what she was hinting at? That Dorian is someone I know who's gorgeous beyond words?

Do I know anyone like that, other than Dia?

Oh my gosh.

No, it can't be. It can't.

I've been played all this time? It wasn't real at all?

They were trying to keep me from him. That's what she said.

Villicus lands at the back door to Goethe Hall and shoves me inside. But not fast enough. Not before it hits me who Dorian Gray is.

It can only be him, too-beautiful *him*.

Dorian Gray is none other than Ben Zin.

thirty

IMPOSSIBLE BEAUTY

VILLICUS FLINGS OPEN THE DOOR TO HIS OFFICE, DIA'S former office. He pushes me in. I stagger in—and stop dead. I can't believe my eyes.

Teddy is standing, quivering, trying to look brave on the opposite side of the room. Pilot is next to him. I fix my glare on that little puke of a punk—no, he's a demon now. Whatever this is, I know Pilot's behind it. I look for Ben, waiting to see him step out of the shadows. Could he really be Dorian Gray? All this time? But why would he play me? Why me? What could Ben—or Dorian—get out of this?

If Ben is Dorian, I don't know how I'll go on. I pray I'm wrong.

"Teddy?" I say in disbelief. "Did he catch you?"

"Shut up," Villicus commands me as he slams the door. He turns to me and slaps me hard with the back of his hand. I flinch and step back, but I don't scream. "You ungrateful bitch."

He hits me across the face again.

I hear Teddy gasp.

Pilot rams his elbow hard into Teddy's side. "Shut up, you lying bastard."

"Pilot!" Villicus warns him to keep it down.

I could kill Pilot. Did he sell me out again?

"I gave you *everything*," Villicus hollers at me. "I gave you this life. I supported you. And now you repay me by doing this? By taking sides with a vile creature that would have you destroy Dia Voletto?"

Villicus knows about Teddy. He knows we set out to destroy him. And he knows I've already completed half of our mission. Does he know *he's* the other half?

"I ran from Hell to escape you," I yell at Villicus. My lip is bleeding into my mouth. "And I gave you my followers. I gave you the Seven Sinning Sisters! We were even when I left."

"Like hell we were!"

He shoves me to the ground. I bang my head and wince.

"Come on, Gia!" he growls, pinning me. "Aren't you gonna come out and fight me?"

Holding me in place, Villicus lures Teddy to him. I shake my head, telling Teddy not to do anything Villicus says.

"And you," he says to Teddy, "what do you have to say for yourself?"

"Let her go," Teddy stammers as he shakes his head. "Please."

He bravely tries to swing his fists at Villicus, but he's not powerful enough. Villicus thrusts him to the floor like he's swatting a fly.

"Anne, I'm so sorry," Teddy says.

"I'm going to kill you!" Pilot shouts at Teddy. He's still halfway across the room. Strangely, he hasn't moved from his spot.

"No," Villicus says, "I think *I* shall kill her. But first? Teddy."

"No!" I cry out.

I can't let Teddy die! How many good people will die on my watch? No, this can't happen. Teddy has sacrificed so many years for the greater good. If I've done anything, as myself or Saligia, it's been for me. I manage to shift Villicus's face so he's looking at me again.

"If anyone should die, Mephisto, it should be me," I declare.

I killed Dia Voletto when he only tried to love and protect me. I believed in Ben when he was secretly Dorian all along. I've enslaved demons and humans alike, all for Ben, for a lie, a lie I was too blind to see. I've left a trail of dead people—people who loved me—in my wake. I should have realized this long ago. It's all anyone's ever told me: I don't belong here. Now I know it's true.

"I'm the bad one," I say.

Teddy swings his gaze my way and weakly shakes his head. But I've already decided. Villicus can kill me instead. With Ben's secret identity and the betrayal it must be hiding—a betrayal I can't understand yet, but something bad enough to make Dia and Superbia try to keep me from him—I have little reason to go on anyway.

"Let me up," I tell Villicus, "and we can come to an agreement. Just—just don't kill Teddy. He's the only good thing in this world."

"Anne!" Pilot screams.

Villicus turns to Pilot and silences him with a look. Literally takes his voice away. I watch Pilot's mouth move madly, but not a peep comes out.

"If you want me to kill you instead of killing your precious Teddy, I can't," Villicus says, releasing me and standing. "You're alive in the true world. And, as much as I'd love to kill a mortal with my bare hands, I am forbidden."

"I know. But if I were to," I look around for an idea, "if I could surrender my soul in place of his."

"Your soul."

"Just let him go. You must want my soul, don't you? I've got a lot of Dia's followers. They'll be yours. I'll be yours. Like…like old times."

Villicus holds out his hands to help me up. "You would do that?"

Pilot waves his arms wildly at me. He's shaking his head.

Why doesn't he budge from that spot?

Why did Villicus take his voice away?

"Tell me exactly what exchange you have in mind," Villicus says as I straighten what little is left of my uniform. My heart's racing. "I need to hear the words."

I can't stop looking at Pilot.

Something's not right about this.

Voices in my head whisper, *Look closer.*

"Miss Merchant?" Villicus urges. "You were saying you would surrender your soul to save Teddy's life. Can I take that as a promise?"

I watch Pilot. He's freaking out.

"What's Pilot doing here?" I ask Villicus.

Relief seems to wash over Pilot's face. He nods at me.

"Anne," Teddy says, "please focus. Don't let that terrible boy distract you. I—I can't die. What would happen to your mother's plan?"

"Simply say the word, Miss Merchant, and I will take your soul and release Teddy's."

Pilot's trying to tell me something. He's been vocal about hating Teddy, but he's never said why. So why?

My stare shifts to Teddy. He knows so much about Saligia. He told me everything—who she was, how she longed to destroy Dia, how she once loved Mephisto and only escaped the underworld to escape Dia, not her mentor Mephisto. He told me she wanted to work with him, to help him. He said Gia was his good friend in the underworld.

But when he read my soul last September, I was completely creeped out by him. If he was reading Gia and they were friends, shouldn't Gia have, even then, responded well to Teddy? Shouldn't it have been like my soul was connecting with a soul mate?

And then Teddy was there in the hospital room. Bringing me back here. As Mephisto wanted. Under the guise that my mom wanted me here. Knowing I couldn't confirm that story. Knowing he could turn me any which way with the mention of my mom.

But when I made Scout connect me with him on Battleship Island, he must have known that I could just as easily ask Lance Crenmost to connect me with my mom, and if that had worked, I could have asked her about him, and if he'd been lying, he would have been found out. So he couldn't have been lying about working with my mom. Which means he's telling the truth. He must be. Except I didn't end up connecting with my mom. I couldn't. Why couldn't I?

"Miss Merchant, Teddy's existence hangs in the balance."

What do I absolutely know about Teddy? I trusted him because he mentioned my mom. But could he have simply been saying that to get me back here? For Mephisto? Or—or to kill Dia? Or to offer my soul to free his now? Why would he want that?

I've had so few interactions with Teddy. I can count them almost on one hand. The memories come at me in flashes. Teddy in his tuxedo, looking back at me as we marched up to the dance. He quoted Mephistopheles then. And when we were in the woods after the Scrutiny and he was telling me about my past as Saligia, he said the line, "To define is to limit"—I'm sure of it. That's a line pulled straight from *The Picture of Dorian Gray*; I know because Superbia discussed it in class. In fact, during our talk in the woods, Teddy seemed to be quoting someone else several times. Didn't Superbia teach us that Dorian rarely said anything interesting on his own but rather quoted others? Dorian had no original thought. She then told me...

"Any artist would be wise to steer clear of Dorian," I whisper, repeating her warning.

"Sorry?" Teddy asks.

Villicus staggers backward. He's even smiling a little.

That's when I know I'm on to something.

Because I've seen that smile before. I saw it when I outsmarted Pilot in Valedictorian Hall. It's the smile of a proud parent, or someone who considers himself my real father.

"*The truth is written plainly on your face*," I say, turning to Teddy as I recite Superbia's words, spoken just this morning. "Dorian Gray was beautiful at first, but his true self was miserably ugly. The gruesomeness of his soul was written on every line of his hideous face."

Teddy's jaw tightens.

He told me once that he'd been beautiful in a previous life. I just didn't listen.

"Dia sent you away," I say to him. "That was how he tried to separate us. I thought Superbia was talking about Ben. I thought he was the beautiful one—" Ben hasn't betrayed me. I wish I had time to celebrate. "But it was *you* they were separating me from. My Guardian. The person with absolute influence over my life. My thoughts. My actions. Dia sent you away almost instantly. He loved me enough to do that. He did—he came here to protect me. From you, Teddy. And from someone more powerful than you, more powerful than any of us."

I look at Villicus.

"From you. You and Teddy. Superbia tried to warn me."

Villicus scoffs.

"Why did you silence Pilot?" I ask him.

But I know why. Pilot called Teddy a lying bastard. Pilot knows. Maybe he's known all along. He's hated Teddy. If what Dia said is true—if Pilot couldn't reveal the plot of a superior demon—then Pilot couldn't have told me what he knew of Teddy and Mephisto, both of whom rank far higher than he does.

"Anne," Teddy says softly, "Superbia filled your head with lies. I told you not to listen to her."

"You're Dorian Gray."

"You outrank him, Gia," Villicus says. "Force him to tell you."

But I just stare at Teddy. He doesn't deny it.

"What the hell do you want with me?" I ask—just as the door to the office flies open, and Molly tears in.

thirty-one

REVELATIONS

"MISS WATSO!" VILLICUS EXCLAIMS. "LEAVE US!"

"No," she utters coldly, securing her glare on him and charging toward us. "You leave her."

"Mol—" I begin.

She slashes through the air, and Villicus drops to his knees. Again, she slashes, and he swings the other way. Teddy dives for the open door, but she holds up her hand, and he stops on the spot.

"Oh my gosh," I whisper. Molly's got some kind of power. "Molly?"

She throws me a little smile and a shrug. As if that's that. I'm speechless. I can only stand idiotically and watch while my petite friend, who's always seemed too bold for one small body, pulls Villicus up to his feet with little more than a glare.

He growls at her. "Whatever you are, you are unwelcome here. I have dominion over this land."

Molly stands, in her uniform, hands on her hips, and stares back at him. "This is not your land," she says. Her voice is the sound of power. "You traded the Seven Sinning Sisters to Dia Voletto for this island."

"I earned it fairly in an exchange. It's mine, you moronic child."

Molly smirks. Before our eyes, she blossoms until she is at least ten feet tall. Her dark hair rolls in waves like the sea down her back. Stunned, I drop to my knees.

"But, as you can see," she says, "Dia's original exchange to secure the island is, contractually, null and void. He failed to properly vivify Molly Watso. The soul that inhabits her body is not hers."

"Who are you?" Villicus demands.

"I took possession of Miss Watso's physical form." She throws me a sideways smile. "Don't worry, Annie. She let me."

For a moment, Molly's glow softens, and I see the face of her spirit. Unless I'm hallucinating, I now know why Lance Crenmost couldn't connect me with my mom.

"You should remember me, Mephistopheles," she says. "I once asked you for a child."

All this time, I thought I was talking to Molly.

But it was my mom.

Now all of those little lapses in Molly's memory make sense. Why she didn't want to fill in her page. Or even talk about what Villicus did to her. It was because she wasn't there when they happened!

"Ah, you! Nicolette Merchant," Villicus scoffs. "Your precious daughter condemned you to die, you realize."

Her expression turns stony. "Don't ever speak of my child."

"Mom?" I stammer.

"I'll deal with you in a second," she says to me. I haven't been in trouble from my mom in so long, I don't even mind hearing that tone. I'd give anything to hear it again and again for the rest of my life. "Mephistopheles, because Dia Voletto failed to vivify Molly Watso—"

"A technicality!"

"—your contract is null and void, and this island returns to the ownership of the Abenaki people." She uses his own words on him: "A technicality, yes. And a good one. Good-bye."

In true Mephistophelian form, Villicus, furious, shoves his heel into the floor, making a long crack. He is about to leap into it when he pauses, looks at me, and opens his mouth to speak. But Molly won't stand for it; she shoves him, and with a deep cry he disappears.

Only Teddy and Pilot remain with us.

Teddy looks mortified.

Pilot doesn't look that surprised, actually. With Mephisto gone, Pilot's voice returns. He's coughing and trying to catch his breath.

"Explain yourself," she commands Teddy.

"I'm so sorry!"

"Explain. Your. Actions."

"Mephisto wanted the soul of Saligia back," Teddy says quickly. "That's your daughter, you know! The girl you think is so perfect she has to be protected. She doesn't! She's bad to the core."

Molly blinks, and Teddy cowers.

"I know the truth!" Pilot shouts. He staggers toward us. "I knew all along. We all knew."

"Why didn't you tell me?" I ask him.

"I couldn't, Anne. It involved Mephisto. His rank protected him and kept our lips sealed. But I did try to steer you away from Teddy. You know I did."

Pilot explains that the plot to hobble Saligia—to take her legions from her and the love of her life from her—all started before she even left the underworld.

"Mephisto wanted to knock Gia down to size," Pilot says. "She was becoming too powerful in the underworld. When she asked to become your daughter, Mrs. Merchant, because she wanted to experience real love—the kind of love that doesn't exist Downstairs—she gave him her followers. But that wasn't enough for him." He glances at me. "He wanted her soul. He wanted her to serve him, which is something she would never have done, not even for her mentor."

"You and Mephisto struck a deal," I spit at Teddy.

"He's the deal-maker," Teddy says, as if that makes everything okay. "When you became a student here, he brought me in. Said if I could get you to surrender your soul to him—so you'd be his again—he'd give me a new life."

"Disgusting," I grumble.

"Anne, that's enough," Molly says.

"What did Dia have to do with any of this?" I ask Teddy.

He looks at Molly. "Give me life, and I'll tell you."

She narrows her gaze just a little, and he twists in agony. He begs for mercy. But he refuses to spill the truth without getting something for it.

That's when Pilot recites an incantation. At once we are standing in Valedictorian Hall as it was the night I battled Villicus, the
night everything changed for me. Villicus and Teddy—or the memories of them—are standing near the very duct I climbed out of that
night, as if they're real. We can hear them speaking quietly. I glance
at Pilot and realize, as I do, that he never told me his power. Now
it's clear: Pilot, the demon now known as Sammie M. Firestone, is
gifted with the ability to *manifest memories.*

"Miss Merchant knows the truth of her existence," Teddy says to
Villicus.

"Of her coma? Or of Saligia?"

"Just her coma."

Villicus nods. "It's only a matter of time."

"But what if…"

"If?"

"What if we could use this moment to our benefit?"

"Our benefit? There is no our, Dorian. You are my servant."

"Your willing servant, Master. But I'm speaking now of growing your
power as never before. Saligia once challenged your power with her legions,
but you managed to shift her out of the underworld. Now only one devil
compares to you."

"Dia Voletto."

"Her ex-lover."

"Your proposition?"

"An exchange."

"Naturally."

"Miss Merchant is on her way here even now," Teddy says. "I told you I
would get her soul for you. But what if I could get you even more?"

"I'm listening."

"What if you were to… let her win tonight? Let yourself be publicly
humiliated by her. Let her escape—for a moment. And let Dia Voletto come
here to take this school from you. He would rush at the chance to see his
beloved Saligia again."

"He was the one who encouraged her to leave the underworld. He'd rush
to protect her, if anything."

"So be it, Master! Bring Dia here. I'll keep Miss Merchant here with a
story that will tug at the very heartstrings that made her so unsuitable for the
underworld. I'll convince her that her purpose here is to destroy Dia. She'll

end his life—he won't see it coming, not from his great love. You'll reap the benefits."

"Why do I sense an 'and'?"

Teddy chuckles. "If I can both destroy Dia and get Anne to surrender her soul to you, will you give me what I always wanted? Will you give me the life of eternal youth and beauty I left behind?"

"It's agreed, Dorian."

They both glance up at the duct, which is open above them. Villicus transforms into Hiltop, who flies up the wall at the same time Teddy disintegrates. No sooner has Hiltop shoved her scrawny arm into the duct than I see myself, pulled out and thrust to the hard floor of the hall.

The memory vanishes. Teddy, engrossed in it, gasps and stares ahead, as if seeing his perfect vision disappear.

"It was all I ever wanted," he says. "My beauty."

I can't believe I destroyed Dia Voletto to help Dorian Gray feed his vanity.

He collapses to his knees and throws himself at Molly's feet. She's her normal size again, but even still she seems too large and powerful for one small body.

"Have mercy!" Teddy cries. "If you knew the ways of the underworld, you would know my need to leave it. I'm not built to survive it. I was desperate. Please!"

"Go to Hell," she says.

A wind rushes up from the gash in the floor. It pulls Teddy toward it.

"This won't stop anything!" He clings to the rugs, chair legs, sculptures as he is tugged toward the crack in the floor. "I found a new land. The expansion is starting. I'll tell you where it is if you'll let me—"

He disappears into the crack, which seals after him.

Molly looks at Pilot. He stands, trembling, and looks at us uncertainly, as if he's not sure where he'll be sent. After all, the crack in the floor is sealed. He keeps his gaze on it.

"Molly," he says quietly. "Or Mrs. Merchant. Or—I don't…"

"Why did you work so hard to build up Anne's followers, Pilot?"

"In part because…because I hoped Anne would outrank Mephisto, and then I could tell her the truth about this plan."

"And in part because?" Molly asks. "Be honest."

Slowly, timidly, he lifts his head. And he looks at me. "Because you were my second chance, Anne. You were my ticket out. I'm sorry." His voice is quivering and thick with emotion. "I'm sorry for everything, especially for doing it for all the wrong reasons."

Molly turns to me. She looks at me as only my mom can. Which is weird.

"I'm sorry, too," I say to Pilot. "I'm sorry for destroying your vial. And for breaking my promise to help you get a new life."

"Go then," she says to him.

Without another word, he vanishes.

"Where did he go?"

"Home."

"Like home-home?" I point up, gesturing to Heaven, which I'm pretty sure isn't in the sky, but whatever. "Or home to the under-world?"

"Home to California. He can try to prove his worth once more."

"A second chance."

"You all deserve one, Anne."

I can't look at her now. "Even me?"

She lifts my chin, but she's too beautiful to gaze at, like an eclipse that could blind me.

"You are the best second chance I ever had," she says. "I was wrong to start your life on such a shaky foundation. I'll never deserve to be your mother. But I'm so glad I got the chance to try."

"You were an amazing mom," I say. "You still are."

She brushes at my tears. Her touch makes me feel a thousand times stronger.

"Mom?"

"Yes?"

"Why didn't you tell me Teddy was Dorian?"

Caught off guard, she laughs. "I didn't know. I'm not privy to the workings of the underworld. But I knew there was something amiss when you told me he said he was working with me. I couldn't tell you he was lying without, well, revealing myself. Instead, I simply tried to guide you away from him."

"So, then, why *did* you come here?" I ask, hoping to hear she missed me just a fraction as much as I've missed her.

"Because I'm sorry." She drops her eyes. "I brought a devil into your life. I was desperate, Anne—desperate to have you when I asked Mephisto for you. When your dad sent you here, I kept watch over you, but I needed to get closer. To protect you."

"I really can protect myself," I whisper.

"You can't blame me—or even Dia—for trying. Your friend Molly understood, when I asked her to do me this favor. She's just as protective as I am. Since dying, she's been darting in and out of God knows what—squirrels and birds and trees—to watch over her grandpa."

"You met Molly?" I can't help but smile.

"Mouthy girl. But a great girl. And a great friend to you."

It occurs to me that, over the course of the year, I shared an awful lot with someone I *thought* was Molly. Which means my mom not only knows everything about every single time Ben and I kissed… but, um, didn't she tell me to "wax my lady parts" once? I'm torn between cringing and laughing.

"You're sneaky," I say to her. "Aren't you supposed to be a better role model for me?"

She laughs. "Now, sweetheart, are you ready to wake up?"

"No, stay with me. Let's just stay here forever."

"Your dad is waiting for you. He needs you, Annie."

It occurs to me that Molly and my dad looked at each other like they knew each other. He felt my mom's spirit even when I didn't. They really loved each other.

"Can I tell him I saw you?" I ask.

"That might freak him out a bit."

"But, the thing is,"—I pause—"I'm kinda done keeping secrets."

She smiles. "Then tell him everything."

"I'll be grounded for eternity."

"Probably."

I can anticipate her leaving. I can practically hear the beeping of the hospital room. Before she waves her hand or does some tiny, simple gesture that sends me back to California, I throw my arms around her and sink into her embrace. This is it. This is good-bye. Knowing this is the last time I'll be able to hug my mom—and the last I'll ever see of Molly—I cling hard to her for as long as I can.

My face is pressed into her shoulder when I ask her one last question. "Why did you send me back into a coma that night, Mom?"

"The night you woke? In the hospital?"

"Yeah. When Dad went to get the nurse."

"Do you remember who was waiting for you in Gigi's house when you woke up?"

I will never forget. "Ben," I say, and my face heats up. He was spooning me.

"Do you remember rolling onto a certain sheet of paper?"

"The sketch I did of him."

"You needed to know."

I lean away and look her in the eyes. "You sent me back for…a boy." I smile through my tears. "Seriously?"

"For love. Is there anything better I could have sent you back here for?"

"I dunno, maybe to save 200 souls from the clutches of the devil?"

"You don't need me to tell you to do that."

It occurs to me that, in all the chaos and wonder of my mom's return, I have no idea where Ben is now. What will become of him?

"If Mephisto's gone, how will Ben be vivified?" I ask her. "You saved Pilot. Can you save him, too, Mom? Can you bring Ben back?"

"I could," she says. "Or you could." She runs her hands over my eyes. "Make me proud."

Her voice is the last thing I hear before the excited rush of doctors racing into my hospital room awakens me. And I find myself, once again, in California.

ABOUT THE AUTHOR

Joanna Wiebe is a graduate of the University of Alberta's Honors English program, where she received the James Patrick Folinsbee Memorial Scholarship in Creative Writing. She lives in Victoria, British Columbia, with her partner, Lance. Find her online at joannawiebefiction.com.